Unchained Memories

Book II of
"The Commitment" Series

BLUE FEATHER BOOKS, LTD.

I will always have a fondness for this book, as the stories contained within are the catalyst that set my life in a new direction and changed it in ways I could only imagine in my wildest dreams. It was through these stories that I discovered the woman within and emerged a whole and complete individual... happily in love with life and all the future had to offer. I dedicate this book to those who made that possible, and those who accepted the metamorphosis without blinking an eye. That is truly what love... and family, are all about.

ALSO WRITTEN BY KAREN D. BADGER AND
AVAILABLE FROM BLUE FEATHER BOOKS:

❖ ON A WING AND A PRAYER
❖ YESTERDAY ONCE MORE
❖ IN A FAMILY WAY

www.bluefeatherbooks.com

Unchained Memories

A BLUE FEATHER BOOK

by

Karen D. Badger

This is a work of fiction. All characters, locales and events are either products of the author's imagination or are used fictitiously.

UNCHAINED MEMORIES: BOOK II OF "THE COMMITMENT" SERIES

Copyright © 2011 by Karen D. Badger

Cover design by Ann Phillips

A Blue Feather Book
Published by Blue Feather Books, Ltd.
133 Merck Rd
Cleveland, GA 30527

www.bluefeatherbooks.com

ISBN: 978-1-935627-87-6

First edition: October, 2011

Printed in the United States of America and in the United Kingdom

Acknowledgements

Many thanks to the following people for the love, support, and knowledge provided during the writing and editing of this book:

To Bliss for her unwavering love and for unscrewing me from the ceiling when I was convinced my editor was being mean to me. Thanks for making me see the editor's job is not only to produce a polished novel, but also, to help me to grow as a writer. I love you, baby. To Heath and Dane for providing the models for Seth and Tara. How does it feel to be immortalized in print? To Big Guy (Sheri Barnett) for her medical expertise and advice. You've saved my butt from looking eternally ignorant once more, my friend. Love you much. To Ellie for not only being my Mom, but for her unconditional love, friendship, and acceptance, not to mention her superb abilities as a beta reader. You rock! To Verda and Nann for your excellent editing services. I appreciate all your feedback—even when it catapulted me into the ceiling. To Emily and Jane for having faith in my abilities and providing a forum for my work. Finally, to all my friends and family who stood by me while I morphed into the woman I am today, and for accepting that change with unconditional support and love. Without your love and acceptance, this book would not have been possible.

Part I:
Promise Me Paradise

Chapter 1

Cat pulled up to the curbside mailbox and removed several business-size envelopes. "Bill, bill, junk, bill," she said as she sifted through the mail. She stopped when she came upon an envelope larger and thicker than the rest, labeled "Occupant."

"Ma, hurry. My show's on," Seth said from the backseat. Cat tucked the stack of envelopes on the seat just under her leg and steered the car into the driveway. Seth released his seatbelt and reached over the backseat. "Can I have the keys?"

Cat pulled the keys out of the ignition and gave them to him. "Be sure to put them on the kitchen table so we don't have to go on a witch hunt for them tomorrow morning," she called after his retreating form. She glanced into the rearview mirror. "Tara, honey, could you please unhook your sister?"

Cat collected the mail and her handbag and followed the girls into the house. She threw the mail on the kitchen counter and set up the coffeepot to brew. As the enticing aroma of freshly brewed coffee filled the room, she clasped her hands above her head and stretched from side to side to work out the stiffness that accumulated while spending six consecutive hours anesthetizing her patient during surgery. She enjoyed her work as an anesthesiologist, but the occasional long surgery left her stiff and sore.

When the coffee finished, she poured herself a cup and sipped the rich dark liquid. She sighed. "Oh, that's good." She leaned against the countertop, thought about what to make for dinner, and decided on pizza. Pizza was a favorite of Billie and the kids.

Cat smiled as she thought about Billie. It seemed like yesterday, but nearly five years had passed since she walked into Billie's aerobics class. There, at the front of the class, was a tall, dark-haired beauty with the bluest eyes she'd ever seen. The attraction was immediate, and it rendered her helpless and even more uncoordinated than usual as she proceeded to literally fall on her face in the middle of class. Luckily, Billie took pity on her and agreed to private lessons.

4

Cat was grateful for the life she had built with Billie, although the road to happiness was paved with what felt, at times, like insurmountable obstacles. First, Cat learned Billie had a son, Seth, who when they met, lay in a coma after being hit by a car while getting off the school bus. Seth was blond and had blue eyes like his mother. Seth's illness had caused Billie to put her bar exams on hold while she worked as a paralegal to supplement his medical expenses. She had since passed the bar and was a junior partner in a local law firm.

Seth was two years older than Cat's daughter, Tara, who with red hair and spitfire green eyes, was a miniature of herself. Then there was Skylar, who was conceived in the most heinous of manners, but who truly pulled them together as a family. Five years younger than Tara, she also sported Cat's red hair but had the same blue eyes as Seth. Now Seth was eleven years old, Tara was nine, and Skylar was nearly four.

Cat finished her coffee and headed toward the stairs to change into a pair of shorts and a T-shirt before starting dinner. She passed Seth lounging on the couch as he watched his favorite cartoon. She stopped to kiss him on the forehead. "Don't forget, scout, homework right after this show, okay?"

"Yeah, I know."

Cat ruffled his hair and continued toward the stairs. She peeked into Tara's room along the way. Tara and Skylar were playing with their dolls. "Homework tonight, Tara?"

Tara regarded her mother. "I have some spelling words to do."

"Okay. You have about a half hour to play, then you'll need to get it done before supper is ready."

"Ah, Mama," Tara said.

"What is it with you two? You know how it goes," Cat said.

A short time later, she sat down at the table to go through the mail. Cat's attention was drawn to the thick envelope marked Occupant. The phone rang just as she lifted the corner of the flap.

Cat crossed the kitchen and grabbed the phone from the cradle on the wall. "Hello?" She trapped the phone between her shoulder and ear as she continued to peel the flap away from the envelope.

"Hi, baby," Cat heard from the receiver.

Cat leaned against the wall with the half-opened envelope in her hand. She closed her eyes and sighed at the sound of Billie's voice.

"Hi, sweetheart," Cat said as she continued to open the envelope. "What's up?"

"I called to let you know I'll be home just a bit late. I'm in the middle of an emergency meeting with a domestic violence case we took on last week. It'll be about an hour before we wrap it up."

"Is everything all right?" Cat reached into the envelope while she spoke.

"It will be. She's beaten up pretty badly."

Cat heard the distress in Billie's voice. "I know this hits close to home, but please don't let it get personal for you. I don't want to see you get hurt."

"I can't help it. He beat her son too. Bad enough to put him into the hospital."

"God. How old is the child?"

"Three, just a bit younger than Skylar. If anyone hurt our children, I'd—"

"I know, sweetheart. I understand."

Cat reached into the package and extracted several photographs.

"Anyway," Billie said. "I'll be about an hour late."

Cat gasped.

"Cat?" Billie asked. "Are you there? Talk to me."

"Oh my God," Cat said as she stared at the pictures.

Billie grabbed her jacket and keys and pulled her senior partner and friend, Art McDonough, aside. "Art, I have an emergency to deal with at home. You'll have to finish preparing the brief without me."

"No problem. Don't give it another thought. I hope things are all right with Cat and the kids. See you tomorrow."

Billie brought her car to a screeching halt in the driveway and ran into the house. She found Cat sitting on the kitchen floor, with her back against the wall. The phone and a large envelope were on the floor by her side. Tears streamed down her face.

Billie cautiously approached Cat and crouched down in front of her. She noticed Seth and Tara in the doorway a few feet away, fear and confusion on their faces.

"Seth, take your sister and go into the other room, please."

Seth stood there, unresponsive.

"Now!" Billie yelled, louder than she intended. The children jumped and scurried into the other room.

Billie's curt tone brought Cat to her senses. "Don't you ever yell at them like that again."

"I'm sorry." Billie reached to help Cat up.

Cat slapped her hands away. "Don't touch me. Don't touch me. Just leave."

"Cat, what's wrong? Talk to me."

"I want you to pack a bag and leave."

Billie was shocked. She sat back on her heels. "What did you just say?"

"I said, get out."

"I'm not going anywhere. At least not until you tell me what's going on here."

Cat climbed to her feet and walked a few steps away. "I'm not the one who should be explaining herself."

Billie rose and attempted to wrap her arms around Cat. "Cat, please…"

Billie lost her hold as Cat flung her arms outward. The venom she saw in Cat's eyes made her take a step backward.

"I told you to leave. Don't make me call the police."

Billie's anger surfaced. She grabbed Cat's arms and pressed her against the wall. "I don't know what this is all about, but you've apparently decided I've done something wrong." Billie's chest heaved with each word.

"Leave her alone."

Billie's attention was drawn to the living room doorway where Seth stood with his fists clenched. Tara stood behind him and was crying.

"Let her go, Mom. I won't let you hurt her."

Billie couldn't believe her son had gall enough to stand up to her. The rational part of her mind acknowledged he was taking sides with Cat against her.

"See that? You've turned my own son against me," Billie said. "Damn you."

Cat's eyes narrowed into slits. "Our son, Billie. Our son. And he's staying here with me. Now leave."

"You're making no sense," Billie said. "I call home to say I'll be late, and the next thing I know, I'm being thrown out of the house. No explanation. No reason. Just get the hell out."

Cat reached for the phone and dialed 9-1-1. "Yes, this is Caitlain Charland, and I need a police officer right away."

Billie grabbed the phone out of Cat's hand and slammed it down onto its cradle. "Why did you have to do that? What in God's name could I have done to deserve this?"

"I will not live with a whore! Now I suggest you leave before the police arrive."

"Whore? What makes you think I've been whoring around?"

"I'm not blind. I know what I saw. Unless you want to go to jail, you'd better get out of here."

"What you saw? You're talking in riddles. I deserve an explanation."

"You deserve nothing!"

Billie was terrified by the rapid rise of emotions within her. Deep inside, a dark, powerful force was building. The longer she stood there, the more she wanted to hurt this woman who accused her of infidelity. She grabbed the sides of her head to quell the pain and dichotomy of wills raging inside. Part of her wanted to release the monster she knew lurked inside, but the stronger part of her held on to the reins of self-control. She had to get away before she did something she'd regret. If she hurt Cat, she'd never forgive herself.

She headed for the door.

"Billie."

She stopped short and faced Cat.

Cat grabbed the large envelope from the floor and thrust it at her. "Take these with you. They make me sick."

Billie stuck the envelope in her coat pocket and stormed out the door.

Cat's resolve crumbled when the door slammed. She slid down the wall into a helpless heap on the floor. Seth and Tara ran to her side and huddled against her.

"I was afraid Mom would hurt you." Seth laid his head on Cat's shoulder.

"Me too," Tara said.

"She didn't hurt me, sweetie—at least not physically."

"Is Mom ever coming back?" Tara asked.

Cat saw the confusion in Tara's eyes and lost her battle to hold back tears. "I don't know, sweetheart. I don't know."

Cat pulled her children close and cried as she thought of what life would be like without Billie.

Chapter 2

Billie drove blindly through the streets. She didn't realize where she was until she pulled into the parking lot of her office building. She parked the car and replayed the confrontation with Cat. She went over the event several times, trying to figure out what she had done. Why would Cat do something so drastic as to throw her out?

These past five years were the most joyful and yet the most challenging of her life. For the first time, she had someone she could be happy with. Cat was the most beautiful woman she had ever seen. Short in stature, coming only to her chin, she had the biggest heart and most generous nature of anyone she had ever known. Cat's red-blonde hair and green eyes captivated her the minute she walked into her aerobics class nearly five years earlier. When they met, Seth was only six years old and destined to spend the rest of his life in a vegetative state, but Cat accepted him and arranged to get him the help he needed to recover. To Cat, Seth was like her own flesh and blood, and Cat's daughter, Tara, wormed her way into Billie's heart the moment she set eyes on her.

They had endured so much together. From the heart-wrenching conception of their daughter, Skylar, to Billie finishing law school and passing the bar, they stood shoulder to shoulder and never wavered in their support for each other. Cat stood by her as she lived through a brutal beating at the hands of assailants who disagreed with her fight to legalize gay marriage. Their legal marriage and adoption of each other's children made them a family in every sense of the word.

Billie cherished her life with Cat and the kids, and pain filled her heart as she wondered how she could live without them. What had happened?

An hour later, Art saw Billie in the office parking lot, slumped over her steering wheel. He tapped on her window.

"Roll the window down." He motioned with his hand.

Billie sat back in her seat and lowered the window.

Art reached into the car and squeezed her shoulder. "Are you all right?"

Billie nodded.

"Are you sure you're okay?"

Billie closed her eyes and rubbed her forehead. "I'm fine."

"Really? I don't think so. Is it Cat? The kids? Talk to me. I don't know how to help you."

Billie sighed and released a stuttered breath. "I've lost them. They hate me."

"Come on, that can't be right. Cat loves you. A blind man could see it."

"No. It's over. I can't go home."

"Then you're coming home with me." Art leaned in, took her keys from the ignition, and helped her out of the car. He settled her in the front passenger seat of his own car and called his wife.

"Honey," he said, "I'm bringing Billie home with me. She's in a bad way. No. No, she's not hurt—just upset. Would you mind getting the guest room ready? We'll be there soon."

Art's heart broke for Billie as she leaned against the door, her head on the window and her arms wrapped around herself. Tears coursed down her face as sobs wracked her body. Ten minutes later, they pulled into the driveway of Art's home.

Marge took charge as soon as Art brought her into the house. After removing Billie's coat and handing it to Art, she led Billie to the couch. She sat beside Billie, wrapped her arm around her shoulder, and held her tight as sounds of sobbing filled the room. She stroked Billie's hair and made soothing sounds in her ear

When Billie's sobs subsided, Marge offered her the glass of water Art had brought from the kitchen. While she drank, Marge pushed the hair out of Billie's face and tucked it behind her ear.

"Do you want to talk about it? Do you want us to call Cat?" she asked.

"She won't talk to me. She threw me out," Billie said. "I've lost her. She hates me. My God, how will I live without her? Without my kids?"

Marge cast a worried glance at Art. He sat down on the other side of Billie and circled her back with his arm. "You don't know that she hates you. What could you have possibly done to make her hate you?"

"She called me a whore. She told me to get out."

Art's eyes grew wide. "Why would she say such a thing? She knows better than that."

"I don't know. I just don't know."

Art knelt down on one knee and squeezed one of Billie's hands in his own. "You know we're here for you—right?"

She rested her head against the back of the couch and closed her eyes. Apparently exhausted, within moments she fell asleep.

"Poor dear." Marge wiped the tears from Billie's tear-stained face. "I'm going to turn down the blankets on the bed in the guest room. Carry her in there for me, will you?"

Art slipped his arms under her knees and around her shoulders. Billie's head rested on his shoulder as he carried her into the room and placed her on the bed. She roused slightly as Marge removed her shoes and tucked the blankets around her.

Marge leaned in and spoke softly. "I don't know what happened between you and Cat, but I want you to know we're ready to listen when you feel like talking about it."

Billie nodded.

Marge kissed her on the forehead. "Try to get some sleep."

Billie closed her eyes and nodded once more, while tears escaped from beneath her lids.

"Cat? This is Art."

"Art," Cat said.

"I think you know why I'm calling."

"She's with you, isn't she?"

"Yes, she is. She's in pretty bad shape. She's not hurt or anything, but she's a total wreck."

Cat remained silent on the other end of the line.

"Cat?"

"Art, it's late. I need to put the children to bed. I've got to go."

"I don't know what's happened between you two, but Billie is devastated."

"Ask her about the photographs. I've got to go, Art. Goodnight."

Art frowned at the receiver in his hand. Photographs? He hung up the phone and went in search of Marge, who had just exited Billie's room.

"How is she?"

"She's finally sleeping," Marge said. "She's dying inside. I'm not sure what it is, but something major happened between them."

"Cat called her a whore. Can you believe it?"

"I know what you mean. I was shocked when Billie told us that. I wonder what prompted it?"

"I don't know. I just talked to Cat, to let her know Billie was here. She seemed very cold. She told me to ask her about the photographs. I don't know what that means, but I intend to find out tomorrow."

* * *

Billie's lids fluttered open then slammed shut to ward off the headache that followed the sunlight into her pale blue eyes. She raised a hand and massaged her temple in an attempt to release the tension that had built during her restless night. When she first awoke, she was disoriented and not sure where she was. She sensed a presence and slowly opened her eyes into thin slits to scan the room. There in a chair by her bed, sat a large, dark-skinned man.

"Welcome back to the land of the living." Art leaned over and moved the bangs from her forehead. "How are you feeling this morning, or should I say this afternoon?"

Billie sat up and grabbed her head as a sharp pain erupted between her eyes. "Damned headache. Afternoon?" she said. "What time is it?"

"It's almost one." Art rose to his feet. "Let me get you a couple of painkillers for that headache."

Billie swung her legs over the side of the bed. "I've got to go. Cat—"

"Cat knows where you are. I called her last night. You're not going anywhere until you tell me what's going on."

Billie thought about confiding in him but changed her mind. "It's nothing. We'll work it out."

"I didn't get that impression last night when I found you in your car, nor when I talked to Cat. It didn't appear to me she's ready to work anything out. She was pretty damned cold," Art said. "I can't help you if you don't tell me what this is all about."

"I didn't ask for your help," Billie said. She regretted the words as soon as they left her lips.

"Well, that's just too bad because you've got it whether you want it or not—you got that?"

Billie's bottom lip quivered. "I'm sorry. I didn't mean it the way it sounded. I just need to work this out myself. It's probably nothing anyway."

"Don't tell me it's nothing. I'm the one who found you last night, remember? You told me Cat called you a whore and threw you out. Damn it, that doesn't sound like nothing to me. Whatever happened between you and Cat yesterday was a little more than nothing to put you in the state you were in when I brought you home. Marge has been worried sick about you, and she wouldn't worry over nothing. Understand? Now you're not going anywhere until you tell me what happened."

Billie rose to her feet and paced like a caged tiger. After several trips, she stopped and glared at Art.

"For some reason, she thinks I've been cheating on her. She called me a whore. Can you believe it? She has no right to treat me that way. I wanted so much to beat the shit out of her. Is that what you wanted to hear? Is it?"

Billie noticed that Art kept his distance. Part of her felt bad she was taking her pain out on him.

"Why do you think she called you a whore?"

"How the hell am I supposed to know? I've been faithful to her from the day we met," Billie shouted. "I called her yesterday to let her know I'd be late, and all of a sudden, there was dead silence on the other end of the line. I rushed home, thinking she or the kids were in trouble, and when I got there, I found her on the floor crying." Billie started pacing once more.

"What happened next?"

"I tried to console her, and she just flew off the handle. She told me not to touch her. She screamed at me to leave." Billie ran her hand through her hair. "Seth and Tara were standing there watching the whole thing. I asked them to go into the other room, and I guess I became a little too loud with them, which only made her angrier."

"You didn't hurt her or the children, did you?"

Billie glanced at him and quickly averted her eyes. "I grabbed Cat and pressed her against the wall. I wanted to hurt her. Part of me was so pissed off I wanted to hurt her bad, but no, I didn't. At least I don't think I did."

"And the kids were there the whole time?"

"Yes. In fact, Seth stood up to me and threatened to defend Cat. My own son turned against me."

Art pulled Billie into his arms. "No, my friend, he didn't turn against you. He was defending Cat. You should be proud of him, not angry."

"What am I going to do? My God, if I only knew what I did wrong. She threw me out for no reason. It's unfair."

Art took Billie by the shoulders and held her at arm's length away from him. "Well, when I called Cat last night, she told me to ask you about the photographs. Do you know what she's talking about?"

Billie's forehead creased in thought. "I didn't see any photographs. Wait. She threw an envelope at me as I was leaving."

"Bingo," Art said. "Where is it?"

"In my coat pocket."

"Okay, wait here and I'll get it. Keep your chin up. We'll get you through this, I promise."

She tried to smile through the pain in her heart. "Thanks, Art." She sat down on the bed and massaged her aching head.

Chapter 3

Billie sat on the bed, surrounded by several photographs. Very compromising photographs—photographs of her in graphically sexual positions with an attractive blonde. Her eyes were wide as she glanced back and forth between Art and the pictures.

Art paced, one hand on his hip, the other moving worriedly across his chin. He stopped in front of her. "This isn't good," he said. "I thought you said you never cheated on her. No wonder she threw you out."

Billie continued to stare at the pictures.

"No offense, Billie, but why? Cat is the sweetest, most perfect woman in the world for you. The two of you complete each other. I've heard you say that a thousand times. How could you do this to her?"

Billie's eyes narrowed into slits. She swung her legs over the edge of the bed and shoved her feet into her shoes. She collected the pictures, stuffed them into the back pocket of her jeans, and faced Art. "I thought you were my friend. How could you even think I could do that to Cat?" Billie pressed her hands into the sides of her head. "I need to get out of here before I do or say something I don't mean." She stormed out of the room, yanked her coat from the entryway closet, and reached for the front doorknob.

"Billie, don't leave. I'm sorry. We need to talk about this." Art grabbed her arm to stop her.

Billie swung around and yanked her arm out of his grasp. "You're no better than she is. Both of you jumped to conclusions. Billie must be fucking some blonde bimbo behind Cat's back—right? Well, you have no idea what's behind those photographs. No idea at all."

"You have to admit, the photographs are pretty damning." He again placed his hand on her arm. "Please stay. Let's talk about this."

"Take your hand off me," Billie said through clenched teeth.

"At least let me drive you to where you want to go."

"No thanks, I'll walk. It'll give me time to think. Tell Marge I said thanks for everything."

"Albany Medical Center. How may I direct your call?"

"I'm looking for Cat, ah, I mean, Caitlain Charland."

"One moment please."

Art held the phone against his ear and waited for Cat to answer.

"Caitlain Charland."

"Cat, this is Art."

"Art," Cat said. "If you're calling about Billie, I don't want to discuss it, okay?"

"Listen to me," Art said. "Billie just—"

"Did she show you the photographs?"

"Yes, she did. In fact, it was obvious to me it was the first time she'd looked at them. I can't blame you for being angry."

"I have to go back to work. Is there something you needed to tell me?"

"Yes. Billie just left here pissed off. I've never seen her so disturbed. She told me about yesterday's encounter with you and how she had to stop herself from hurting you. I'm worried about her, and I'm worried about you."

"You don't think she'll—"

"I don't know what she's capable of. I've seen a side of her I didn't know existed. She's not herself. She was an emotional wreck last night, and she complained of a headache. Come to think of it, she had the headache when she went to bed last night and still had it in the morning. I've never seen her in such bad shape. It was as though some dark force was controlling her temper. She thinks she's lost you and the kids, and she's desperate. Desperation has driven people to do awful things."

"Art, I've got to go."

"One thing I've got to know before I hang up," Art said. "Do you still love her?"

Without hesitation, Cat said, "I'll always love her. I just don't know if I'll ever trust her again."

"I understand," he said. "She set out on foot. We're too far from the office for her to walk there, so I don't think that's where she's headed. I'll search around the immediate area first. If I find her, I'll give you a call. Okay?"

"Okay. Thanks."

Billie shoved her hands deep into the pockets of her coat and stared straight ahead as she walked away from Art's house.

"Damn you, Art," she shouted. "How could you? How could Cat?" She walked for miles and ducked between buildings when cars approached. She saw Art drive by several times. Soon she found herself in the downtown area, in a part of the city nicknamed Hell's Hole.

She ducked into a bar as she saw Art's car approach for what felt like the 100th time. She ordered a drink and carried it to a table in the far corner of the room where she could see the entire bar at a glance. She pulled the photographs from her pocket and spread them out on the table. She stared at them as she sipped her drink. Waves of fear and disgust filled her heart as the photographs prompted memories of her painful past.

"What do we have here?" a gravel-tinged voice asked from behind Billie's shoulder.

A large scruffy man leaned over her. The smell of liquor and body odor made her queasy.

"Whoa, there. These are hot." The man picked up one picture to examine it closer. "This is you, isn't it? Why don't you and me go find your little friend here in the picture and the three of us can have a good time?" He rubbed his free hand up and down his crotch.

Billie sneered at the man with disgust. "You're not my type, tripod. I think I'll pass."

"I can see from the picture what your type is, sweetheart. Thought you'd like a nice hard man for a change."

"You thought wrong." Billie grabbed the picture from his hand and threw it back with the others on the table. "Now I'd appreciate it if you'd leave me alone."

"Your loss, dyke." The man walked away and took a seat at the bar.

Several hours and more than a few drinks later, Billie pushed the pictures into a pile and shoved them back into her pocket. She stood, then swayed on her feet and fell back into her chair.

The next thing she knew, she was being helped to her feet by the same man who propositioned her earlier in the evening. Her inebriated state made her helpless to resist as he dragged her out of the bar and into the alley.

"Let go of me, asshole." Billie tried to yank her arm out of his grasp.

The man increased his hold as he half-carried and half-dragged her through the alley.

"I said, let go of me, cocksucker!" Billie screamed as she landed a punch on the man's jaw.

The punch glanced off him. His backhand sent her crashing into the wall where she slumped to the ground. "We'll see who the cocksucker is," he said.

The man grabbed her by the hair, pulled her to her feet, and pushed her deeper into the alley. He slammed her against the wall behind the trash dumpster and pressed his sweaty body against her.

Billie gagged at the smell of him.

He grabbed her by the throat and smashed her head against the brick building. Billie's half-drunk attempts at martial arts didn't faze him. He backhanded her a second time and sent her into a pile of boxes and bags.

The man laughed as he yanked her to her feet and landed a punch to her stomach. She fell to her knees and threw up the countless drinks she had consumed. He kicked her in the side, grabbed her shirt, and pulled her to her feet once again. He pressed her against the wall where he groped her with one dirty hand, while he unbuckled his belt with the other.

Billie forced herself to remain calm while the man unzipped his jeans and exposed himself to her. He grabbed the front of Billie's jeans and tugged until the zipper broke. Moments later, he had her jeans and underpants down below her buttocks. He released the front of her shirt to use both hands to finish removing her jeans.

Billie saw her opportunity. She thrust her knee into sharp contact with his exposed genitalia. The man buckled at the waist and fell forward, knocking both of them to the ground.

"Get off me, you filthy piece of shit!" Billie fought to get away. She almost succeeded, but he grabbed her ankle and pulled her back.

"You whore!" He struggled to hold her down while he pulled his belt from the loops around the waist of his jeans. "You're gonna pay for this, bitch."

Billie filled with terror as flashbacks of beatings at the hands of her ex-husband raced through her mind. *No, this can't be happening again. No, Brian. No more. Please. I won't do it again, I promise.* She covered her head with her hands and did her best to protect her face, while the wide strap bit into her back.

The last thing she remembered before she lost consciousness was her assailant lying on the ground beside her.

Chapter 4

Cat was awakened by a persistent banging. She bolted upright and scanned the room. Where was that noise coming from? She scooted out of bed and pulled on her robe. Carrying a baseball bat she got from Seth's room, she crept down the stairs. As she tiptoed through the living room, she heard the banging again. Someone was pounding on the kitchen door. She reached into the kitchen and turned on the light before she stepped inside. She could see Art through the back-door window. He struggled to hold something in one arm while he banged on the door with the other.

Cat ran over to the door and opened it. She muffled a scream when she saw what he was holding, or rather, who he was holding.

"She's hurt," Art said. He dragged Billie inside and laid her on the floor.

Cat's medical training took over as she examined Billie. "Please carry her to our room, up the stairs and at the end of the hall. I need to get her clothes off to see the extent of the damage… and please try to be quiet. I don't want to wake the kids."

Art lifted Billie and carried her up the stairs to her room. Cat followed behind. She took a deep breath to regain her composure before she entered their room and closed the door.

"Lay her on the bed and help me remove her clothes," Cat said as she collected her medical bag from the desk in the corner.

Within minutes, they had her clothes off. When Art saw Billie's battered body, he ran into the adjoining bathroom. Cat heard him vomit into the toilet. When he returned to the bedroom, Cat was examining Billie's eyes with a small light, testing the responsiveness of her pupils.

"Why didn't you take her to the hospital?" Her hands shook as she examined Billie.

"She refused to go. She made me promise to take her home."

Cat's eyes filled with tears. "What happened to her?" she whispered.

Art knelt by the side of the bed and took one of Billie's hands in his. "She tried to drown her sorrows in one of the seediest bars in town. Some creep had her in the alley and beat the shit out of her. I hope to God nothing else happened, but she was partially unclothed and the man had his pants down around his ankles when I found them."

Cat gasped as the knowledge of what Billie might have endured sunk in. "Art, I need to see if she's been violated. Please go into the bathroom down the hall and soak some white towels in hot water while I examine her, okay?"

Art nodded and rose to his feet.

While he was gone, Cat spread Billie's legs and examined her for signs of sexual violation. When it became obvious Billie had escaped that horror, Cat lowered her head to the bed and cried silent, thankful tears.

Moments later, Art returned with the towels. "Was she…"

Cat shook her head.

Art released a breath and wrapped his arms around Cat. He hugged her and kissed her on top of the head. "

What can I do to help?" he asked.

Cat handed him some of the towels as they worked together to clean the blood and dirt off Billie. When they rolled her over to examine her back, Cat almost passed out at the sight of the welt marks crisscrossing her back and shoulders.

She cried as she washed the angry red stripes on Billie's back. "My God, she must have been terrified."

"Cat, let me finish here, okay? Go make us some tea while I clean her up."

Cat nodded and rose to her feet. She shuffled out of the room and came back later with two cups of hot mint tea. She handed one to Art, placed her own on the nightstand, and resumed her examination. Noting the large bruise on Billie's side, she pressed the palm of her hand into it to determine if there were any broken ribs. Billie moaned at the contact.

"Help me to sit her up. I need to wrap her ribs. I don't think anything's broken, but she's pretty well banged up."

After a few more minutes, they had tended to all of Billie's wounds, wrapped her ribs, and rubbed salve into the welts on her back. Cat slipped a clean flannel nightshirt over Billie's head and laid her on the bed. She pulled the sheet up to cover her just above her breasts. She leaned over, brushed a stray lock of hair from her forehead, and motioned Art out of the room ahead her.

She carried second cups of tea to the table for her and Art and placed her hand on his arm. "You should have taken her to the hospital."

Art studied the contents of his cup and glanced at Cat. "She wouldn't go. She insisted I bring her here. She said if she was going to die, she wanted it to be in your arms."

Cat was startled. "She said that? Her injuries aren't severe enough for her to die."

"I know. I think she went to the bar on purpose, hoping someone would put her out of her misery."

"No. Billie has too much to live for to have a death wish."

"Does she? She doesn't think so. She thinks she's lost you and the children for good. I think she went to the bar fully aware this could happen."

"If that's true, then she's more unstable than I thought," Cat said.

Art extended his hand to her, palm up. Cat willingly placed her hand in his. "No, I don't think so. She's not unstable, just distraught. She thinks she's lost the most precious things in her life. I think she just gave up, not wanting to live without you and the kids."

"You saw the photographs."

Art sighed. "Yes, I did, and like I said on the phone, I don't blame you for being angry. But maybe, just maybe, there's an explanation for all of this."

Cat raised her eyebrows. "I know what I saw. Hell, even you admit the photographs are incriminating."

"Yes, they are, but Billie was adamant about her innocence. In fact, she was pissed at me for jumping to the same conclusions you did."

Cat stood her ground. "What other explanation could there be?"

"Did you ask her for one?"

A cloud of regret fell over Cat's mind. "No, I didn't. I just reacted. Maybe I should have let her explain."

"Billie said you called her some pretty hurtful names."

"Yes, I did. I called her a name appropriate to the situation."

Art squeezed her hand. "You don't need to forgive her yet. Give her time to heal and let her explain before you decide to open your heart again. Okay?"

"I don't know if I can trust her."

Art nodded. "I understand how you're feeling, but do you want to spend the rest of your life wondering?"

Cat shook her head.

"Then give her a chance to explain. Do it for her. Do it for you, and for the kids. If you still feel this way after her explanation, at least you'll know. All right?"

Cat closed her eyes. "All right."

Chapter 5

Cat checked on Billie one more time before climbing into bed with Tara for the night. Within moments, she fell into a light sleep, her subconscious mind listening to Billie in the next room. Before long, sounds of moans and protests woke her up.

She rose from the bed, careful not to disturb Tara, and went to her own bedroom. She checked in on Billie and saw her twisting in the bed. Her head thrashed from side to side and sweat poured from her hairline while a bead of moisture formed on her upper lip. A string of protests came from her throat.

"Brian, no more. Please. I promise not to do it again. Please, no more."

The fear and pain in Billie's voice filled Cat with remorse. What hell Billie must have lived through while married to Brian.

"My God, what did he do to you?" Cat whispered.

Cat ached as she stood in the doorway and watched the keeper of her heart struggle. Unable to stay away, she approached the bed and crawled under the covers. She pulled Billie into her embrace and held her tight while reciting soothing words of comfort into her ear. Soon, Billie settled down and fell back into a deep sleep.

Try as she might, Cat couldn't let go of the pain in her heart as she waited for Billie to calm down. When she was sure Billie was sleeping quietly, she slipped out of bed and rejoined Tara for the rest of the night.

Cat was awakened the next morning by Seth. "Mama, Mom's here. She's in your room and she's hurt," he said.

Cat got up and ran her hand through her hair. She saw Tara was out of bed. "Where's your sister?"

"Tara's downstairs watching cartoons. Sky's with Mom."

Cat took him by the shoulders and lowered her face to his. "Seth, Uncle Art brought Mom home last night. A bad man beat her up, that's why she's hurt. She's going to be fine, honey. All right?"

A string of emotions crossed Seth's face. "Are you and Mom still fighting?"

"No, we're not fighting. Mom just needs time to recover from her injuries."

"Is she staying with us?"

Cat cupped one side of his face with her hand. "I don't know what's going to happen. We'll take it one day at a time and see, okay?"

Seth nodded and hugged her. "I won't let her hurt you, Mama, I promise."

"I don't think you have to worry about Mom hurting me, or any of you for that matter. True, we might fight now and then, but there's never been any hitting—never."

"I know," Seth said, "but Dad used to hit Mom, and—"

Cat pulled him close and agonized over what he had witnessed between Billie and Brian at such a young age. "I know, but please don't worry." She kissed him on the head. "I care a great deal about your mom. Trust me when I say that. We just have some things to work out, but I promise you, no hitting. Okay?"

"Okay."

She ruffled his hair. "Go watch TV with your sister. I'll be down soon to make breakfast."

Seth scampered out of the room. Cat headed toward her own bedroom. She pushed the door open and saw Billie lying on her side, curled around a still sleeping Skylar, who must have crawled in with her in the middle of the night. Cat leaned on the doorframe and stifled a sob with her hand.

Full of aches and pains, Billie held Skylar in her arms and headed toward the kitchen. She stopped in the doorway and watched the scene before her. It was a day like many others. Cat held a spatula over a tall plate of pancakes. "Who wants more?"

Seth and Tara held out their plates.

"Me too, Mama," Skylar said, announcing their presence.

Cat looked up. "You're awake," she said. "Sit. I'll get a dish for you." Billie noticed that her gaze lingered only momentarily. She was almost certain she felt the chill emanating from Cat's cold shoulder.

She winced as she walked toward the table. She placed Skylar in her seat and sat down in the empty chair beside her. She opened her arms to the older children. Both of them rose from the table and approached her warily.

"It's all right. Come here." She tried hard to stifle a painful grunt as they ran into her arms. She wrapped her arms around them and held them close. With a kiss for each child, she sent them back to their seats to finish their breakfast.

Gingerly, she rose to her feet once more and approached the counter where she poured herself a cup of coffee and refilled the cup Cat was drinking from. She carried them to the table.

Cat followed her with a clean plate and utensils. "Sit. Help yourself." She placed a stack of fresh pancakes and sausage in the center of the table.

"Thanks, but I'll pass on the food." Billie drank her coffee in silence, while noting the nervous glances Seth and Tara shot in her direction.

"Mom, what happened to you?" Tara asked.

Billie paused for a moment before answering. "I ran into someone last night who wasn't very nice. Let's just say he got a few more punches in than I did."

"Is he in jail now?" Tara asked.

"I don't know. I don't remember much of what happened."

"Well he belongs in jail. Hey, pass the pancakes, will you?" Tara said to her brother.

Billie sipped her coffee as she listened to the children chatter about their plans to go to the park with their friends, Stevie and Karissa, later in the day. As she watched her family interact, she prayed to whatever God was listening that Cat would allow her stay.

After the children finished eating, Billie rose from the table and helped Cat clear away the breakfast dishes. As usual, Billie rinsed them and handed them to Cat, who arranged them in the dishwasher. As the last dish was loaded, their eyes met and held for a moment. A frown crossed Cat's brow. She looked away, grabbed the dishcloth from the counter, and washed the table.

"Cat," Billie said.

Cat continued to wash the table. "Billie, please. Not now."

Billie lowered her chin to her chest and sighed. She pushed herself off the counter she was leaning against and headed back to their room. Several minutes later, she was dressed and descending the stairs to the living room. She went to each child and kissed them. She told them each she loved them and would see them soon.

Cat, who had been downstairs in the laundry room, carried a laundry basket of clothes up the cellar stairs into the kitchen just as Billie reached for the doorknob. All three children were standing in the doorway between the kitchen and living room, crying. Billie also had tears rolling down her cheeks.

Cat stopped short and said, a little more sternly than she intended, "Where the hell do you think you're going?"

Confusion masked Billie's face. "You said—"

"I said I didn't want to talk about it. It's too fresh. I need some time to deal with it, okay? I didn't mean for you to leave. You're in no condition to go anywhere."

Tara wiped the tears from her face, walked over, and took Billie's hand. "Wanna watch Barney with us, Mom?"

"Barney! Barney!" Skylar chanted as she jumped up and down.

Instead of the traditional groan usually invoked by any mention of the purple monster's name, a grin crossed Billie's face.

"I'd love nothing more than to watch Barney with you, sweetie." Billie allowed herself to be led to the living room by a daughter on each hand.

Cat sat down into a kitchen chair and dropped the basket of clothes on the floor. A pair of small arms circled her neck as Seth hugged her.

"Thanks, Mama," he said. He kissed her cheek, released her, and ran into the living room to join his mother and sisters.

This is not going to be easy, Cat thought.

Chapter 6

Cat walked through the living room on her way upstairs, carrying a pile of folded clothes to be put away. As she passed by the couch, she observed Billie's long form surrounded by children. Billie sat on the couch, watching a purple dinosaur dance across the screen. Skylar was on her lap, wrapped in her arms, and Seth and Tara were book-ending her. Each held onto an arm and leaned into her. Cat's heart ached at the thought that this loving scene could be nothing more than a farce.

Moments later, Cat reminded the children to get ready for their trip to the park with Stevie and Karissa. "Come on guys, you need to get dressed. Jen will be here to pick you up in a few minutes."

Three excited children jumped up and headed for their rooms to get dressed, leaving Billie on the couch alone.

Billie noticed Cat had dragged the vacuum cleaner out earlier. She held her ribs, struggled to her feet, and plugged the machine in. She stepped on the foot pedal to turn it on and began to vacuum the rug. Seconds later, the vacuum shut off. She turned around as fast as her injuries would allow and saw Cat standing behind her with the electrical plug in her hand.

"What are you doing?" Cat asked.

Billie shifted her weight to one hip and narrowed her eyes. "What does it look like I'm doing?"

"I didn't ask for your help."

"I wasn't aware I had to have permission to do chores in my own home," Billie said.

Cat threw the plug on the floor and stomped out of the room.

Billie took a deep, painful breath and sighed. She bent over to pick up the cord, plugged the vacuum back in, and finished cleaning the rug. She wrapped the cord around the built-in holder on the vacuum and rolled it into the hall closet. The whole time, she could hear Cat banging dishes around in the kitchen.

27

Billie walked to the kitchen and stopped in the doorway. "Cat, we need to talk."

Cat stood at the sink with her back to Billie. She raised her hands out to the sides. "Not now. Leave me alone. Please. This isn't a good time."

"Not a good time?" Billie said, her voice tinged with anger. "When will it be a good time? Tell me that much, will you?"

At that moment, Jen burst through the kitchen door. "Hey, neighbors," she said in her usual cheerful manner. The expression changed on Jen's face as she took in the scene before her. "This is not good," she said.

"I'll get the kids, Jen," Cat said. "They should be just about ready to go." She tossed the dishtowel onto the kitchen table and left the room.

Billie shifted from foot to foot and avoided Jen's gaze. Jen was their closest friend, but this situation was too personal to share. She felt Jen's hand on her arm and winced at the contact. Still, she avoided her gaze.

"Billie," Jen said.

Billie allowed Jen to take her chin in hand so she had a full-on view of the cuts and bruises.

"My God. What happened?"

"Stupidity. Mine."

Jen buried her hands in the back pockets of her jeans. "Want to talk about it?"

"Yes, I do, but the one I need to talk to isn't talking to me."

Jen gasped. "Cat? Tell me Cat didn't do this to you."

"No, she didn't."

The sound of children coming down the stairs drew the attention of both women.

Billie placed her hand on Jen's shoulder. "This is something I need to work out with Cat. Taking the kids today is good timing. I'm hoping I can get her to sit down and listen to me while they're gone."

Jen nodded, her attention diverted to the kids who scampered into the room—all except Seth. "All set?" she asked.

Seth walked slowly into the kitchen, with his hands buried deep in his pockets. "Maybe I should stay here, Mom."

Billie knew he was worried about another conflict between Cat and herself. To be honest, she was too, and she didn't want him around to witness it.

Billie motioned for Jen to take the girls out to the car. Cat followed while Billie held Seth back. She knelt down on one knee and took him by the arms. "Sweetie, I know you're worried about Mama," she said. "I won't hurt her—I promise. I love Mama very much, and I swear to you I won't hurt her, okay?"

"You promise?" he said.

"I promise."

Seth hugged her.

She kissed him on the forehead. "Go on now. Have fun."

Seth ran out the door just as Cat was coming back in. He stopped and hugged her as well before running out to the car.

Cat closed the kitchen door and leaned against it. Billie struggled back to her feet through the pain. Sweat broke out on her brow and upper lip from the effort. She pulled out a chair and sat down. Crossing her arms before her on the table, she rested her forehead on them.

Cat broke the silence. "You wanted to talk? Then talk."

Cat's annoyance with Billie rose as she took an interminable amount of time to respond. When Billie did raise her head from her arms, Cat was startled and concerned by the almost unrecognizable expression on her face. Billie's eyes glazed over, and a sneer crossed her normally beautiful features.

She sat back in her chair and pushed another chair out with her foot. "Sit down, Cat."

"No. No, I think I'm fine right here." Cat continued to lean against the door with her arms crossed in front of her.

Too late, Cat realized her refusal to cooperate, most likely combined with the pain Billie was in, angered Billie beyond reason. She stood her ground as Billie rose to her feet and placed her hands on the table.

"I asked you to sit down. I won't be so nice the next time. Now do it," Billie said in a near growl.

Cat's defiance matched Billie's anger. "I don't think so. You're my wife, not my boss."

Cat knew she was pushing the limits of Billie's patience and half-expected her to explode. She was surprised when Billie's brow creased and her face clouded over with confusion as she lowered herself back into her chair. Billie placed her elbows on the table and held her head between her hands.

"Please make it stop," she said.

"Make what stop?"

"The ringing. It hurts."

Cat resisted the urge to help as she watched Billie's mannerisms from her position at the door. As quickly as Billie had succumbed to the pain, she appeared to shake off the confusion. She lifted her head from the table and turned venom-filled eyes toward Cat.

She slammed her fist down onto the table. "Damn you, Cat. Get your ass over here before you make me do something I'll regret later."

Billie was aghast by the words coming from her own mouth, but she was helpless to stop them. It was as though a demon controlled her words and actions.

Cat's stubborn nature held. "Judging by those photographs, I'd say you've already done something you'll regret later."

Billie stood, grabbed her chair, and threw it across the room. She stomped close to Cat and stopped within inches of her face. Her hands were clenched in tight fists at her sides, and her face was a mask of anger and pain. She tried hard to calm the raging tide churning in her chest, but her anger took over. She placed both hands against the door on either side of Cat and trapped her there. "I promised my son I wouldn't hurt you. Otherwise I'd—"

"Otherwise what? Does it make you feel good to threaten someone weaker than you, Billie? Or should I say, Brian?"

Billie reached forward as though to wrap her hands around Cat's throat. She struggled to hold herself back. The veins in her neck bulged and threatened to burst. Her hands shook with controlled restraint.

She looked into Cat's eyes and allowed all the pain and hatred she felt during her life with Brian to enter into them. She dropped her hands to her sides and walked a step away. A safer distance away. She lifted her right hand and pointed a finger in Cat's face. "Don't you ever call me Brian again. You have no idea what he's capable of."

Cat leaned against the kitchen door with her arms crossed in front of her. "Are you forgetting your ex-husband raped me? I'm well aware of what he's capable of."

"The rape was a walk in the park compared to what I lived through at the hands of that bastard. You don't know the half of it."

Cat pushed herself away from the door and took a step toward Billie. "How dare you minimize what he did to me?"

Billie narrowed her eyes and opened and closed her fists at her sides. "I'm not minimizing anything. You don't know how deviant his mind is. I lived with it every day for years. I'll say it again—you have no idea what he's capable of."

"Okay, I'll bite. Just what is he capable of?"

Billie's breathing was labored. Each breath sent waves of pain through her bruised ribs. She backed away a few more steps until she came in contact with the wall. She leaned against it for support, grabbed both sides of her head, and closed her eyes in an attempt to ease the confusion that threatened to take over once more.

She took a deep breath and forced herself to calm down. "Do you want to see what he was capable of? Do you? Okay, you've got it."

Billie grabbed Cat by the arm and dragged her to the table. She shoved her into a chair. "Don't you dare move," she said before leaving the room.

When Billie came back into the room, she was panting and holding her side from her painful run up the stairs and back. She tossed the photographs that started this whole mess on the table in front of Cat.

"That is what he's capable of." She pointed to the pictures.

Cat crossed her arms and held Billie's gaze. "I don't want to see them."

"Right now, I don't care what you want. You jumped to your own conclusions earlier because of these photographs. You assumed guilt before you even asked me about them. I deserve the right to defend myself, and you owe me the respect of listening with an open mind."

"I know what I saw," Cat said.

"No. You don't know what you saw. You couldn't possibly know what you saw. I lived it. Trust me. What you think you saw is not what's really there. Now look at the pictures."

"No."

Billie grabbed a handful of Cat's hair and forced her to look at the pictures. With her free hand, she spread them out before her.

"Look at them, Cat. Look closely."

Billie noticed Cat had closed her eyes. She slammed her hand onto the table. "Damn it, Cat, open your eyes. You're so convinced I'm guilty, yet you won't give me a chance to defend myself. Now open your eyes or I'll walk out that door right now and never come back! Please," she added in a much softer voice. "I don't want to leave. Please don't force me to."

At the soft tone of the plea, Cat opened her eyes. She saw every emotion Billie was capable of in the azure depths of her eyes. Cat knew she held their future in her hands at that very moment, and her next action would either begin to heal the wounds between them or tear Billie's heart out. She took a deep breath and examined the pictures.

She stared at them for long moments, but her heart saw only hurt and betrayal. She covered her eyes with her hands for several moments to regain her composure before looking at them again.

Billie leaned down and whispered in Cat's ear. "Both you and Art allowed your minds to see only the big picture. You allowed your first impression to let you see just what these pictures intended for you to see. Ignore the obvious. The truth is in the details."

With shaky hands, Cat picked up two of the images and studied them for several moments. Suddenly, she saw things she hadn't seen before. She reached out and picked up several more photos.

Cat looked at Billie, who had settled in an adjacent chair and now sat with her hands folded in front of her on the table.

"My God." Cat laid the photos back on the table. "These pictures... How old are they?"

"They were taken when Seth was almost two, and before you ask, Brian took them."

Cat rose to her feet and circled behind Billie. She lifted the back of Billie's shirt, examined the whip marks given to her by the man in the bar, and compared them to the subtle shadows in the pictures. Cat bent down and kissed the marks on Billie's back. She felt a shudder run through Billie before she lowered her shirt and sat again at the table.

Cat clasped her hands in front of her as remorse filled her. "Why did he beat you?" she whispered.

Billie picked up several of the photos. "I told him I wanted a divorce. He beat me and tied me to the bed while he went out and hired the prostitute in this picture. He forced me to pose for these photographs, threatening me with more beatings, and threatening to hurt Seth if I didn't cooperate. In the end, when it was all over, he beat me again anyway."

"Why? What did he think he would gain by photographing you like this?"

Billie shrugged. The pain in Billie's eyes was tangible. "Back then, he used these pictures to control me. By threatening to show them to my parents, he managed to delay the divorce for another year. After my parents were killed, he lost his leverage. It's pretty obvious these photos came from him, but after all this time, I don't know what he hopes to gain. My parents are dead. He no longer has that to hold against me."

Cat touched Billie's hand. Billie instinctively recoiled. "I'm so sorry. I was wrong. I'll never forgive myself," Cat said before whispering, "What are we going to do?"

"We?"

Cat reached out again. This time she took Billie's hand in her own and didn't allow her to pull away. "We," Cat said. Billie had lowered her gaze to the table.

Cat lifted Billie's chin. "I feel like a total ass. I know now I overreacted. I'm so sorry. You have every right to be angry with me. I deserve whatever punishment you can think of, but please, don't hate me. I've been a jealous fool. I wouldn't have reacted that way if I didn't love you."

Billie opened her arms. Cat closed the distance between them as she slid onto Billie's lap and pulled Billie's head to her chest. She recited terms of endearment and apology over and over into Billie's ear.

"I'm sorry too," Billie said. "I shouldn't have treated you that way. I don't know what got into me. I was so angry. Please know I wouldn't have harmed you."

"I know. What do you think gave me the courage to stand up to you?"

"Talk about losing leverage."

Cat cupped Billie's face. "I'm so sorry. I should've known you'd never betray me. I'll never doubt you again." She raised her lips for a tender kiss.

Billie pulled her in closer and the kiss intensified. "God, Cat, I want to ravish you from head to toe."

Cat pulled away from the caress. She traced Billie's lips with her fingertips. "I don't think so. You're in no condition to make love to me right now." Cat saw the distress on Billie's face. "But that doesn't mean I can't hold you while you sleep." She rose to her feet and helped Billie up. "Come with me," she said and led Billie upstairs to their bedroom.

In their room, Cat sat Billie on the edge of the bed and removed her own clothing, being careful to stay just beyond Billie's reach. "No, no," she said. "If you can't behave, you'll have to nap alone."

Billie sighed and clasped her hands in her lap.

Finally, Cat stepped into Billie's embrace and kissed her. She lifted Billie's shirt over her head, being careful not to disturb her ribs. After she dropped the garment to the floor, she encouraged Billie to lie on the bed and removed her shoes and shorts.

"Can you sit up while I take care of your injuries?" Cat asked.

"If a cute little redhead I know helps me, I think I can manage it."

Several minutes later, Billie's ribs were rewrapped and her wounds massaged with ointment. Cat helped her pull a clean T-shirt over her head and pushed her down under the covers. Cat stretched out beside her and draped her arm over Billie's waist. "Close your eyes. Sleep will do you good. I'll be here when you wake."

After a time, Cat felt Billie relax. "Feel better?" she asked.

"Yes, but I still want you."

"Right now you need to recover so you can take some of that animal prowess I witnessed downstairs and apply it to our lovemaking later," Cat said with a wicked grin.

A wave of guilt crossed Billie's face, and she turned away. "I'm sorry," she said. "I don't know what came over me. Part of me wanted to hurt you, and part of me tried so hard to control the anger. It was like I was standing outside of myself. It scared the shit out of me."

Cat regretted the hurt she had caused with her careless comments. "Billie, baby, I'm sorry. I shouldn't have said that. Down deep I know you wouldn't intentionally hurt me. It was inconsiderate of me to mention it. Forgive me?"

Billie closed her eyes. When she opened them again, they shone brightly. "You've done nothing to apologize for. Please, let's put it behind us."

Chapter 7

Billie walked into the office on Monday morning, conscious of the stares and curious glances she received from her coworkers and office staff. Cat tried to talk her into taking vacation until the bruises faded, but her workload and the domestic abuse case she was working on wouldn't allow it.

She sat at her desk and read the case file on Peggy McBride, age twenty-eight, married for four years to Roger McBride. One son, Travis, age three. Peggy had been hospitalized no less than three times in the past four years for internal injuries. Causes of injuries were listed as accidents: a fall down the cellar stairs, a skiing accident, and a fall from a tree while building a clubhouse for her son. In addition to her hospital stays, there were several visits to the emergency room for various broken bones and sprains.

Each injury was blamed on an accident or just plain clumsiness, until her three-year-old son Travis was hospitalized with broken ribs and head injuries. An astute nurse in the emergency room noticed a trend in Peggy's file that the hospital reported to the police, and thirty-three-year-old Roger McBride was arrested on suspicion of spousal and child abuse. He was currently free on bail, but a restraining order required him to keep his distance from Peggy and Travis.

Billie read through the paperwork in the folder until she came across photographs of the victims' most recent injuries. She stared at the eight-by-ten pictures and realized they could very well be pictures of Cat had she not controlled herself two days earlier. Her gut clenched into a tight knot as she replayed the scenes in her head: pinning Cat against the door, reaching for her throat, grabbing her arm, and forcing her into the kitchen chair. And what about Seth and Tara? Losing her temper and screaming at them was uncalled for. God, what was happening to her?

She crossed her arms on the desk and rested her forehead on them in an attempt to control the headache running rampant between her temples. The headaches seemed to be more frequent of late, and the intensity was beginning to worry her. She felt so out of control when they occurred. She made a mental note to schedule a physical.

Billie's internal struggle was interrupted by the telephone.

"Hey, Billie," Art said, "how are you this morning?"

"Better than I could have been. Thanks for the help Friday night."

"I'm glad I was there. I shudder to think what might have happened if I wasn't."

"Yeah, me too."

"Billie, I want to talk to you about the McBride case. Can you come to my office?"

"Sure, I'll be there in a few minutes."

"Okay. I'm running to the cafeteria for a coffee first. Can I pick one up for you?"

"Please. Large, black, and thanks,"

"Tall, strong, and black, just like me, huh?"

"Yeah, just like you, you moron."

"See you in a bit."

Billie hung up and smiled. She found herself thanking the heavens above for Art. He had grown to be a very close and trusted friend, and she could always count on him for help. She grabbed the McBride folder and headed to his office, with a stop at the restroom on the way.

Billie reached Art's office at about the same time he did. He pushed the door open with his hip and allowed her to walk in ahead of him. He circled around the desk and placed her coffee in front of her.

She sat in a chair on the opposite side of the desk and reached for the coffee. "Thanks. I need the caffeine this morning."

Art studied her while he sipped his coffee. "That guy sure did a number on you."

Billie traced the bruises along her jawline. "Yeah, I guess he did." Her hand shook as she lowered her coffee cup to the desk, spilling a small amount. "Sorry. I'm a little shaky today."

"You know, you could have taken a few days off to let the bruises fade."

"Cat encouraged me to do just that, but we've got a lot of work to do on the McBride case. It just didn't feel right to take time off."

"Speaking of Cat, how is she?"

Billie lowered her gaze to the desk. Moments passed in silence.

"Billie? You didn't hurt her, did you?"

Billie felt her anger rise and struggled to keep it in check. She knew Art was concerned for both of them. "No, I didn't hurt her, although I came close—too close for comfort."

Art's brow furrowed. "What do you mean?"

Billie grabbed the McBride file and found the photographs. She pulled them out of the folder and placed them on the desk in front of him. She pointed at the bruised face of Peggy McBride. "I came within a hair's breadth of doing that to Cat this weekend."

Art rose to his feet and placed his hands on the desk, leaning forward. "What happened?"

Billie stood and walked a few feet away. When she turned around, her bottom lip quivered with emotion. "Saturday morning, after Jen took the kids to the park, I forced Cat into a discussion about the pictures we received in the mail." Billie started to pace. "She was being so damned stubborn. I had her pinned against the kitchen door, my hands almost wrapped around her neck. I... I don't know what came over me. It's like I was a different person. I wanted to beat the shit out of her."

"But you didn't."

"No, I didn't."

Art took a deep breath. "Tell me to mind my own business if you want, but that son of a bitch you were married to beat you, didn't he?"

Billie made eye contact with him. "More times than I can count."

"You want to talk about it?"

"Those pictures you saw—the ones Cat was so upset over— were taken several years ago by my ex-husband. He had just beaten me for asking for a divorce. The other woman in the picture was some whore he hired to do just what the pictures accomplished with Cat. They contaminated the minds of the people I love."

"I don't understand," Art said.

Billie stopped pacing and walked back to her chair. She took her coffee from Art's desk and savored the rich, dark liquid before returning to the discussion at hand. "My parents were still alive when I came out to Brian. They had no idea about my sexual orientation, and I didn't want them to know. I made the fatal mistake of begging Brian not to tell them. Knowing he was about to lose me and Seth, he beat me senseless then staged those photographs to use against me. To force me to stay with him. He lost leverage a year later when my parents died in a car accident."

"So, Cat somehow found the photographs and assumed they were current. No wonder she was pissed."

Billie stared at a spot on the floor in front of her. "Actually, someone sent them to us in the mail. She wouldn't listen to me. She automatically assumed I was guilty. You both did."

Art placed his hand on her shoulder. "You have my deepest apology for that, but even you have to admit the evidence was pretty damning."

"On the surface it was, but this is me we're talking about. You should have trusted me. Cat should have trusted me as well."

"So, did she finally listen?"

Billie's head bobbed up and down. "Yes, she did."

"And?"

"And things are fine now. She feels awful about accusing me now that she knows the whole story."

"Who on earth would have sent the photographs?"

"Brian, of course. As far as I know, he's the only one who had them."

"Damn." Art sat on the edge of his desk facing Billie. "How's Cat feeling about all of this?"

"Cat's fine. She's a little scared, but she's okay."

"How's Billie?" he asked.

Tears rolled down her cheeks. "Billie's not so fine."

Art stood and reached out his hand. "Come here," he said.

Billie put her coffee on the desk, rose to her feet, and walked into the circle of her friend's strong arms. He held her close.

"Let it go," he said. "Let it out. I've got you."

After a time, Billie regained control of her emotions and broke free of Art's embrace. She walked over to the Kleenex box on the credenza and grabbed a handful of tissues to wipe her tears and blow her nose. After regaining her composure, she faced Art.

"The first thing I did when I got here this morning was go through the McBride file. I read the report and came across the pictures." She stifled a sob and tried to regain her composure. "When I saw the pictures, I realized they could have just as easily been pictures of Cat."

Art crossed his arms in front of him. "As of right now, you're off the McBride case."

Billie's eyes grew wide. "No. Don't you dare do that to me!" She grabbed his arm as he tried to walk away from her.

Art swung back around to face her. "You're too close to this. You can't detach yourself from this one. Emotional involvement leads to carelessness. You're off the case."

"I won't let you do this. My personal experience will help this case. Please don't do this."

"And what will your personal experience do to you and Cat?"

"If this case adversely affects Cat, or the kids, then I'll voluntarily pull out. I promise."

Art ran his hand through his hair. "This is against my better judgment. I'm warning you, Charland, any indication at all that Cat or the kids are suffering, and I'll pull you off this case and beat the shit out of you myself. Understand?"

Billie smiled through her tears and offered her hand to him. "Understood," she said as her hand was enveloped in his.

* * *

Billie returned to her desk and contemplated her conversation with Art. Deep down, she knew he was right about her level of personal involvement in this case. The case photos alone brought back horrible nightmares of her own abuse. Uncontrollable waves of anger and hatred surfaced with each memory. Near the end, she thought about how she voluntarily lent herself to the abuse to prevent Brian from taking his anger out on Seth. The McBride boy wasn't so lucky. She promised herself she would do everything in her power to see McBride go down for this.

Where to start? she thought as she planned her research for this case. She decided she needed help to do a search on Roger McBride's history, so she picked up the phone and called Jimmy in Criminal Law. Jimmy was the firm's Internet expert, with access to state and national criminal records. In his younger years, he had quite a reputation as a beat cop. Although he moved to a desk job when his age made it difficult to maintain his daily beat, he still had connections all over the city. If there was information to be found, Jimmy would find it.

"James Callahan," the voice on the other end of the line said.

"Jimmy. This is Billie Charland."

"Hey there, missy. What can I do for you?"

"I've got a challenge for you. I need a background check on one Roger McBride, including the details on any criminal activities he may have been involved in over the past, say... ten years."

"Is he a local fellow?"

"Yes."

"Piece of cake. I'll have the information for you lickity-split."

"Thanks. I knew I could count on you."

"Anytime. Say hello to the missus for me, would you?"

"I sure will. Thanks again, Jimmy."

Her next task was to set up interviews with Peggy McBride and the boy, Travis. Dealing with the victims would be the most difficult part of the case. She had seen so many domestic abuse cases ruled in favor of the accused because the victim was too terrified to testify against them or felt some sense of loyalty to the abuser. So many times, the victim went back to the abuser, only to allow the cycle to repeat itself months, weeks, or even days later.

Billie sat at her desk and stared straight ahead as her mind wandered to events nine years earlier. She was working on her law degree and taking classes at night. One night in particular, she was late getting home. She stopped to have coffee with another woman in her class. Seth was almost a year and a half old.

When she got home, the first thing she noticed was Seth crying. She found him standing in his crib, sobbing his heart out. Cradling him in her arms, she realized he was soaking wet. Brian had neglected him the entire evening. She cleaned Seth up, changed his diapers, and dressed him in clean pajamas. She got a bottle from the refrigerator, sat down with him in the rocking chair in his bedroom, and sang to him until he fell asleep. After laying him in his crib, she covered him up and went to confront Brian.

She found him lying on the living room couch, with several empty beer bottles scattered around him and the television remote in his hand. Before she had a chance to say anything, he was off the couch like a shot and grabbed her by the neck.

"Why are you late, bitch?"

Billie found it difficult to reply through the stranglehold he had on her throat. "I was hav... having coffee."

"You were out fucking around on me, weren't you? Weren't you?"

"No. No, I wasn't. Please let go."

He backed her up against the wall and slammed her head into it over and over. "You belong here with me, taking care of that little bastard in the other room," he screamed. "Not out screwing everything in sight."

"I... I wasn't."

"Don't lie to me, you filthy whore."

"Brian, stop. Please."

"I'll teach you to run out on me, bitch." While he reached for his belt buckle, Billie kicked him in the shin. He let out a howl and fell to the floor, releasing the hold he had on her neck only when she fell on top of him. She scrambled away, but he caught her foot and yanked on it as hard as he could. He twisted it and caused an audible snap. Climbing up and sitting across her stomach, he threw blow after close-fisted blow at her face. About half of the blows landed on target, the other half blocked by Billie's flailing hands. When he stopped, he removed his belt and whaled it across her back until stripes of blood could be seen through her blouse.

Afterward, he rolled off her, staggered to his feet, and passed out on the couch in the living room. Billie managed to crawl into Seth's room, where she locked the door and laid on the floor, trembling from anger, pain, and fear through the remainder of the night.

It wasn't the first time he'd hit her, but it was one of the most severe. It all went downhill from there. Not long after that, Brian found Billie's diary and discovered her preference for women. He beat her again, and she couldn't get out of bed for two days. Next, came the photographs with the prostitute, and the blackmail, vowing to reveal her "dirty little secrets," as he liked to call them, to her parents. She couldn't let him break her parents' hearts, no matter what she had to endure.

The beatings became more frequent, but he was careful about where he hit her. Having to make up excuses for her injuries had been difficult, so she had learned to hide the abuse. For another full year, she lived in her secret hell, until one fateful day her parents were killed in a car accident and Brian lost his hold over her. In her parents' death, she found the freedom to divorce him and run away with Seth.

She reported him for the abuse, but his wealthy parents managed to buy his freedom. He never paid a penalty for his crimes. Not until she met Cat. Not until he made the mistake of hurting his son and raping the woman she loved. It took the pain of others to make her act on years of hate and anger that had built up inside of her.

And now, that hate was back to haunt her. She found herself on the verge of hurting the one person who gave her life meaning. She found herself falling into Brian's patterns.

God, please don't let me hurt her, or the children, Billie prayed to whatever God was listening. She closed her eyes and allowed the tears to cleanse her memory as they ran down her face.

Chapter 8

Billie drew herself out of her self-imposed hellhole of memories and checked her watch. It was only one p.m. She fidgeted, feeling emotionally out of control. She didn't like who she was becoming. Her anxiety level was very high and caused waves of desperation to run through her. Unable to hold back any longer, she picked up the phone and dialed the hospital. After several minutes, Cat came on the line.

"This is Cat Charland."

"Cat," Billie said, her voice weak and shaky.

"Billie? Billie, are you all right?"

"Can you get out of work? Can you meet me at home?"

"What's wrong? You're scaring me."

"I need you."

"I'm on my way. I'll see you at home in a few minutes."

Billie grabbed her car keys and headed out the door. She ran to her car. Ten minutes later, she pulled into the driveway of her house. Cat wasn't there yet. Billie paced the living room for the next five minutes until Cat stepped into the kitchen.

"Billie, where are you?" Cat called as she walked into the living room.

Billie ran to her and pulled her close. She couldn't stop trembling as Cat's hands ran up and down her back.

"Shhh. Whatever it is, it'll be all right. I love you. Shhh."

Billie took Cat's hand and led her up the stairs and to their bedroom. They lay on the bed, and Billie held Cat close. "Please forgive me," Billie whispered. "I'll spend the rest of my life showing you how sorry I am, and I'll never give you reason to doubt me again. Please believe that."

Cat traced her finger across Billie's brow and down her cheek. "Don't be afraid. I'm here for you. I'll always be here for you. And as far as forever goes, you're stuck with me. Yep—stuck like glue."

Billie smiled at Cat's attempted humor. "Thank you."

"We'll get through this. I promise." Cat pulled the quilt up around them. "Sleep now and know that I'll be here when you awake."

* * *

Billie only slept an hour. Cat didn't sleep at all as she stood guard over Billie's heart. Finally, Billie stirred.

"Hi," Cat said.

Billie just smiled.

"Are you ready to talk about it?"

Billie sat up and reclined against the headboard. She pulled the quilt up with her and tucked it around her waist. For several moments, she held Cat's gaze without speaking a word.

"Billie?" Cat took Billie's hand in her own.

"I need help."

"Help? What kind of help?"

"Professional help."

"I don't understand."

"There's so much you don't know about my past. So much I've been holding inside, keeping from you. I need help dealing with it before I end up hurting you or the children. Please try to understand."

Cat saw how much this meant to Billie. "Okay. Help is good," she said. She tucked a few stray locks of strawberry blonde hair behind her ears. "Do you have someone in mind?"

"I thought we could start with the doctor we saw after the rape."

"Dr. Connor. She's good. Okay, I'll call to make the appointment." Cat paused and studied Billie for a long time. "I'll be right back," she said. Cat went to the living room to make the call.

Moments later, she returned. "We're in luck," she said. "Dr. Connor has an opening at four this afternoon. That's just an hour away. Let me give Jen a call to see if she can pick the kids up at daycare."

Billie nodded and Cat made the call. "All set. Do you want anything to eat before we leave?" Cat was uncomfortable with the situation. She had never seen Billie in this kind of funk, and she didn't know how to deal with it.

Billie shook her head.

"Is there anything else I can do for you while we wait?"

"Can you hold me?"

Cat held her close to her heart and whispered, "I love you."

"I'm sorry, Cat."

"For what?"

"I came so close to hurting you the other day."

"You wouldn't have hurt me. I trust you completely."

"Don't be so quick to trust me. You could end up hurt if you do."

"Never," Cat said. "Never."

* * *

Billie and Cat sat side by side in the waiting room of Dr. Connor's office, hands clasped, neither saying a word. Finally, the door opened and the doctor motioned Billie into the room. Billie rose to her feet and sent a silent plea with her eyes. Cat rose and followed Billie.

Billie held Cat's hand as they sat opposite Dr. Connor.

"It's been awhile since I've seen you," Dr. Connor said as she read through notes from previous sessions. "Let me see—ah yes, almost five years ago when you were dealing with the rape trauma." Dr. Connor laid the notes in her lap. "What brings you here today? Billie, let's start with you."

Billie looked at Cat, then back at the doctor. "I... ah... I... Damn, this is hard."

"Would it be easier if Cat left the room?" Dr. Connor asked.

"No," Billie said vehemently. "This concerns her. She has a right to be here."

"Billie, it's okay. I can wait—"

"No. I need you here with me. Please don't go."

"Okay."

Billie brought Cat's hand up and kissed her knuckles. "Thank you." She directed her attention at Dr. Connor again. "I'm afraid of hurting Cat and the children."

Dr. Connor leaned forward. "Why would you be afraid of hurting your wife and children?"

"Because it's all I know."

"Billie," Cat said, "we've been together for nearly five years, and you've never once hurt any of us in anger. How can you say that?"

"Yes, I have. Two days ago, I yelled at the kids for no reason. I had you pinned against the door. I wanted to hurt you during that argument. I sat at my desk today at work, thinking about that fight. I panicked. The anxiety was overwhelming. That's why I called you. I needed to feel you, to know you still loved me, even though I treated you like that."

Cat opened her arms and took Billie into them. "Of course I still love you. You didn't hurt me. Please stop beating yourself up for something you didn't do."

Dr. Connor interrupted. "Cat, did Billie pin you against the door?"

"Yes, she did, but—"

"And did she threaten you?"

"Yes, she did, but she didn't do it. She couldn't."

"Couldn't she?"

"No. I don't believe for one minute she could." Cat rose to her feet. "I trust her. I may have learned the hard way, but I trust her."

Dr. Connor looked at Billie. "Do you believe you could do it?"

"Sometimes I feel I need to hurt others the way I've been hurt."

Cat sat down and took Billie's hands in hers. "I've never hurt you. How can you say that?"

Billie freed one of her hands and cupped the side of Cat's face. "Not you. Never you."

"Brian?" Cat asked.

Cat and Dr. Connor spent the next hour listening to the horror that Billie's marriage to Brian had been.

By the time Billie finished, she and Cat were total wrecks. While Billie spoke, Cat paced the room and finally settled herself in a far corner, leaning against the wall. Dr. Connor rose from her chair and picked up a water pitcher and glasses from a nearby table. She put them on her desk and poured some water. She approached Cat and led her back to the chair next to Billie. Several moments of silence followed as the women composed themselves.

"I knew he was abusive," Cat said, "but I had no idea."

"Billie, what do you think prompted these memories and these feelings now?" Dr. Connor asked.

Billie sipped her water and cradled the glass in her lap between her hands. "I've been assigned to a domestic abuse case at work. The victim is about the age I was when Brian... well, you know. Her son is a year older than our son, Seth, was when I left Brian."

"So the case brought back the memories?" Dr. Connor asked.

"In part, yes."

"In part?"

"Yes. You see, a few days ago, a package of photographs arrived at our home. They were pictures Brian had taken of me and a prostitute. He beat me then staged the photos as emotional blackmail to hold me hostage in the marriage."

"When I saw the photographs," Cat said, "I assumed the worst. I feel horrible about that."

"The photographs in the mail were the final straw," Billie said.

"Where do you think the photos came from?" Dr. Connor asked.

"Probably Brian," Billie said. "I want to confront him, but—"

"I don't want you anywhere near that bastard," Cat said.

"He can't hurt me now," Billie said.

"He can't? Why do you think you're here? He's not only hurting you, he's killing you!"

"I need closure on this. I don't know what else to do."

"And if he denies it and abuses you further—even verbally? Then what?"

Billie shook her head. "I don't know."

"Do you think it's a good idea for you to work on this domestic abuse case?" Dr. Connor asked.

"Now you sound like Art," Billie said.

"Art?"

Billie's face broke into a half-grin. "Yeah, my partner in crime at work. Actually, he's my superior, but don't tell him that or he might actually think he can boss me around."

"I'm happy to see you still have a sense of humor," Dr. Connor said.

"Art threatened to take me off the case because I was taking it too personally. He made me promise I'd withdraw from it if my family ended up in danger because of it. I suspect he thinks the danger would come from me."

"I can't believe Art said that," Cat said.

"Uh-huh," Billie replied.

"Why that son of a—" Billie clamped a hand over Cat's mouth and shot an apologetic grin at Dr. Connor.

When she removed her hand, Cat continued to say, "... four-flushing, knock-kneed, two-toed billy goat. He's going to get a piece of my mind."

"Do you think you can handle the case, Billie?" Dr. Connor asked.

Billie paused a moment. "I think I have to. I could never forgive myself if I didn't help this woman break the cycle. Her son's in the hospital because of her husband. I don't want to see her end up there as well, or in the morgue for that matter."

"And you think you can do that without putting yourself or your family in jeopardy?"

"I don't know."

Chapter 9

The drive home was quiet. Cat drove while Billie sat with her head leaning against the passenger door window. Several times, Cat reached over to run her hand up and down Billie's arm. When they pulled into the driveway, Billie sat up.

"Thanks for coming with me," she said in a soft voice.

Cat took Billie's hand and kissed the palm. She placed it on the side of her own face and leaned into the touch. "Thank you for letting me share that with you. It must have been hard for you to talk about it."

"I didn't realize how much pain was building up inside of me. I guess this case just brought it all to the surface. Unfortunately, you became the unintended target for that pain. Can you ever forgive me?"

"Billie, I've already told you there's nothing to forgive. Sweetheart, you didn't do anything wrong. You didn't hurt me. What else can I do to convince you?"

"I could have. God knows, I wanted to."

"But you didn't. Don't you see? You didn't do it, because you couldn't. Please believe that."

"I want to." Billie rubbed her forehead.

Cat saw the gesture. "Are you all right, love?"

"Yeah, just a headache."

Cat had noticed the headaches were coming more frequently. She felt Billie's forehead. "No fever. You know Mom and Dad are coming home for the summer in about a week. I'd like Daddy to take a few CAT scans, and maybe an MRI, of the area around the gunshot wound. Maybe there's a reason for these headaches."

"It's just a headache, Cat. It'll go away."

"And when did you get your medical degree?"

"Come on, don't make such a fuss."

"At least think about it."

"I actually planned to call earlier today for an appointment, but the day kind of got away from me. Right now I need a couple of painkillers and a nice warm bed."

"All right, let's get you settled, and I'll fetch the kids from Jen's." Cat got out of the car and followed Billie into the house.

A half hour later, Billie was tucked into bed and Cat sat at Jen's kitchen table nursing a hot cup of tea and staring into space.

"Do you want to talk about it?" Jen asked.

Cat was pulled out of her thoughts by the sound of her friend's voice. "Huh? I'm sorry, my mind was somewhere else. What did you say?"

"I said, do you want to talk about it? It's clear something's bothering you."

"I'm okay."

"No, you're not okay. I walked in on a pretty intense scene the other day. Billie looked like she'd been dragged through a meat grinder, and you were so angry you were spitting nails. For crying out loud, the tension was so thick you could cut it with a knife. I've seen you two argue before, and it wasn't anything like what I witnessed Saturday. Don't tell me things are okay."

Cat wanted to discuss this with her best friend, but she didn't want to betray Billie's trust. She stared into her mug for several moments. "I can't say any more. I really want to, but I can't. I hope you understand. I promise I'll tell you all about it when I can."

Jen sighed. "I hate to see you two in so much pain. I'll be patient, but know I'll be here if there's anything you need. Promise you'll call me if there's anything I can do."

"I'll let you know. You can count on it, although I feel like we take advantage of you way too often."

"Cat, I could never repay the debt we owe the two of you. Billie ran into our burning house and saved my family, and you opened your home to us while our home was rebuilt. I'd walk barefoot on broken glass to help you in any way I can. Am I making myself clear?"

"You've long since repaid that debt, Jen. Please don't feel like you owe us. Just know we appreciate you very much."

"Ditto. How about a refill?"

"God, no. Thanks anyway. It's already six o'clock. I've got to get the kids home and start supper." Cat poked her head into the living room and told the kids to get ready. She returned to the kitchen, wrapped her arms around Jen, and hugged her fiercely. "Thanks for picking up the kids. It was a big help."

"Anytime, kiddo. Give the tall one a kiss for me, okay?"

"Sure," Cat said, beaming. "That's one message I don't mind delivering."

Within minutes, Cat and the children arrived home. Cat sent them into the family room to play until suppertime so they wouldn't disturb Billie. After she put the casserole into the oven, she climbed the stairs to the second story and pushed open her bedroom door. Billie was sprawled out across the bed, holding her head in her hands. The bed was torn apart, the blankets in a tangle around her body. She was obviously in a great deal of pain.

Cat made her way to Billie's side and slipped into bed behind her. She sat with her back against the headboard and rolled Billie over until her head was lying in Cat's lap. Billie's eyes were shut.

"It hurts. God, it hurts."

"Relax, love." Cat placed her fingertips on Billie's temples and rolled them around in small circles. "Let it go. Don't fight it, honey. Relax." She continued the massage, speaking in soft, soothing tones at the same time. Soon, Billie's body visibly relaxed and she sank into the bed. Cat continued the ministrations for several more minutes, until she was sure Billie was sleeping. After a time, she worked her way out from beneath her, pulled a quilt over her, and closed the drapes. She placed a gentle kiss on her forehead and left the room.

* * *

Billie rose the next morning feeling better than she had in days. The last thing she remembered from the day before was drifting off in Cat's arms while the ache in her temples was soothed away by miracle fingers. This morning, she felt great. She woke up long before the alarm and lay there, savoring the look and feel of the beautiful woman asleep beside her.

Billie studied Cat's face and noted tiny lines at the corners of her eyes and across her brow. Worry lines. She frowned and thought about the roles they played in each other's lives and within their family. After deep contemplation, she realized Cat had taken on the role of caretaker for the family. Not that Billie didn't help, but it appeared Cat always took the initiative to get things done. On the other hand, Billie was the self-appointed protector, trying very hard to keep everyone safe and warm.

While Billie saw herself as the playful parent, that role forced Cat into the position of disciplinarian and teacher and she held herself responsible for the emotional health of their family. The small worry lines etched into Cat's face were evidence of the stress such a responsibility placed on her.

Billie placed tender kisses across Cat's brow, honoring the sacrifices she had made for their family. "I love you, kitten," she whispered as she watched the corners of Cat's mouth twitch while she slept.

Billie rolled out of bed, stretched her arms high over her head, and leaned side to as far as her injured ribs would allow. She walked to the window and lifted the shade to reveal a beautiful sunrise peeking over the horizon. No sense wasting a beautiful day, she thought as she pulled on a T-shirt, shorts, and a pair of running shoes. She grabbed her hooded sweatshirt and left the room.

Once outside, she took a few moments to stretch some more before starting her walk. As she reached the end of the driveway, she noticed Jen coming down the road, out for her usual early morning power walk.

Billie waved. "Morning, Jen. Mind if I join you?"

"Sure. Maybe I'll actually be able to keep up with you this morning, considering the Goddess of Tall Women is not running on all cylinders."

"Watch yourself. Just because I'm injured doesn't mean you've got one up on me." Billie jabbed Jen in the arm.

"Hey, no fair. I can't hit you back."

Billie jabbed at Jen's arm again.

"Damn it. If you don't stop, I'll kick your ass."

"Ooh. I'm afraid." Billie continued to annoy Jen with playful jabs.

"All right then, I'll sic Cat on you."

Billie stopped. "I know when I'm outclassed."

Soon they fell into a steady walk with Jen setting the pace. After about a half mile, Billie was holding her side. "Maybe this walk wasn't such a good idea. Do you mind slowing down a bit?" she asked Jen.

Jen slowed her pace. "We're almost to the park. Maybe we can sit for a while."

"Sounds good to me."

Jen and Billie sat on a park bench to allow Billie to catch her breath. Jen locked arms with Billie. "So, are you feeling better?"

"Yeah. Damned headaches. I get them every now and then. They knock the wind right out of my sails. Thank God for Cat's magic fingers."

Jen raised her eyebrows. "Don't go there, girlfriend. That's way more information than I need."

It took a second for Billie to realize Jen had misunderstood her. She punched Jen in the arm. "Get your mind out of the gutter. Geesh. Cat gives great neck massages. Her fingers are good for things other than that, you know."

A sly expression crossed Jen's face. "That? What do you mean... that? Explain yourself."

Billie closed her eyes into narrow slits. "Jennifer."

"Yikes." Jen took off running.

"Hey! Wait for me," Billie said as she struggled to her feet.

Jen ran back and jogged in front of Billie. "Only if you promise not to pulverize me."

"Deal. Now give me a hand."

Jen once again grasped Billie's elbow and they set out for a leisurely walk back home.

"So," Jen said, "how many rounds did you go with that guy?"

Billie fell silent.

"I'm sorry. I shouldn't have made that comment. Forgive me?"

"I guess I can't blame you for being curious. Let's just say I tried to drown my sorrows after Cat and I had a fight, and I ran into a very big brick wall."

Jen touched the side of Billie's face with her palm. "Are you all right? I mean, did he..."

Billie took Jen's hand between her own. "No, he didn't. Thank God, Art found me just in time."

"Enough said. No more of this depressing talk. We're supposed to be exercising. What's up with you, soldier? Tired? Can't walk anymore?"

"I'll show you who can't walk. Last one home grills the burgers at the next cookout," Billie said as she took off as fast as her injuries would allow.

Jen stood there with her hands on her hips and yelled. "Hey, that's not fair. If I beat you home I'll have to eat your cooking!"

Billie stopped and grinned at Jen. "I never issue a challenge I can't win."

"How does Cat put up with you?" Jen said, as they walked the rest of the way home.

* * *

Cat was still asleep when Billie returned from her run, so she tiptoed to the bathroom and climbed into the shower. Seconds later, she stood under the warm spray and delighted in the tingle of the water as it danced across her skin. Suddenly, a pair of arms circled her waist and a warm, soft body pressed against her from behind.

"Jen?" she said, with a wide grin on her face.

That remark earned her a slap on the bare butt. "Ow!"

"I'll Jen you, Billie Charland," Cat said before she claimed Billie's body from behind once more. She reached around Billie, grabbed the soap from the tray, and rubbed a rich lather into her hands.

Billie took the soap from Cat and placed it in the tray. She leaned her head back and moaned as Cat's hands circled up and around her breasts, teasing each one into a peak of awareness, then slipping to her lower abs, hips, and buttocks, kneading the supple flesh as they moved. Billie pressed back against her in an attempt to remove all space between them. Without warning, Cat's hand plunged between her legs repeatedly, the soap paving the way with slickness.

"Oh my God," Billie screamed as she doubled over into the abyss of ecstasy.

Billie allowed Cat to support her weight for several moments as tremors tore through her body. It was a long time before her knees were steady beneath her. Finally, Billie pulled Cat into her arms for a mind-shattering kiss. She forced Cat backward against the shower wall and proceeded to return the favor, until Cat too was a trembling pile of mush in her arms.

"How are you feeling?" Cat asked several moments later.

"Like I've just made love to the most beautiful woman in the world," Billie said. She kissed Cat again. "It doesn't get any better than this."

* * *

When Billie arrived at work that morning, the first thing she did was drop by Jimmy's desk to check on the query she had asked him to do on Roger McBride the day before. Unfortunately, Jimmy was in a meeting, so she resolved to check with him later in the day.

She detoured to the vending machine and purchased a coffee. Carrying it, she went to her desk to go through her mail and organize her workload for the day. She checked her calendar and saw she had an appointment at one o'clock with Peggy McBride and a meeting at three with Art on the McBride case. In the meantime, she had briefs to file on the case and interviews to set up with the McBrides' friends, family, and neighbors.

It was almost eleven by the time she sorted through her mail and scheduled the appointments. Needing a break, she grabbed her coffee cup and headed to the vending area for a refill. Her phone rang before she got two feet from her desk.

"Billie Charland," she said into the receiver.

"Ms. Charland, this is Sergeant Lang at the Albany Police Department."

Billie's heart rose to her throat. "Yes, Sergeant Lang. What can I do for you?"

"Ms. Charland, we have a Caitlain Charland here. She says she's your, ah, wife?"

Oh God—Cat. "Yes, she is. Is she all right?"

"She's fine. Ms. Charland, can you come to the police station right away? We have a few questions for you before we release her."

"Release her?" Billie said. "Why is she being held?"

"Ms. Charland, your wife was arrested about an hour ago at the county correctional facility for assaulting one Brian Charland."

"What?" Billie said in disbelief. She regained her senses and said, "Yes, of course. I'll be right there."

Billie grabbed her keys and headed to her car. *Damn it, Cat. What the hell is going through your mind?*

Billie arrived at the police station twenty minutes later and identified herself at the front desk. She was led into a dingy office at the back of the station house. A few minutes later, an attractive woman entered and introduced herself as Detective Matheson. Billie extended her hand. "I'm Billie Charland. Where's Cat?"

Detective Matheson reached for Billie's hand. "She's in a holding cell at the moment." She didn't immediately release Billie's hand.

Billie took a moment to study the detective, who had a death grip on her hand. Detective Matheson was a beauty, with long auburn hair, green eyes, and a deep cleft in her chin, all complemented by a peaches-and-cream Irish complexion. Billie's attention was drawn to their clasped hands, and she realized where the detective's intentions lay. She pulled her hand out of the woman's grasp. "I want to see my wife, Detective."

Matheson walked a circle around Billie. "Yes, in a moment. First I have some questions for you. Please sit down." She indicated the chair Billie had just vacated.

Billie sat.

Matheson pulled out a chair and sat in front of Billie. She crossed her legs and leaned forward, showing her ample cleavage. She tilted her head to one side.

Oh, you're good! Time to teach this rookie a lesson. Billie also leaned forward and smiled into the woman's face.

"Tell me, Ms. Charland," Detective Matheson said.

"Billie, call me Billie."

"Billie. Yes. Tell me, is your wife always this violent?"

"Only in bed." Billie pulled her bottom lip in between her teeth.

Matheson gulped. "Really?"

"Oh, yeah." Billie wiggled her eyebrows for emphasis. "How do you think I got these bruises?"

Matheson rose and walked around to stand behind her own chair. Billie sat back and crossed her legs. She rested her forearms on the arms of the chair and tilted her chin down toward her chest so that she had to glance up at the detective through her eyelashes. Billie's skirt had risen to mid-thigh and exposed a mile of skin. Billie could see a bead of sweat form on her upper lip.

"What is your relationship to Brian Charland?"

"He's my ex-husband, father of my son, creator of my worst nightmares. Why do you ask?"

"I'm just trying to figure out why your wife would attack him. His police record says he raped her, but that was nearly five years ago, so I can't imagine that being her motive."

Billie rose and approached the detective, backing her up against the wall. In two-inch heels, Billie had a good five inches on her in height. "Well, if you're through with your little seduction attempt, let me see her and I might be able to help you with that question."

A deep blush colored Matheson's cheeks. She slipped out from between Billie and the wall. "Follow me. I'll take you to her."

Billie stepped into the holding cell and heard the door close and lock behind her. She leaned back against the bars and crossed her arms and ankles. Cat sat on the cot on the far side of the room, her hands folded in her lap. Her gaze met Billie's. Billie could see the anger smoldering in her eyes.

"Want to tell me what happened?" Billie asked.

Cat grimaced and shook her head. She lowered her gaze to the floor.

Billie opened her arms wide. "Come here."

Cat walked into Billie's embrace and wrapped her arms around her. Billie held her close. "Are you all right?"

"They took my wedding rings," Cat said.

"Huh?"

"They took my rings. They took everything—my watch, my earrings, my wallet."

Billie cupped Cat's face with her palm. "That's standard procedure. You'll get them back when we leave."

"I promised I'd never take them off. Damn them."

"It's okay. Right now we have more pressing matters to take care of. What possessed you to attack Brian?"

Cat pulled out of Billie's embrace and walked to the other side of the cell, arranging the bangs on her forehead with her hand as she went. She stopped and pivoted back toward Billie. "I'm sick of his shit. First the photos, then the letter."

"The letter? What letter?"

"We received a letter today, addressed to me. They took that from me too."

Billie pulled Cat over to the cot and sat down with her. "What did it say?"

"It was awful. He made several references to our 'sick kind of love' and about us settling for each other because we couldn't keep a man satisfied. He even mentioned writing to the editor of the paper about how we're living in sin and raising children in an environment filled with evil lust. That was the final straw." Cat jumped to her feet and paced back and forth. "I will not stand by and let him blemish our name or harm our kids."

"So you decided to just waltz into the prison and put an end to it?"

Cat marched over to Billie and shook a finger in her face. "Don't you talk to me in that tone. You'd have done the same thing. Don't you dare deny it."

Billie stared at her wide-eyed. She hated to admit it, but Cat was right. She would indeed have done the same thing.

Billie walked to the door and leaned her back against it. "So what happened at the prison?"

"They escorted me to a visitor's room and went to get Brian. He was so smug when he came in, I just wanted to scratch his eyes out right there and then. We sat down at the table across from each other. My skin crawled just being that close to him. I wanted to puke."

"So why did they arrest you?"

"I asked Brian to stop harassing us, and he acted ignorant about the whole thing. I told him I didn't appreciate the pictures he sent, nor the letter. He just laughed in my face and said, 'You reap what you sow, bitch.' He was so smug and arrogant, I couldn't take it any longer, so I lunged at him across the table."

Billie couldn't hide her grin.

"He's got a nice scratch down the left side of his face to show for his arrogance. I would have done more, but the guard pulled me off him, and now here I am." Cat raised her hands out to the sides.

"You'll have to go to court for this if he presses charges," Billie said.

Cat walked into Billie's arms. "That's okay, I've got the best lawyer in town. Hey, don't you have to check my briefs or something?"

Billie kissed her on the nose. "You're incorrigible. Come on, let's get you out of here."

Chapter 10

Detective Matheson released Cat from custody pending the filing of official assault charges against her by Brian. While they waited for the clerk to collect Cat's belongings, Billie felt Matheson eyeing her from across the room. Determined to hold her own, Billie baited her by leaning back in her chair and crossing her legs. She challenged Matheson's bold stare with one of her own, while Cat paced back and forth.

Finally, the clerk handed a large yellow envelope to Cat and pushed a sign-out log in front of her for her signature. Cat tore open the envelope and pulled out her wedding rings. Cat handed the rings to Billie as she joined her at the desk. They both grinned as Billie slid them over Cat's knuckle. When Cat pulled the rest of her personal effects from the envelope, the last item was the letter. Billie took the letter from Cat and noticed something wasn't quite right about it. She made a mental note to look at it closer that evening and handed it back to her. "Are you ready to go, sweetheart?" She took Cat's elbow and guided her toward the door.

Matheson blocked her path. She leaned in and whispered to Billie, "It could have been good, you know."

Before Billie could reply, she was pushed back by Cat who wormed her way between them. "Back off," Cat said.

Billie noticed the shocked expression on Matheson's face. She grabbed Cat's arm to restrain her. "Watch out, this Cat has claws. Just ask Brian." Billie chuckled and led Cat around the woman and out the door.

Billie gave Cat a lift back to the prison to pick up her car. She parked, leaned over to take Cat into her embrace, and kissed her.

"Not that I'm complaining, mind you, but what was that for?" Cat asked.

"For defending me against the she-wolf, my little tiger."

"You hardly needed defending. I just wanted to set the record straight with her. You belong to me, so hands off."

"Oh, I think she got the message," Billie said, then added, "I've got an appointment at one with a domestic abuse victim and another at three with Art. I should be home by four-thirty. Think you can stay out of trouble for that long?"

"I'll show you trouble."

Billie waggled her eyebrows. "Promise?"

"Oh, yeah." Cat kissed her again. "I'll see you tonight."

*   *   *

When Billie returned to the office, she logged on to her computer and found an e-mail from Jimmy. She glanced at the digital display at the bottom of her computer screen. She would be late for her one o'clock meeting if she opened it. She had only enough time to scan the subject line before Peggy McBride arrived. It said "Roger McBride Criminal Record." Her attention was drawn from the computer screen by a soft buzzing coming from her telephone.

Billie pushed the intercom button. "Yes, Deb?"

"Your one o'clock appointment is here."

"Please show her in."

As Billie directed Peggy McBride to a seat opposite her desk, she reviewed what she had read about Peggy's age. Late twenties. She seems much older than that, Billie thought. It must be all those years she lived with that abusive asshole. God, I could have ended up like her.

"Please make yourself comfortable. Can I offer you something to drink? Coffee, tea, or water?"

"Coffee would be nice," Peggy said.

Billie frowned and kept her gaze trained on her client as she paged her secretary with a request for two cups of coffee. She hung up the phone. "Peggy, do you mind if I record this conversation?"

Peggy glanced up. "No. Go ahead."

"Thanks. Okay, let's get started by reviewing the formalities of prosecuting this case. We need to put together a background on the relationship with your estranged husband and chronicle the history of abuse. Are you up to that?"

Peggy nodded.

"Oh, here's our coffee. Thanks, Deb." Deb set a tray on the table complete with two cups of coffee, spoons, packets of sugar and creamer, and napkins. Billie waited for her secretary to leave the room. "All right then. How did you meet Roger?"

"We've known each other since high school."

"So you've known him for maybe fifteen years. Is that right?"

"Yes."

"What was he like?" Billie watched a small smile form at the corners of Peggy's mouth. *Uh-oh—that's not a good sign. She still has feelings for him.*

"He was nice… and very handsome. I considered myself lucky he paid me any attention at all."

"What do you mean?"

"I wasn't exactly part of the popular crowd, and he was the captain of the football team. To be truthful, I was somewhat of a wallflower. I was surprised when he seemed to be attracted to me."

Billie reached over the desk and covered Peggy's hand with her own. "Don't sell yourself short, Peggy. You're a very attractive woman."

Peggy chuckled. "Not when I was in high school. I wore thick glasses and was pretty gawky. To this day, I don't understand why he singled me out."

"So what was your courtship like?" Billie asked.

"He was attentive and respectful and very charming. He won my family over immediately."

That sounds familiar. "So, your parents liked him, did they?"

"They thought he was wonderful. So much so, Daddy offered him an apprenticeship job at the bank, every summer during high school and college, and guaranteed him a position after we were married."

Billie sat back in her seat. She could see where this was going.

"When did you marry Roger?"

"Right out of college."

"Let me see—you would have known each other for eight years by the time you graduated from college. According to your records, you're twenty-eight, so you would have been twenty-five when your son Travis was born. That means you were married at age twenty-one. Is that right?"

"Yes."

"So how did Roger treat you after you were married?"

"For the first three or four years, it was great. We entertained a lot. Almost every weekend we had a dinner party for corporate clients with the largest bank accounts. He was a good provider. Never once did he refuse to give me an allowance."

Billie sat back abruptly. "Whoa—stop right there. He gave you an allowance?"

"Yes. I almost never had to ask for it."

Billie scanned the data sheet on her desk. "Peggy, your fact sheet indicates you went to college and have a degree in accounting. Didn't you work?"

"Oh, no. Roger wouldn't hear of it."

"He forbade you to work?" Billie was amazed at the woman's complacency.

"Of course. How would that look for a prominent banker's wife to be working?"

Billie could feel the anger rise in her chest. "Is that what he told you?"

"Well, yes. I mean—my mother never worked either. I just thought that's the way it was supposed to be."

Billie inhaled to control her own emotions. "So you were married for about four years before Travis was born. How was Roger during the pregnancy?"

Peggy frowned and didn't answer right away.

"Is there something disturbing about that question?"

Peggy fidgeted with the napkin in her hands. "Yes and no. You see, when we first learned I was pregnant, Roger wasn't very happy about it. He blamed me for letting it happen."

"Why would he be unhappy with the prospect of being a father?"

"I don't think it was that. I just think the timing was bad. At least that's what he said. He was climbing the executive ladder at work, and he thought having a child would interfere with his career."

"You said at first he was unhappy with the prospect of having a child. What changed his mind?"

"Daddy did."

"Your father?"

"Yes. Daddy was ecstatic about being a grandfather, and he rewarded Roger for it with a promotion sooner than he expected. After that, Roger seemed to warm up to the idea."

Jesus Christ. It sounded like both her father and husband were egotistical control freaks. "So tell me, Peggy, how did Travis's birth affect Roger?"

Peggy fell silent again. She raised the napkin to her eye and wiped away a tear.

"Peggy—are you all right?"

"I'm okay. It's just that everything changed after Travis was born. Roger became a different person."

"How so?"

"He became withdrawn and verbally abusive. I gained a lot of weight during the pregnancy, and he never let me forget it. Some of the names he called me aren't even repeatable. He also stopped giving me my allowance and forbade me to attend social events—especially those associated with his job."

"How was he with Travis?"

"Distant. Impatient. Barely tolerant."

Billie walked around the corner of her desk and sat on the edge. "Why do you suppose that was?"

Peggy shook her head. "I don't know. Maybe he was jealous. I just don't know."

"Jealous? Of the child?"

Peggy nodded. "Travis required a lot of attention when he was a baby. He was colicky and he cried and fussed a lot. The crying made Roger nervous. He would scream at me to shut him up."

Billie couldn't imagine Cat or her being jealous of the kids' presence in their lives.

Peggy looked at Billie. "Do you have children, Ms. Charland?"

Billie smiled. "Call me Billie, and yes, I have three, a boy and two girls."

"Then you must understand what it's like to have a fussy child. I can't blame Roger. Travis did cry all the time. It even wore on my nerves on occasion."

Billie put a hand on Peggy's shoulder. "I do understand how a crying baby can be nerve-wracking, but I don't understand how violence can be a solution for it. Don't be so quick to defend his actions."

"Who are you to tell me what not to defend?" she asked.

"I'm someone who's been where you are right now," Billie said. "The only difference is I didn't let him get to my son."

Peggy's gaze dropped to her lap again, and she whispered, "I'm sorry. I didn't know."

"It's all right. Like you, I took the steps necessary to get out of the marriage. It took three years of beatings for me to realize I could do it, but I did."

"And what about the future? Is there a future for me if I leave Roger?" she asked through tears.

"Yes, there is. The rest of your life is waiting for you, but you need to get rid of the baggage before you can move on."

"And you, did you move on?"

"Yes, I did. I'm married to the most perfect person in the world, and we have two daughters besides our son. I moved on, and so can you."

Billie walked to the office door. "Deb, could you bring more coffee? Thanks." She walked back to her desk and sat down. "Okay, my friend, this is the hard part. I need you to tell me about the beatings—in detail—and don't leave anything out. Do you understand?"

Two hours later, Billie closed the door behind Peggy and leaned against it. She was exhausted by the interview and bleeding emotionally from old wounds that had been reopened. She liked Peggy. She hoped Peggy was strong enough to break the cycle of abuse she'd allowed herself to become entangled in.

Billie checked her watch. It was time for her meeting with Art. She grabbed her briefs and the notes she took during the interview with Peggy and headed to Art's office.

* * *

Billie fought her way through the kitchen door when she got home. Shoes and school bags littered the doorway, creating a virtual minefield of booby traps to trip over. She stepped over the mess, put her briefcase and jacket in the coat closet, and headed to the living room. She stopped in the archway between the living room and kitchen and crossed her arms over her chest. The kids were lying disarrayed all over the furniture, watching cartoons.

"Funny, you don't look like the Three Little Pigs."

The sound of her voice caught their attention. "Huh?" Seth said.

Billie crooked her index finger at them in a "come hither" fashion. All three children scampered to their feet and followed her back to the kitchen. She stopped just short of the mess in front of the back door. "You guys know better than this. Let's get it cleaned up, okay?"

"Aw, Mom," they said together as they picked up their things.

Soon the mess was organized and put away. The children dispersed to the living room to resume watching their show, and Billie went upstairs to change out of her work clothes. She met Cat coming down the stairs. She stopped her in mid-flight and, without saying a word, took Cat's hand and led her back up the stairs to their room. She closed the door behind them.

"Is everything all right?" Cat asked.

Billie backed Cat up against the door. "Everything's fine. I just need a little help getting out of these clothes. Know anyone who can do that for me?"

"I might." Cat pulled her head down for a kiss.

Billie groaned as she allowed Cat's tongue to force her lips apart for an invasive kiss before moving to her chin and ear. Billie tilted her head back to give Cat free access to her neck and willed her legs to support her as bolts of desire shot from her neck to her groin. She wrapped her arms around Cat and grasped her firm bottom to pull her in closer to her own heated center. "Do you have any idea what you're doing to me?" she whispered.

Cat reached down and lifted Billie's skirt. "I don't know... Let's see." She pushed Billie's panties down and slid her hand between the wet folds. Billie moaned. The invasion was sudden and deep, and Billie's knees buckled. "Oh God."

In one swift movement, Billie found herself swung around and trapped between the door and Cat as the invasion continued. Billie pressed her head against the door and held onto Cat's shoulders as her body surrendered to wave after wave of convulsions, each leaving an intense feeling of warmth and lightheaded euphoria in its wake.

As the last of the tremors left her body, Billie rose back to her full height and pulled Cat close to her. "I love you, Cat. Let me show you how much."

Just then, a knock was heard on the door behind them. "Mama?"

Billie groaned and lowered her forehead to Cat's. "Tonight... I promise," she whispered.

"I'll hold you to that," Cat said.

Chapter 11

Cat and Billie decided to treat the kids to pizza and miniature golf that night. After two complete games, they called it quits and started for the parking lot. On the way, Seth bragged about his winning scores.

"Hey, when you're good, you're good," he said.

"You cheated," Tara said.

"Did not."

"Did too."

"Did not."

"Well, I think you all cheated," Billie said.

Cat gave her a hip check while they walked along. "You're just mad you got the worst scores."

"Yeah, Mommy, even I beat you and I'm just little," Skylar said as she walked along holding Billie's hand.

Billie leaned down and scooped her youngest child into her arms. Skylar instinctively wrapped her legs around Billie's waist and her arms around her neck. Billie planted a loud raspberry into Skylar's neck as the little girl giggled with glee. Addressing all of them, she said, "Well, I was at a disadvantage."

"Oh, really?" Cat's eyebrows raised into her hairline.

"Yes, really. Those little clubs are too short for my height."

"Face it, Mom," Seth said. "You just stink at miniature golf."

"I'll show you who stinks, young man," Billie said as she put Skylar down and reached for him.

Seth grinned and took off at a dead run toward the car, with Billie right on his heels. Within seconds, she had him thrown across the trunk of the car and had tickled him into submission.

As Seth recovered from his torture, Cat and the girls approached them. A movement to Cat's left caught Billie's eye. It took a few seconds for her brain to register the car speeding toward her family.

"Look out!" she shouted.

Billie ran toward them as Cat turned to see the car bearing down on them. She grabbed the girls and thrust them toward Billie before the car clipped her on the side. Billie watched helplessly as Cat spun around and crashed to the ground while the car sped away.

"Cat! Oh my God! Seth, take the girls to the car." Billie ran toward Cat. She reached her in seconds. "Cat, honey, are you hurt?"

Cat was conscious and lying on her side with her upper body propped up on her hands. "The girls?"

"They're okay, thanks to you." All three children ran to them. Skylar cried and Tara picked up stones and threw them in the direction of the car that had long sped away. Seth knelt beside Cat and took her hand.

"Seth, I told you to get the girls into the car," Billie said.

"They wouldn't go," Seth said as he held Cat's hand.

"Are you hurt?" Billie asked again.

"I don't think so." Cat tried to sit up but fell back and grasped her hip. "Well, maybe. Help me up."

Billie pulled her cell phone out of her pocket. "Maybe I should call an ambulance."

"No, I'm all right, I don't think anything's broken, just bruised. Give me a hand here."

"Seth, get the other side," Billie said as she offered her hand to Cat. With Seth on one side and Billie on the other, they helped her to her feet as she tested her weight on her legs. Skylar stopped crying and had wrapped herself around Cat's waist. Billie peeled Skylar off Cat and picked her up.

Skylar rested her head on her mother's shoulder. Billie whispered in her ear, "It's okay, Sky... Mama will be all right, I promise."

Between Billie and Seth, Cat was able to limp to the car and climb into the front seat. Soon the family was headed toward home. Billie glanced at Cat during the ride and noticed every bump caused her to wince in pain. "I'm taking you to the hospital, and I don't want an argument." She held up her hand when Cat started to interrupt. "You're a doctor for Christ's sake. You know you could be hurt worse than you think."

Ten minutes later, Billie and the kids sat in the emergency room while Cat was being examined. At Billie's request, the receptionist called the police to report the incident. The police officer was just beginning to interview Billie when Cat hobbled out of the examining room on crutches.

Billie rushed to Cat's side and helped her to a chair.

"Mrs. Charland, is there anyone you're currently at odds with?" the officer asked.

"I can't think of anyone who would want to hurt me," Cat said.

"I can," Billie said, "but he's in jail, so it couldn't be him."

"Can you tell me what type of car it was?" the officer asked.

"Yeah," Seth said. "It was a black 2005 Buick Regal."

The officer raised his eyebrows.

"Trust him," Billie said. "He's a huge race-car fan. He knows his cars."

"Okay, then," the officer said. "I'll let you know if we find anything. Have a nice evening."

"Seth, keep an eye on your sisters for me while I bring the car closer to the door, okay?" Billie said.

Seth nodded and Billie ruffled his hair. She placed a light kiss on Cat's forehead and said, "I'll be right back... Don't move."

* * *

"Okay, bed for you," Billie said as she helped Cat hobble into the house.

"I don't need to go to bed. I'm bruised, not sick."

"True, but I still think you'll be more comfortable in bed with your leg propped up."

"Fine, but I don't think I can maneuver the stairs. I guess it's the guest room for me for the next few days."

"Fair enough," Billie said. "Seth, do me a favor and fill the tub for your sisters' bath while I make Mama comfortable. It's late and you three need to get to bed."

With baths over and children tucked into bed, Billie joined Cat in the guest room. When she entered the room, she noticed the deep frown on Cat's face as she massaged her leg. She sat on the edge of the bed and pushed Cat's bangs out of her eyes. "Hurts, huh?"

Cat nodded.

"I'll get you a couple of painkillers."

"All right."

Billie made the rounds of the house to turn off lights and lock the doors. She took a couple of extra-strength pain relievers from the medicine cabinet. As she passed through the dark living room on the way back to the guest room, she noticed the red light blinking on the answering machine. She pushed the play button. A man's muffled voice came over the speaker.

"Tonight's accident was just a warning. Next time, I won't be so easy on you. Back off."

Billie was stunned. *Back off? Back off from what?* Realizing she still held Cat's painkillers in her hand, she rushed to the guest room. She handed the pills and water to Cat and paced at the foot of the bed while she waited for Cat to take the meds.

Cat set the water glass on the nightstand and turned to Billie. "You're pacing like a caged animal. What's wrong?"

Billie stopped. "What happened to you tonight was no accident."

Cat drew her brows together in a frown. "What do you mean?"

"Come with me." Billie helped Cat to her feet and offered her arm as support while Cat hobbled beside her toward the answering machine.

"Listen to this." Billie pushed the Play button. She could see the fear in Cat's face.

"Who is it?" Cat asked.

"I don't know, but I intend to find out. Here, let me help you back to bed."

Billie resumed pacing once Cat was settled in.

"What are we going to do?" Cat asked.

Billie stopped. "Where's the letter you received in the mail?"

"You mean the one Brian sent? It's in my purse near the telephone in the hall."

"I'll be right back." A few moments later, Billie stared at the envelope as she sat on the edge of Cat's bed. She narrowed her eyes into slits and pulled the letter out of the sleeve. She unfolded the letter and read it out loud.

"You two sick bitches disgust me. It's a sad day when a woman needs another to find the kind of fulfillment that can only be provided by a man. I'm sure your sick kind of love is a direct result of not being able to satisfy a man. You are sorry excuses for women. You will always be the weaker sex—in every way. You are inferior. You are living in sin and raising children in an environment filled with evil lust. I'm of a mind to write a letter to the editor condemning your sick relationship. How dare you thrust your evilness upon the rest of us by changing the laws to legalize your putrid lifestyle? You deserve nothing short of death. Watch your backs and mind your own business, or you just might get what you deserve."

Billie frowned. "Brian didn't write this."

"What do you mean?"

"This isn't his handwriting."

"Are you sure?"

"Honey, I lived with the man for three years. I'm sure. This is not his handwriting."

"Oh God. Do you mean there's someone out there stalking us? Billie, the kids... I..."

Billie climbed into the bed beside Cat and pulled her into her arms. "Shhh. It's okay. I'll think of something. First thing in the morning, I'll see if I can put a trace on this letter to find out where it came from. I have an idea who might be behind this. I'll investigate it as soon as I get to work tomorrow."

"You know who's behind it?"

"I said I have an idea. I don't want to say anything until I'm sure. Right now, you need to sleep. How do you feel?"

"The meds are starting to kick in. The pain is still there, but manageable."

"Good. Lie down then. Let me hold you while you sleep. I love you. I won't let anyone harm you or our children. Trust me."

"I do trust you."

*   *   *

As soon as she got to work the next morning, Billie checked the e-mail Jimmy sent to her on Roger McBride. He was Billie's primary suspect. The McBride case was the only one she was working on at the moment, and the warning to mind her own business was loud and clear in the letter. The file attached to the e-mail was organized in descending order, with the latest offenses listed first. The most recent entry was his arrest for spousal and child abuse, followed by several entries over the past three years for aggravated assault involving barroom confrontations. Without warning, a name jumped out at Billie and hit her in the gut, knocking the wind out of her... Brian Charland.

"Bingo," she said out loud as she read how Brian had been a passenger in the car when McBride was issued a speeding ticket at age 16. There's the connection, she thought. She logged off her account and grabbed her car keys. Moments later, she pointed her car in the direction of the prison. Brian had a lot of explaining to do.

An hour later, Billie sat across the table from him. She noted the long, angry scratch that ran down the left side of his face. *Good girl, Cat.*

"What do you want?" he asked. "You and your girlfriend have caused me enough trouble already."

"Wife, Brian. She's my wife."

"You're a sick bitch... you know that?"

"Look, I'm not here to talk about my love life. I want to know why you sent those photographs and that letter to Cat."

"Go to hell, slut. I don't have to answer your questions."

"Okay. Have it your way." Billie rose to her feet. "I'll be back in about an hour with your mother in tow." She started walking toward the door.

"Wait," Brian said. "Jesus Christ. Do you have to be such a fucking bitch? She'll rag on me until the day I die if you get her involved in this, and you know it."

Billie walked back to the table, leaned over it, and supported her weight on her hands. "I only want answers. My family is in danger here, and I'll do anything to protect them, including getting your mother involved. Have I made myself clear?"

"Shit." Brian pushed his chair back violently and walked to the opposite side of the room. He ran his hand through his hair as he went. "Shit," he said again.

"Well?"

He gestured with his hands. "All right... all right. I didn't write the letter. Roger did. I did give him the pictures though. Actually, I had my lawyer get them from the safe deposit box and send them to Roger."

"You kept them in a safe deposit box?"

"Of course. They needed to be where I could access them without you knowing where they were."

"Now who's the sick one?" Billie sat down and clasped her hands in front of her on the table. "Why did you give them to McBride?"

"With the kind of record Roger has, he'll end up here for a very long time if you convict him of beating his wife and kid. He was desperate. When he discovered your last name was Charland, he called my parents looking for me. My mother told him where I was, so he contacted me to see if I knew you. When he found out you were my ex-wife, he asked for my help to stop you."

"And you were oh-so-eager to help him, weren't you?"

"Why not? You never did me any favors. In fact, I'm locked in here today because of you."

"You're locked in here because of your own deviant mind. You are one sick bastard. Don't you care you're hurting your son and daughter as well?"

"They're not mine anymore. You saw to that when you forced me to sign the papers giving them up."

Billie stood. "Just so you know, Cat was almost run down by a hit-and-run driver last night. I have reason to believe it was McBride. That makes you an accomplice. I'd advise you to get a life and stay out of mine from now on, or I just might decide to tell the authorities you've been aiding McBride. Do I make myself clear?" Billie started to leave and stopped at the door. "And by the way, that scratch on your face... It didn't happen, right?"

He looked at her for a long time. She stood firm, refusing to break the stalemate. Finally, he lowered his gaze and said, "Right."

Chapter 12

Billie called Cat on the way back to the office from the prison.

"Hello?" a voice said from the other end of the phone.

"Jen?" Billie asked.

"Hey, tall, dark, and dangerous. What's up?"

"I'm calling to see how Cat's doing."

"She's being a cranky bitch. How do you put up with her anyway?"

"I figured she might be. Are the kids driving her nuts?"

"No. The kids have been good. They're all in the family room playing. She's just tired of being stuck in bed."

"Did she tell you what happened yesterday?"

"Yeah, she did. It's kind of scary. That's why the kids are downstairs and not outside. She didn't want them out in the open."

"Good move. I'm hoping it won't be for long. I'm on to a lead I think will solve the problem. I just called to tell Cat about it. Is she asleep?"

"Hell, no. She's in the guest room plotting ways to make us all as miserable as she is. Hold on while I get her for you."

A few moments later, Billie heard the click of the phone.

"Billie?"

"Hi, love. I just called to see how you're doing and to give you some news."

"How am I? I'm going out of my mind. I hate this. Christ, I can't even go pee without help."

"You need help to pee?" Billie said, chuckling.

"It isn't funny."

"I know. I'm sorry. I called to tell you I've confirmed who the stalker is."

"Who?"

"Roger McBride."

"McBride. Isn't he the one you're prosecuting for beating his wife and child?"

"Yes, and do you want to hear something funny? He knows Brian. In fact, he not only sent the photographs, he got them from Brian."

"It figures that rat bastard's involved. Why would McBride want to hurt me? What have I ever done to him?"

"He's trying to get to me through you. He knows he'll go to jail for a long time if he's convicted, and he wants me to back off—just like he said on the answering machine message."

"Damn. What are we going to do about it?"

"Well, first, I'm going to visit with his wife, just to verify the letter was written by him. Then I'm going to the police. After that, I'm resigning from the case."

"You're what? You can't do that!"

"I promised you and Art I wouldn't allow this case to endanger my family. Well, I've failed. I can't risk you or the kids again."

"Billie, you can't quit now. There's no one better to handle this case. Do you want to walk away?"

"No, but I will for your safety… and the kids'. I can't risk it."

"If you're right about McBride, I'm sure there's something the police can do to stop him from getting too close again."

"Well, with his wife's affirmation he wrote the letter, I'm sure the police will put him under surveillance."

"Okay, then there's no reason to quit."

"Are you sure?"

"I'm sure. Peggy McBride has the best working for her. It wouldn't be right to walk away from her, and it wouldn't be right for Travis either. Just please be careful."

"I'll be careful. I promise."

* * *

The first thing Billie did when she arrived back at work was call Peggy McBride.

"Peggy, this is Billie Charland. I need to see you as soon as possible. Can I come over?"

Peggy hesitated. "Ah… Ah… I guess so," she said.

"Is everything all right?"

"Yes, everything's fine. Can I ask what you need to see me about?"

"I have some notes to go over with you and some questions to ask. It's very important, or I'd set up a meeting here at the office. Is now a good time?"

"Now is fine, but can I meet you somewhere?"

Warning bells went off in Billie's head. "Okay. We can meet at the coffee shop on the corner of Main and Maple. I'll meet you there in about fifteen minutes."

Ten minutes later, Billie was sitting in a booth in the corner of the diner, waiting for Peggy to arrive. Twenty minutes later, she was convinced Peggy wasn't going to show. She had all but given up and was ready to leave when Peggy walked in the door. She was wearing oversized sunglasses and a decorative scarf around her neck. "Damn," Billie said under her breath.

Peggy spotted her across the room and waved. Moments later, she slid into the booth across the table from Billie. She didn't remove the glasses.

Billie watched Peggy squirm under her scrutiny. "Peggy…"

"What is it you need help with?" Peggy said.

Billie took a deep breath and let it out. *Okay, I can take a hint.* "I have a question for you about Roger. It will sound kind of odd, but it has some bearing on this case."

"Okay." Peggy adjusted her sunglasses.

"How does Roger feel about homosexuals?"

Peggy visibly started. Her hand flew up to arrange her hair. "Ho… homosexuals?"

"Yes. Gays, lesbians. Has he ever voiced his opinion to you about that particular subject?"

Peggy fidgeted in her seat. "Yes. He hates them."

Billie sat back in the booth and crossed her arms. She narrowed her eyes. "Does he know you're gay?"

"I… I… Oh God." Peggy lowered her chin to her chest and began to cry. "How did you know?"

"Part of the investigation into your case required a background check on you as well as Roger. We interviewed several of your friends and family members."

"Rachel?" Peggy asked.

"Yes. She pretty much volunteered the information. She said you and she developed a relationship that crossed the boundaries of mere friendship. It didn't take a rocket scientist to figure out what she was saying."

"How is she?"

"She seemed fine, but we didn't go into a lot of detail with her. However, she did want me to ask you to contact her after the divorce is final."

Peggy wiped her eyes with a Kleenex she dug out of her purse. "I'm surprised she still cares."

"Why shouldn't she?"

"Rachel and I volunteered together at the local food shelf... you know, wives of prominent businessmen are expected to be active in charitable causes. Anyway, we spent a lot of time together and found we had a lot in common. Before long, the friendship developed into something much deeper. I found myself anticipating every moment we had together, and one day, she kissed me—quite unexpectedly—and I felt the most intense desire and longing. I thought I would never recover from it. She felt the same way. When I realized I was in love with her, I told Roger. He went ape-shit and almost killed me. He threatened to kill Rachel as well, so I broke it off with her to keep her out of danger. I just dumped her without an explanation. I haven't seen her since."

Billie heard anger and bitterness in her voice. "Is that why Roger beats you?"

"Is that why your husband beat you?"

Billie's lips thinned. "Okay, I deserved that, I guess, but to answer your question, no. My husband started beating me long before he knew I preferred women."

"To be honest, Travis's birth was pretty much coincidental with my coming out and the beatings started not long after that. I can't be totally sure whether he was beating me because I was gay or because he was just unhappy in our marriage. Considering his feelings about homosexuality, I tend to believe it's the former."

Billie placed her hand on top of Peggy's smaller one. "I'm sorry."

Peggy composed herself. "What made you ask that question?"

Billie removed her hand. "I have reason to believe Roger has been stalking my family in an attempt to get me to back off this case. We received some photographs and a letter that came from someone who hates the concept of gay relationships. Some of the things in the letter were so vile it made me ill to read it. Also, my wife and daughters were almost run down by a speeding car that I believe was driven by the same person who sent the letter. I thought at first it was my ex-husband, but after confronting him, in jail I might add, and doing a criminal records search on Roger, I'm convinced Roger's behind it."

Billie pulled the letter out of her pocket and dropped it on the table. Peggy gasped. "It's his handwriting, isn't it?"

"Yes."

"Go ahead and read it if you'd like."

Several minutes later, Peggy handed the letter back. "I don't know what to say except I'm sorry."

"It's not your fault. You've given me what I need to go after him, and for that, I thank you."

Peggy rose to her feet. "I must be going. Is there anything else?"

Billie rose with her. "Yes, there is. I want you to promise you'll call me if you need help." She handed Peggy a business card with her work and cell numbers on it. "Call me anytime, night or day. I mean that."

Peggy took the card, murmured her gratitude, and left the diner.

* * *

Before going home that night, Billie filed a formal complaint against Roger McBride for stalking, harassment, and assault, adding one more offense to his long list of crimes. A restraining order was issued, although Billie knew it was only as good as the paper it was written on. If McBride chose to violate the order, it would be too late to do anything about it until after it happened. After seeing what he had done to his own wife and child, she had no qualms about him being capable of doing the same, or worse, to Cat and the kids. So, she spent the next couple of weeks holding her breath and praying to God he would be smart enough to stay away.

The legal case progressed against McBride at a steady pace. Interviews with friends and family produced mixed results, ranging from "Roger's a great guy," to "I expect one day he'll kill her."

Billie was convinced the outcome of the case would depend on Peggy McBride. Her testimony and medical records were vital to the success of the prosecution. For this reason, and out of genuine fear for the woman, Billie became alarmed when she was unable to make contact with Peggy for an entire week. She left voice messages on her answering machine, mailed notices to her house, and even went to her home a couple of times to seek her out. Each time, she was unavailable.

Billie was on the verge of filing a missing person's report when Peggy surfaced. Billie was home, relaxing with Cat and the children in the family room, eating popcorn, and watching a movie. She was cuddling on the oversized sofa with Cat, while the children were lying at all angles around and on top of them. This was Billie's favorite time of day. She craved the emotional and physical affection she received from her family. They were her life, and she would do anything for them.

When the phone rang, Billie shifted Skylar off her lap and onto Cat's as she rose to answer it. When she stood, the kids seemed to flow in to fill the void she had just vacated on the couch, scooting a little closer to Cat.

Billie picked up the phone. "Hello?"

"Billie?"

"Yes."

"I understand you've been looking for me."

"Peggy? Peggy, are you all right? Your voice sounds funny."

"I'm fine, just a little cold."

Billie didn't believe her. "Where are you?"

"Home. Sorry I've missed you, I've been in and out a lot."

Billie heard a painful groan from the other end. "Peggy, what's happening? Talk to me."

"I'm fine, really. He didn't mean to…"

"I'm on my way."

"No! No. I'm fine. Don't come over. You'll only make it worse."

"Peggy."

"Please don't. Please."

By this time, Cat had joined Billie at the phone. She placed a hand on Billie's arm and looked at her questioningly.

Billie wrapped her free arm around Cat and pulled her close.

"Is he there with you now?" Billie asked.

"Yes. He's in the bathroom right now. I've got to go. He won't be in there long."

"I want you out of there. Promise me you'll leave when he falls asleep. Promise me, or by God, I'll drive over there right now."

"All right. I promise. I've got to go."

Billie stood there, listening to the dial tone coming from the phone in her hand.

* * *

Billie felt like a caged tiger. Nervous energy caused her to pace across their bedroom.

"Billie, please come to bed. She'll call if she needs you."

"I have a very bad feeling about this. Very bad. I want to go over there."

"Honey, if you're that worried, call the police. I'm sure they'll send a car over to check things out. After all, he's not supposed to be around her, right? If he's there, they can arrest him for violating the restraining order."

Billie stopped pacing. "You're right." She sat on the edge of the bed and kissed her. "You always know what to say, don't you? I'll be right back. Don't go anywhere, okay?"

"You're kidding, right? I have plans for all that pent-up energy you seem to have. I wouldn't dream of moving a muscle. Hurry back."

Billie placed a call to the police, and after much argument, convinced them there was reason to at least check the situation out. That accomplished, she took Cat up on her offer.

Several hours later, they lay spent in each other's arms, skin against skin, sweat and essences mingling together in a sexual afterglow that permeated the room. Billie shifted so she was lying on top of Cat, their noses a fraction of an inch away from each other. "I love you with all of my heart. Thank you for trusting in us. God knows, I've given you reason not to. I'll cut off my own hands before I ever do anything to hurt you or the children. I promise."

"Billie," Cat said, "I've assured you over and over that I trust you. I know you'd never hurt us. Please let it go. It's over." She pushed an errant lock of hair behind Billie's ear. "Now lie down and let me hold you."

Billie shifted her weight to the side to lay her head on Cat's shoulder and wrap her arm around her.

Cat kissed Billie on the head. "Sleep well, dear heart," she said as they both drifted off to sleep.

Chapter 13

Billie was in the shower the next morning when her cell phone rang. Cat, who had been cheating the clock to get a few more minutes of sleep, rolled over and grabbed it from the nightstand. She glanced at the time, and 5:15 a.m. flashed in the semidarkness. She wondered who could be calling at such an hour. "Hello?" she said.

"Help me," the weak, broken voice on the line said. "Help me, please…"

"Peggy? Is that you?" Cat covered the receiver with her hand. "Billie, come quick," she yelled.

Billie was out of the shower in a shot and ran into the bedroom, naked and dripping wet. "Cat?"

Cat handed her the phone. "It's Peggy."

Billie grabbed the phone. "Peggy?"

"Help me."

Billie heard a thumping noise and then nothing at all. "Peggy," she shouted. "Peggy, honey, talk to me. Peggy!"

Reacting to the panic in Billie's voice, Cat scrambled out of bed and quickly dressed. She woke Seth and sent him over to fetch Jen. When she came back to the bedroom, Billie was still standing there, naked and wet, holding the silent phone in her hand. She took the phone and hung it up. "Billie," she said. "Honey, get dressed. I've sent Seth over to get Jen. We'll leave as soon as she gets here, okay?"

Billie didn't say a word. She just nodded, and Cat went downstairs to collect her medical bag and wait for Seth and Jen.

Minutes later, Jen came charging into the house behind Seth. "What is it with you two?" she asked. "Geesh. Your lives are like a soap opera. What happened this time?"

Cat filled Jen in on what was happening with Billie's client. "I'm sorry to pull you out of bed. I know we depend on you too much," Cat said.

Jen grabbed Cat's shoulders. "Don't you ever let me hear you apologize again for needing my help, got it? Haven't you figured out yet that Fred and I would do anything for you? Anything. Is that clear?"

Billie entered the kitchen just in time to catch the last part of Jen's speech. She wrapped her long arms around both of them and hugged them close. "Thanks, Jen. We love you too. Thanks for helping us out again." She placed a kiss on Jen's head.

"You're welcome. Now go help your client and don't worry about things here."

Billie grabbed her jacket and approached Seth, who was sitting at the kitchen table, his face a mask of worry. She leaned over and hugged him. "Thank you, sweetie. Go on back to bed, okay? We'll be back soon." She kissed him on the forehead and swatted him on the butt lightly as he headed back upstairs.

*   *   *

Billie was silent as she drove through the predawn morning. Cat sat close to her in the car and rubbed her hand up and down Billie's thigh to maintain a comforting contact. The way Peggy sounded on the phone, Cat assumed what they might find when they got there wouldn't be good. Billie's dark profile showed she was of the same mind.

When they had driven about halfway, Cat said, "Maybe I should call the police and an ambulance." Billie nodded and Cat reached for her cell phone. "What's the address?" Cat asked as she placed the call.

Minutes later, they pulled into the driveway of Peggy's home. Gaining entry into the house wasn't a problem, as the front door was wide open. They searched the downstairs, but found no evidence of foul play. Cat followed Billie up the stairs to the second floor. After searching two empty bedrooms, they came across Peggy lying in the middle of a king-size bed. There was blood everywhere: on the bed, on the floor, and even splattered on the wall. Billie ran to the bed and turned Peggy over. She was still alive. Her face had been beaten so it was almost unrecognizable.

"Oh God." Billie climbed onto the bed and cradled Peggy's head in her lap. "Cat, help her, please."

Cat examined her. Her blood pressure was dangerously low, and one pupil was unresponsive, indicating a head injury. Cat avoided eye contact with Billie, knowing the prognosis would show on her face.

Peggy's eyes fluttered open.

"Hold on. Cat's a doctor. Don't give up. We're doing everything we can to help you."

Peggy grasped Billie's arm with a bloodied, broken hand. Her voice was raspy and ragged. "Don't let him have Travis. Please."

"I won't. I promise," Billie said as Peggy sank into the bed and closed her eyes.

Cat dropped her chin to her chest and sighed after finding no pulse.

"Cat?"

Cat shook her head. "I'm so sorry."

Billie dissolved into tears.

A noise from downstairs alerted them to the arrival of the ambulance crew. "I'll send them up," Cat said.

* * *

It was well into the morning before the homicide department finished with the scene, photographing the body and the room and taking blood, hair, and fiber samples. After the police left, Cat and Billie sat in the car in front of Peggy's house. Billie stared straight ahead.

Cat reached out to rub Billie's arm. "Hey, love. Are you ready to go?"

Billie stared at Cat as though she were seeing her for the first time. Her eyes filled with tears. "I can't leave," she said.

"What do you mean? There's nothing you can do here."

Billie threw the car door open and got out. She walked around the car and opened Cat's door. "Take the car and go home. I'll be all right. I'll catch a cab later."

Cat refused to get out of the car. "No. I won't leave you. I go where you go."

"Cat, I don't want you here."

"I won't leave you."

"Damn it, Cat! Get your ass in the fucking driver's seat and leave before I beat the shit out of you!"

Cat felt as though she'd been slapped across the face. Never before had Billie used such force and language with her, even during their fight over the photographs a few weeks earlier.

Overwhelmed by hurt and anger, she got out of the car and stomped around to the other side. She slid into the driver's seat and slammed the door. The squeal of tires and tread marks on the pavement marked her departure.

She drove through the streets, not wanting to go home and let the kids see her in this state. She knew they'd be all right with Jen, so she drove around in circles. Finally, she stopped at the park. Almost by instinct, she found herself sitting under the tree they always used for family picnics. They called it their healing tree. It was under this very tree she sat, nine months pregnant with Skylar, when her water broke.

In her mind's eye, she could see Seth and Tara climbing on the monkey bars while Skylar played in the sandbox. She and Billie would relax under the tree, with her leaning against the trunk and Billie lying with her head in her lap. They would share whatever they happened to be eating, grapes, chips, crackers; suck the crumbs off each other's fingers; and silently promise paradise to each other later that evening.

Cat stifled a sob as she lowered herself to lie in the grass. Soon, she fell into a light sleep.

Several hours later, a cool breeze awakened her. She glanced at her watch and saw it was almost dinnertime. She sat up, a little disoriented. It took a few moments for her to remember why she was there, and her heart broke all over again. Then, she surprised herself. Instead of crying, she began to get angry. *Damn you, Billie Charland. You had no right to treat me like that, and you're not going to get away with it.*

She climbed to her feet and ran back to the car where she called home on her cell phone.

"Hello?" a tiny voice said.

"Sky? It's Mama."

"Hi, Mama, when are you and Mom coming home?"

So Billie's not home yet. "Sweetie, can you please tell Jen Mama needs to talk to her?" She heard Skylar yell for Jen as she waited.

"Cat?" Jen said.

"Yes. How are the kids?"

"The kids are fine. Where are you?"

"It's a long story. Remind me to tell you about it sometime. Has Billie called?"

"She's not with you?"

"No, she isn't. We, ah... we... Let's just say I've got a few things to settle with her once I get my hands on her."

"Whoa, girl. Remember the last time you flew off the handle without listening first."

"Jen, she told me to get my ass in the fucking car before she beat the shit out of me. Now, don't you think I have a reason to be angry with her?"

"Ouch," Jen said. "Boy, when she blows it, she blows it big time, doesn't she?"

"Big isn't the word for it. I'm not sure how late we'll be—"

"Don't worry about it. I'll take the kids home with me for the night. That'll give you some fighting room without little ears around listening. Okay?"

"You know, it seems they sleep more often at your house than in their own beds. I love you. You know that, don't you?"

"Ditto, little sister, ditto. Now go find your lady and get this mess straightened out."

"I'll try. And thanks again. We owe you."

"And don't you forget it," Jen said. "See you later, sweetie."

*　*　*

Billie stood in the darkness, her body pressed against the wall near the front door as she listened to the rhythm of her own breathing. Her nerves were strained as she poised to react. Her knuckles were white from the death-grip she held on the rolling pin she had found in the kitchen. After what seemed like an eternity, she heard a car door slam, followed by the distinctive whoosh of the front door as it cleared its threshold. Billie struggled to control her breathing as she waited for her visitor to step inside. As the shadow passed before her, she raised her weapon and brought it down, hitting her target with as much force as she could muster within the short distance she had. Her victim fell to the floor with a thud.

She reached down and rolled the body over in the darkness. *This isn't a man.* She rose to her feet and reached for the table lamp. There, lying unconscious on the floor, was Cat. The contents of Billie's stomach threatened to mutiny as she realized what she had done. She fell to her knees next to Cat and examined the bump she'd just put on her head.

"Damn you, Cat. Why can't you ever do what you're told? Why does everything have to be an argument with you? Now look at what you made me do."

Billie fell back to sit on the floor and rested her forearms on her knees.

"Well, well, well, it appears someone did me a favor here," a voice said. "That was intended for me, wasn't it?"

Billie spun around and looked Roger McBride in the face. "You bastard!" she screamed and scrambled to her feet. All the rage, anger, and hurt she had locked away through three long years of abuse came to the surface as she unleashed her fury on McBride. She caught him off guard with her sudden attack and was able to place a roundhouse kick to his head, sending him across the room. He didn't stand a chance. She rained blow after blow upon his body, nonstop, until he was reduced to a pile of quivering flesh. When she saw he wasn't getting back up after the last kick, she straddled his body and started on his face with her fists. He was unconscious after the third punch, but Billie continued to hit him.

As she pulled her fist back for another blow, her arm was grabbed. She whipped her head around, ready to attack whoever was restraining her, until she realized it was Cat.

Cat was terrified by the hatred and bloodlust she saw in Billie's eyes. She knew in that instant Billie was capable of murdering this man. She also knew she had to stop her, no matter what. If Billie crossed that line, there would be no going back, no way to recover what they had together, and no way for them to return to their peaceful and loving life.

Billie snapped out of her trance and regained her composure. She climbed off McBride and allowed Cat to take her into her arms, holding her as she trembled. Cat led her to the couch and sat her down before she picked up the phone and made an anonymous call to the police. After placing the phone back into its cradle, she took Billie's hand and led her out of the house and into the car. Moments later, they pulled into the parking lot at the park. Cat helped Billie out of the car and led her to the healing tree where they sat and leaned against the trunk. She lowered Billie's head into her lap and began to stroke her long hair. Not a word was spoken between them. Soon, Billie relaxed and slept, while Cat stood guard over the treasure that was her heart.

Chapter 14

Billie opened her eyes and peered into Cat's face. She smiled as Cat brushed the bangs from her forehead. She felt Cat's fingers linger over the slight scar that disappeared into her hairline.

She took a deep breath and sighed. It was hard to believe it had only been two short weeks since she lay in this same position, under this same tree in the park, her head in Cat's lap. Only then, it was late at night. Her hands were covered with the blood of a madman, and her heart was filled with anger and rage. Cat saved her life that night, for if she had carried out her plan, McBride would be dead and the darkness would have overtaken her forever.

Billie reached up and touched Cat's face. "I love you," she said.

"I know."

"I can't stop thinking about that night, about how I almost—"

Cat covered Billie's lips with two fingers. "Shhh. No more. I don't want any more apologies. You didn't know it was me. Pure and simple."

Billie kissed the fingers covering her lips and took pleasure in the moan that escaped from Cat's lips.

She took Cat's hand from her mouth and placed it over her heart. "This is yours. I give it to you freely. Please don't ever give it back."

"I'll protect it with my life."

"You saved me, Cat. I almost killed him, you know."

"But you didn't. McBride is in jail where he belongs, and with the evidence the police have against him, he'll stay there for the rest of his life. Peggy's murder will be avenged. Everything seems to have worked itself out. Travis is healthy again and living with his grandparents, and we're here, together and intact, even after all we've been through."

"Things wouldn't have worked out this well if not for you. You saved me from destroying my soul. I'll never be able to repay that debt, but I promise to spend the rest of my life trying."

"It was a matter of self preservation, my love," Cat said. "You're the other half of my soul. If I let you destroy yours, then I'd be lost as well."

"I hope, with your help, I can keep my dark side in check. I'm so afraid one day I won't be able to control it, and I'll end up hurting you, hurting us."

"Never. As Dr. Connor said, as long as we have each other, there's no darkness we can't control. I'm glad you decided to continue with therapy. I'll be there with you, every step of the way. We'll get through this. I promise."

Billie rose to her elbows and reached up to pull Cat down into a searing kiss.

"Promise me Paradise," Cat said.

"I promise." Billie pulled her down for another kiss.

"Hey! You two gonna do that all day? The ice cream truck is here. Can we have some?"

Billie broke the kiss. Seth stood in front of them, grinning ear to ear.

"Well?" He flung his hands out to the side to emphasize his point. Tara and Skylar were jumping up and down on each side of him chanting, "Ice cream. Ice cream. Ice cream."

Billie laughed, then lunged at Seth and pulled him down to the ground in a wrestling hold.

The girls jumped on top of them.

"Hey, no fair," Seth said.

Billie lowered her face close to Seth's. "I'll make you a deal. You let me win at miniature golf next time, and I'll buy you an ice cream." She chuckled at the stubborn set to his jaw.

By this time, Cat had made her way around the pile of bodies and was lying facedown on the grass so her head was within inches of Seth's and Billie's. She brushed the corn-silk-colored hair from his forehead. "Well, sport, ice cream does sound good."

The girls, who were both sitting on top of Billie, who was on top of Seth, chimed in. "Come on, Seth, give. We want ice cream."

Seth stood his ground. "Maybe I've changed my mind. Maybe I don't want ice cream."

"Mo-omm," both of the girls said together.

Billie twisted around. "Don't be such 'Whine-erellas.' If your brother doesn't want ice cream, then I guess we'll just have to tickle him." Billie formed her hands into claws and dove into his belly for the full torture treatment. Cat rolled over and laughed as Billie's sudden movements caused both girls to tumble off her back and right onto her.

Moments later, after laughing himself into hiccups, Seth gave up and agreed to get ice cream. Billie climbed to her feet and lent him a hand.

"Go save us a place in line," she said, and he and his sisters scampered off toward the ice cream truck.

Billie offered her hand to Cat, who was still on the ground, wiping tears of laughter from her face. She pulled Cat to her feet and into her embrace.

Cat reached up and placed her open palm on the side of Billie's face. "Thank you," she said.

"For what?"

"For keeping your promise."

"My promise?" Billie smiled and draped an arm across Cat's shoulders, pulling her close.

Cat slipped her arm around Billie's waist as they strolled toward the ice cream truck to join the kids. "Yes," she said, sweeping her hand in an arc, taking in everything, including their family. "Just like you promised. You delivered Paradise."

Part II:
While I Was Gone

Chapter 15

Cat rolled over in her sleep and instantly missed the warm body she was accustomed to cuddling against. The time on the clock flashed 2:14 a.m. A few more moments passed before she was fully awake. She looked to her right and realized what had awakened her. Billie wasn't there.

The room was pitch black. Not even the moon illuminated the sky this night. She squinted, trying to make out shapes in the darkness. "Billie?"

"Over here, by the window."

Cat wiped the sleep from her eyes with one hand while supporting her weight with the other.

"Are you all right?"

"I'll live. Couldn't sleep."

"You'll live?" Concerned, Cat rose from the bed and approached Billie at the window. She wrapped herself around Billie from behind and said into her shoulder blades, "I don't like the sound of that. Are you sure you're all right?"

Billie pulled Cat into a warm embrace. "Another headache."

Cat could barely make out Billie's face in the darkness. She cupped her cheek with one palm. "Did you make that appointment with your doctor?"

"I was going to, but I was distracted by the McBride case. Now that Doc and Mom are home from Florida, I plan to set it up with him. I've been feeling okay lately, so it slipped my mind."

"Well, I don't think we should let this go on any longer. When Brian shot you, he made you susceptible to headaches that could be life threatening. I'll talk to Daddy in the morning about scheduling a series of CAT scans and MRIs."

"Do you really think the gunshot wound could be causing it? That injury was what—three years ago? Wouldn't the danger have passed by now?"

"Maybe, but your headaches have been occurring closer together and severe enough to keep you up at night. Those aren't normal headaches. It's even possible the damage resulting from that gunshot could have caused you to blow up a few weeks ago over those photographs. I'm sorry to dredge up painful memories, but this is important. You acted out of character that day, and I wonder if damage from the shooting might have caused it."

"You overreacted to those pictures, Cat. My behavior that day was an attempt to vindicate myself."

"I don't agree. In my wildest imagination, I would never believe you'd be violent with me. I feel horrible, and I'll never forgive myself for not trusting you, but you were definitely not yourself. Brain damage from the shooting might explain your behavior that day."

"Stop making excuses for my behavior over those few days, Cat. I was wrong. It's just that simple. I don't want to put the blame on anyone or anything else."

"I know. All I'm saying is, it's possible. Look, I can't live the rest of my life wondering when it will happen again. I love you, and I trust you. Believe me, I do, but if brain damage caused the outburst, then how do we know it won't happen again, or that you'd be able to control it the next time?"

"I can't argue with you on this one. You're certainly in a better position to understand this than I am. I appreciate you setting things up with Doc."

"You're welcome," Cat said. "Let me get you a couple of painkillers, then it's back to bed with you." She led Billie to the bed and pushed her down to sit on the edge of it.

Cat collected the meds from the cabinet in the bathroom and brought them to Billie, along with a small glass of water. Billie swallowed the pills, handed the cup back to her, and allowed Cat to tuck her into bed. Cat climbed over Billie's prone form and snuggled under the covers with Billie wrapped in her arms.

Before long, Cat felt violent tremors rattle Billie's body. "Sweetheart, what's wrong?"

"Cat, I'm so sorry. I'll never forgive myself for what I put you through those few days. I hurt you, and I hurt the children—maybe not physically, but it was still hurtful. I was out of control. Promise me, Cat. Promise me you'll leave if it happens again. Promise you'll take the children and get as far away from me as you can, to a safe place. Promise me."

"Billie, that's why we need to schedule the exams, so it doesn't happen again."

"That's assuming the gunshot wound caused the outburst. It might not have. Promise me, Cat."

"All right, all right, I promise. But it's a promise I don't ever intend to keep. You got that?"

"Got it."

Soft whimpering nudged Cat awake for the second time that night. She rolled over and saw Billie leaning against the headboard, crying. She maneuvered herself into a seated position and reached an arm around Billie's shoulder to pull her head down into her lap. In slow, even circles, she massaged Billie's temples until the crying stopped and she was sleeping. Cat sat there for a long time brushing Billie's silky hair with her hand, fearing the worst for her, but hoping for the best. Finally exhausted, she lay down, pulled Billie's head onto her shoulder, and continued to stroke her hair.

Before long, she, too, fell sound asleep.

Chapter 16

Cat woke the next morning to find Billie still in bed. Normally, Billie was up, showered, and ready for work by the time Cat rolled out of bed, all of this after taking her usual five-mile morning run. Cat reached over Billie, who was facing away from her, and brushed long dark locks out of her face. Expecting the caress to wake her, she was surprised when there was no reaction. She felt Billie's forehead and found it cool, but Billie didn't wake up. Cat frowned and shook her shoulder. "Billie. Billie, honey, time to get up. You'll be late for work." Still, there was no response.

Cat became frantic. She shook harder, and when there was still no reaction, she rolled Billie over. Billie's arm flopped onto the bed, limp, as she settled onto her back. Cat took Billie's chin in her hand and turned her face toward her. She gently slapped the side of her cheek.

"Come on, Billie. Wake up, love, come on." She fought the medically trained part of her brain that told her heart something it didn't want to hear.

Billie's face remained calm, eyes closed, seemingly in a deep sleep.

"Oh God." Cat scrambled off the bed to fetch her medical bag from the desk in the corner.

She rushed back to check Billie's vital signs. Her pulse and blood pressure were stable, but her breathing was shallow, her pupils were nonreactive, and her reflexes were all but nonexistent.

Tears coursed down Cat's face as she reached for the phone to call her father, thanking God her parents had come home from Florida a week earlier. "Daddy?" she said when he picked up the phone. "Daddy, it's Cat. I need help. Billie's sick." Cat's voice cracked through the tears.

"Caitlain, honey, calm down and tell me what's wrong."

Cat tried hard to detach herself from the situation. "She's been having a lot of headaches lately. She had a severe one last night, and now I can't wake her up. Her pupils are unresponsive and she has no reflexes."

"She isn't responding to outside stimuli at all?"

"Nothing. I've tried shaking her and slapping her face. There's no reaction."

"I'll call an ambulance and meet you at the hospital."

Cat hung up the phone and dialed Jen's number. Five minutes later, Jen was standing in Cat's bedroom, holding her as she cried.

"Cat, sweetie, it'll be okay, you'll see," Jen said. "Pull yourself together. I hear the ambulance coming. I'll go downstairs and meet them, okay?"

"Okay." Cat pulled her jeans and sweatshirt on over her nightshirt as the ambulance crew carried the stretcher up the stairs.

Jen entered the bedroom behind the ambulance crew and stood off to the side as they loaded Billie onto the stretcher. Cat hovered over their every move.

As the EMTs strapped Billie down, Cat faced Jen. Jen placed two fingers on Cat's lips. "Don't worry about the kids. I'll be here for them when they wake up. You just concentrate on Billie."

"I... I..."

"Yeah, yeah, I know. You don't know what you'd do without me... yada, yada, yada. You're welcome, and I love you too. Now go on and take care of your lady." Jen pushed Cat along behind the stretcher. "And don't forget to call me as soon as you know something."

* * *

Cat paced back and forth in the waiting area of the emergency room. With each passing moment, her fears escalated out of control. When Doc exited the examination room, she was frantic. She ran to him and grabbed his arms.

"Daddy?"

"Kitten, come with me. We need to talk."

Cat's hands flew to her mouth. "Oh God, no."

"Cat, please. She's alive, but in serious condition. I've ordered CAT scans and an MRI. Depending on what they show, you may have some decisions to make. Come on. Let's go to my office while they take her down to Radiology."

Cat followed her father through the maze of hallways and into his office. She closed the door, leaned against it, and sank to the floor. She covered her face with her hands and wept.

Doc sat on the edge of his desk. He crossed his arms and ankles and watched Cat cry herself out. After a few moments, he helped her to her feet and wrapped her in his arms.

"Daddy, I can't lose her. I need her. The kids need her."

Doc led her to the couch and sat her down. "Kitten, I don't think we'll lose her, but my preliminary examination suggests a blockage of sorts in her brain, around the area of the gunshot wound. The blockage, most likely scar tissue, is causing leakage from the blood vessels. As you know, this leakage causes the brain to swell, and because the capacity of the skull is limited, the swelling will cause pressure to rise and the brain to compress. If the pressure increases enough, it will affect the flow of blood to her brain, ultimately preventing the brain cells from eliminating toxins… and it could kill her if not corrected. This type of injury almost always requires surgery to remove the blockage and repair the leaky blood vessels."

Doc paused while Cat took in the full extent of Billie's condition. Continuing, he said, "As her spouse, you need to decide whether or not to allow this surgery. Without it, she has about a ten percent chance it will repair itself, with a high probability of severe brain damage. On the other hand, if we proceed…" He hesitated.

"Daddy? If you proceed, what? Tell me."

Doc sighed. "With this type of surgery, there might be some serious consequences."

"What kind of consequences?"

"I'm not inclined to say right now. I'd rather not go there until we know more about what we're dealing with. The CAT scans and MRI will be more conclusive. We'll talk more when the results come in, okay?"

"No, I need to know. You're asking me to make a life-and-death decision for her. How can I do that without knowing the risks? Now tell me, what kind of consequences?"

"Cat…"

Cat jumped to her feet. "Damn it. We're talking about Billie here. My wife. My heart. The one person I can't live without. If she dies, I die. Understand? Please, tell me. Please."

Doc lowered his chin to his chest for a moment then looked at Cat. "She could end up with permanent brain damage and be handicapped."

Cat just stood there staring at him.

"What should we do, kitten?"

"Save her, Daddy. Do what you have to. Just save her," Cat said before crumpling into a heap on the couch.

* * *

Cat sat in her father's office for what seemed like an eternity. Over and over, she agonized about Billie's plight. Deep down, she knew Billie wouldn't want to live as an invalid. She wouldn't want to be a burden to her and the children, but Cat couldn't bring herself to let her die.

She was still in his office when Doc came back two hours later. He sat beside her on the couch and rubbed her back. "The test results are back. Come with me, I have something to show you."

Cat followed him to the Radiology lab. She sat as he displayed Billie's CAT scan and MRI results on the computer monitor. Cat stared at the images, not wanting to see what was so obvious to her trained eye.

"Do you see it?" Doc asked.

Tears filled Cat's eyes as she nodded. "Daddy, I can't let her die."

"I know, baby, I know." He sat next to her and wrapped one arm around her. Cat laid her head on his shoulder.

"Now that you've seen the scans, have the risks changed, Daddy?"

Doc rose to his feet and walked closer to the monitor. "We're dealing with a blockage caused by this scar tissue right here." He pointed to a spot near the front of Billie's brain. "As I said before, if we do nothing, there's a huge chance the blockage will cause enough swelling to starve the brain of much-needed blood supply, and death will result. The wound occurred in the frontal lobe. That part of the brain deals with planning, organizing, problem-solving, attention, personality, behavior, and emotions. It also contains the pre-motor and motor areas that affect movement. The temporal lobe, which is located just below it, is the next high-risk area that might be affected. This area controls memory. If we operate, there's a chance of paralysis, seizures, sensory disorders, and personality shifts. If we don't operate, she will, in all probability, die."

Cat stared at her hands folded in her lap as she listened to her father. Tears flowed down her cheeks. The decision of life over death was not in question, but the burden of what she might be condemning Billie to for the rest of her life was overwhelming.

Doc pulled her into his embrace. "We need a decision, kitten. The sooner we operate, the sooner we'll know how much we can do for her."

"Operate. I'd rather live with her hate than her death."

"Are you sure?"

Cat nodded. "I'm sure."

Chapter 17

"Art?" Cat said as he picked up the phone. "This is Cat."

"Hi, Cat. I was wondering when one of you would call. Has Billie decided to play hooky from work today?"

"Billie's in the hospital."

Cat's declaration was met by silence on the other end of the line.

"Art?"

"What's wrong?"

"She's in a lot of trouble, Art. I couldn't wake her up this morning. She had one of her headaches last night. Daddy has scheduled her for brain surgery tomorrow morning."

"Brain surgery? Jesus Christ. I'm on my way."

"No. There's nothing you can do here. She's unconscious and unresponsive. There's no use in both of us just sitting around, waiting."

"At least let me keep you company."

"I'm fine. Just keep her in your thoughts, okay? I'll keep you posted as things change."

"I want you to call me if you need anything. Promise me."

"I promise. Thanks for being such a good friend. I'll talk to you later."

* * *

Billie was scheduled for surgery the next morning. The rest of the afternoon was spent running her through a series of tests to gauge her responsiveness and to use the CAT scans, along with other methods, to attempt to pinpoint the exact area of the brain affected by the damaged tissue. Cat spent this time pacing in the corridor outside Billie's room or standing in the picture window in the solarium at the end of the hall, which is where Jen found her as the dinner hour approached.

Cat stood with her forehead pressed against the window, taking in the city bathed in sunset. At any other time, the orange hue blanketing everything would have been breathtaking. Tonight, Cat was oblivious to everything but the passing time. She was so absorbed in her own inner turmoil, she almost didn't feel Jen's arms circle her from behind and pull her into a warm embrace.

Jen pressed her cheek up against the side of Cat's face. "Hi," she said.

Cat pivoted around and rested her head on Jen's shoulder. Her arms went around Jen's waist. "Hi," she whispered back as she snuggled in close.

After long moments, Jen stepped back. "How are things going?"

"I don't know. She's been in Radiology for most of the afternoon. Daddy's with her."

"Are you hungry?"

Cat shook her head. Suddenly, she realized Jen wasn't at home with the kids. "Jen, the kids?"

"Your mom came to relieve me. She took them home with her, and before you ask, I sat them down and told them Billie was sick. They're worried, especially Seth. You might want to call them a little later."

"Thanks, I will." She spotted her father coming down the hallway. She pulled out of Jen's embrace and ran to him, with Jen following close behind.

Cat stopped just short of him. "Daddy?"

Doc took her arm and led her back to the solarium. "Have a seat."

Cat sat next to her father and reached for his hand while Jen chose a chair close by.

"The tests indicate her comatose state is due more to the body's natural defense mechanisms than to existing brain damage."

"That's good, isn't it?" Cat asked.

"Well, it's better than I'd hoped for. It means she has a fighting chance of making it through the surgery with minimal effects. If she has any impairment afterward, it will be the result of the surgery, rather than anything caused by traumatic brain injury. After all, she's been functioning all right since the shooting."

Cat looked at Jen, then back at her father. "Daddy, I'm not so sure that's true."

"What do you mean?"

"She's been having these headaches. They're so bad I need to massage her temples to ease the pressure, and she has to sleep for a few hours to get rid of them."

"Is that all?" Doc asked.

"No." She felt Jen's hand slip into her own in a show of support. Cat squeezed her hand. "You said traumatic brain injury can cause behavioral changes, right?"

"Yes. Depression and anxiety are the most common. About fifty percent of TBI victims suffer from it. Mood swings, irritability, and crying are also symptoms, as well as volatile emotions. According to the research, brain injury can cause a change in the way people express their emotions. Traumatic brain injury often causes a person to lose their inhibitions. For example, a person could spend a lifetime suppressing personality traits toward violent or abusive behavior only to have TBI provide an outlet for the behavior to surface, through the loss of inhibitions." Doc paused. "Has Billie suffered from any of those since the shooting?"

"Several weeks ago, Billie, well, she blew up. She lost control."

"Did she hurt you or the children?"

"No, she didn't. She had enough strength and control not to let that happen."

Doc rose to his feet and paced, while running his hand through his hair. He stopped in front of her and looked her straight in the face. "Are you telling me you and the children are at risk for domestic abuse?"

"She didn't hurt us. She couldn't."

"Caitlain, it's possible TBI caused Billie's outburst. The next time, she might not be able to control herself. Maybe you should consider moving in with your mother and me when she's released from the hospital, at least until we're sure."

"No. I won't leave her. She needs me now more than ever. She also needs the children. They're her life. Take them away from her, and she'll die."

"Cat—"

"How about a compromise? At the first sign of agitated behavior, I'll move in with you, okay? But I won't leave her. Not now."

Doc sighed. "I hope you know what you're doing."

"I do, Daddy. Believe me, I do."

Chapter 18

"Hi, Seth, this is Mama," Cat said into the phone.

"Ma, how's Mom?"

"She's in her room resting right now."

"Is she going to die?"

Cat covered her mouth to stifle a sob and breathed deeply to control her emotions. "No, honey, I don't think so. Grandpa thinks she'll be okay, but she's going to be sick for a while." She tried to keep her voice from breaking.

"Are you going to stay at the hospital with her?"

"I'm going to stay here for as long as she needs me, sweetie. I want you and your sisters to behave for Grandma, okay?"

"We will, Ma, and tell Mom I miss her."

"You bet. Now let me talk to your sisters, okay?"

Ten minutes later, Cat hung up the phone and walked back to Billie's room. She paused in the doorway, leaned her shoulder and head against the frame, and crossed her arms in front of her chest. *She seems so peaceful.*

Cat pushed herself away from the door and sat in the chair next to Billie's bed. She lifted Billie's hand to her mouth and kissed the back of it before holding it close to her heart. The blank expression on Billie's face caused her to break down into heart-wrenching sobs as she rested her head beside Billie on the bed.

"Billie, how did you ever live through this with Seth? I'm out of my mind with grief. Please come back to me. I need you. Your babies need you."

Several minutes passed before the sobbing calmed and sleep claimed her.

* * *

Cat was awakened by a sharp knock to her head. She bolted into a sitting position, disoriented. Suddenly she realized where she

102

was, and what caused her rude awakening. Billie was thrashing around on the bed, her arms flailing. Cat was caught in the crossfire.

"Billie. Billie, honey, you're dreaming. Come on, love, wake up."

Cat sat on the edge of the bed and attempted to pin Billie's arms to the pillow on both sides of her head. "Its okay, Billie. Shhh, it's all right. Calm down. You're safe. I've got you, shhh." Billie relaxed, but continued to rock her head side to side.

"I know it hurts, sweetheart. Here, let me help you." Cat shifted her weight so she was leaning against the headboard. She reached around Billie's head and massaged her temples until she was still. She slid her body down sideways until she was lying across the top of Billie's pillows, her face just a hair's breadth away from Billie's head. She kissed her, closed her eyes, and let sleep take her away.

"Caitlain. Caitlain, wake up."

Cat lifted her head. "What?" The first thing she noticed was Billie's head right in front of her. She stroked the silky dark hair and kissed her forehead.

The sound of someone clearing their throat drew her attention.

She straightened herself into a sitting position. "Daddy?"

"How did you end up there?" he asked.

"She was thrashing around. She was in pain. I had to help her."

"That was very foolish. We don't know what she's capable of."

"I've already told you, she won't hurt me."

"In her right mind, she wouldn't, but we don't know what her state of mind is right now. For your own safety, stay away from her when she's like that."

"I can't. I won't. She needed me. I'd do it again in a heartbeat."

Doc raised his eyebrows. "More like your mother everyday," he muttered under his breath.

Cat smiled at his comment.

"They'll be here soon to take her to surgery."

Cat's expression darkened as the realization of what Billie would be going through settled in. "I want to be there," she said.

"No. Absolutely not. Don't argue with me on this, do you understand? That OR is no place for you to be during this procedure."

"But—"

Doc grabbed her arms. "No. Now don't ask again."

Their argument was interrupted by the orderlies who appeared at the door to transfer Billie to a gurney for her trip to the OR.

Cat held her hand up to stop them and approached Billie's bedside. She sat on the edge and placed her palm on the side of Billie's face. She leaned in close to Billie's ear and said, "I love you, Billie. I know you can hear me. Fight. Fight for us, and for the children. We need you. Please come back to us." She placed a tender kiss on Billie's lips and wiped away one of her own tears that had fallen on Billie's cheek.

The orderlies transferred Billie to the gurney and rolled her out of the room as Cat stood in the circle of her father's arms and cried.

* * *

Where am I? What is this place? It's so cold in here. What are those voices, and that humming sound? Why can't I open my eyes? I can't move. What's happening to me? I need to get out of here. So sleepy.

"Scalpel."

She's so helpless... Please, whoever's listening, please let her make it. Hang on, my love. Daddy would kill me if he knew I was in here. They've shaved off all your beautiful hair. Come on, Billie, fight. Don't you dare leave me. Seth, Tara, Skylar—your babies need you. Don't give up, sweetheart. My life would not be worth living without waking each morning to drown in your beautiful blue eyes. I love you move than life itself. God, Billie, please hang on... please.

"Scalpel."

"Doctor O'Grady," the anesthesiologist said. "She's showing signs of regaining consciousness."

"Good, just on time," Doc said as he observed over the surgeon's shoulder. He leaned down next to Billie's ear. "Okay, daughter, this is where you take over. You need to guide us here." He gently slapped the side of Billie's face.

Billie regained consciousness. Her eyes scanned the room and settled on a point near the ceiling. Her face lit up as she whispered one word, "Cat," before her face went blank again.

Doc followed Billie's gaze upward to the observation deck above the operating theater. There, grinning ear to ear, was Cat.

Chapter 19

Doc scowled at Cat. "Caitlain, get your ass out of here."

"I'm not leaving."

Doc glanced at the attending surgeon and saw humor in his eyes. "It's not funny, Bert. She shouldn't be here."

Bert looked down at Billie and back at Doc. "Wouldn't you be, if you were in her shoes?"

Doc raised his hands to the sides. "I can't win here, can I?" He peered up at Cat. "Okay, you can stay, but I don't want to hear a peep out of you. Do you understand?"

Cat made the sign of the cross on her chest in promise.

"Okay, Billie-girl, are you ready?" Doc asked. He frowned when the expression on Billie's face indicated she didn't know who he was. "Billie, do you know where you are? Who I am?"

"No." The frown on her brow and the mist in her eyes was unmistakable to Doc. He spared a glance at Cat in the balcony above them. Concern and confusion were evident on her face as well.

"What's happening?" Cat asked.

"Cat, I can't have you second-guessing me. You promised to be quiet. If you can't, I'll have you removed from the balcony."

"I'm sorry. I'll be quiet."

Doc sighed and addressed Billie. "Billie, I'm Doc O'Grady. You're in the operating room of the Albany Medical Center. We're attempting to repair some damage in your brain caused by scar tissue. Do you understand?"

"Doc?" Billie said.

"Yes, Billie. We need your help here, daughter. You need to tell us what you're feeling while we remove the damaged area. Do you understand?"

"Are you my father?"

"No, but I am your father-in-law. You're married to my daughter, Caitlain."

Doc watched Billie's face as her gaze darted to the observation deck. A flash of panic and confusion crossed her features. "That's not possible."

Doc tilted his head to one side. "Why is that not possible?" he asked.

"Because I'm a woman."

Doc's attention was drawn to the balcony by an audible gasp. He looked up in time to see Cat retreat from the upper deck.

"Damn," he cursed under his breath as he realized the damage was already done.

*　*　*

Cat ran from the observation deck in a panic and didn't stop until she reached the grassy courtyard nestled in the intersection of the four wings of the hospital. She sat down on one of the benches and held her head in her hands, trying to make sense of what had just happened in the OR. *She recognized me when she opened her eyes. She said my name. I know she recognized me.*

Cat wrapped her arms around her midsection and rocked back and forth. *What did she say? 'That's not possible, because I'm a woman'? Billie, what does that mean? Don't you remember me? Don't you remember our love?*

Cat spent the next hour pacing across the grass, fearing she'd lost everything in that one sentence. *Billie, I can't live without you. Please remember me. Remember your children. We need you.* Cat lifted her eyes skyward. *Please bring her back to us. We need her more than you do.*

*　*　*

Throughout the operation, Doc repeatedly glanced into the balcony for signs of Cat. He struggled with the ethical issues surrounding Cat's presence in the room during surgery. It was enough he was in there, operating on his own daughter-in-law, which in itself was bordering on unethical. But considering the soonest a neurosurgeon could be brought in was days away, he opted to push ethics aside and do what he could to help this woman he had come to love as a daughter.

Billie lost consciousness two hours into the procedure, and the anesthesiologist was unable to rouse her a second time, so Doc finished the operation without her guidance. It was his preference for the patient to be awake during this type of surgery, as it made the success rate higher if they were able to gauge the patient's reaction to the invasion of brain tissue before cutting it away. Losing Billie's cooperation so early in the operation was unfortunate.

* * *

In the surgical ward waiting room, Cat alternated between pacing, crying, and sitting, all the while fretting about Billie's fate and their future together. After one long, exhausting stretch of pacing, she sat and rested the back of her head against the wall. She closed her eyes against the pain in her temples. Soon, she felt a presence beside her.

"Here, drink this while it's still hot."

Cat opened her eyes and saw Jen sitting beside her, a cup of coffee extended toward her. "You're a lifesaver."

"How's Billie?" Jen asked.

"She's still in surgery."

"How long?"

Cat looked at the clock on the wall. "About four hours."

Jen took Cat's chin in her hand. "Cat, look at me. That's better. How are you holding up?"

Cat broke down into tears as soon as her gaze met Jen's.

Jen took her coffee and set both cups on the table in front of them. She opened her arms wide, and Cat fell into them. "It's okay. It's okay," Jen said.

Jen held her for long moments until Cat broke the embrace and sat up. She wiped her eyes with the napkin Jen handed her. "No, it's not okay. She doesn't know who I am. She doesn't remember us."

"What do you mean?"

Cat explained everything. About the nightmare and headache the night before, about her sneaking into the observation deck of the OR, about Billie opening her eyes on the operating table and saying her name, about Billie mistaking Doc for her own father. Finally, Cat told her about Billie's comment regarding their marriage. Jen's arms tightened around her, and Cat leaned her head on Jen's shoulder.

"Cat, I'm sure it's only temporary, a side effect of the operation."

"No. I don't think so. All of this happened before the operation. Her comment upset me, and I left the OR and ran. After a while I calmed down, and I've been sitting here ever since." Cat blew her nose. "I can't live without her. I don't want to live without her."

"You know Billie loves you. How can she just forget that?" Jen asked.

"I don't know. What if she never remembers?"

"Then you'll just have to make her fall in love with you all over again."

"What if this new Billie isn't attracted to women? Her comment in the OR kind of implied that."

Jen took Cat's hand in hers. "Tell me, Cat, why are you attracted to women?"

"What's that got to do with anything? I'm not the one lying on the table in there," she said, pointing to the OR door.

"Think about it. Why are you attracted to women?" Jen asked again. "Humor me."

"I don't know. I was born this way."

"That's right. You were born that way. It's biological... not a matter of choice. Right?"

"Right."

"Do you think Billie's attraction to women is a matter of choice?"

Cat's eyes opened wide. "I think you're trying to tell me Billie's inherent biological makeup hasn't changed, so don't worry about it, right?"

"Right."

"So I'll just have to make her fall in love with me all over again."

"Is there an echo in here?" Jen said, earning her a jab in the ribs.

* * *

The operation lasted 10 hours. By the time Doc allowed his assistants to close the wound, he was exhausted and not a little skeptical about Billie's recovery. He stepped back and watched as the piece of skull that had been removed was carefully replaced and the skin sutured back together.

Be strong, daughter. Your family needs you. We all do. You've made my Caitlain happier than I've ever seen her before. Please put a smile back on her face as only you can do. We need you, Billie. Come back to us.

Chapter 20

Cat and Jen sat in the OR waiting room, watching the hours tick by on the clock. The two spent six hours talking, reading, and napping, each one alternately using the other's lap as a pillow. As the minute hand fell upon 6:12 in the afternoon, the door to the OR opened and a very tired Doc exited. Cat ran to his side.

"Daddy?"

"She came through the operation with flying colors. She's a strong woman. I wouldn't be surprised to see her awake by tomorrow morning."

Cat hugged him tight while Jen grinned from ear to ear.

Cat pulled out of his embrace. "How did it go?"

Doc took a deep breath and ran a hand through his hair. "We'll know more in a few days. She lost consciousness about two hours into it, so most of the operation was done by referencing the CAT scans, X-Rays, and MRIs. Only time will tell how successful we were and how much damage resulted from the operation."

"Damage?" Jen said from her position on the couch.

Cat took Jen's hand. "Billie had major brain surgery. There's always the risk of damage when you start cutting away pieces of the brain."

Jen jumped to her feet. "You cut away pieces of her brain?"

"Calm down," Doc said. "We only did what was medically necessary to save her life. Her brain would have been starved of a much-needed blood supply without the operation. She would have died if we hadn't done it."

Jen paced back and forth. "Jesus Christ! Jesus Christ!" She stopped in front of Cat. "You do realize how pissed she'll be if she ends up handicapped because of this?"

"I thought of that, but it's a risk I was willing to take, for her and for us. It wasn't an easy decision. In fact, it was the most painful decision I've ever had to make. The brain is such a mysterious organ. It has the remarkable ability to help the body balance itself. If she ends up with permanent damage, there's a good chance she can learn to compensate. I'll help her."

Jen walked up to Cat and stopped within inches of her. "Who are you trying to convince, me or you?" Jen held this position for a few seconds before walking away. "I'm going home," she said and left the room.

Jen marched down the corridor and out of sight. Cat faced Doc and saw sympathy and understanding on his face.

"What?" Cat asked.

"She's right, you know. There's a chance Billie will come out of this with a permanent disability. As a doctor, I'm sure you understood the risks going into this. I hope to God she'll come out of this intact, but Jen's right. If she doesn't, there'll be hell to pay, in more ways than one."

"But she might have died without the operation."

Doc nodded. "In all probability, she would have. I hope we haven't just saved her physical life in exchange for her emotional health. There's a chance her quality of life will degrade, and she'll be angry if things don't end well." He lifted Cat's chin. "If that happens, she may blame you and—just like her death—her resentment might result in the end of your life together."

"I couldn't let her die. I couldn't."

"I know, kitten. I would have made the same decision if it had been your mother, but I'd feel a lot better about the prognosis if there weren't signs of memory loss before the brain tissue was removed."

"That's not what I want to hear, Daddy."

"Well, it's not what I want to tell you, either, but her obvious confusion on the operating table made it pretty apparent to me that brain damage had already occurred as a result of the injury three years ago. I'm afraid a three-year-old injury might not be as reversible as one that happened in a more recent time frame."

"What are you saying?"

"I'm saying the possibility of a full recovery is slimmer with such an old injury."

* * *

A half hour later, Billie was transferred to the ICU. Cat sat on the edge of the bed and looked at the white bandage wrapped around her head, and at the tangle of tubes and wires connected to various parts of her body.

"Billie, I know this isn't how you'd want to live your life," she said. "Please don't hate me for doing this to you. You know I made this decision because I can't bear to lose you. Remember when Seth had surgery? Remember we agreed we would love him and nurture him no matter what his abilities were? The kids and I, we feel the same about you. We want you in our lives regardless of how this turns out."

Cat stood and walked to the window where she stared out over the city. *You need to keep your wits about you, Cat. She needs you now, more than ever. Have faith in her. Have faith in what you have together.*

Cat walked back across the room and stood at the foot of Billie's bed. Needing physical contact, she reached over and touched Billie's left foot, which jerked at the contact. Cat yanked her hand back at the unexpected reaction. A grin spread across Cat's face. "It moved," she said out loud. "It moved."

"What moved?"

Cat's gaze darted to the doorway to see her father standing there, holding Billie's chart in his hands. "Her foot," Cat said. "I reached out and touched it, and it moved. That's a good sign, isn't it? It means she isn't paralyzed, doesn't it?"

Doc slipped the chart into the pocket at the bottom of the bed. He placed an arm around Cat's shoulder and pulled her head down to kiss the top of it. "It gives us reason to hope. It could have been an involuntary reflex, but it's too soon to draw conclusions. She's only been out of surgery for an hour. It'll be tomorrow morning at the earliest before she even wakes up."

Doc released his embrace and reached for both of Cat's hands. "Honey, why don't you go home and get some sleep? There's not much any of us can do until she wakes up. Go home, get some sleep, and come back tomorrow morning."

"No. I can't stay away all night. I'll go home and shower, but I'll be back in a couple of hours."

"You've been saying no a lot to me lately, young lady. When did you get a mind of your own?"

Cat saw the twinkle in his eyes. "The day you delivered me in the car on the way to the hospital." She rose on tiptoe to kiss his cheek.

"I should've known you'd be trouble when you wouldn't wait." He chuckled as he picked up Billie's chart and left the room.

Cat walked to the bed and leaned over Billie's still form. She placed several kisses on her mouth and cheeks and leaned in closer to whisper in her ear. "I'll be back. Don't go anywhere, okay? I love you." She kissed her once more before she left.

All the way home, Cat thought about Jen's reaction to her decision for Billie to undergo surgery. As she thought about it, her feelings seesawed between understanding and anger. In the end, anger won. *Friends were supposed to support each other, have faith in each other. I needed you, and you turned on me.*

By the time Cat pulled into her driveway, she was furious. She climbed out of the car, slammed the door, and stomped over to Jen's house. Jen was loading the dishwasher when Cat walked into the kitchen. Cat walked toward her, grabbed her arm, and dragged her into the bathroom just off the kitchen.

She slammed the door and leaned against it. Jen positioned herself on the edge of the bathroom sink and crossed her arms.

"What the hell was that all about at the hospital?" Cat said.

"I'm not so sure you made the right decision, Cat."

Cat raised her hands in a helpless gesture. "What did you expect me to do? Let her die? What would you have done? Tell me, what would you have done?"

Cat's eyes locked with Jen's, and she waited for a reply.

"I don't know. I hope to God I never have to make that decision. But what I do know is this. Billie may not thank you for saving her life, not if it means spending it in a wheelchair or hooked to a respirator. I think if the decision was hers, she'd have chosen death over a lifetime of being a burden to you and the kids."

Cat sank to the floor and pulled her knees up to her chest. "I couldn't do it. I couldn't let her die."

Jen sat on the floor beside her and pulled her into a hug. "Cat, it's water under the bridge at this point. The decision is irreversible. We both know there's a chance she'll live the rest of her life as a cripple. If that happens, the pity and sympathy will kill her, but what we need to do now is hope for the best and work our asses off to see she recovers."

Cat nodded and wiped the tears from her cheeks.

"I'm sorry I was such a bitch at the hospital. I had no right to treat you like that. Forgive me?"

Another nod from Cat.

"All right then," Jen said. "I want you to stay with us tonight. You shouldn't be alone."

"I can't. I'm going to shower and head back to the hospital. I want to be there in case she wakes up during the night."

Jen squeezed her tight for a moment then released her and rose to her feet. She offered a hand to Cat. "Then I'm going with you. Come on, on your feet."

Cat went home to shower and change while Jen said goodnight to her family. Twenty minutes later, they were in Cat's car on the way to the hospital.

Chapter 21

Cat and Jen arrived at the hospital fifteen minutes later. As they approached the ICU, Cat noticed a barrage of activity going on around Billie's room. Panic filled her when she saw a trauma cart being wheeled into the room. "Oh, no!" She ran the rest of the way down the hall with Jen right on her heels.

Cat fought her way through the bodies surrounding Billie on the bed and broke through to see her in the clutches of a seizure. Her body jerked and twitched, making it difficult for the doctors to monitor her vitals.

Cat heard her father's voice. "Time?"

"Four minutes," came the reply from the intern seated at Billie's side.

"It should be over soon," Doc said.

"Daddy?"

Doc's attention was drawn to the sound of her voice. "Monitor her closely. If the seizure doesn't stop in another four to five minutes, notify me immediately." He took Cat's arm and dragged her across the room.

"You and Jen need to wait in the hall. You'll do her no good in here."

"She needs me," Cat said.

"Right now, she has no awareness of anything or anyone around her. Not even you. Now do as I say and go wait in the hall. I won't take no for an answer this time. I promise to come get you if her condition worsens, all right?"

Jen approached Cat and took her by the hand. "Come on, sweetie. Do as Doc says. I'm sure Billie will be fine."

Cat allowed Jen to lead her to the waiting area just beyond Billie's room.

Cat was in a daze. Her heart ached to think about what Billie was going through. She looked at Jen and their clasped hands as Jen brought them to her lips and kissed Cat's knuckles. The gesture was so like Billie, tears welled up and threatened to spill over. No words passed between them as the minutes ticked by.

After what felt like an eternity, Doc joined them in the waiting area and took a seat next to Cat. "I'm sorry for my abrupt tone in there, but there was nothing you could have done. You didn't need to see that. However, if my suspicions are right, you might have to get used to it and learn how to deal with it."

Cat eyed him questioningly. The knot in her throat made it difficult to breathe.

"Caitlain, you've seen this before. I'm sure it's happened to a random patient while you've had them under anesthesia, so you know she's in no real danger from the seizure alone. However, so soon after injury, there's always the concern the jerking and twitching might cause excessive movement of her already swollen brain inside the skull cavity. That's the last thing she needs right now."

"So what happened in there? What caused the seizure?" Jen asked.

"A seizure occurs when there's an abnormal electrical discharge from a group of cells in the brain. This abnormal discharge can be caused by a head injury that results in scarring of the brain tissue, as is the case with Billie. What you saw in there was Billie in the throes of a grand mal. These seizures are typically partial, meaning they affect a localized area of the brain, but sometimes they become generalized, encompassing the entire brain. I believe the seizure she just endured was generalized."

"You said she was in no danger from the seizure," Jen said, "but it seemed pretty bad."

"Most seizures are harmless. In fact, if a person is unconscious during a seizure, they may feel nothing at all. There's a type of seizure called 'status epilepticus' that is characterized by several hours of prolonged seizure activity. That could be life threatening. However, the type of seizure Billie had lasts one to seven minutes and almost never requires medical attention. It's much scarier for the people around her than it is for her to experience."

"What did you mean I might have to get used to it?" Cat said when she regained her voice.

Doc took a keep breath. "It's too early to tell, and we'll need to run several tests, but it's possible the injury may have caused Billie to develop epilepsy."

* * *

Cat stood in the window of Billie's room and stared out into the darkness while Jen sat in the chair by the bed. Billie lay a few feet away, wires from the electrocardiogram extending from pads placed strategically on her chest and head in an octopus-like fashion. An intracranial pressure monitor was attached to her skull. Intravenous tubing, which fed her fluids from the bag hanging on the rack next to her bed, extended from her arm and was taped to a board on her left forearm. A transducer to detect and measure heart rate and blood pressure completed the assortment of monitoring devices attached to her body.

Cat turned around and leaned against the windowsill. Her heart went out to Billie lying so frail and helpless in the midst of all that gadgetry. Cat's thoughts dwelled on the comments Billie had made on the operating table. *That's not possible. I'm a woman.*

Cat's attention was drawn to Jen when her friend's chin slowly lowered to her chest. Cat approached Jen and shook her. "Jen, honey, wake up."

Jen rubbed her eyes. "Is she awake?"

"No. I don't expect her to regain consciousness before tomorrow morning. Why don't you take my car and go home. Get some sleep, okay?"

"I don't want to leave you here alone."

"I'm not alone. Billie's here with me."

Jen nodded. "Of course. Are you sure you don't mind?"

"No, I don't mind. I'm not leaving her side anyway. There's no sense in both of us sitting here watching her sleep. I insist. Go home. I'll see you tomorrow."

"All right. I'll be back bright and early, okay?"

"Sure. Oh, before I forget, could you stop by and pick up a change of clothing for me? I'll shower here in the morning."

"No problem." Jen took the keys from Cat and hugged her close. She kissed the side of Cat's head and whispered in her ear, "Be strong, my friend. She's going to need you."

"I will. Now go home. Get some sleep."

Jen walked over to the bed and kissed Billie on the cheek. "Hey, big guy, you've got one hell of a lady waiting here for you, so get well soon, okay?"

Then Jen was gone.

Cat sat in the chair next to the bed and held Billie's hand close to her heart. She stared at her for long moments. By midnight, she was unable to stay awake, so she laid her head on the bed next to Billie and fell asleep.

"Cat. Cat, come on, wake up," Doc said as he shook her.

Cat's eyes fluttered open. "Daddy?"

"You fell asleep, kitten."

Cat looked at Billie and saw there was no change from the night before. Stiff from sleeping bent over all night, she stretched her back and leaned over to kiss Billie on the forehead. "Good morning, love." She watched Billie's face for some type of reaction but was disappointed to see none.

"Cat," Doc said. "I need to examine her. The monitors show stable readings throughout the night except for a very brief period around midnight when it appeared her heart rate increased."

Cat stood back and watched as her father examined Billie. There was virtually no response to stimuli tests, including those designed to evoke movement and reaction to pain and sound. Her heart sank as Billie failed test after test. Finally, Doc was finished.

"She's in a coma, isn't she?" Cat asked.

"I'm afraid so. Hard to tell how long it will last."

Cat tried to mask her disappointment.

"Caitlain, go home and get some decent sleep. You'll be no good to her if you end up sick yourself."

"I can't. I can't leave her. Please don't ask me to."

Doc squeezed her shoulder. "All right. I know when I'm defeated. I'll be back a little later to check in on her." He kissed Cat on the cheek and left the room.

Soon afterwards, Jen came in, juggling a small suitcase, a bag of pastries, and two coffees. She handed the food to Cat and placed the suitcase at the foot of the bed so she could embrace her. "Good morning," she said. "Any change?"

"She's in a coma. Daddy put her through a battery of tests this morning, and she failed to respond, even to those intended to test her pain level." Cat handed a coffee back to Jen.

"That's not good, is it? I mean, being in a coma is serious, isn't it?"

"It can be serious when it's associated with some type of traumatic event, but there are times when the body will put itself into a coma so the necessary healing resources can focus on the source of the illness. It appears Billie's coma is self-induced. Daddy feels certain neither the operation nor the seizure caused it."

"So that's a good thing," Jen said.

"Yes. We're choosing to believe Billie's coma is a positive sign."

"Let's hope so. Here, eat something. You must be starved."

Cat declined the pastries, but welcomed the coffee. "Oh, this is delicious coffee. Thank you."

"I brought a few days' worth of clothes, since I figured you wouldn't want to leave Billie."

"You thought right. Thank you for thinking ahead."

"No problem."

"I need to shower. Could you keep an eye on her while I'm in there?"

"Absolutely."

"And let me know the minute she twitches, all right?"

Jen raised her right hand in the air. "Scout's honor."

While Cat was in the shower, Jen held a nonstop talk with Billie. "Well, tall, dark, and gorgeous, how are you today? You know, you'll have to get your lazy butt out of bed pretty soon. I miss my five a.m. running partner. The kids say hi. You've got some wonderful kids. Seth is pretty worried about his mom. He's a great kid, that one. Very sensitive and softhearted. Tara and Sky can't wait for you to come home, so hurry up and come back to us, okay?" Jen paused to take a sip of coffee.

She traced the edge of the bandage that ran across Billie's forehead and let the back of her hand trail down along Billie's cheek to her jaw. "You're pretty damned cute in a turban. Don't tell Miss Spitfire in there I said that though, she might get jealous. Quite honestly, she'd look pretty ridiculous in a turban—yep—she's kind of too short, know what I mean? She'd pretty much resemble a Q-tip." Jen laughed at her own joke and continued her monologue.

"You know, I wasn't so sure about you and Cat when you moved into the neighborhood. I have to confess I was ignorant about relationships like yours. Before you two, I don't think I'd ever met a lesbian, never mind find myself a soul mate with two of them. All I could think when you moved in was there goes the neighborhood. Well, my friend, I was right, the neighborhood did change, from a bigoted, opinionated bunch of pompous asses, to a group of people who have come to care for one another.

"I know I've grown as a result of your friendship, and Fred has too. We have you and Cat to thank for that. You know, it never occurred to me to teach my kids that love is love, regardless of how it's packaged. Not that I wanted them to be prejudiced, who could possibly want that? I just never thought about how careless and hurtful ignorance and intolerance can be—hurtful to us as well as to you. I'm so happy you came into our lives at a point when my children were still young enough not to have formed ideas about people who are different from them. Stevie and Karissa think of you as family. Hell, you are family, you and Cat both, and your kids. You have a wonderful life waiting for you when you get home, Billie. Don't you dare screw it up. Do you hear me?" Jen paused again to regain her composure.

"Cat's having a rough time with this. She's worried to death. That wife of yours is one stubborn woman. You're so lucky to have her. She loves you a lot. She refuses to go home, you know. She's afraid to leave you alone. You've got a lot of people who need you, including me. Yeah, I know, I might seem like just the pesky neighbor to you, but, oh hell, I love you too. It breaks my heart to see you lying there. I want so much to take you in my arms and tell you it'll be all right. It will be—all right, I mean."

Finally, Jen rose to her feet and leaned over Billie. She whispered in her ear, "Please come back," and placed a kiss on her cheek. Unable to go on, she wiped a tear from her eye as Cat came out of the bathroom, dressed in jeans and a T-shirt.

Jen looked at her. "That was a quick shower."

"I didn't want to be away from her for too long. Been talking her ear off?"

"Yeah. It's the only time she's actually listened to me without interrupting."

Cat laughed and approached Billie's bed. She stopped short a few feet from her destination. Startled blue eyes met green.

"Oh my God! Billie!"

Chapter 22

"Jen, get Daddy. Please hurry."

Cat was unsure of Billie's state of mind, so she approached her cautiously and reached out to touch her cheek. Billie's eyes widened. The fear evident on her face froze Cat in place.

Doc rushed into the room with Jen right behind him. He approached Billie and sat on the edge of her bed. Billie's gaze darted to him.

"Good morning, young lady," he said. "You've given us quite a scare. How do you feel this morning?"

Billie stared at Doc. "Who are you? Where am I?" she asked. Her speech sounded strange, like her tongue was too thick.

Cat took another step forward. Billie's gaze quickly moved to her.

"Billie—"

Doc silenced her with an upheld hand.

Doc's voice once again drew Billie's attention. "You're in the hospital. You've just undergone brain surgery. I'm Doctor O'Grady. This is your friend Jen," he said, pointing to Jen, "and this is Cat, your wife."

Billie's eyes grew very wide. "I'm confused. I don't understand. M... my wife?"

"Yes. You've been married for almost two years," Doc said.

"No... no." Billie's eyes misted over, and she was unable to continue.

Cat felt Jen wrap her arms around her from behind. "Hold it together, Cat. She just doesn't remember yet," Jen said.

Doc took Billie's hand in his. Tears flowed freely from Billie's eyes. He turned to Cat. "Caitlain, I need you and Jen to leave the room for a little while."

"Daddy—no, I can't."

"Please don't argue with me on this."

Cat's face contorted as she struggled with Doc's request. Finally, she relented and allowed Jen to lead her out into the hallway where she broke down and cried in Jen's arms.

Doc continued to hold Billie's hand while she cried. When she stopped crying, he reached for a tissue from the bedside table and wiped the tears from her cheeks. "I know you're frightened. You have every right to be, but I promise, you're surrounded by people who love you very much, and who'll keep you safe. Do you understand?"

"What happened to me? Why am I here?" she asked. "Why can't I talk right?"

"A previous head injury ruptured inside your skull, causing the need for emergency brain surgery. That was yesterday. It's affected your speech among other things. Do you understand what I'm saying?"

Billie felt the bandage around her head and frowned. "Brain surgery?"

"Yes," Doc said. "Now, I need to examine you, all right?"

"All right."

After an hour and a barrage of tests, Doc was finished. Billie remained silent throughout the testing process. Doc sat on the edge of the bed and took her hand once more. "Billie, do you mind if I ask Cat to come back into the room so I can explain the test results to both of you?"

"Why does she say she's my wife?" Billie asked.

"I know this is difficult for you to understand right now, but you and Cat have been married for about two years."

"But I... I'm a woman. She's a woman too. We can't be married."

"Don't worry about that now, daughter. You need to concentrate on getting well. We'll deal with all of this in due time."

"Are you my father?"

Doc started. This was the second time Billie had asked that. "As much as I wish I were, no, I'm not your father. I'm Cat's father and your father-in-law. But in my heart, yes—I guess you could say I'm your father. Now, if it's okay with you, I'll ask Cat to come back into the room now."

"Okay."

Doc met Cat and Jen in the hall. "Cat, you can go in now, but I encourage you not to move too fast. She's experiencing memory loss, so you'll need to be careful around her until her memories resurface." He addressed Jen. "I apologize, Jen, but I'll have to ask you to wait out here for now. I don't want to overwhelm her with too much too fast."

"I understand," Jen said. "Maybe I'll head home for a while. Call if you need me, Cat, and I'll be here in an instant."

Moments later, Cat sat by Billie's bedside, but she made no attempt to touch her. Billie stared at Cat.

Doc sat on the opposite side of the bed. "Billie, let me begin by asking you what you remember."

Billie's gaze veered to Doc and back to Cat.

Doc continued. "Do you know who you are?"

Billie turned her eyes toward Doc once more. "No."

"Do you recognize any of us?" he asked.

Billie closed her eyes for a moment. "No."

"Okay. Things may come back with time," Doc said. "For now, let me summarize what I know. First, you have amnesia. That's quite normal after brain surgery. We'll work very hard to help you recover your memory, if we can. Sometimes memory comes back all at once, sometimes it comes back in pieces, and sometimes it doesn't come back at all. Second, you lack mobility. The results of the sensory testing indicate the pre-motor and motor skills housed in the frontal lobe of the brain will have to be relearned. We'll set up a program of physical therapy, occupational therapy, and counseling to help you deal with that. Do you understand what I'm telling you?"

Billie pulled her gaze away from Cat once more to look at Doc. "I... I'm paralyzed and I don't remember anyone," Billie said.

"It's clear the intellectual parts of your brain have been unaffected by the brain injury. You're correct, except you're not paralyzed. Paralysis implies nerve damage in the spine. That's not what your condition is. You have the ability to move your muscles, but your brain has forgotten how to move them in a coordinated manner, kind of like a newborn. You'll have to relearn how to grasp objects, walk, feed yourself—things like that. The good news is, those skills are learned at a rapid pace, so I expect you'll be on your feet in no time. I'm going to arrange therapy sessions and meet with your team of doctors to set things in motion here. Now, before I go, do you have any questions?"

"How did this happen? Was I in an accident?"

"This is going to sound somewhat incredible to you right now, but your injury was caused by a gunshot wound to the head three years ago."

Billie looked startled. "Someone shot me in the head? Who?"

"That's not important right now. Just know that the scar tissue building up around the injury site over the past few years was beginning to jeopardize your health."

"Does my family know? Have they been contacted?"

Cat stepped forward. "We are your family, Billie. You have no other living relatives."

Billie became agitated. "You're not my family."

Doc placed his hand on Billie's shoulder. "That's enough for now. Things may become clearer with time as your memories return. Do you have any other questions?"

"No."

Doc rose to his feet and kissed Billie on the cheek. "I'll see you later, then. Caitlain, could I speak with you in the hallway?"

Out in the hall, Doc took Cat into his arms and hugged her close. Cat clung to him for dear life, shaking like a leaf. "She'll be fine, kitten," he said.

"But will she ever be Billie again?"

"Only time will tell. In the meantime, you'll need to be as supportive and as patient with her as possible. You can't push her. She's very confused and won't react well to pressure. If she regains any memory at all, it'll have to be on her terms, not yours. She'll be moody and may even lash out at you. Be prepared to deal with that."

"I love her with all my heart, Daddy. I don't care what I have to endure, as long as we get her back. I'm prepared to work my ass off to see that we do."

"How can we fail with determination like that?" Doc said as he tweaked her nose.

Cat started to go back into Billie's room but stopped short. "Daddy, I have to call Art and Marge to let them know she's awake."

"Give me the number. I'll call them." Doc wrote the number down as Cat recited it.

"Thanks, Daddy."

Cat approached Billie's bed. Billie's eyes were closed. Unsure whether she was asleep or not, Cat touched her hand. Cat jumped back when Billie's eyes flew open. The terror in Billie's eyes broke her heart.

"I'm sorry. I didn't mean to startle you."

Billie continued to stare at Cat but didn't respond to the apology.

"May I sit down?" Cat asked.

A slight nod was answer enough for Cat as she pulled the chair closer to Billie's bedside.

"Billie," Cat said. "I know this is all very confusing to you right now, but I promise I'll help you through it. I love you, with all my heart."

"We can't be married. We're both women."

"Yes, we are. We've overcome a lot of obstacles, one of which was the legality of gay marriage."

"I'm not gay," Billie said.

Cat's heart sank. *Remember what Jen said, Billie's inherent biological makeup hasn't changed.* She studied her hands clenched in her lap and took a deep breath to compose herself. "Billie, I think we need to concentrate on getting you well. We can deal with our relationship later."

Billie looked away from Cat. "I'm not gay," she said again as Cat's heart crumbled into pieces.

Chapter 23

Cat was asleep in the chair beside Billie's bed when Doc arrived the next morning. He shook her shoulder. "Cat, wake up."

"What is it?" Cat said. "Is Billie okay?"

"She's sleeping. Come into the hall with me," he whispered.

Cat rose from the chair and followed him into the hall.

Doc shoved his hands into his lab-coat pockets. "Caitlain, I forbid you to spend every night sleeping in that chair."

"You forbid me?"

"You'll be of no use to Billie if you don't take care of yourself. You need to go home and sleep in your own bed. You need to reconnect with your children. Billie's in capable hands. She can survive the nights without you."

"Daddy—"

"I insist."

Cat tried hard to stand her ground against her father's piercing gaze, but she had to admit she was tired. "Oh, all right. All right. I'll go home at night. Geesh."

"Good decision. Now, let's go see how that lady of yours is this morning."

Cat led the way into the room just as Billie began to stir. She went directly to her bedside and kissed her on the forehead. "Good, you're awake. How are you feeling this morning?"

Billie frowned at Cat and shifted her attention to Doc. "I'm okay."

Doc picked up her chart from the pocket at the foot of the bed and read through the notes from the night shift. "Everything appears to be fine here. All indications are that you had an easy night."

"How long will I be here?" Billie asked.

Doc put the chart back and sat on the edge of the bed. "That depends on you. We'll need to set up a physical therapy schedule as soon as the swelling has subsided enough for valid baseline measurements."

Cat stepped forward and placed her hand on Billie's arm. "You remember, Billie—just like when Seth was recovering from brain surgery."

"Seth? Who is Seth?"

"There'll be time to talk about that later," Doc said. "Right now, I'll go schedule a battery of tests that can be carried out over the next few days so we can get you home as soon as possible. Now if you ladies will excuse me."

Cat sat in the space vacated by Doc. She reached for Billie's hand, only to be disappointed when Billie pulled it away. Cat forced herself not to react.

"Things really will be better when you can come home," Cat said.

"Where's home? Where do I live?"

"You live with me. Don't you remember Doc telling you we're married?"

"No, we're not. We're both women. I told you I'm not gay. Why are you trying to force yourself on me?"

Cat was losing her battle to keep her temper in check. She inhaled deeply to calm herself. "I'm doing nothing of the kind. I just want you to know I'm here for you. Soon your memories will come back, and you'll understand just what I feel for you."

Cat could see the confusion on Billie's face. "I'm not gay."

"Howdy, howdy." The cheerful hello from the doorway drew Cat's attention.

Cat's face lit up. "Jen. Good morning."

Jen swept into the room and enveloped Cat in a warm hug and tender kiss on the cheek. She then hugged and kissed Billie. "How are my best friends this morning?"

Cat yawned. "A little tired, but good."

Jen directed her next question at Billie. "How about you, big guy?"

"Big guy?" Billie said.

Jen lay across the bottom of Billie's bed. "Yep, that's my favorite name for you. Big guy—all bark and no bite."

Billie grinned, a fact not lost on Cat.

Cat stood and grabbed her jacket from the back of the chair. "If you don't mind keeping Billie company for a while, I think I'll head home and get a shower."

"Sure. No problem," Jen said.

Cat attempted to kiss Billie on the cheek before leaving, but Billie turned her face away.

"I'm sorry. I can't," she said.

Cat stepped back and closed her eyes against the pain. "It's okay. I understand. I'll see you a little later today."

Jen climbed off the bed and walked Cat to the door. Cat felt warm and secure wrapped in her friend's arms. "Don't worry, she'll come around," Jen whispered.

"I hope so. I'll be back soon."

"I've got it covered. Take your time. Love you," Jen said as she kissed Cat once more.

"Love you back."

Jen closed the door behind Cat and sat on the edge of Billie's bed. "How are you feeling today?"

"I have a headache, and I'm confused and afraid."

"Afraid? Why?"

"Cat insists we're married."

"You are."

"Why can't I remember it? Why don't I feel something for her? How can I possibly be married to her when I'm not gay? I don't even know who she is."

"It'll come back in time."

"You care a lot for her."

"I love her," Jen said. "She's a wonderful woman. I love you too."

Billie frowned. "What is it about lesbians? Do they all act like that? Did you and Cat and I have a *ménage a trois* or something?"

Jen fell back onto the bed and laughed heartily, her blonde curls splayed over the side of the bed.

"What's so funny?"

"You. You're funny. I've often thought about that very thing. You two are so cute together, I can't help but be jealous of your relationship, but a *ménage a trois?* That's a little over the top. There's no way I could deal with a threesome. Can you imagine the drama? Yikes!"

"I'm sorry. I assumed..."

Jen sat closer to Billie and grasped her hands. "There's nothing to be sorry about, big guy. I'd be honored to be part of a threesome with you and Cat, but lesbian drama is something I'd rather avoid."

"I'm not a lesbian, Jen. I'm not."

"Just promise me you'll keep an open mind, okay? Cat will grow on you, you'll see. Promise?"

Billie met Jen's gaze. "I promise."

Cat arrived back at the hospital just as Billie was being wheeled down the hall in her bed. She caught up with Doc who was walking alongside the bed. "Daddy, where are they taking her?"

"To the PT lab. We're doing the baseline testing this afternoon."

Cat followed them onto the elevator.

"Where's Jen?"

"She left when the orderlies came to get me," Billie said. "She'll be back later."

Cat was surprised to hear Billie answer. "Oh. Okay. Thanks."

"All right, here we are," Doc said when the elevator stopped. "I hope you ate your Wheaties this morning, Billie, we have a long day of testing ahead of us."

Later that afternoon, Doc met Cat and Billie in Billie's room. "Good afternoon, ladies. I have Billie's PT schedule for the next few weeks."

"Few weeks? Will it really take that long?" Billie asked.

"I've scheduled you for three weeks. Whether we need all that time will depend on your progress. It's possible you may need even more time than that. However, the better you do, the faster you'll be able to go home."

Cat pulled a chair close to Billie's bed and waited for Doc to begin.

"Okay, the plan calls for an early start each morning with a quick examination and collection of vital statistics. After breakfast there'll be an hour-long physical therapy session for gross motor skill development and an hour of occupational therapy for fine motor skills. Following lunch and a nap, you'll have a session with a counselor. Finally, another physical therapy session followed by dinner. Each day will end around six o'clock."

"That sounds grueling," Cat said.

"It's designed to be," Doc said. "Immersion therapy will give Billie's body the quickest chance at recovery." Doc looked at each of them. "Do you have any questions?"

Cat noticed that Billie fell silent during Doc's explanation, staring at her hands folded in her lap. When she realized Billie was not going to reply, she answered her father. "Not right now. I'm sure we'll have plenty once PT begins."

"Okay then, I guess I'll head home and see you in the morning."

After Doc left, Cat sat on the edge of Billie's bed. "You were pretty quiet during Daddy's explanation."

"There wasn't much to say. He's the doctor. I assume he knows what he's doing."

"That he does."

Cat waited for Billie to say something else, but it became apparent to her Billie was deep in thought.

"I'll be here in the morning to help with your therapy," Cat said.

"How is it you have so much time to spend here? Don't you work?"

"As a matter of fact, I do. I'm a doctor. An anesthesiologist to be exact. I've arranged to take some time off except for emergency calls so I can participate in your recovery."

"And what about me? What do I do for a living?"

"You're a lawyer—a very successful one. You almost single-handedly argued the case for gay marriage in this state—and you won."

"I did? I don't remember."

"You did. I've never been so proud of anyone in my life."

Billie yawned.

"It's been a tough day, huh?" Cat asked.

"Do you mind leaving early tonight? I'm kind of tired."

"But we haven't had much time together today. I don't mind sitting here while you sleep."

"No. I'm tired and I'd like some time alone. Please."

Cat retracted her hand and stood by the bed. She tried not to allow her hurt feelings to show on her face. "Okay then. I guess I'll see you in the morning." She leaned down to kiss Billie and was once again met with Billie's cheek. She kissed the cheek offered to her and stood to leave.

"Thank you for understanding," Billie said.

"I'll see you in the morning."

*   *   *

Breakfast on the first morning of therapy was tense. Cat adjusted Billie's bed so she was partially sitting, but her balance was so poor, she had to support her on either side with pillows.

Cat wedged the final pillow between Billie and the bed rail. "There. That ought to do it. Can I help feed you?"

"No. I'll do it myself."

"Okay, suit yourself, but I'm here to help if you need me."

"I don't need you."

Cat felt the sting of Billie's comment and retreated to the chair by the window to nurse her hurt feelings. Billie struggled to guide the spoon from the bowl to her mouth. After two spoonfuls of oatmeal ended up on her face and shirt, Billie flung the spoon across the room.

Cat cringed and approached her cautiously. "Let me help you."

"No! Get away. Don't touch me."

"Billie, you've got to eat. You'll need to keep up your strength for therapy."

"I said no."

Cat clenched her fists at her sides to suppress her anger. When she was calm enough to deal with Billie without losing her temper, she picked up the spoon from the floor and put it on Billie's tray. "It's up to you if you don't want to eat, but at least let me clean you up."

Cat ignored the scowl on Billie's face as she wiped the oatmeal from her chin and shirt.

She finished cleaning the oatmeal from Billie's face just as the therapist arrived, promptly at nine a.m. Cat could almost touch the air of arrogance that surrounded the man as he entered the room and folded his arms across his chest. He was a large man, well over six feet tall.

He approached Billie and extended his hand. "My name is Joseph, and if I do my job right, I'll be your worst nightmare."

Cat watched Billie's face for her reaction. She sat there stoically. Joseph seemed unfazed that Billie ignored his greeting.

He lowered the safety bar. "Your injury is to your brain, not your spine or muscles, but in order to reestablish the correct electrical impulses associated with gross motor movement, we'll be working primarily today with your arms and legs. We'll begin with range of motion tests."

Cat eyed Joseph warily as she stood off to the side and watched him manipulate Billie's limbs. As tall as Billie was, she was dwarfed by Joseph's large frame. She had to admit he was very good-looking—broad shoulders, muscular chest and arms, dark, wavy, shoulder-length hair, goatee—but there something about him Cat didn't trust. She decided she'd keep her eye on him.

At first, when Joseph worked Billie's muscles, the movements were simple gentle extensions and contractions of her arms and legs. Before long, he became more aggressive, applying more pressure and demanding more counteractive force from Billie. Cat could see the pain on Billie's face. Billie clutched the sheets with her hands and gritted her teeth while Joseph pushed her bent knee toward her chest.

After almost an hour, Billie objected. "Stop, please. It hurts."

"Sorry, no can do. Now come on, push harder." Joseph pushed her knee toward her chest.

"I can't. It hurts."

"Push," Joseph said loudly.

"No." Tears streaked Billie's cheeks.

Cat couldn't take it anymore. She took a step forward. "That's enough," she said.

Joseph leveled a harsh look at Cat and pointed his finger in her face. "You—back off."

"You're hurting her."

"I'm doing my job. Now either you back away, or I'll call her doctors and let them take care of you."

Cat raised her hands in resignation and walked back to her place against the wall. She clenched her teeth as she listened to Billie's cries for the remaining fifteen minutes of the session.

No sooner had Joseph left, than the Occupational Therapist arrived. The OT was a young woman named Julie. Cat liked her immediately. Her warm, bubbly personality was a welcome relief after Joseph's gruffness. Cat walked over to the window and peered out as Julie put Billie through fine motor skill training. Mild cursing came from the bed behind her as Cat listened to Billie trying to fit various shaped pegs into their proper slots on the pegboard. Julie's soft voice provided gentle coaching when Billie struggled and hearty congratulations when she completed the entire board. After an hour, the session was over and lunch arrived. Julie remained with Billie through lunch, using this time for additional therapy.

Cat stayed by the window and watched Julie work with Billie. By the end of the meal, Billie was able to guide her spoon from her soup bowl to her mouth. She had a great deal of soup on the front of her hospital gown, but she learned to maneuver the utensil in the general direction of her mouth. Cat felt a sense of joy at Billie's accomplishments, but she also felt jealousy and resentment that she wasn't the one instrumental in Billie's success.

When Julie left, Cat grabbed a fresh gown from the closet and approached Billie.

"What are you doing?" Billie asked.

"You need to get out of that soiled garment."

Cat watched as Billie pulled the soiled gown tighter around her.

"I'll do it." Billie awkwardly reached out for the gown.

Cat once more quelled feelings of impatience and anger and handed the garment to Billie. "At least let me untie the back for you."

Billie allowed Cat access to her back. Seconds later, the gown was ready to remove. Cat saw the expectant expression on Billie's face. When she realized what Billie wanted, she released a frustrated sigh and turned her back. Cat heard mild cursing for several minutes.

"Okay. It's on. You can turn around now."

Cat approached Billie and pulled her forward, leaning her against one of her own shoulders as she reached behind to tie the gown into place. She felt Billie shudder at the physical contact between them, but she forced herself not to react. She eased Billie back onto the pillows and pulled the covers up to her waist.

"Thank you," Billie said without making eye contact.

"You're welcome, love."

Billie looked up abruptly. "Why do you call me that?"

Cat sat down in the chair next to the bed. "Call you what?"

"Love."

"Because I do. I love you with all my heart. You're the other half of my soul."

Billie held her gaze for several moments before replying. "I... I don't remember you. I'm sorry."

Cat's eyes became heavy with unshed tears. She touched Billie's hand and tried not to let the tears escape when Billie jerked her hand out of her reach. She forced a smile onto her face. "Well, give it time. I'll wait." She stood and walked out of the room.

Cat made her way to the solarium at the end of the hall and lay on the couch where she cried herself to sleep.

* * *

"I don't remember her," Billie said. "She scares me. She says she's my wife. That can't be."

"Why can't that be, Billie?" Dr. Connor asked.

"What's wrong with everyone? Look at us. We're both women. Why isn't that as obvious to everyone else as it is to me?"

"Yes, you're both women. But that didn't stop you from fighting City Hall for the privilege of getting married. You and Cat have been seeing me for a while now, and within the first ten minutes it became apparent to me how devoted you were to each other. Are you telling me you have no memories at all of your life with Cat?"

Billie nodded. "That's right. I have none."

"I see," Dr. Connor said. "What is it about her that scares you?"

Billie's gaze roamed around the room and settled back on the doctor. "She wants to be with me, but I'm not gay."

"You're not gay?"

"No."

* * *

Cat awoke and pulled herself into a seated position on the solarium couch. She smiled when she spotted Jen. "Hi."

"Right back atcha. You look like hell, my friend."

"I love you too, Jen. How long have you been watching me sleep?"

"Not long. I arrived less than an hour ago. There was a Do Not Disturb sign on Billie's door, so I thought I'd wait here. I was surprised to see you sleeping here. How're you feeling?"

"Like the most important person in my life has gone and left me."

Jen got up from her chair, sat next to Cat, and pulled her into an embrace. Cat started to cry.

"Let it out. I've got you. I'm here for as long as you need me." Jen placed a kiss on Cat's temple. "It'll be okay."

After several minutes, Cat brought her crying under control. She pulled out of Jen's embrace, embarrassed. "I'm sorry. I've been doing that a lot lately."

"Don't ever be sorry for feeling. I'm glad to be here for you."

"Thanks." Cat glanced at her watch. "Damn. I've missed Billie's counseling session. Damn it." She rose from the couch and cast a helpless glance at Jen.

"It's okay. I'll wait here," Jen said.

Cat headed toward Billie's room just as Dr. Connor exited it. She ran down the hall to catch her and called out her name. Dr. Connor stopped.

"I'm so sorry," Cat said. "I fell asleep in the solarium. I wanted to be there for Billie."

"Calm down," Dr. Connor said. "It's okay. I would have asked you to leave the room anyway."

"Why?"

"Because Billie needs to vent a few feelings without you there. She's not the same Billie who's been visiting me for the past month."

Cat shook her head. "Please don't say that."

"It's true. She's different. We have no way of knowing if it's permanent or not, but right now she's not the same person."

Cat leaned against the wall. "God, I don't know what to do. I can't lose her. I can't."

"All I can say is you need to be as supportive, as positive, and as strong as possible for her over the next few weeks. She has a very steep hill to climb, physically and emotionally, and she'll be able to climb it more effectively if she has a strong support network behind her. You're the center of that network. Your love for her is her safety net, whether she realizes it or not."

Cat nodded. "I can't lose her. I'll do whatever it takes."

"You won't be able to help her at all if you don't help yourself first," Dr. Connor said. "You need to get some rest—away from this hospital. You'll do her no good if you fall sick from exhaustion." Dr. Connor paused and then continued. "Her physical therapist is in there with her right now. Take this time to get some rest."

"What! God, no. I've got to go. That bastard is brutal to her," Cat said as she headed toward the door.

Cat came to an abrupt halt as Dr. Connor caught her arm. "Cat, stop. Stop it right now. You can't go barging in there all angry with her therapist. He's only doing his job. I understand it's painful for her, but it's necessary. Surely you understand that?"

Cat nodded.

"Okay, then. If she needs you, by all means, go. But control yourself. You don't want to make her any more afraid of you than she already is."

"Billie's afraid of me?" she asked, shocked at this revelation.

"Yes, she is. Don't make it worse."

Cat stood by the door to the hospital room, clenching and unclenching her fists as Billie cried out in pain. Finally, when she was on the verge of giving in to her protective instincts, the session was over. Her heart broke as she watched Billie, tears streaking down her face and muscles quivering. Cat wanted to slap the smugness from Joseph's face as he sneered at her and left the room without even complimenting Billie on her efforts.

Cat approached the bed and squeezed Billie's shoulder. "I wish there was something I could do to ease your discomfort."

"That would be my job," a voice said from the doorway.

Cat saw an attractive woman dressed in scrubs standing there.

The woman entered the room and extended her hand to Cat. "I'm Laura, Joseph's assistant. Part of my job is to mop up after him. Massage is my game."

"Nice to meet you," Cat said. "I hear a southern accent. South Carolina?"

"Exactly. Most people put me in the general vicinity of the south, but few pinpoint it dead on."

"My grandmothers live in Charleston. I spent many summers there as a child. It's a beautiful state."

"That it is." Laura directed her attention to Billie. "So, you're Billie, right?"

Billie nodded.

Laura rubbed her arm. "Rough session, huh? Well, I'm hoping you'll feel a lot better by the time I leave."

For the next hour, Laura magically dissolved Billie's pain and helped her relax. When the massage was finished, she left them alone again.

Cat walked to Billie's bedside and sat down. Billie glanced at her then looked away.

"I'm sorry," Cat said.

"For what?"

"For scaring you and for treating your therapist like shit, even though he deserves it." Cat thought she saw the corner of Billie's mouth twitch at the mention of her confrontation with the therapist. "And for pushing myself on you before you're ready to accept it."

Billie looked at her. "Cat—"

Someone knocked on the door. "Ms. Charland?"

Cat saw the confusion on Billie's face and realized she hadn't yet been told her last name.

Cat rose to her feet and said, "Yes. This is Billie Charland."

"I'm Joselin. Speech therapist."

Cat turned back to Billie. "I'll leave you to your therapy, okay? I should be back by dinnertime." She left the room and went toward the solarium.

Cat was surprised to find Jen still there. "I thought you might have gone home by now," she said. "I'm sorry I deserted you."

Jen put down the magazine she was reading and rose to her feet. "No apology necessary. How's tough guy doing?"

"The speech therapist is with her for the next hour. They'll serve her dinner after that," Cat said. "God, it's been a long day."

Jen draped an arm around Cat's shoulder. "Come on. Let's see what kind of swill the hospital cafeteria has to offer while Billie is tied up, okay?"

"Okay," Cat said. "I guess I could eat."

"Have you eaten at all today?"

"Well—"

"Jesus, woman. I don't need both of my best friends sick in the hospital."

"You just don't want to be stuck with my kids," Cat said. "Speaking of which, I need to call them after dinner."

"Sounds like a plan. Let's go."

"Sky, honey, this is Mama."

"Mama, where are you? When can we come home?"

"I don't know, sweetheart. Mommy is very sick right now, and I need to stay with her for a while. You need to stay with Grandma so I can go the hospital whenever I'm needed—even in the middle of the night. Do you understand?"

"Yeah, but I miss you."

"I know, honey. I miss you too. I'll see you soon, I promise," she said. "Let me talk to your brother and sister, okay?"

"Hi, Mama," Tara said cheerfully.

Cat was always amazed how this child let problems roll right off her back.

"Hey, sweetie," Cat said. "Are you behaving for Grandma?"

"Yep. Is Mom all better yet?" she asked. "I can't wait until she comes home. Seth and Sky are no fun to play with—not like Mom is."

The thought of Billie and Tara engaging in hand-to-hand combat on the living room rug lifted her spirits.

"She'll be here for a while yet. But I hope she'll be able to come home soon."

"Okay, Mama. Here, Seth is bug'n me for the phone," Tara said.

"Hi, Ma," Seth said.

Cat's voice almost choked at the sound of her son's voice—Billie's son. "Hi, scout."

"Is Mom gonna be all right?"

"Yes, she is. She's awake and alert. In fact, she had a very busy day with therapy."

"When can we come see her?"

"I'm not sure. I need to talk to Grandpa about that. Is he home?"

"Yeah. Grandpa, it's Mama," Seth yelled, causing Cat to wince as he blasted her eardrum. "Here he comes. Tell Mom I love her, okay?"

"I will, honey. Be good for Grandma."

"Caitlain?" Doc said. "Is everything all right?"

"As right as it can be. Billie had a pretty rough day. Her therapist is brutal. Daddy, I need to know when I can bring the kids to visit. I'm a little apprehensive about it."

"Before you bring them, you'll have to explain the situation to them, and to Billie. Do you understand what I'm saying?"

"Yes, I do."

"I'll be there shortly. We can talk to Billie about this together, okay?"

"Okay. I'll see you soon."

Cat and Doc arrived at Billie's room just as her occupational therapist left, carrying Billie's dinner tray. Billie sat in bed, propped up between pillows as she watched Cat pace across the room.

"Caitlain, sit down, you're making me nervous," Doc said.

"Sorry." Cat sat in the chair next to Billie's bed. Doc walked over to the opposite side of the bed and sat down on the edge.

Doc took Billie's hand. Cat was envious of the fact that Billie didn't pull away from the contact. "Billie," Doc said, "Caitlain and I have something to tell you. I want you to have an open mind and hear us out, okay?"

Billie raised her eyebrows in question.

Cat looked at Doc and Billie before starting to speak. "Billie," she said, "you've already been told we're married."

Billie became agitated. Cat raised a hand to stop her. "I know. I know you're confused about that, but please hear me out." Cat paused then continued. "We have children."

"What?"

Cat reached for Billie's hand. Billie whipped it away fiercely. "No. Don't touch me," she yelled, setting Cat back in her seat.

"All right now," Doc said. "You just calm yourself down. Cat is telling the truth. You have three children between you, a son and two daughters."

Billie's gaze darted around before settling back on Cat's face. "Where are they?"

"They're staying with Cat's mother and me," Doc said, "until one or both of you are able to be home with them."

Billie pressed her head back onto the pillows and stared at the ceiling.

Cat regained her composure and willed herself not to cry. "They've been asking to see you. I want to bring them here after dinner tomorrow. Is that all right with you?"

Billie nodded yes.

"Thank you."

Cat sat in the chair beside Billie's bed and listened to the sound of her even breathing as she slept. She leaned her head back, yawned, and fought exhaustion brought on by the busy day. She could only imagine how Billie felt. The next day promised to be even more traumatic for all of them. As she sat there, she prayed things would work out for them. Life would not be worth living with only half a soul.

She glanced at her watch and noted it was 10:47 p.m. She knew she should go home to get some sleep, but she felt wired—keyed up over the children's visit the next day. She worried it wouldn't go well. She worried Billie wouldn't remember them and the visit would leave them traumatized. For long moments, she allowed the anxiety to paralyze her. Finally, she forced herself to rise from her chair and donned her jacket. She placed a tender kiss on Billie's cheek and bade her goodnight before leaving her room and walking down the hall toward the elevator. When she rounded the corner, she ran headlong into Jen.

"Jen! What are you doing here? Do you know how late it is?"

Jen was disheveled, like she had been roused out of bed. She grabbed Cat by the shoulders. "Cat, is Billie all right? Are you all right? Where are you going?"

"Whoa, slow down. One question at a time. I'm fine. Billie's fine, and I'm going home. I'm exhausted." She noted the odd expression on Jen's face. "What's wrong?"

Jen raked a hand through her hair. "I don't know," she said. "I was sleeping, when I woke up with this panicky, unsettled feeling. My first thought was that something was wrong with you or Billie, so I pulled on some shoes and a jacket and headed here."

Cat's eyes narrowed. "Did you happen to notice the time when you woke up?"

"Yes, it was 10:47. Why?"

"Jesus!" Cat locked arms with Jen and pushed the Down button on the elevator. "Walk me to my car, and while you're at it, explain to me just how you got into my head."

Jen and Cat stepped into the elevator.

"And by the way," Cat said, "you look real funky in fuzzy slippers and Fred's hunting jacket."

Chapter 24

The next morning, Cat reclined against the windowsill, sipping a cup of coffee, when Joseph arrived to begin Billie's second day of therapy. She'd tried since she arrived that morning to pull Billie out of the funk she was in, to no avail. Cat noted the scowl that crossed Billie's face when Joseph entered the room. She refused to acknowledge his presence.

"Okay, Billie," he said, after nodding hello to Cat. "Time to get to work."

"No," Billie said.

"No? Did you say no?"

"What part of no don't you understand?"

"Well, considering that word isn't in my vocabulary, I don't take no for an answer. I'm here to do a job, and like it or not, you're going to cooperate."

"I said, no."

Joseph leaned over the end of the bed and grasped Billie's ankles. "Well, I said yes." He gave her legs a steady pull until she was lying flat on her back, walked around to the side of the bed, and began manipulating her legs.

Cat was shocked at his use of physical force in an attempt to make Billie cooperate.

"Damn you," Billie shouted as she struggled. "Leave me alone."

"I suggest you cooperate before you hurt yourself." Joseph continued his manipulations.

Cat put her coffee cup down and readied herself to interfere. All she needed was a sign from Billie.

"Don't touch me!" Billie yelled.

Cat caught the desperate glance Billie cast in her direction. Interpreting it as a silent plea, she launched herself at Joseph, and soon found herself flat on her back, lying across Billie's legs.

"Cat!" Billie shouted.

Cat could only surmise Joseph had seen her coming and intercepted her tackle, swinging her up and around and landing her on the bed in front of him, across Billie's legs.

"You know, I really don't know what you see in her," he said to Billie.

Then, without warning, Cat found herself thrown over Joseph's shoulder and carried out of the room.

Joseph deposited her in a chair in the hallway and blocked the door to Billie's room. "Until you can learn to behave yourself in there, therapy sessions are off limits to you. Understand?"

Cat was speechless as she watched him go back into Billie's room and shut the door. She spent the next hour and a half fretting over the torture he was surely administering to Billie.

Finally, he came out again and stopped in front of Cat who was still sitting in the chair. "I apologize if I got a little rough earlier, but sometimes drastic measures are called for. I know what I do hurts in the beginning, but it's necessary." He glanced back over his shoulder into Billie's room. "She needs you right now," he said and walked away.

Cat scrambled to her feet and entered Billie's room. Billie was lying on the bed, the sheets in wild disarray around her. It was obvious she had given him a hard time throughout the entire session. Cat walked over to Billie's bedside and reached for her hand. Billie turned her tear-streaked face toward Cat.

"I'm sorry, Billie. I tried to stop him."

Billie pressed her head in the pillow. "Thank you," she whispered.

The door to her room opened, admitting Julie to begin her occupational therapy.

* * *

Cat went to her parents' house while Billie was progressing through OT, lunch, and her afternoon nap before seeing Dr. Connor. Cat needed to prepare the children for their visit with Billie that evening.

A small body launched itself at her the moment she walked through the door. She wrapped her arms around the child. "Sky-baby, I've missed you so much. Where's my kiss?"

Skylar took Cat's face in her hands and planted a big sloppy kiss on Cat's mouth before hugging her again. "Where's Mommy?"

"Mommy's still in the hospital. Want to go see her tonight?"

"Yippie." Skylar clapped. "Can we go now?"

"Tonight, after you've had dinner. Grandpa will take you, okay?"

"Where will you be?"

"I'll be with Mommy, waiting for you, Tara, and Seth to come visit. Where are your brother and sister?"

"They're in the family room playing Nintendo. Want me to get them?"

"Would you, sweetheart?" Cat said and Skylar ran out of the room.

"How is she, Caitlain?" a voice said from behind her.

Cat swung around to see her mother in the doorway of the kitchen, a dishtowel slung over her shoulder. Their eyes met as a meaningful glance passed between them. Cat covered her mouth with her hand to prevent a sob from escaping and ran to her mother's open arms. Several minutes later, Cat felt another set of arms circle around her and looked down to see Seth snuggling close into her side. Cat's mother took a step back so Cat could comfort him.

"Hey, sweetie," Cat whispered into Seth's hair. "You okay?"

He nodded and Cat pretended not to notice how he tried to hide the tear that escaped from his eye. "Do you feel up to visiting with Mom tonight?"

Seth's eyes brightened. "Really?"

"Really. After dinner, okay?"

"Great!"

She smoothed his hair. "There are a few things you need to know before tonight, so if you want to go drag your sister away from that video game, we need to have a talk. Okay?"

"I'll get her," Seth said. Moments later, he was back with an irritated Tara in tow.

"Mama, I was almost beating the game and Seth shut it off on me," she said, sticking her tongue out at him.

"Don't blame your brother. I sent him after you. And is that any way to greet your mother whom you haven't seen in two days?"

Tara ran into Cat's open arms, jumping up at the last moment so her legs straddled Cat's waist. "You're getting kind of big to be doing that, pip-squeak. Pretty soon, you'll be knocking me over." Cat placed a raspberry in Tara's neck, making her squeal and wriggle away to drop to the floor.

Finally, she had them all in the same room together. She sat cross-legged on the floor, and the children gathered around her.

"Okay," she said. "Tara, I've already told Seth and Sky this, but I want to take you to visit Mom tonight." Three grinning faces peered up at her. "There's something you need to know before you get there."

"What?" Tara asked.

"Well, she... she won't know any of you."

"What do you mean?" Seth said.

"Seth, honey, you know she's had brain surgery, right?" She waited as he nodded. "Well, sometimes after brain surgery, the patient wakes up and doesn't have any memories. That's what's happened to Mom."

"Does she know you?" Seth asked.

"No, she doesn't. She doesn't recognize Grandpa either."

"Will she get her memory back?" Tara said.

"We hope so, but right now, she's pretty scared. She doesn't even know who she is."

"I wanna see Mommy," Skylar said.

Cat opened her arms for Skylar to climb into. "Grandpa and I have talked to her about you. She knows you're coming to see her tonight, but I don't want you to be upset if she doesn't recognize you or remember your names, okay?"

Seth and Tara nodded while Skylar snuggled in closer. "Okay. Any more questions?"

"Can I color her some pictures?" Tara asked.

Cat touched Tara's cheek. "I'm sure she'd like that. She'd like that a lot."

"I made a bead necklace in Cub Scouts last night. Do you think she'd like that?" Seth asked.

Cat was touched by the children's offers. "Yes, I think she would."

"I'll color some pictures too," Skylar said.

"Mom and I are the luckiest mothers in the world. Thank you, sweeties. Now, how about helping your old mother to her feet so I can get back to the hospital?"

Seth lent Cat a hand. She hugged each of them and promised to see them later that night. She kissed them goodbye before hugging her mother and heading out the door.

She arrived back at the hospital just in time for Billie's counseling session with Dr. Connor. Her spirits were much improved after spending time with the kids. Deciding to use her father's direct approach, she waltzed into the room like there was nothing wrong and perched herself on the edge of Billie's bed. "Hi," she said, cheerfully. "How'd your OT go?"

Billie's gaze locked with Cat's. "Fine," was all she said; however, she continued to stare at Cat.

Cat got the distinct impression Billie was waging some internal battle as she watched a wide range of emotions parade across her face. You're not the only fighter in this family, she thought as she refused to break the stare.

Long moments passed before their silent confrontation was interrupted by Dr. Connor's arrival. Cat expected to be asked to leave when Dr. Connor came in, so she was surprised when Billie consented for her to stay. She chose the chair by the window, to allow Dr. Connor a closer position to Billie by the bed.

"Cat, bring your chair closer," Dr. Connor said. "Over there next to Billie. Now, let's get started."

"How are you feeling today, Billie?" Dr. Connor asked.

"Scared."

"How so?"

"Cat's bringing the kids to visit tonight."

"What about that scares you?"

"I don't remember them. I didn't even know I had children until Cat told me about them. This is all so unsettling. I don't know who I am. I don't know where I live."

Cat reached for Billie's hand but pulled it back quickly. "Billie, you live with me—with our children. We want you to come home."

"Cat, why did you pull your hand back just now?" Dr. Connor asked.

"Billie doesn't like me to touch her."

Dr. Connor looked at Billie. "Why not?"

Billie's brows knit together as she looked back and forth between Dr. Connor and Cat. "I don't know."

Dr. Connor got out of the chair and sat on the edge of Billie's bed. "Billie, give me your hand."

Billie did as she was told.

"Now you, Cat."

Cat placed her hand in Dr. Connor's.

Dr. Connor turned Billie's hand palm up and placed Cat's hand, palm down, into it. "Now close your hands," she said to them.

Cat slid her fingers between Billie's and closed her hand but was disappointed when Billie didn't follow suit.

"Billie," Dr. Connor said.

Billie glanced at Dr. Connor and then at their hands. Slowly, her fingers closed over Cat's, and Cat's smaller hand all but disappeared into Billie's. Cat found it difficult to breathe as the love she felt for Billie flowed directly to their intertwined hands.

"Cat," Billie said in a whisper.

Cat looked expectantly at Billie.

"I'm sorry." Billie abruptly released Cat's hand. Cat felt like she'd been thrown a lifeline, only to have it snatched away. She took a huge gulp of air. Her body shuddered with emotion.

Billie clasped her hands together on her lap.

"Billie, look at me," Cat said.

Billie was unable, or unwilling, to meet Cat's eyes a second time.

The rest of the session was a blur for Cat. After Billie's rejection, she stood at the window and stared out over the city. Her heart was broken in a million pieces, and she was beginning to think it would never be put back together again. How could Billie be so cold? Even an angry Billie was easier to deal with than this indifferent one.

Billie sat on the bed, propped up on both sides by pillows, and watched Cat stand by the window. Somewhere in the recesses of her mind, an emotion began to build. Guilt, anger, or anxiety? Billie wasn't sure, but it was undeniable. Cat's hand felt so soft, she thought. So soft, yet so strong and familiar. God, I don't know what to do. This scares me so. She inhaled and said out loud, "Cat?" At that very moment, a deep voice from the doorway said, "Okay, Red, get out."

"Excuse me?" Cat said.

"I said out. You know the rules," Joseph said.

"I'm not leaving."

Joseph narrowed his eyes. "You've got balls, lady. I like that. Okay, I'll make you a deal. You stay back and out of the way with no interference, unless I ask you for some, and I'll let you stay. Deal?" He reached out his hand to Cat.

Cat placed her hand in his. "Deal."

Billie grinned as Cat won the battle of wills. Over the next half hour, she found herself grateful for Cat's support as Joseph put her through a warm-up routine. Several times, she had to resist crying out when Joseph pushed her beyond her comfort zone. When the warm up was over, he climbed onto the bed and sat back on his knees, straddling her shins.

"Now, give me your hands," he said.

Although wary of his motives, Billie complied .

"Good. Now I want you to use me as an anchor and pull yourself into a sitting position."

Billie looked at him as though he were out of his mind.

"Come on, you can do it. Pull against my hands. That's it… pull. Good," he said.

Billie used every ounce of energy she had to lift her head and upper body off the bed and pull herself toward Joseph. When she managed to pull herself up enough so her upper body was at a ninety-degree angle to her legs, Joseph wrapped his big arms around her and hugged her tight.

"I knew you could do it," he said before lowering her back down. He made a move to climb off the bed. Billie stopped him with a hand on his arm. "No. I want to do it again," she said.

"I think that's enough for today."

"Please?"

Joseph held out his hands, "All right. One more time."

Chapter 25

After Joseph left, Laura came in to massage Billie's muscles. This time Cat asked her questions throughout the whole routine, hoping to be able to pick up enough knowledge to be of some help to Billie later. Finally, the massage was over and Cat was left alone with Billie once more.

"You did a very good job in therapy this afternoon." Cat knew she was making idle chitchat, but she felt too awkward with the silence to let it continue for long.

"Thank you."

Cat's heart melted when Billie cast the crooked smile she loved so much. "I was very proud of you when you pulled yourself up," she said. A blush rose to Billie's cheeks. Cat wanted to tease her about the nice shade of red, but she wasn't sure how Billie would take it.

Billie's dinner tray was brought in and set in front of her. Cat walked over and took the cover off the tray. "Yummy," she said.

"Want some?"

"No, that's all right. I'm not very hungry."

"You, not hungry? That's a first," Billie said.

Cat's eyes grew wide. "What did you say?"

"I... I'm sorry. I don't know why I said that."

Cat's heart was beating a mile a minute as she struggled to calm herself. It was obvious from the shocked expression on Billie's face the response had been involuntary. *Don't push her, Cat. You'll only scare her again. Let it go.*

Cat opened Billie's milk carton, unwrapped her straw, and put it in the milk. She placed the carton back on the tray. "Are you nervous about tonight?"

Billie nodded. "Are any of them mine?" she asked as she led a spoonful of mashed potatoes to her mouth. Cat was pleased at how much better Billie was becoming at fine motor skill coordination after only two days.

148

Cat reached for Billie's fork and knife and cut the meat loaf into bite-size pieces. "They're our children—both of ours—but to answer your question, our son is biologically yours. The girls are mine."

"I have a son?"

"And two daughters."

"Yes, of course. What are their names?"

Cat felt her face glowing as she thought of their children. She leaned forward so her forearms rested on her thighs. "Seth is eleven years old, almost twelve. He's a beautiful and sensitive child. He has corn silk hair and blue, blue eyes—like yours. He's our little man. Tara is nine and very much an outspoken free spirit. She's stubborn as all hell and quite a tomboy. She has red-gold hair and green eyes like mine. Skylar is the baby. We call her Sky for short. You named her, Billie. She's four years old and still very cuddly. She likes to curl up in your arms and cuddle into your neck when she's tired. Skylar also has red-gold hair, but her eyes are blue like yours and Seth's."

"Where are their fathers?"

Cat sighed and sat back in her chair. "Tara's father was an anonymous sperm donor, so I have no idea who or where he is. Seth and Sky's father is in jail for kidnapping, assault, attempted murder, and rape." Billie's eyes widened with each offense Cat listed.

Billie paused in mid chew. "Seth and Sky have the same father?"

"Yes. He was your ex-husband when I met you. We'd known each other for less than a year when he raped me." She paused for a moment. "Skylar is the product of that rape."

Billie watched Cat intently. "I'm sorry."

"Yeah, well, that's in the past, where it belongs. I try not to dwell on it. If I linger too much on what's already past, I just might stumble over what's in front of me, and besides, we have a beautiful daughter as a result, despite how she was conceived."

Billie sat back against the pillows.

"All finished?" Cat asked.

Billie nodded as Cat cleaned up her tray and pushed it aside. She noticed the contemplative expression on Billie's face. "What are you thinking?" she asked.

"How long have we been together?"

"Well, Sky is four and I became pregnant less than a year after we met, so we've been together for just under five years."

"I had Seth before we met, then."

"Yes. You divorced Brian when Seth was three."

"Why did I divorce him?"

Cat reached out to touch Billie's hand but pulled hers away at the last moment.

"It's okay," Billie said as she extended her hand to Cat.

Cat's heart leaped for joy, and she placed her hand inside Billie's.

"Tell me about Brian."

"Brian wasn't a very nice man. In fact, during your marriage he was abusive... physically abusive. You divorced him when you realized you were attracted to women."

Billie retracted her hand and crossed her arms in front of her. Cat sat back, startled. "I told you I'm not gay," Billie said.

Cat rubbed her temples with both hands. She was becoming more and more impatient with Billie's attitude about their relationship. She thanked the stars above that Billie's speech therapist chose that moment to walk into the room, saving her from having to deal with Billie's comment.

"I think I'll get some fresh air during your therapy," Cat said. She grabbed her sweater and headed out the door without waiting for Billie's response. She hoped a walk in the cool evening air would give her the strength and renewal to deal with the children's visit.

The hospital grounds were beautiful. All around were well-manicured lawns, colorful arrays of flowers, and benches dotting the landscape. Being cooped up in the hospital almost nonstop for the past several days had been very tiring.

She filled her lungs with fresh air and released it as she thought again about Billie. She promised herself, as soon as Billie was recovered, she would plan something special for her and for their family.

Cat sat on the bench for almost an hour, enjoying the breeze, sunshine, and solitude of the day. She looked at her watch. The speech session would be ending soon, so she rose and stretched and headed back inside.

She reached Billie's room just as the therapist was leaving. Before she could step into the room, though, she spotted her family walking down the hall toward her. The kids saw her, and against all warnings from Doc, they took off running and almost knocked her over when they made contact. By the time Cat had the situation under control, Doc reached them, and they entered Billie's room together.

Seth and Tara held Cat's hands, while Doc carried Skylar. As they walked into the room, Cat noticed the nervous expression on Billie's face.

"Mommy, how come you're wearing that funny hat?" Skylar said.

Billie laughed. Skylar wriggled out of Doc's hold, slid to the floor, and climbed into Billie's open arms. As Cat predicted, she curled up into Billie's neck and kissed her on the cheek. "I missed you, Mommy."

Billie extended an arm out to the other two children. It didn't take long for Seth and Tara to get onto the bed and into Billie's arms.

Cat stood by the door and watched Billie interact with the children, hoping she would see some sign of recognition. Skylar was curled up in Billie right arm, while Seth sat on her left, leaning against her. Tara straddled her thighs, facing her, hands flying out in all directions as she talked nonstop about the Nintendo game she was trying to master.

"...and then I kicked him and he went flying and he jumped up and did a flip, but I super kicked him across the room... and... and then three more guys came out and I had to fight them too, and..." Tara almost whacked Seth across the head with one of her arms.

Seeing Tara was becoming a little too animated, Cat approached the bed and took her by the shoulders. "Tara, honey, calm down. You almost clocked your brother across the head, and if you're not careful, you'll hit Mom too. Why don't you get down for now."

"No, let her stay. She's okay," Billie said.

"Are you sure?"

Billie nodded and turned her attention back to the children while Cat sat in the chair next to the bed.

"Mom, why do you talk funny?" Tara asked, earning a punch from Seth.

"Hey, scout, none of that," Billie said.

Cat gasped at Billie's use of Seth's nickname.

"As for your question, Tara, my brain has forgotten how to talk. I have to learn how again. That's why I talk slow and sometimes stutter."

"Too bad your brain didn't forget how to talk, Tara," Seth said.

"Mom, tell him to shut up," Tara said.

"Scout, come on now, be nice," Billie scolded her son.

Tara grinned as Seth was being reprimanded. She cocked her head at an angle. "Did they cut off all your hair?" she asked.

"I think so. I haven't seen it without the bandages. Maybe Mama knows. Cat?"

"Oh yeah, it's all gone. But it'll grow back pretty fast," Cat said.

Seth leaned forward. "All of it?"

"All of it," Cat said. "Does that bother you, honey?"

"A little. I kinda liked Mom's long hair," he said.

"I was kind of partial to it myself," Cat said. "But then, I think she's beautiful, no matter how much hair she has." She peeked over to see a blush rising up Billie's neck.

"Mommy's bald," Skylar said giggling.

"You'd better watch it, pip-squeak, or I'll have to tickle you." Billie formed her left hand into a claw. Skylar squealed with delight while Cat sat by stunned at Billie's familiarity with the children. *I'll bet she isn't even aware of it.*

Knowing the threat would develop into a full-blown tickle war, Cat put a stop to it before someone got hurt. "Okay, you two, that's enough." She took Skylar out of Billie's arms and rested her on her hip. Billie looked disappointed.

"Hey, don't you have something for Mom?" Cat asked them.

"Oh yeah, I almost forgot." Tara jumped off the bed and ran to the bag they had left by the door. Skylar squirmed her way out of Cat's arms to join her.

While his sisters were busy digging their prizes out of the bag, Seth climbed off the bed and walked around to the other side, slipping onto Cat's lap. Cat wrapped her arms around him and kissed the side of his head as he leaned back into her. Her gaze met Billie's, and she reveled in the interest Billie appeared to be taking in her interaction with Seth.

Tara and Skylar walked side by side to the bed while trying to hide something behind their backs. "Close your eyes, Mom, and no peeking," Tara said and Billie obeyed.

The girls laid the pictures they had colored on her lap, like a treasure.

"Okay, Mommy, you can look," Skylar said.

Billie uncovered her eyes and saw the pictures on her lap. Her eyes filled with tears, and she reached down and touched them with a shaky hand.

"You don't like them?" Tara asked.

Billie looked at her daughters. Tara was standing ramrod straight at the edge of the bed, while Skylar was leaning forward, her upper body supported by her forearms on the bed. Both children's eyes were wide with anticipation.

Billie touched the side of Tara's face. "Of course I like them. They're beautiful. Thank you." She opened her arms for the children to climb into. "I'll ask Mama to hang them up for me on the wall. Okay?"

While Billie thanked them, Cat whispered in Seth's ear, "Don't you have something for Mom?"

"I wanna give it to her in private," he said.

Cat could see Billie was starting to tire. It had been a long and difficult day with therapy, and Billie needed to sleep to be fresh for the challenges that awaited her tomorrow. Cat rose to her feet and motioned for the girls to join her. "Come on, girls, Mom's tired. Hugs and kisses, then we've got to get going, okay?"

"Awww, Mama," the girls said together, but they climbed off the bed to leave after depositing big, wet, sloppy kisses and lots of hugs on Billie.

While the girls were saying their good-byes, Cat leaned in to Seth and whispered that he was to stay with Billie until she and the girls found Grandpa to take them home.

Cat and the girls left Seth standing in the middle of the room, alone with Billie.

"Seth, are you all right?" Billie asked.

Seth pulled something out of his pocket and hid it in his fist. He approached her and stood by her bed. "I made something for you in Cub Scouts last night." He opened his hand and extended it toward his mother.

Billie began to cry when she saw his gift. She reached for the colorful beaded necklace and held it high in front of her. She closed her eyes and allowed tears to escape down her cheeks before looking at her son once more. "It's beautiful. I love it. Thank you," she managed to say, and opened her arms for a warm hug.

After a moment, Billie released Seth and asked him to help her put the necklace on. He closed the clasp and stepped back. "It fits you real good," he said.

Billie was about to say something when a searing pain shot through her head. She cried out and grasped her head with both hands.

Seth climbed onto the bed and grabbed Billie's arm. "Mom! Are you all right?"

Billie closed her eyes, rested her head against the pillows, and rubbed her temples. When she opened her eyes, she saw Seth lying in a hospital bed.

"Hey, buddy-boy, how're you doing today?" she said as she entered his room. Seth lay passively in his bed, with his eyes closed. It was so discouraging sometimes, to come in day after day and face such unresponsiveness.

Disturbed with the scene before her, Billie closed her eyes once more.

"Mom?" she heard a voice say next to her.

She opened her eyes. A rush of heat rose from the pit of her stomach to her brain. She took Seth by the shoulders and stared intently at him. Seth slipped off the bed and took a step backward.

"Come here, Seth. Let me look at you. Turn around."

Seth obeyed while Billie checked him over. When he swung back around to face her, she took his face between her hands and kissed his forehead.

"Mom? Are you all right?"

"Seth, you're awake! Come up here. Please."

Seth climbed back onto the bed and sat next to Billie as she wrapped her arms around him. "Oh God, my baby. I can't believe you're all right. I told those doctors you'd wake up. I told them."

"Mom, I woke up five years ago."

Billie frowned. "How can that be? I just saw you in the hospital."

"But I did. Mom, I'm eleven years old now."

Billie stared at him. He was six years old when he was hit by the car. This child sitting beside her was older than six.

"Seth? Oh God..." Billie lost consciousness.

Cat was in the chair by the window, with Skylar asleep in her arms. Seth and Tara had settled on the floor with their backs against the wall as they watched Doc examine Billie. After a few moments, Doc sat on the edge of the bed, facing Cat and the kids.

"Daddy, what happened to her?"

"I can't be positive, but she may have had a seizure." He turned to Seth. "Son, can you tell me what happened with your mom before she fainted?"

"She was acting kinda weird. She thought I was still six, and she was surprised I was awake. She thought I was still in the hospital."

"She's remembering," Cat said, almost in a whisper.

"Seth, was she upset, or excited, or anything like that before she fainted?" Doc asked.

"She was acting real worried and confused... and she looked scared. Grandpa, is she gonna be all right?"

"She'll be fine," Doc said. To Cat, he added, "I'm going to order an EEG to see if there's any evidence of abnormal electrical activity in the brain, and depending on what that shows, we might need to follow it up with a CAT scan and MRI. The EEG results will tell us a lot."

"What if it shows normal brain activity?"

"Then it might not be epilepsy. However, I'm not ready to rule that out yet."

"But the seizures—" Cat said.

"Seizures can be triggered by a lot of things, including low blood sugar, fainting, heart disease, stroke, migraines, kinked blood vessels, anxiety, and stress, to name a few. Billie's in pretty good shape, so a few simple tests can rule out most of those causes. But if her memory is indeed returning, extreme stress and anxiety would not be unexpected," he said. "It's late. I'll order the EEG to be hooked up tonight so we can monitor brain activity while she sleeps." Doc leaned down and lifted a sleeping Skylar out of Cat's arms. "Come on, little ones, let's go home."

Cat kissed her children goodnight, holding Seth just a little longer than normal. "Mom will be all right. I promise," she whispered to him. She leaned against the doorframe and watched her family walk down the hall until they rounded the corner to the elevators. She released a deep sigh, walked back into the room, and sat by Billie's bed. It was going to be a long night.

Chapter 26

Cat chose to stay in the hospital with Billie that night rather than go home. The nursing staff accommodated her with a portable cot set up beside Billie's bed. Between the hum of the EEG monitors and nurses checking on Billie during the night, she got very little sleep. She was standing at the window, watching the sunrise when she heard movement come from the direction of Billie's bed. She spun around and sat on the edge of the chair by Billie's bed. "Good morning. You gave us a scare last night. Daddy thinks you might have had a seizure. That explains the wires and monitors. How are you feeling?"

Billie's brows knit together. "Where's Seth?"

Billie's gruff attitude hit Cat the wrong way. She let herself fall back into the chair. "I'm fine, Cat, thank you for asking," she answered for Billie sarcastically. She rubbed the dull ache in her forehead. "Seth is home with Mom and Dad, doing what normal eleven-year-old boys do at five a.m.—sleeping."

Billie's eyes narrowed. "Why didn't you tell me he woke up from his coma?"

"Billie, he woke up five years ago," Cat said, a little harsher than she intended. She realized she was starting to lose patience with the whole situation. She rose to her feet and paced with her arms crossed at her chest. She stopped at the foot of Billie's bed.

"Billie, what do you remember?"

Billie leveled a gaze at her, but remained silent.

"Do you know who you are?"

"Yes."

"Who are you?"

"You know who I am."

"Damn it! Yes, I know who you are. I want to know if you know."

Billie sneered at her. "I'm Billie Charland, mother, legal assistant, aerobics instructor," she shouted back.

"Well that's almost right. You're a lawyer. I told you that yesterday."

"I don't remember finishing law school."

"Well you did. Now, who am I?"

"I don't know. I don't know. Is that what you want to hear? All I know is you have my son. I want him back. He's all I've got." Billie broke down into powerful sobs.

Cat's heart ached for her. Risking rejection, she sat on the edge of the bed. She took Billie into her arms and held her as she cried, whispering over and over, "You're not alone, my love, you've got me and the girls as well as Seth. We're a family. Let us love you."

Cat kissed the side of Billie's head and rocked her as she held her. Billie didn't pull away.

Doc entered Billie's room about a half hour later and found her sleeping in Cat's arms. He approached Cat's side of the bed and squeezed her shoulder.

"Good morning," he said softly.

"'Morning, Daddy."

He nodded in Billie's direction. "When did this happen?"

"Very early this morning. We had a bit of a confrontation, and she let me comfort her."

"Good. You've got about an hour before breakfast arrives. Try to sleep. You look like hell."

"I love you too, Daddy," Cat said. She snuggled closer to Billie, closed her eyes, and drifted off.

An hour later, breakfast arrived, rousing the two women from sleep.

Billie jumped when she opened her eyes and saw Cat's face mere inches away from hers. "What are you doing in my bed?" she asked.

"Good morning to you too." Cat sat up and slid off the bed.

"How did this happen?"

"It's not the end of the world, Billie. You were upset last night. You allowed me to comfort you. Don't you remember? Anyway, I fell asleep. It's not a big deal."

"Well, it is to me."

"I'm sorry. Look, I'm going to get a coffee. I should be back in time for your PT."

Cat returned to Billie's room a few minutes after PT began. Still smarting from Billie's abrupt manner that morning, she chose to sit in the corner where she could sip her coffee and watch passively from the sidelines rather than be an active participant in the session.

Most of the session focused on helping Billie balance herself in a sitting position. She used Joseph as an anchor while Laura provided the stability she needed to keep from falling over. Try as Cat might to hold on to her anger, she felt it melting away as her heart filled with pride with each bit of progress Billie made. By the time the session was over, Billie was sitting up unassisted for several moments.

Joseph left the room, and Laura helped Billie resettle into bed. Billie sat on the edge of the bed, feet dangling over the side, with Laura standing in front of her. "Cat, Would you come over here please?" Laura said. "I'd like to straighten the bed while Billie's sitting up, and I need you to keep her balanced while I do that, Okay?"

Cat got up from the chair and stood in front of Billie. Cat noticed that Billie avoided her gaze.

"Okay, put your hands out like this." Laura demonstrated by holding her hands at waist height, palms up, in front of Billie. "That's right. Good. Now Billie, place your hands in Cat's and hold on."

"Give me your hands," Cat said. "I won't bite you."

Billie relented and placed her hands in Cat's but avoided her gaze.

Laura took her time straightening out the bed behind Billie. At one point, she winked at Cat over Billie's shoulder and continued moving at a turtle's pace. Cat had all she could do to keep the grin from her face.

When Laura finished, she came back around and helped to lower Billie onto the bed. She headed to the door. "See you this afternoon, ladies," she said as she left.

Cat pulled the covers around Billie's waist and began to arrange the pillows on either side of her.

"No, leave them," Billie said. "I need to work on my balance without the pillows."

"Okay, good idea." Cat adjusted the blankets and the height of the bed. "You worked very hard in your PT. I was proud of the progress you made."

"Thanks."

"Good morning, ladies," a cheery voice said from the doorway.

"Good morning, Julie," Cat said. "She's all yours. Billie, I'm going to find Daddy and talk to him about the EEG tests he collected last night. I'll be back soon."

"What do you think?"

"Well, kitten," Doc said. "See this right here… and here?" He pointed to a couple of high points on the EEG graph. "They indicate some sort of abnormal electrical activity, but it's not very pronounced. It's hard to tell from this data whether epilepsy is the cause of it. We can take another CAT scan and MRI, but with readings this mild on the EEG, I'm afraid we'll be wasting our time there too. I hate to say it, but we might just have to wait and see if it happens again."

"Can't we start her on anticonvulsants now to prevent another seizure?"

"That is an option, but I'd rather wait until we have a confirmed epilepsy diagnosis. I'd rather not medicate her for a condition she might not even have."

Cat lowered her chin to her chest and reached a hand up to rub her brow. "Daddy, I hate to see her suffer. I hate not knowing."

Doc pulled Cat into his embrace. "You need a hug," he said as she burrowed down deep into his shoulder. "I know this has been hard on you. She'll get better. I promise."

"I know she will," Cat said into his shoulder, "but I want her more than well. I want her back."

"You know, you can let go of my hand," Cat said as she and Doc walked toward the hospital cafeteria.

"Not a chance. This is the only way I can be sure you're eating."

"But I'm not hungry."

"Caitlain Maureen O'Grady Charland, I won't take no for an answer, do you understand? You haven't eaten enough to keep a bird alive over the past three days. Now, you're going to have lunch with me if I have to hog-tie you to the chair. Is that clear?"

Cat grinned. "I knew I'd lost the battle when you used my full name. All right, all right. I'll eat."

Moments later, Cat and Doc sat across from each other at a small table in the hospital dining room.

"Caitlain, you need to eat more," Doc said. "That salad isn't big enough to fill a bird's stomach."

"I'm not very hungry. This is fine." Cat pushed the greens around her plate.

"It might be, if you'd actually eat some of it."

Cat put her fork down and pushed her plate away. "I don't have much of an appetite. I guess I'm just too worried about Billie."

Doc put his own fork down and sat back in his chair. "Spill it," he said.

"Huh?"

"I said, spill it. What's keeping you from eating and sleeping?"

"How do you know I haven't been sleeping?"

"I have my spies."

Cat focused on her hands clasped on the table in front of her. "I'm afraid, Daddy. Afraid she'll never remember me. I'm afraid of losing her, and Seth."

"Seth?"

"She's starting to remember. She knows who she is, and she remembers Seth."

"That's wonderful news."

"I hope so." Cat paused for a moment. "We had an argument this morning over why I hadn't told her Seth was out of his coma. She's the Billie I met five years ago. She doesn't know me. She's living in a time just before we met."

Cat put her hand inside the one offered to her by Doc.

"Give her time, Cat. Take this as a good sign. If she's recovered part of her memory, there's a good chance she'll recover the rest. Keep your chin up, okay?"

"I'll try."

Cat pulled her cell phone from her pocket and called Jen. She answered after two rings.

"Hi, Jen. Just checking in."

"All right, what's up?" Jen asked.

"What do you mean?"

"Spill it, girlfriend. I know something's wrong. I can hear it in your voice."

"Damn it. You know me too well for my own good. All right, all right. The visit with the kids was great. You should have seen how Billie was with them. It was like nothing was wrong. Several times throughout the visit, she called them by their pet names—

quite naturally, I might add. Glimpses of the old Billie kept showing through, but I don't think she realized it."

"That's great. You were worried it would be tough on the kids."

"Well, I've only told you part of it. I left Seth with her while the girls and I went to find Daddy to take them home, and while we were gone, Billie had a spell. Poor Seth. It appears memories of him from five years ago when he was still in the hospital came flooding back. She passed out on him."

"Oh my God! Is he all right? Is Billie all right?"

"Yes, to both questions. The good news is she remembers who she and Seth are now. The bad news is her memories stop when he was hospitalized at six years old."

"Before or after she met you?"

"Before."

"Well, it's a start. We have reason to hope now. I have a good feeling about this. It'll work out. I know it will."

"Jen, what would I do without you? I can't thank you enough for your support."

"No thanks necessary. I'm glad I can help."

"Well, I've got to go. Billie's counseling session begins soon, and I don't want to miss it."

"All right then, I'll see you soon. Kiss the big guy for me, okay?"

"Only if she lets me kiss her for me first."

"You might know—too selfish to share." Jen laughed. "Promise to call me later if you need to talk."

"I will. Thanks."

One more phone call, Cat thought as she punched the keys on her cell phone.

"Hello, Art?"

"Cat? How is Billie?"

"She's improving. She's starting to remember. She knows who she is now, and who Seth is, but her memories stop just before she and I met. In her mind, she's still a legal assistant. If you come to visit her, she'll no doubt recognize you, but she won't remember she's a practicing lawyer. Just keep that in mind, okay?"

"She must be confused, huh?"

"Yes, she is."

"Any idea when she'll be going home?"

"I'd say in another week or so."

"Maybe it would be better if Marge and I wait to visit until after she goes home. That will be one less thing she'll have to deal with in the hospital. What do you think?"

"I think that's a good idea. I'll tell her I spoke with you and you'll see her soon."

Cat rushed back to Billie's room just in time for her session with Dr. Connor. When she got there, she was surprised to see Laura manipulating Billie's legs.

"Hi," Cat said as she walked into the room. "Where's Doctor Connor?"

Laura looked over her shoulder at Cat. "Hi, Cat. No sessions on Saturday. The doc's on call though, if you'd like us to reach her."

"No, that's all right. Is it Saturday already?"

"That it is, Red," Laura said. "Pretty easy to lose track of time around here, isn't it?"

"Oh, yeah." Cat watched Laura exercise Billie's arms and legs. "What are you doing?" she asked.

"Yeah, what are you doing?" Billie echoed from the bed.

"So, you can talk," Laura said. "I was beginning to wonder, when you didn't say a word in this morning's session. I'm warming your muscles up. We have a pretty taxing workout planned for this afternoon."

"Is Ivan the Terrible going to be here?" Billie asked.

Laura chuckled. "You must mean Joseph, huh? Yes, he'll be here. Great nickname by the way."

"What's so taxing about this afternoon's session?" Cat asked.

"Can you say, 'On your feet, soldier'?"

Cat knew she and Billie sported identical expressions, eyes wide, mouths agape, and eyebrows raised into their hairlines.

Laura laughed and, in her best Mae West voice, said, "Close your mouth, you're catchin' flies."

"Plant your heels on the floor and push yourself up," Joseph said. "Laura won't let you fall. You can do it."

Billie gritted her teeth and pushed into the floor with all her strength, to no avail.

Joseph lowered his face to hers. "Lean forward as you push. You'll be able to feel where the fulcrum point is. The moment you feel like you're falling forward, allow your thighs to take over and push your heels into the floor."

Billie leaned forward and nearly fell off the bed, save for the hold Laura had on the belt around her waist. "I can't do it," Billie said.

"Yes, you can."

Billie shot a desperate glance toward Cat, who was watching from her chair in the corner.

"Red isn't going to help you. She knows better. Now do as I say and try again," Joseph said.

Billie unsuccessfully tried again and fell back onto the bed. "Damn it! I can't do it. There's no use in trying. I've had enough."

"Oh no you don't." Joseph bent down and invaded Billie's personal space. "No quitting. You don't understand. My patients don't quit on me."

Billie grabbed his shirt front and pulled him down nose to nose with her. "You don't understand. It hurts. I can't do it."

"Yes, you can." He grabbed her shoulders and pulled her into a standing position. "Now do it," he said and released her arms.

Billie was so angry she didn't realize she was indeed standing. Laura had a firm grasp on the belt around her middle. Cat rose from her chair in the corner and clasped her hands over her mouth in surprise.

Billie scowled into his face. The smirk he was wearing only made her angrier. "You bastard."

Joseph grinned and took a step back. "I've been called worse," he said as his eyes drew her attention to the fact she was standing on her own.

When Billie realized no one was holding her up, her knees began to buckle.

"I've got you," Laura said as she wrapped an arm around Billie's waist and lowered her to a sitting position on the bed.

Billie's eyes were wide with awe at what she had just accomplished. They misted over as she broke into a grin. "I did it," she said. "I did it."

Joseph walked toward the door and stopped to address Billie. "Like I said, my patients don't quit on me. Tomorrow, we start the real fun. See you then."

"Cat, you need to go home, see the kids, get some sleep," Billie said.

"No. I won't leave you."

"I'll be all right. Go home."

"No." Cat sat on the edge of her own cot and crossed her arms across her chest.

"Please?"

"No... no... no... no... no. Got it?"

Billie inhaled deeply. "I don't want you to get sick. At least lie down and get some sleep."

Cat yawned and closed her eyes. "Just a nap." Within seconds of lying down, she was sound asleep.

Billie rested her head against her pillows and stared at the ceiling. *Who are you, Cat? Why can't I remember you?* Finally, exhausted from a day filled with therapy, she felt her own lids grow heavy and she too drifted off to sleep.

Chapter 27

Billie awoke the next morning feeling refreshed. The first thing she noticed was Cat on the cot on the other side of the room. She was lying on her side, her left hand tucked under her cheek and the blanket pulled up to her neck. Red-gold hair spilled out over her face. Billie had the overwhelming urge to brush her hair back and place a kiss on her brow.

Now where did that come from? She was startled by the intensity of the emotion. She closed her eyes and took a deep breath to calm her rapidly beating heart. When she opened them again, she was staring into two of the greenest eyes she'd ever seen.

"Cat," she said, unnerved by Cat's intense stare.

"Good morning."

"You must feel better this morning," Billie said. "You looked like hell last night."

Cat sat up on the edge of the bed and combed her hair with her fingers. "Why does everyone keep saying that?"

"Because it's true. You're not taking care of yourself. I want you to go home tonight. You need to eat a good meal and sleep in a real bed."

"I'll think about it. I do need to check in at work to arrange another week's vacation. Let's see how things go today, okay?"

"All right," Billie said, smiling.

"God, how I miss that."

"Miss what?"

"Your smile. It's so beautiful. You're so beautiful."

Billie blushed.

Cat sat on the edge of the bed, facing Billie. She traced a finger down the side of Billie's face. "I've embarrassed you. I'm sorry."

Billie looked at Cat with uncertainty in her eyes. She took a deep breath and forced a crooked smile. "You got a thing for bald women?"

"Only if they have eyes the color of the sky on a sunny spring morning. Know where I can find someone like that?"

Billie blushed again.

Cat's attention was diverted as Billie's breakfast was brought into the room. "Breakfast is here."

"Help me to sit up."

"Do you think you should?"

"Yes. I'm sick of eating lying down." Billie rolled onto her side, maneuvered herself onto her elbow, and pushed her body upright.

Cat grabbed Billie's ankles and swung them over the side of the mattress as Billie grasped the edge of the bed with her free hand to pull herself into a seated position. Billie balanced herself while Cat moved the bed tray in front of her and locked the wheels. Billie grinned as she reached for her fork and began to eat her breakfast.

Laura arrived at nine a.m., pushing a wheelchair in front of her. "Good morning, ladies." She positioned the wheelchair close to the bed and locked the wheels. Standing in front of Billie with her hands on her hips, she said, "I'm surprised to see you sitting up. Pretty proud of yourself, huh?"

"Yes, I am."

Laura extended her hands to Billie. "Are you ready for a workout, missy?"

Billie put her hands in Laura's. "Just tell me what to do, coach."

"Okay, shift your weight forward and press your heels into the floor, just like yesterday. That's it. I've got you. I won't let you fall."

Billie rose to her full height and shifted her body sideways as Laura helped lower her into the chair.

"Comfy?" Laura asked after adjusting the footrests.

Billie nodded.

Laura unlocked the wheels. "You coming, Cat?"

"Wouldn't miss it." She followed them out.

Laura wheeled Billie into the Physical Therapy room, parked her chair in front of the parallel bars, and locked the wheels. Joseph stood beside the parallel bars, his arms crossed in front of his chest. "Good morning, Billie. You're not going to quit on me today, are you?"

"I'd like to see you make me," Billie said without breaking eye contact with him.

"You're on." He took a step backward and placed one of his hands on each bar. "Grab the bars."

Billie kept her eyes on Joseph as she did what she was told.

"Now stand up."

She pulled on the bars with all her might and pushed her heels into the floor. Her face contorted with the effort and sweat broke out on her brow. Halfway up, her strength gave out and she fell back into the chair, which Laura had kept close behind her.

Billie's chest heaved with exhaustion and anger as she made her second and third attempts. Over and over, she failed and fell back into the chair. Joseph stood there, a hand on each bar, leaning forward. He watched her intently as Cat stood nearby.

In the midst of the fourth attempt, Billie was drenched in sweat. Her muscles quivered, and tears ran down her cheeks.

"Help her," Cat yelled at Joseph.

Joseph pointed at her. "I warned you before about interfering. Now either shut up or get out."

Billie was pissed. She summoned all her anger and pulled herself to her feet, coming face-to-face with Joseph. "Don't you ever talk to her like that again. Got it?"

Joseph grinned. "Congratulations, Billie. You did it."

Billie's knuckles were white from holding on so tightly to the bars. Her face and neck were covered with sweat, and her entire body trembled. She felt Laura's arms slip under hers as she helped her back into the chair. Billie looked at Cat, who had backed up against the wall in reaction to Joseph's outburst. Billie's heart lifted as Cat smiled at her.

An entire hour had passed during Billie's attempts to stand. She was exhausted and weak as Laura wheeled her back to her room and helped her into the straight-backed chair by the window. Her body shook from exertion and shock.

Laura took a blanket from the closet and wrapped it around Billie's legs. She squeezed one of Billie's knees. "You did real good this morning. Better than expected."

Cat, who had been sitting on the edge of Billie's bed during this exchange, jumped down and approached Laura. "Laura, why does he antagonize her so?"

"I agree Joseph's methods are a little unorthodox, but he does produce results," Laura said.

"He makes me so angry," Cat said, "I just want to slap that smug expression off his face."

Laura laughed. "Oh, girl, I know what you mean. Sometimes he even gets to me, but I've learned to butt out. Like I said, he gets results. He's good at what he does."

"He won't be doing it much longer if he attacks Cat again," Billie said.

Laura chuckled. "Something tells me Joseph has met his match with you, Billie. Your OT should be here soon. I'll be back after lunch to help you back to bed. You should take a nap before this afternoon's session. Okay?"

"All right. Thanks Laura," Billie said and Laura left the room.

Billie's OT went well. Before the therapist left, she indicated their sessions were about to end, as Billie's progress was rapidly becoming self propelled. During OT, Cat curled up on Billie's bed and fell asleep. Billie watched her with interest as she waited for her lunch to arrive. Something felt so familiar about her, yet so foreign. Billie felt more and more comfortable with her as time went on. No one had mentioned their marriage for a couple of days, but the nagging thought was always there at the back of her mind. *She said I was beautiful. I can feel her love for me. Why can't I feel anything for her? Who are you, Cat? Who are you?*

Billie pondered these questions as her lunch arrived. Without Cat to wait on her, she found it a little more of a challenge, but soon, she managed to open her milk carton by herself and spread the mayonnaise on her turkey sandwich without making too much of a mess.

As promised, Laura arrived when lunch was over to help her into bed. She wheeled the chair over to her, locked the brakes, and held her hands out to Billie. Using Laura as an anchor, Billie struggled to her feet, pivoted her body, and lowered herself into the chair. "You're getting pretty good at that, girl." Laura wheeled her over to the bed.

Billie stopped Laura from waking Cat. "No, leave her."

"You sure?"

"Yes."

"Okay, up you go then." She helped Billie to her feet and lowered her to the bed. "Pleasant dreams, Billie," Laura said as she left.

Billie lay back carefully, so as to not awaken Cat. Cat's hair spilled over onto Billie's pillow. Billie raised a lock of hair and held it. *So soft.* She rolled onto her side, spooned behind Cat, and draped her arm around Cat's middle. Moments later, she joined her in the arms of sleep.

Cat shifted in her sleep and felt a familiar weight around her waist. She rolled part way over and peeked over her shoulder. Her heart flip-flopped when she saw she was wrapped in Billie's arms. *Is this really happening?* She shifted a little more and felt Billie's arm tighten around her and pull her closer. *Oh yeah, this is definitely happening.* Cat snuggled into the embrace and allowed herself to gather warmth and comfort from Billie's arms before falling back to sleep.

Laura shook Billie's arm. "Ladies, ladies, time to get up. Wakey, wakey."

"Huh?" Billie rolled onto her back. When she pulled away from Cat, she felt a tremendous sense of loss and separation. Confused and disoriented, she glanced at Cat, who was still sleeping, and back at Laura.

"You okay?" Laura asked her.

"Yeah, I think so." She glanced again at Cat.

"Should we wake her?" Laura asked.

"If we don't, she'll be upset that she missed the PT."

"Do you want to do the honors, or shall I?"

"I'll do it. She's hard to get up sometimes." *Now how did I know that?* Billie thought as she shook Cat several times before she roused from sleep.

"Whaa...? Oh, is it time to go?" Cat rubbed the sleep from her eyes.

"Yes, ma'am," Laura answered. She moved the wheelchair within Billie's reach. "Come on, Billie. Ivan will get impatient if we're late."

"Okay, Billie, now that you've mastered pulling yourself up out of the chair, let's see if you can take a few steps," Joseph said.

Billie stood between the parallel bars with Joseph in front of her. Laura was behind her, grasping the belt around her waist. Once again, Cat was relegated to the sidelines, with strict orders from Joseph to keep her mouth shut.

"Try to move one of your feet," Joseph said.

Billie felt like her feet were glued to the floor. Using her hands for support and Laura's touch on the belt for balance, she struggled to move her right foot forward. Suddenly her knees gave out and she almost went down, save for Laura's strong arms around her waist. Laura helped her back to her feet and whispered words of encouragement in her ear as Billie regained her balance. This process was repeated for an hour, with Billie stumbling several times.

Angry, humiliated, and frustrated beyond all comprehension, she lashed out at Joseph, and even at Laura, as tears streaked down her face. Partway through the session, Cat fled the room.

When Billie was on the verge of giving up, Joseph assisted her with simulated leg movements and helped her take several steps along the length of the parallel bars to her wheelchair.

Laura wheeled her back to her room, where Cat sat staring out the window. Laura helped Billie into bed. She massaged the knots out of Billie's tired muscles, wished the women a good evening, and left them alone.

"I'm sorry," Cat said.

"For what?"

Cat faced her. "For deserting you in there. I'm sorry, but I couldn't take it anymore. My heart was breaking for you."

"I understand. I wish I could have gone with you."

Cat approached the bed. "Do you still want me to go home tonight?"

"No."

Cat nodded.

"Cat?"

"Yes?"

"We're married, right?"

"Yes, we are. You fought very hard in court for the right to make it legal."

"Will you tell me about it—about us? Will you tell me about our life?"

Cat took Billie's hand in her own and raised it to her lips. She kissed her knuckles and held the hand close to her heart. "Of course I will, love. Of course I will."

Billie moved over on the bed to make room for Cat to lie next to her. Cat climbed in and lay facing Billie. Their noses were only inches part.

"Once upon a time, there was a beautiful dark-haired aerobics instructor and a very clumsy redhead..."

Part III:
Unchained Memories

Chapter 28

Billie opened her eyes the next morning and found herself looking straight into twin emerald orbs. She was lying in the same position she had fallen asleep: on her side, hands tucked under her cheek, facing Cat. The same held true for her companion. Their faces were mere inches apart as they kept their gaze. Neither of them seemed willing to break the spell that held them captive.

Who are you, Cat? Out loud, Billie said, "Your story last night was incredible."

"Our story. Yours and mine, and it's all true—every word."

"I believe you. I'm sorry I can't remember." Billie rolled onto her back and covered her eyes with her arm.

"But you remember you, right? You remember you're attracted to women?"

Billie nodded without removing her arm from her eyes.

Cat propped herself on her elbow. "Billie, I know this scares you. It scares me too."

Billie removed her arm from her face and narrowed her eyes at Cat. "Why are you scared? Your memories are intact. You know who you are and what your dreams are. What have you got to be afraid of?"

"You're kidding, right? You want to know what I have to be afraid of? I'm afraid you'll never remember me, that you'll never remember us. I'm afraid of facing a future without the one person who completes me—who makes me feel whole. I'm afraid the day you leave this hospital, you'll walk out of my life forever, and you'll take my son away from me when you go. I'm afraid I'll never again wake up in the morning and see those beautiful blue eyes looking back at me. I'm afraid we'll never experience the joy of seeing our children marry, or witness the birth of our first grandchild together. I'm afraid of facing each and every day with the memory of your touch, your smile, and your kiss lingering on my mind, but beyond my reach. I'm afraid of lying on my deathbed longing for your love and knowing it would never be mine again.

My entire future is centered around you, Billie. I'm afraid that future is but a fleeting hope, which is losing its grip on reality. These are the things I'm afraid of." Cat closed her eyes, releasing the tears teetering on her lids.

Billie was not so lucky. As she listened to Cat expose her heart, the tears flowed unchecked. When it became obvious Cat had finished, she reached out to touch her cheek. "I'm so sorry. I wish I could remember, but I can't. I'm sorry."

"Just know I love you, Billie. I'll wait for you, and I hope and pray you'll come back to me someday. No matter how long it takes, I'll be waiting."

Tears rolled down the sides of Billie's face to the pillow. She allowed Cat to wipe them dry and place a tender kiss on her forehead

"A nice strong cup of coffee sounds real good right now. What do you say?" Cat asked.

Billie nodded.

"Okay, I guess we'd better get up then. I'll go see about that coffee while we wait for your breakfast, then I've got to take a shower. I'll be right back."

Moments later, Cat returned, helped Billie into a sitting position, and left to get a shower.

Billie thanked the cafeteria attendant who brought her breakfast, along with an additional cup of coffee for Cat. As soon as the attendant left, Billie's attention was drawn to the doorway by the arrival of Jen, who walked into the room carrying coffee and donuts.

"Good morning, tough guy. Wow, I'm impressed. You're sitting up on your own." Jen wrapped her arms around Billie and kissed her on the mouth.

Billie was startled at her boldness. A blush rose rapidly to her face.

Jen laughed. "You look pretty in pink." She scanned the room. "Where's Red?"

"In the shower. You're our neighbor, right?"

"That would be me. Neighbor extraordinaire. I can't wait for you to come home. I kind of miss running with you in the morning. Without those long legs of yours giving me a challenge, I'm afraid I'm getting soft."

"I run with you?"

"Every morning."

"I'm sorry, I don't remember."

Jen sat next to Billie and wrapped an arm around her shoulder. "Don't worry, it'll come back. It just takes time."

Cat came out of the bathroom in time to see the little tête à tête. It was on the tip of her tongue to ask Jen if she was putting the moves on her woman, but she thought better of it, afraid a comment like that might scare Billie. So, instead, she opened her arms for Jen, who quickly rose from the bed and embraced her tightly. She held her for long moments with her head resting on Jen's shoulder while Jen rubbed her hand up and down Cat's back.

Jen released Cat. "I brought some coffee and donuts. Eat. You need to keep up your strength."

Cat accepted the coffee that had come for her with Billie's breakfast and the one Jen brought, but she declined the food.

Jen took the chair by the bed while Cat sat next to Billie and sipped her coffee. Billie reached a hand over and placed it on Cat's thigh.

"Cat," Billie said. "Please eat something."

"I'm not hun—"

"Please."

"Okay, okay." She took one of the donuts.

"So, what's on the agenda for today?" Jen asked.

"I've got to check in with Anesthesiology to see if I'm scheduled for any operations this week," Cat said.

"You're a doctor?" Billie asked.

"I'm an anesthesiologist, Billie. We chatted about this just a short time ago. I work here at this hospital."

"I must have forgotten. I guess that explains how you know so much about my condition."

"What's on the schedule for you today, Billie?" Jen asked.

"I have physical therapy in about a half hour." Billie frowned.

"That's not one of your prettier faces, my friend. Something tells me you're not fond of your therapy," Jen said.

"Not fond of her therapist is more like it. The man's a slave driver. I'd actually like to deck him myself," Cat said.

Billie laughed. "You've already tried that."

Jen pushed Cat's shoulder. "Get out of Dodge!"

Billie's eyes sparkled with mirth. "He and I had a little disagreement about my therapy. Cat tried to make him see the light. He took exception. Cat ended up on her back."

Cat poked Billie in the ribs with her elbow. "It wasn't funny. He tossed me around like a rag doll. He threw me over his shoulder, carried me out of the room, and plunked me down in a chair in the hallway. I was banned from therapy for the rest of the session."

Jen laughed out loud.

"It wasn't funny," Cat said.

"I'm sorry, but I can just see you trying to defend your lady's honor against the dragon. It's a pretty funny image." Jen chuckled and Billie joined in.

Cat raised her hands in exasperation. "What am I going to do with the two of you?" she asked.

"Do you really want to know?" Jen asked.

"Don't go there, girlfriend," Cat said, causing Jen to laugh and Billie to frown.

Changing the subject, Jen asked Cat how the kids were.

"They're fine. I talked to them on the phone last night. They miss us of course, but Mom and Dad are spoiling them rotten."

"I'd like to see them again," Billie said.

"Of course. How about tonight, after dinner?"

"That sounds good."

"Tell you what," Jen said, "I'll pick them up and bring them to visit. Afterward, they can come and spend the night with Stevie and Karissa."

"You have children?" Billie asked.

"Sure do. A boy and a girl. They're pretty close in age to Seth and Tara."

"Are you sure you won't mind having five kids in the house?" Cat said.

"You know I love the little rugrats like they were my own. It'll be fine. And besides, it'll give your parents a break and let them spend quality time alone."

Cat hugged Jen. "Thank you. I really appreciate it."

Billie narrowed her eyes at Jen.

Their attention was drawn to the doorway by the arrival of Laura pushing the wheelchair in front of her. "'Morning, ladies."

"Good morning," Cat said. "Laura, this is our friend and neighbor, Jen Swenson. Jen, this is Laura, friend and savior. Laura is the therapist's assistant. She does a good job cleaning up after the dragon has made mincemeat out of Billie. She works wonders with Billie's muscles after a tough session."

Laura took Jen's hand in her own for a firm handshake. "Nice to meet you, Jen." She looked at Billie. "Are you ready to go to work? We don't want to make the dragon angry at our tardiness. He just might decide to eat you for breakfast."

Billie grumbled, but held out her hands for Laura to help her up. Moments later, she was secured in the wheelchair and ready to go. She touched Cat's arm. "Are you coming back?"

"Yes, I am. I need to check the OR schedule and let Anesthesiology know where I'll be in case of an emergency. I'll be along after that." She kissed the top of Billie's head.

"All right. See you soon," Billie said, and Laura wheeled her away.

Jen placed her arm around Cat's shoulder, and Cat's arm found its way around Jen's waist. "Come on," Jen said, "Walk me to the elevator."

Billie frowned as she watched Cat and Jen walk down the hallway.

Laura stopped the chair and came around to face Billie. "Don't like that much, do you?"

"She says she loves me, but she acts so casual with Jen."

"Is Jen gay?"

"It's my understanding she has a partner."

"So what do you have to worry about then?"

"Having a partner doesn't mean she's faithful."

"Point taken."

"Sometimes I wonder if Jen's in love with her. Sometimes I think she'd be better off with her."

Laura placed her hands on her hips. "Don't let Cat hear you talk like that. She'll have your hide."

Billie's misty gaze met Laura's. "It's true. Jen and Cat already act like they're a couple. At least Jen wouldn't be a burden to her."

Laura lifted Billie's chin to make eye contact. "I don't think Cat is worried about you being a burden. She loves you very much. Never doubt that."

Billie looked down and somehow managed to hold her tears in check.

"Now, let's concentrate on working hard this morning. The quicker you recover, the quicker you'll be able to go home—with Cat."

Chapter 29

Billie stood between the parallel bars with Laura grasping the belt around her waist. Joseph was in front of her.

"Come on, lift your foot. Try harder," Joseph urged.

"Damn it. I'm trying as hard as I can." Sweat ran down Billie's back.

"Concentrate. Use your mind as well as your muscles."

Cat slipped into the room and stood against the wall near the door.

Billie closed her eyes and grasped the bars. She channeled all her willpower into her legs and grunted with effort as she moved her right foot forward a full step. Her eyes snapped open as she looked at Joseph.

"That's it, Billie. You're doing it. Now come on, try it again with the other foot."

Billie shifted her weight to her right foot and moved her left foot forward. Now it was her turn to grin. "I'm doing it! I'm really doing it."

"Yes, you are," Laura said from behind her.

Again, the right foot moved forward then the left. Billie's muscles trembled with the effort.

"Okay, that's enough for this morning," Joseph said.

"No. I want to keep going."

"If you overdo it, you'll only set yourself back. We don't want that."

"He's right," Laura said. "You need to rest. We can try again this afternoon."

Billie gave in and allowed Laura to lower her into the wheelchair. They wheeled around and came face-to-face with Cat.

Cat leaned over and placed a tender kiss on Billie's lips. "I'm so proud of you."

Billie grinned and said to Laura. "Home, James."

Laura chuckled as she wheeled her back to her room.

Laura left Billie sitting in the straight-backed chair by the window while Cat lay on her stomach on the bed, facing Billie.

"Do you have to work today?" Billie asked.

"No, but I'm on the schedule for surgery tomorrow morning. I'll miss your morning PT."

Billie fell silent for a few minutes. "Cat, about Jen... She seems kind of, I don't know, too comfortable with us—especially with you."

Cat wasn't sure where this was headed, but she had an idea. "Yes, she is. She's a good friend."

"How good?"

Cat's gut flip-flopped. *Don't you dare insist I break off that friendship.* "Very good. She loves both of us a great deal. Why do you ask?"

Billie shrugged. "I don't know. Forget I asked."

Cat rose from the bed and knelt in front of Billie. She touched the side of Billie's face. "You wouldn't have asked if it wasn't important to you. Please tell me what's wrong. What makes you so uncomfortable with Jen?"

"Sh... she loves you."

"Yes, she does. She loves you and our children too. She's a good friend to both of us."

"She's a big flirt."

"You've got that right." Cat laughed. "I have to admit she's an incredibly beautiful and sexy woman, and she uses that to her advantage, but before you call the kettle black, dear heart, you should look in the mirror. I don't know who flirts more, Jen with you, or you with Jen."

"I flirt with Jen?"

Cat was amused by the shocked expression on Billie's face. "Oh, yeah."

"Are you jealous about that?"

"Not in the least. In fact, I couldn't be happier about our relationship with Jen."

"You think she's sexy?"

"Oh yeah—she's very sexy."

"What about her do you find sexy?"

"Billie, where is this going?"

"Answer me. What about her do you find attractive?"

Cat sat back on her heels. "Well, she's cute with those bouncy blonde ringlets and the cleft in her chin. She has a beautiful smile and a wonderful sense of humor. The whole package is very attractive, but I think her best feature is her personality. She's warm and caring and the most genuine friend I've ever had."

A play of emotions crossed Billie's face. Cat saw doubt and something else she couldn't identify.

"Are you all right, Billie? Is there something else you want to say to me?"

Billie seemed as though she were going to speak before she shrugged it off and shook her head.

"Good. Now where's that gorgeous smile I love so much?"

Billie complied.

"My God, you're beautiful."

"You're kind of easy on the eyes yourself, Red."

"Thanks." Cat was thrilled that Billie used one of her favorite nicknames. She cried from happiness, and Billie joined her.

Doc walked in on the crying women. "Dang blast it. What is it about you two? You make a guy want to go out and buy stock in Kleenex."

Cat and Billie both laughed.

"That's better. Now, how are you feeling today?" he asked Billie.

"Not too bad. Sore, but okay."

"Daddy, you should have seen her in PT this morning. She took a few steps on her own at the parallel bars."

"That's wonderful news. Won't be long now, and you'll be able to go home."

Billie tensed at this proclamation.

Cat placed a hand on her arm. "Billie, are you all right?"

"Yeah, I'm fine. I just... I just haven't thought much about going home yet."

Cat rubbed her hand up and down the length of Billie's arm. "I understand. It'll be all right. I promise."

"It'll be another week or so," Doc said. "A lot can happen with your memory in that amount of time. Until then, we need to concentrate on getting your body healthy. Now, I'm going to remove the bandage from your head."

Billie touched the bandage. "No," she said.

Doc raised his eyebrows. "I need to check the incision. We need to expose it to the air to allow it to heal."

"I... I..."

"Billie," Cat said. "It'll be okay. Trust me. Trust us."

Billie held Cat's gaze for long moments before she lowered her hand. "All right."

A few minutes later, the bandage was removed. Billie ran her hand up and over the short bristles of hair growing back in. Her eyes were wide with emotion.

Cat once again knelt in front of Billie and took her face in both hands. "Billie, you are the most beautiful woman I have ever laid eyes on, with or without hair. It's okay, love. It'll grow back."

Billie began to cry.

"Okay, now, let me examine that incision," Doc said. "It appears to be healing nicely. Oh, and before I forget..." He reached into his coat pocket and pulled out a baseball cap. "Here. A present from Seth. He'd like you to wear it so he'll be on your mind, so to speak." Doc chuckled at his own joke.

"Oh, that was bad, Daddy. Don't give up your day job," Cat said.

Billie's tears turned to laughter, and she slipped the cap onto her head.

Billie and Cat sat side by side on the edge of the bed while Dr. Connor sat opposite them in the chair.

"Okay, ladies," Dr. Connor said. "It's obvious to me that a lot has changed since the last time we met. Here you are, sitting side by side, shoulders touching, and no effort to break the contact. Tell me—what's been happening?"

Billie nodded at Cat and visually gave her permission to speak for both of them.

"Well," Cat said, "I brought the kids in to visit a couple of days ago, and Seth spurred some memory recall. Billie knows who she is now, and who Seth is, but the memories stop five years ago— just before we met."

Dr. Connor looked at Billie. "Tell me how you felt when your memories returned."

"Confused, angry, anxious—and relieved Seth was all right."

Dr. Connor raised her eyebrows in question.

"Seth had been in the hospital," Cat said, "in a coma for six months by the time we met. He was hit by a car getting off the school bus when he was six years old."

"Billie, how do you feel now? About your life, about Cat, about the future?"

"I'm afraid," Billie said. "I still don't remember Cat. I... I'm afraid I'll never remember her."

"And the future?" Dr. Connor asked.

Billie looked at Cat with sadness in her eyes and back at Dr. Connor. "I... I don't know. Cat wants me to go home with her, but... I don't know if I can."

Cat sat next to Billie, spine ramrod straight, eyes closed, and chin lowered to her chest.

"Billie, what will you do if you don't go home with Cat?"

"Find an apartment, I guess. One big enough for Seth and me."

"No. Seth is my son too. Please don't take him away from me." Cat's eyes misted up.

Billie reached for her hand.

"The children won't understand if you don't come home," Cat said. "Seth knows you're his mother, and Tara knows she belongs to me. She was four years old when we met, but Skylar... well, you were there when Sky was born. You cut the umbilical cord. You've been her mother from the moment she took her first breath. Skylar's birth made us a real family. You adopted her and Tara, and I adopted Seth. As far as the children are concerned, we are both their mothers, in every way. They'll be devastated if you don't come home, and they'll be devastated if you take Seth away from us."

A variety of emotions played across Billie's face with each new piece of information about their lives together.

"I'm sorry, Cat. I don't know what else to do."

Cat touched the side of Billie's face. "Please don't decide right now. Give me a chance to prove you belong with us—both you and Seth. No pressure. I promise. Give it some time, and after a while, if you still want to leave, I won't stop you, no matter how much it hurts. Okay?"

Billie looked at Cat for a long time. A slight nod was her only answer.

"Thank you," Cat whispered.

Chapter 30

Laura set the brakes on the chair while Billie grasped the rails. In one smooth motion, Billie pulled her way into a standing position.

Cat stood against the wall on the opposite side of the room.

"Okay, Miss La-Dee-Da, let's see how you do through the bars," Joseph said.

Billie stood face-to-face with Joseph. "You just watch me, Ivan."

Joseph chuckled as Billie struggled to put her legs into motion.

Fifteen minutes later, she made it all the way through the bars, with just Laura's gentle support on the belt to help her along. As she took her last step at the end, Cat jumped up and yelled, "Yes," with her arms extended high into the air. The pride and love Billie saw in Cat's eyes warmed her heart.

Then, Billie did the unexpected. She turned herself around, despite protests from both Laura and Joseph, and headed back in the direction she had come. This time, after making it through the bars, she was exhausted and didn't argue when Laura lowered her into the wheelchair.

Cat hugged Billie. "I'm so proud of you." She squealed when Billie pulled her down into her lap and gave Laura her cue to return to the room.

Back in the room, Laura massaged the kinks out of Billie's muscles while Cat watched. When the massage was over, Billie touched Laura's hand. "Do you think you can arrange a bath for me?"

Laura snorted. "I was wondering what that smell was."

Billie slapped her arm.

"Okay, okay, I give. Of course. I'll see what I can do." Laura walked out of the room chuckling.

Cat waited in Billie's room as Laura returned with an aide and lowered Billie into the warm tub. Twenty minutes later, they emerged from the bathroom, with a freshly bathed Billie in tow, and helped her into a sitting position on the edge of the bed to wait for dinner.

"Your shirt is all wet," Cat said to Laura.

Laura laughed and raised her hands out to the side. "Paybacks are a bitch. My punishment for telling her she stinks."

Billie sat on the edge of the bed with the devil mischievously dancing in her eyes.

Dinner was quiet. Once again, Billie offered to share her meal with Cat, and once again, Cat refused.

"Cat, I'm worried about you."

"I'm fine. I'm just not hungry, that's all."

"All you've had to eat was that donut this morning. You've got to eat more than that. We don't want you getting sick as—"

The sounds of children running down the hallway interrupted her. In seconds, three small bodies covered her bed, all clamoring to give her hugs and kisses.

"Take it easy, rugrats, there's plenty for all of you," Billie said.

"You need to be gentle with Mom," Cat said.

A movement in the doorway drew Billie's attention from the children. She looked up just as Jen entered the room and took Cat into her arms from behind.

"Hi," Jen said.

An intense feeling of anxiety filled Billie's chest as she watched Cat press her head back into Jen's shoulder. Her hands came to rest on Jen's arms wrapped around her midsection.

"Hi, yourself," Cat replied.

Billie scowled at the sight, before redirecting her attention back to the children, who were talking to her all at once.

Jen released Cat and went over to plant a kiss on Billie's cheek. "Hey, spike. How are you feeling?"

I'll spike you… right into the middle of next week, Billie thought. "I'm fine, Jen. Thanks for asking." After a slight pause, she said, "Jen, I need you to do me a favor."

"Anything. Just ask."

"I'd like you to take Cat somewhere and make her eat."

"Billie," Cat said in a deep, warning voice.

Jen interrupted Cat. "Don't tell me you haven't eaten anything since that donut this morning."

"No she hasn't," Billie replied for her.

"Damn you, Cat. Let's go—now." Jen dragged Cat toward the door. She stopped and looked back at Billie. "Will you be all right here with the kids?"

"We'll be fine. Just make her eat something."

"You got it," Jen said as she dragged a protesting Cat out the door.

By the time Cat and Jen came back, Skylar was asleep on Billie's chest. Tara and Seth lay on each side of her watching the end of a Disney movie on TV. Billie smiled as Cat and Jen entered the room.

"It appears like we have a casualty, Mom," Cat said to Billie as she lifted Skylar into her arms.

"She fell asleep about a half hour ago. Did you eat?"

"Yes, I ate, thanks to you and that pushy bitch over there."

"That's Miss Pushy Bitch, to you," Jen replied.

"Thanks, Jen. I appreciate it," Billie said.

"Anytime."

Cat handed Skylar to Jen. "All right, you two," she said to Seth and Tara. "Time to head home with Jen."

"We're going to Jen's?" Seth asked.

"Yes, you are, sweetie," Jen replied for Cat. "Stevie and Karissa have been bugging me to invite you for a sleepover."

Seth and Tara rose to their knees and slid off the bed. "Yeah. Let's go."

"Hugs and kisses first," Cat said, and the children climbed back onto the bed and showered Billie with hugs.

"Let's go, Jen." Seth headed toward the door.

"Hey, what about me?" Cat asked.

Seth and Tara hugged Cat and once again waited at the door. "Come on, Jen, we want to play with Stevie and Karissa."

"Can you feel the love?" Jen said.

Cat hugged and kissed her. "Thank you, Jen. You're a good friend, even if you did collaborate with the pain-in-the-ass on the bed over there to make me eat."

"You know I'd do anything for you two."

"I know. We love you too. Thanks again."

"No problem. Are you rugrats ready to go?"

Seth and Tara responded by pushing Jen toward the door.

"Okay, I get the message. I'll see you tomorrow, Cat."

Cat sat on the edge of Billie's bed. Billie's drooping eyelids made it obvious the day's PT had taken a lot out of her. "Are you tired, my love?"

Billie responded with a nod.

Cat kissed her forehead. "Sleep then. I'll sit with you for a while then climb into my bed. I'm kind of beat too."

Soon, Billie was asleep. Cat pulled the blankets around her and kissed her on the cheek. "Pleasant dreams," she whispered. She changed into her nightshirt and climbed into her cot.

Chapter 31

Cat rose the next morning and showered while Billie was still asleep. She scribbled a few words on a sheet of paper and left it propped up on the bedside table before leaving for work.

About an hour later, Billie was awakened by a nurse who reminded her that breakfast would be arriving soon. She shifted into a sitting position and spotted the note on the table.

It read, "Billie, I didn't have the heart to wake you this morning. You're a beautiful angel when you sleep. I'm off to work. God, how I hate Mondays. I'm sorry I'll miss your morning PT. I'll see you sometime this afternoon. Keep your chin up and don't be too hard on Mr. Terrible. Down deep I don't think he's such a bad guy. Say hi to Laura for me. I'll see you later. Good luck today. Love, Cat."

Billie sighed as she refolded the paper and put it back on the table.

She maneuvered herself into a sitting position just in time for the cafeteria attendant to deliver breakfast. Before long, Laura appeared and escorted her to PT.

Laura positioned her chair in front of the parallel bars. Billie reached forward, grasped the rails, and pulled herself to a standing position. She kept her gaze trained on her feet as she made her way through the bars. Near the end, she saw Joseph standing there, sporting his usual arrogant pose.

"Are you ready for a new challenge?" he asked.

"Bring it on."

Joseph stepped aside and exposed a metal walker to Billie's view.

Billie eyed the walker suspiciously. "You're kidding, right?"

"Do I look like I'm kidding?"

Billie noted the stern expression on his face. "No, I guess you'd need a sense of humor for that." She eyed the walker again. "It doesn't seem very sturdy. Are you sure it'll hold my weight?"

"It's not supposed to hold your weight. It's to teach you balance. Now, reach out and grasp it. Laura will keep the wheelchair behind you."

Billie released one of the parallel bars, grabbed the walker, and repeated the motion with the other hand. She found herself stuck in a bent-over position, arms reaching forward, holding onto the walker with her hands. Her legs were too far behind her to stand upright. Panic rose in her chest, and her arms trembled with exertion.

Joseph stepped up to the front of the walker and pressed down on it with his hands. He bent over close to her ear. "Okay, Billie. The walker won't move. I've got it. Now, move your feet forward, one at a time, until you're standing upright."

Billie had no choice but to trust him and Laura, who still held the chair close behind her. She concentrated all her effort on moving her feet and soon found herself standing within the arc of the walker. Afraid of tipping the walker over by leaning too far forward, backward, or sideways, she was forced to concentrate on maintaining her balance. She wavered but managed to keep herself upright for several minutes before Joseph encouraged her to sit down in the chair and relax. This process was repeated several times, until Joseph called a halt and ordered her back to her room to rest.

At about the same time Billie was heading for her morning PT, Cat reported for a briefing on the surgery she was scheduled to anesthetize. She sat at the conference table and reviewed X-rays while listening to the chief surgeon discuss the patient and describe the surgery. Without warning, she felt a burning sensation rise from her neck and into her head. A loud ringing in her ears drowned out the droning voice of the surgeon. A sheen of sweat broke out all over her body. Nausea overtook her. She struggled to her feet, intending to rush off to the bathroom before she became sick in front of her colleagues. Halfway to her feet, she collapsed.

Doc was waiting for Billie in her room at the end of her PT. Billie could tell by the expression on his face that something was wrong. Her feeling of dread increased as Doc motioned for Laura to leave her in the wheelchair. Laura did as she was asked and slipped out of the room.

Billie scanned the room. "Where's Cat? What happened?"

Doc placed his hand on her shoulder. "First, calm down. She's fine. She passed out in her presurgery briefing this morning."

"She passed out? Where is she? I've got to see her."

"You're not going anywhere until you calm down," Doc said. "I'll take you to her, but you'll do her no good if you're in a snit yourself."

Billie took a deep breath. "Yes, of course, I'm sorry. Please take me to her."

"All right." Doc pushed her toward the elevator.

Moments later, Billie and Doc were at Cat's bedside. Cat was sleeping, and an IV was inserted into her left arm.

Intense anxiety filled Billie's chest. "Why did she pass out?"

"She passed out because she's a stubborn little shit. She hasn't been taking care of herself. She hasn't been eating or sleeping very well."

"Damn you, Cat," Billie said, almost under her breath. "I told you. Why do you have to be so damned stubborn all the time?" Billie looked at Doc. "How long will she be confined to bed?"

"A day or two... if she takes care of herself."

"Can you move her to my room?"

Doc nodded. "It can be arranged."

Lunch was waiting for Billie when she and Doc arrived back at her room, but she had very little appetite. Doc helped her into the chair by the window and wheeled the table in front of her. She pushed it away.

Doc pushed it back. "Eat. I don't need to be worrying about both of you."

That made sense. Billie did as she was told and ate about half of her meal before Cat's bed was wheeled into her room. Cat was still asleep. Doc hung around to see her settled in her new room. Before he left, he helped Billie back into the wheelchair and moved her to Cat's bedside.

Billie lifted Cat's hand and held it in her own. She studied Cat's face carefully as she slept. Without warning, a searing pain streaked through her head, forcing her to close her eyes. When she opened them, she was still in the hospital, but in another room, and at another time.

She sat on the edge of the bed and took Cat's hand in hers. "Cat, it took almost losing you to give me the courage to say this...

I love you. I think I have since you walked into my class that day. I didn't realize how much until this happened."

Billie closed her eyes against the pain. When she reopened them, she was back in her room, watching Cat sleep. *Was that a memory?* She stared at Cat for long moments until Laura came to claim her for her afternoon PT.

"You're early," Billie said.

"Yeah, a little." Laura stood beside Cat's bed. "Is she okay?"

"Doc said she'll be all right. She just needs food and rest."

Laura pulled a chair next to Billie and sat down. "This is all pretty confusing, isn't it?" she asked.

Billie nodded without moving her gaze from Cat's face.

"I wish I could tell you it will all work out in the end, but I can't. So much of this depends on how much you'll remember and what you choose to do with what you have now. But what I can say is this... Cat loves you very much. She's in this bed right now because she's put you above all else, even her own health. Don't give up on that—not yet. Okay?"

"I'll try."

As with the morning PT, Billie started out with a walk through the parallel bars, which she accomplished with little difficulty. Once again, the walker was waiting for her at the end of the bars. She grasped the walker and righted herself into a standing position, struggling hard to remain balanced. Laura was a constant presence standing behind her, her light touch on the belt giving Billie the added confidence to push herself a little further.

"Okay," Joseph said, "lift the walker, move it forward, and place it down again. Be sure to maintain your balance while you lift it."

Billie lifted the walker and teetered side to side before thrusting it forward and lowering it back to the floor.

"Good. Now take a step with each foot."

An echo came from deep within her mind: Come on, Billie, just like on the parallel bars. You can do it. Do it for Cat. With determined steps, she moved forward, first with one foot, and then with the other.

"Again," Joseph said.

Billie repeated the sequence until she crossed the room.

Joseph stood in front of her, his hands covering hers on the walker while Laura fetched the wheelchair. He held her gaze the whole time. Before he released her hands, he said, "Good job. I knew you weren't a quitter." He walked away, and Laura helped her into her chair and wheeled her back to her room.

Billie kept her gaze directed at Cat during the entire post-therapy massage.

"She's going to be fine." Laura rubbed the soreness out of Billie's muscles.

"I know. It's just... I can't help but feel this is my fault."

"It was her own decision to neglect her health, not yours."

"But she did it for me."

"Yes, she did, but she's a big girl, and from what I've seen, a stubborn one at that. She's a doctor. She knows the consequences of not eating and sleeping well. Sometimes common sense flies out the window where matters of the heart are concerned." Laura completed her rubdown and helped Billie change into a clean gown for bed.

"Laura, before you leave, I'd like you to help me over to her bed."

"For the night?"

"Yes."

"All right. You stay put. I'll be right back." Several moments later, Laura reappeared with the walker Billie used in PT. She put it down near Billie's bed, folded up the wheelchair, and rolled it off to the side. "You won't need that anymore." She positioned the walker in front of Billie. "Okay, on your feet."

Billie grasped the walker, and with Laura holding on to her waist, she rose to her feet.

"Okay, you know the routine."

"Balance, lift, forward, lower, step, step," Billie repeated to herself. She made her way over to Cat's bed while Laura walked very close beside her. Finally, she sat on the edge of Cat's bed, smiling ear to ear. "Thank you."

"You're welcome. Can you handle it from here?"

"Yes. Thanks again."

"All right. Pleasant dreams. I'll see you in the morning." Laura left, pushing the wheelchair before her.

"Goodnight," Billie said. She lay down next to Cat and pulled the covers over herself.

Chapter 32

Cat awoke the next morning to find herself trapped on the bed. She wore Billie like a body suit. Billie's legs were entwined around hers like braided rope. Her arm was thrown over Cat's chest, and her face was nuzzled deep into her neck. She desperately wanted to stay right where she was, except nature was calling.

She moved her head so she was almost face-to-face with Billie and kissed her eyelids until she woke up. She grinned. "Billie, as much as I'm enjoying this closeness, I've got to pee."

Billie took in their current positions. She quickly moved away, giving Cat plenty of room. "I'm sorry."

"Don't apologize. You didn't hear me complaining, did you? I just need to use the bathroom before I embarrass both of us."

Cat slid her legs over the side of the bed and was about to rise when a wave of dizziness came over her. "Whoa!" She fell back onto the bed. Suddenly, she noticed the IV in her arm and that there were two beds in Billie's room. "What's going on here?"

"You passed out in a meeting yesterday," Billie said.

"What do you mean, I passed out?"

"You passed out from lack of sleep and food. I told you..."

"Please don't say, 'I told you so.'"

"You scared the shit out of me. I was worried."

Cat realized how harsh she sounded and felt guilty. "Honey, I'm sorry. I shouldn't have snapped at you. I know you warned me. I just... hell, I don't know what. I screwed up. I'm sorry." Cat tried once more to get out of bed, rising slowly to keep the dizziness at bay. She grabbed the portable IV rack that held the drip bag and walked it into the bathroom in front of her.

While Cat was in the bathroom, Billie pushed herself into a sitting position on the edge of the bed. She grasped the walker that Laura had left close by and very slowly pulled herself to her feet just as Doc came into the room.

"What in blazes are you doing?" He rushed to her side. "And where is Caitlain?"

"She's in the bathroom, which is where I'm headed. By the time I make it around the bed, she'll be out."

Billie saw Doc frown at her attempted humor and steeled herself for a lecture.

"Billie, I'm happy to see you on your feet, but it's too soon in your therapy to do this without assistance. Do you understand? If you need to go somewhere, call for help first."

"Yes, Daddy."

"I mean it."

"All right, all right. I'll call for help next time, I promise."

"That's better," he said, just as the bathroom door opened and Cat shuffled out.

"I'm next," Billie said.

"Billie, you're walking!"

Billie's face radiated pride as she made her way past Cat and into the bathroom, with Doc at her side. Billie stopped at the door and gave Doc a pointed look.

"I can't let you go in there alone, Billie."

"Like hell you can't," she replied as she stood her ground.

"Oh, hell. Between you and Cat, I've broken so many rules I guess one more won't matter. Please be careful in there, and call for help if you need it."

"I promise." Billie shuffled the rest of the way into the bathroom.

Cat sat on the edge of her bed and watched her father pace.

"Caitlain, I warned you to take better care of yourself."

"Yes, you did."

"Damn it, you're a doctor. I would think you'd know better."

"You're right."

"From now on, you're going to listen to me and do what you're told. Understand?"

"Yes, Daddy."

"You need to take this seriously, Caitlain. Your health is nothing to fool with. You have a lot of people depending on you to stay healthy right now. Do you understand what I'm saying?"

Cat sighed. "Yes, I understand. I don't know what to say, except I screwed up. I'm sorry."

Doc sat down next to her and wrapped his arm around her shoulder. "You gave me quite a scare. Please promise me you'll take better care of yourself."

"I will. I promise." Cat rested her head on Doc's shoulder for long moments. After a time, she lifted her head. "Maybe we should check on Billie."

Just then, the bathroom door swung open.

Doc was on his feet in an instant and walked beside Billie to the edge of her own bed where she sat and grinned.

"Show off," Cat said.

Doc lounged in the chair by the window while their breakfast trays were rolled in. "Daddy, you don't have to hang around to make sure I eat," Cat said.

"What? Can't I visit with my daughter and daughter-in-law?"

"Yeah, right," Cat mumbled as she started eating.

Doc winked at Billie, drawing a grin from her.

After Cat ate most of her meal, Doc rose to his feet and excused himself.

"He's so transparent," Cat said.

"He loves you, and he's worried about you."

"Well, I've certainly given him reason. I'm sorry. I know it was stupid."

"Just promise me you'll take better care of yourself from now on."

"I will," Cat said as Laura came into the room.

"Ah, my two favorite ladies. Good morning," she said. "Feeling better today?"

"Yes, thank you," Cat said.

She looked at Billie sitting on her own bed and put her hands on her hips. "Okay, missy, how did you get from there," she said, pointing to Cat's bed, "to there?" She pointed to Billie's bed. "You better not have done it by yourself."

"Nope, Doc helped me."

"Good. Okay, are you ready to go for a walk?"

"To the PT room?"

"No, we're all finished in there for a little while. How about a stroll up and down the hall?"

"Don't you mean a shuffle up and down the hall?" Billie joked.

"Walk, shuffle—same church, different pew."

"Can I come along?" Cat asked.

"Sure. The more the merrier. We need to wait for Joseph. He should be here soon." She placed Billie's walker in front of her. "Okay, on your feet."

Laura fastened the belt around Billie's waist while she balanced on the walker. Cat grabbed Seth's baseball cap and slipped in on Billie's head just as Joseph entered the room.

Joseph stood there, arms crossed in front of him. "Well, now we'll see what you're really made of, Billie," he said. "Are you up for a challenge?"

"I can take anything you dish out," she shot back at him. Cat could see the twinkle in Billie's eyes.

He approached her and circled her walker. "Nice hat."

"Get on with it, Ivan," Billie said.

"Okay. Let's see if you can make it to the end of the hall. I'll walk with you on one side, and Laura will be on the other." Joseph looked at Cat. "You can make yourself useful by pushing the wheelchair, Red. She gets a ride back."

If it weren't that she was helping Billie, Cat would have told him where he could stick the wheelchair. Instead, she swallowed her pride, tucked her IV pole between the handles of the wheelchair, and pushed them both behind the slowly moving entourage.

Cat could tell Billie was tired when they finished their walk. It had taken almost a half hour to make it to the end of the hall. A grateful sigh escaped Billie's lips as Laura lowered her into the chair for the ride back to her room.

"You did good," Laura said. "Time to go home."

Laura helped her into a chair in her room. "I'll be back this afternoon for round two. Catch you later." Laura wheeled the chair out of the room in front of her.

"What time is the occupational therapist coming, Cat?"

"Julie's not coming today, remember? She cut your sessions down to Monday, Wednesday, and Friday, because you made so much progress over the past week."

Billie's brows knit together, and she nodded. "Yeah, you're right. I forgot."

Cat sat on the arm of the chair. She wrapped her arm around Billie's shoulder and kissed her on the head. She felt the heat radiating from Billie's skin. "Are you okay? You're a little hot."

"Just tired," Billie said as she rubbed her forehead.

Cat noticed the gesture. "Billie, the headaches are back, aren't they? That would explain why you've forgotten random bits of information over the past few days."

"A little one. Not too bad."

Cat kissed Billie's head again, stood up, and took hold of her IV pole. "I'll be right back. I'm going to find you a couple of pain relievers."

When Cat returned minutes later, Billie was half-asleep in the chair. She nudged Billie awake and handed the meds and water to her.

"Thanks," Billie said. "When's the OT coming?"

Cat frowned. "Honey, I just reminded you that you didn't have a session today. Are you all right?"

"I'm... tired. Help me to bed?"

"Let me call Laura, okay? We shouldn't be doing this without help."

"It's okay. Please, help me to bed." Billie grabbed her walker and tried to pull herself up with it.

Cat steadied the walker as Billie struggled to stand. She wrapped her arm around Billie's waist and helped her move the four feet necessary to make it to the side of her bed. Billie dropped down on the edge and let herself fall back while Cat lifted her feet up and swung them onto the bed. Cat pulled the blanket up to Billie's neck and lifted the bed rails into position before leaning in to kiss her on the cheek.

Billie captured Cat's hand as she attempted to right herself after the kiss. "Join me? Please?"

Cat moved around to the other side of the bed. Making sure not to tangle her IV, she climbed into bed with Billie and snuggled into her shoulder. Billie wrapped her arm around Cat and lowered her cheek to the top of Cat's head. Soon, they were both sleeping, their hearts beating in sync.

"Caitlain, wake up."

Cat rolled over and saw Doc standing beside the bed. "Daddy? Is everything all right?"

"Everything's fine, kitten. I stopped in to let you know your session with Dr. Connor is being rescheduled to this evening. It's nearly time for Billie's afternoon PT. I thought you'd like a chance to eat before then."

Cat saw their lunch trays on the table. "Yeah, you're right. Billie should eat. She needs her strength." Cat rolled back over to shake Billie awake. "Billie, honey, come on, wake up. Time for lunch."

Billie batted her hand away. "No."

"Come on, love. You've got to eat before Laura gets here."

Billie groaned when Cat mentioned Laura's name. "I don't want to walk anymore today."

Cat shook her again. "Billie, come on. Please?"

Billie rolled onto her back. "All right, I'm up." She grinned at Cat and pulled her down onto her shoulder. "Strike that—I changed my mind." She curled up again with Cat in her arms.

Cat rolled onto her stomach and looked Billie in the face. "Billie," she said in a deep, threatening voice.

"What?"

"Up. Now."

"Okay, okay. Geesh. Are you going to get the whip out next?"

Cat chuckled. "Don't even go there."

"TMI!" Doc said as he left the room.

Laura arrived right on time for Billie's afternoon PT. She held the walker down as Billie pulled herself to her feet. Once her balance was secured, they headed down the hall, with Cat in tow, pushing the wheelchair in front of her in case Billie lost her strength during the walk.

It took an hour to walk down the hall and back. As they approached Billie's room, she suddenly stopped and gripped the walker until her knuckles were white.

"Hon, are you all right?" Laura asked.

Billie's gaze darted around, fear and anxiety evident on her face. "I'm hot. God, it's hot all of a sudden." She sniffed the air. "What's that smell?"

Cat pushed the wheelchair closer to Billie. "Laura, get her into the chair and back to her room right now. She's having a seizure. I'll have the desk page Daddy." Cat pushed her IV pole in front of her toward the nurses' station. Within minutes, Doc was there with a team of technicians, hooking Billie up to an EEG.

"Daddy, I've seen these symptoms before. In fact, it happened once while I was anesthetizing a patient. It has the signature of a simple partial seizure," Cat said.

"You're right. Here's our chance to collect enough data to know for sure if Billie is epileptic." Doc hooked the terminals up to Billie's forehead. "Did she experience other symptoms like changes in body temperature, sudden fear or anxiety, abnormalities in speech, sight, or smell? Did she complain of a stomachache, or did you observe any muscle spasms?"

"Changes in body temp for sure. And at one point, she stopped walking and just went stiff."

"You know, I'm right here in the room with you," Billie said as Doc connected the wires to the EEG machine.

"Sorry, Billie," Doc said. "We doctors sometimes get caught up in the moment and forget the patient can hear what we're saying. Just so you know, it does sound like a simple partial seizure. These tests should be more conclusive."

Before long, the technicians finished, leaving Doc to monitor the graph being produced by the EEG, while Cat sat by Billie's bedside, holding her hand.

"Cat, I feel fine," Billie insisted each time Cat cast a worried expression her way.

"Hi there," a voice said from the doorway. "What the hell?"

The expletive drew their attention to Jen standing there. Cat immediately became aware of how bad the situation might appear to her. Billie lay on the bed with multiple pads and wires attached to her head; Cat—an IV coming from her arm—sat next to her, holding her hand; and Doc was in the middle of the whole mess monitoring the equipment hooked up to Billie.

"Will someone tell me what the fuck is going on here?"

Cat rose from the chair and approached Jen, pushing the IV rack along in front of her. "Calm down, Jen."

"My God, Cat, what the hell happened? I leave you alone for less than twenty-four hours, and I come back to this. Explain."

"It's not as bad as it looks."

"How can you say that? Jesus. You've got a drip bag attached to your arm. Billie has wires coming out of her head. Don't you dare tell me it's not as bad as it looks."

Cat grabbed Jen by the shoulders and shook her. "Just shut up and listen to me, damn it."

Jen was stunned into silence.

"That's better. Now I'm going to tell you this just once, so you'd better listen, okay?"

Jen nodded.

"All right. Billie might have had a partial seizure. The wires are connected to an EEG. She's fine. As for me, well, you were right. Yes—all of you were right. I wasn't taking care of myself. I passed out at work, and here I am. The drip bag is for hydration. I'm fine now."

Jen's eyes brimmed with unshed tears. She hugged Cat. "I'm sorry. It's just that you and Billie mean so much to me. You scared the hell out of me."

"We're fine."

"Okay," Doc said as he switched off the EEG. "Finished." He began to remove the pads and wires from Billie's head.

Cat helped him, and soon, the EEG machine was pushed aside. Cat watched over his shoulder as he reviewed the tape it produced. "What do the results say?"

Doc spread the graph paper out on Billie's lap so they could all see what he was pointing at. He started tracing the line on the graph with his finger. "See this ragged line, right here, on the beginning of the graph? This is data collected right after we hooked her up. And this part of the graph, the part that levels out and is straighter and less ragged, is data that was collected just prior to shutting the machine off. The ragged line represents seizure activity, while the straighter, smoother line represents normal brain activity."

"So this data shows there was a seizure," Billie said.

"Correct."

"Epilepsy?" Cat asked, hearing an audible gasp come from Jen.

"Probably, but controllable with medication. There are several different kinds of drugs to treat epilepsy. The choice of drug is determined by the type of seizure and how well the patient tolerates the side effects. Billie, we'll start you on one of these anticonvulsants right away. If we're lucky, we'll find the right one for you relatively fast."

Billie nodded.

"Epilepsy? That's bad, isn't it?" Jen asked.

"Not necessarily," Cat said. "Epilepsy is a neurological disorder, not a disease. In most cases, it's not life threatening and it can be controlled with medication. The seizure we walked in on right after Billie's surgery was pretty severe, yet she's doing fine now."

Jen released a sigh of relief. "Yeah, you're right. Don't mind me, it's just my ignorance showing through. I guess I've got some reading to do."

"I think we all have," Billie said. "Especially me."

"Billie, how did you feel when you learned Cat was ill?" Dr. Connor asked.

"I was scared. In fact, Doc had to force me to calm down before he'd take me to her."

Cat reached her open palm toward Billie, who placed hers on top and folded their fingers together.

"Have any more memories surfaced?"

Billie squeezed Cat's hand. "Only one."

"Would you like to share it?" Dr. Connor asked.

"I'm not sure what it means. It was only a glimpse in time, an isolated moment. I don't know what happened before or after it."

"That's all right. Maybe Cat can help fill in the blanks for you."

"I saw myself sitting at Cat's bedside in the hospital and telling her I loved her, but I didn't realize it until she almost died. She said she had known all her life she would find me, that it was our destiny."

Cat wiped a tear from the corner of her eye.

"Cat, judging by the tears, that must sound familiar to you," Dr. Connor said.

"Yes. I was in the hospital with appendicitis. It was only six or seven weeks after we met. Billie saved my life. I remember telling her I had loved her forever and knew I would find her one day."

"Billie, how did you feel about Cat when you had the vision?"

"Confused."

"Why confused?"

"What I saw in the vision was so intense, I could almost touch it, and when it was over and I looked at Cat, I still didn't know her. I was confused. I had a glimpse of her in my past, but no knowledge of her in my present."

"And what about the future?" Cat asked. "Am I in your future?"

Billie traced Cat's jaw with her free hand. Warmth spread through her abdomen like tentacles. She took a stuttered breath and let it out, all the while, maintaining eye contact with Cat. "Yes."

Chapter 33

Cat was released from the hospital the next morning with strict instructions from both Doc and Billie to take better care of herself. Cat and Billie had slept in the same bed for the last few nights, holding each other close while sharing thoughts and touches.

As much as Cat wanted to make love to Billie, she held back, electing instead to touch and caress her at every opportunity without crossing over the line into sexual advancement. She promised Billie there would be no pressure, and she was determined not to rush her. The last thing Cat wanted was to scare her away. She wanted Billie to make the first move. Cat was certain Billie would let her know when she was ready to take the relationship further. In the meantime, Cat had one goal in mind—a goal planted there by Jen: *You'll just have to make her fall in love with you all over again.*

After breakfast, before Laura arrived for therapy, Cat and Billie discussed another visit from the children.

"I can't wait to see them again," Billie said. "I really enjoyed their last visit. It amazes me how fast they've captured my heart, and it didn't seem to bother them that I'm somewhat limited at the moment."

"They love you very much. It doesn't matter to them that your head is shaved or that your speech is slow. You're their mommy."

"What was I like with them?"

"You're the playful parent, always initiating tickle wars and wrestling matches."

"Really? I wish I could remember."

"Give it time, love. It'll come back."

"I hope so. When do you think they can visit again?"

"I was thinking maybe this evening after dinner. In fact, when Laura's finished and you're doing OT, I'll run home for a change of clothes and then to Mom's to see the kids. I'll talk to them about it then."

When Laura arrived, she and Cat walked Billie up and down the hall with her walker. Billie was making remarkable progress. She beamed with pride as she negotiated the hall with little difficulty. Before returning to the room, the trio spent some time in the solarium, resting, and helping Billie learn how to raise and lower herself into a chair with just the aid of the walker. When they got back to Billie's room, Laura helped her into the chair, gave her a quick hug, and promised to come back later in the afternoon.

Cat placed her hands on the armrests on either side of Billie. Their gazes lingered for long moments. "I'm so proud of you. You've come so far in such a short time. You'll be ready to come home soon, I think."

Billie pulled Cat down to sit across her lap. Cat rested her head on Billie's shoulder. "I've missed this so much," Billie said.

Cat lifted her head. "What did you just say?"

Cat could see the confusion and anxiety in Billie's eyes.

"Did you remember something?"

Billie shook her head. "No, not really. This just feels familiar. It feels right."

Cat nodded. "It is right. It feels right because it is right." She cuddled back into Billie's arms and remained that way until the occupational therapist arrived for Billie's session. Cat left for home.

As Cat pulled into the driveway, she noticed Jen setting out for her power walk. She honked the horn and motioned for Jen to come over.

Jen opened the car door. "Hey, there. Are you taking a break from the hospital?"

Cat climbed out of the car. "Sort of. Billie's in OT, so I thought I'd get a change of clothes and run over to your place to collect the mail."

"Actually, I've been leaving the mail on your kitchen counter."

"Oh, okay. Thanks."

"Are you in a hurry to get back to the hospital?"

"Well, I don't want to be gone too long. Why?"

"I was hoping I could talk you into keeping me company on my walk. I'm betting you can use a little stress relief."

"You got that right. I'd love to go. Give me a few minutes to change."

Moments later, Cat was changed into spandex running shorts, a short T-shirt, and a pair of running shoes. Not wanting to push too hard after Cat's hospital stay, they took a brisk but easy walk. Despite the mildly taxing nature of the workout, they were both covered with sweat by the end of it.

"Come on in the house," Cat said. In the kitchen, she walked over to the growing pile of mail on the counter and sorted through it, filling up the rubbish bin with junk mail. She managed to weed the pile down into a stack of three or four bills. "Not too bad," she said when she finished.

Jen handed Cat a cup of coffee she had brewed while Cat was going through the mail. "Here, drink this. A shot of caffeine is just what you need."

Cat took a sip. "Oh, Jen, this is good. You're right, I needed this."

"How are things going with the big guy?"

Cat gave a big smile. "She's made remarkable progress, even since yesterday."

"Has any more of her memory returned?"

"Not really. I see glimpses of her old self, but it's more behavioral than memory. Does that make sense?"

"Are you saying you're seeing old behaviors, but they're random rather than the result of a memory?"

"That's it exactly." Cat took the last sip of coffee.

"Want some more?" Jen asked as she refilled her own cup.

"No thanks. I need to get into the shower before I visit the kids and get back to the hospital."

"Okay. I'll just finish my coffee and head home."

"All right. Thanks for the walk. It was a nice break. I needed the exercise." Cat hugged Jen and kissed her cheek. "Hey, if you're free, how about coming to visit during Billie's afternoon PT? You can see how much better she's doing."

"I'd like that, but are you sure tall, dark, and dangerous won't mind?"

"Why should she?"

Jen shrugged. "I just don't want to embarrass or upset her, that's all."

Cat slapped her on the arm. "Don't be silly. Of course she won't be upset."

"All right then. It's a date."

"Good. Now I've got to take a shower. I'll see you later."

While Cat was in the shower, Jen lounged against the kitchen counter, finishing her coffee. When she was done, she rinsed her cup, put it in the dishwasher, and shut the coffeepot off. Just as she reached for the doorknob, the phone rang.

Without thinking, she picked it up. "Hello?"

She was momentarily met by silence. "Hello?" she said again.

"Who is this?"

"Billie? Billie, this is Jen."

"Jen, what are you doing there? Where's Cat?"

"Cat's in the shower. We're both kind of sweaty right now. In fact, I was on my way home to clean up too."

"I want to talk to her."

"Sure, hold on. I don't hear the shower running anymore. I'll get her for you."

Moments later, Cat picked up the phone as Jen was leaving. Before speaking into the phone, she called out, "Thanks for everything, Jen. It was fun, and I really needed it. See you this afternoon, hon. Bye." Then, into the phone, Cat said, "Hey, sweetie," just in time to hear a click and a dial tone. Startled, Cat called Billie's room, but no one answered. She peered at the phone and hung it up.

Chapter 34

When Cat arrived at her parents' house she noticed Seth's newly shaved head. She grinned from ear to ear, hugged him close, and whispered to him, "Mom is going to be very touched, honey." He grinned back at her and blushed.

She spent the next hour visiting with her mother and the children.

"Is Mom ready to come home?" Seth asked.

"Not yet. She's getting better, so I expect it will be sometime soon."

"Can she walk now?" Tara asked.

"With a little help, yes, she can."

"Cool."

"Does Mommy still talk funny?" Skylar asked.

"A little, but that's getting better too, except when she's tired or upset."

"I hope she comes home soon," Seth said. "We really miss her."

"Yeah, we really, really, really, miss her," Tara said.

"I miss having her at home too. Let's hope she keeps getting better fast."

"When can we see her again?" Seth asked.

"How about tonight, after dinner?"

"Can we?" Seth turned to his sisters. "Do you want to visit Mom tonight?"

Tara and Skylar jumped up and down and clapped their hands.

Cat hugged each child. "Why don't you go play and give Mama and Grandma some time to talk before I go back to the hospital."

"I call the Nintendo," Seth shouted as he ran into the other room.

"No fair. I want the Nintendo," Tara said.

"There are two controllers—share!" Cat called after them. Skylar wrapped her arms around Cat's leg. Cat brushed wisps of hair away from her forehead. "What about you, lovebug?"

"I'm tired."

"Come here, sweetie." Cat lifted Skylar into her arms and carried her into the living room. She laid her on the couch and tuned in a favorite cartoon on the television. "There. If you feel sleepy, you can just close your eyes. Okay?"

"Okay, Mama."

Cat went back to the kitchen and sat at the table. "I'm beat."

Cat's mother wrapped her arms around Cat and held her close. "I know this is hard for Billie, but I can't help but feel for you as well. Your father told me about your fainting spell at work. Caitlain, you know you need to think of yourself first. Otherwise, you won't be able to be there for everyone else. You're carrying a pretty heavy load right now. If you plan to go on at this pace, you'll need to eat and sleep to keep up your strength."

Cat leaned her head into Ida's arm. "I know, Mom. And you're right, it's been hard." Cat began to cry.

Ida held her closer. "Let it go, sweetheart. I know how difficult this must be for you."

"You don't know the half of it, Mom. Can you imagine Daddy waking up one day and not knowing who you are? I feel like I've lost everything."

"I know it feels that way right now, but it'll get better."

Cat closed her eyes. "I hope you're right, Mom. With everything I am, I hope you're right."

"I know I am. Now let me fix you some lunch."

Cat arrived back at the hospital in a very good mood, hoping Billie's session with Dr. Connor would continue to bring their relationship closer to what it was before her illness. She missed the warm, loving, affectionate woman Billie was. She craved the physical contact and the emotional balance they had together, and she was anticipating the day when all would be restored... *if it can be restored,* said a nagging voice at the back of her mind. Cat tried hard to ignore the voice as she rode the elevator to Billie's floor.

She strolled down the hallway, exchanging pleasantries with the nursing staff on her way by. As she approached Billie's room, she noticed several nurses and orderlies standing outside her door.

Cat's stomach did a flip-flop as she ran the remaining few steps to the room.

Cat pushed her way through the crowd until she made it into the room to find Doc and Laura trying to physically control Billie.

"Leave me alone!" Billie screamed.

"Billie, you need to calm down," Doc said.

Billie picked up the tube of hand cream on her bedside table and threw it at Doc, who effectively dodged it.

"Don't force me to restrain you, Billie," he said.

"Billie! Billie!" Cat yelled, drawing the attention of everyone in the room, including Billie, who immediately stopped the tirade. Cat was startled by the intense anger she saw in Billie's eyes.

"Caitlain," Doc said, "maybe you should leave. She's unstable right now, and I don't want her to hurt you."

"What happened?" she asked, as she watched Laura trying to get Billie back into some semblance of order on the bed.

"We don't know," Doc said. "She asked to use the phone earlier, and the next thing we knew, she was out of control. I don't know who she called, but it upset her."

Cat furrowed her brow and remembered the disconnected phone call Jen said was from Billie. "Daddy, I need to talk to her—alone."

"I'm not leaving you alone with her in this condition."

"Please. I have an idea about what might be bothering her. I need to talk to her alone."

Doc looked at her. "All right, but I'll be right outside the door. If I hear one thing I don't like, I'm coming back in here. Understand?"

Cat nodded and hugged him before approaching Billie's bed. Laura had just pulled the blankets back up to Billie's waist. Billie was calmer but still upset. Laura met Cat's eyes with an expression that clearly said, "Be careful," before she joined Doc in the hallway.

Knowing what Billie was capable of when she was angry, Cat kept herself out of arm's reach until she could determine what the problem was. "Billie?"

Billie continued to glare at her.

Cat took a step closer. "Billie, honey, want to tell me what's wrong?"

"Was it good?"

Cat was perplexed. "Was what good? I don't know what you're asking."

"With Jen. Was it good?" she said again, with even more anger in her voice than before.

Cat's eyebrows rose into her hairline. "Jen?" Getting angry herself, she put her hands on her hips and glared at Billie. "Just what do you think happened with Jen?"

Billie scowled at Cat. "Doesn't Jen have a life of her own? Doesn't she have a partner or something?"

"As a matter of fact, yes, she does."

"And how do they feel about your relationship with Jen?"

Cat crossed her arms in front of her chest. "My relationship? Billie, I'll ask you again—what do you think happened between Jen and me?"

"You fucked her," Billie yelled.

Cat was speechless. Anger rose in her gut as she launched herself over Billie, pinning her to the bed. She knew she was taking a risk, but her heart was ruling her senses at the moment, and she cast caution to the wind.

She sat astride Billie's legs, her hands on both shoulders, and pushed her back into the pillows. She leaned close until their noses were nearly touching and angrily said, "I did nothing of the sort. Do you understand? We're friends and nothing more. I love you. Don't you realize that yet? Are you so blinded by self-pity you can't see how much you mean to me? Jen is like my sister, nothing more. I love her dearly. I always will, but not the way I love you. I refuse to give up my friendship with her because you're being narrow-minded and pigheaded. Now get over it."

Billie's eyes misted. Her tears instantly melted Cat's anger. Cat released her and sat back on Billie's lap. She opened her arms, and Billie went readily into them. Billie rested her head on Cat's breasts and wrapped her arms around her body. Cat held her close to her heart.

"Shhh, it's okay. I love you. Don't ever doubt that," Cat said as she rocked her.

After a time, Cat released her and lowered her back against the inclined bed. She cupped Billie's face in one hand and leaned in to place a gentle featherlight kiss on Billie's mouth. "Do you want to tell me what started all this?"

"I called you at home. I missed you. Jen answered the phone. She said you were in the shower. She said both of you were sweaty."

Cat could see where this was leading. She thought back to what she had said to Jen while she was leaving. *Jen, thanks for everything. It was fun, and I really needed it. See you this afternoon, hon. Bye.* Cat was floored by how that must have sounded to a distraught Billie.

Cat took a deep breath. Her chest felt tight with emotion. "Billie, I went on one of Jen's power walks with her. She caught me just as I got home and talked me into going. After our walk, she came over and we had coffee together—nothing more. I went to take a shower while she finished her coffee before she left. You happened to call just as she was walking out the door."

Billie took Cat's hand in her own. "I'm sorry. I should have trusted you."

Cat traced Billie's right eyebrow and let her finger trail around and down the side of her face to her chin. She tilted Billie's head up and kissed her. "Yes, you should have, but to tell you the truth, I can understand why you were concerned. After all, you're just beginning to know me and trust me. I understand how you could've thought... But nothing happened. Let it go. Okay?"

"Okay," Billie said as the tears began to fall again.

"Well, I guess you don't need me today," a voice said from the doorway.

Dr. Connor was standing there, leaning against the doorframe.

Cat climbed off Billie's lap and sat on the side of the bed. Billie grabbed her hand and prevented her from moving farther away. "How long have you been standing there?" Cat asked.

"At about the point you put that wrestling hold on Billie and pinned her to the bed."

Cat grinned and blushed.

Dr. Connor continued. "Nice move, by the way. Are you two okay?"

Cat and Billie looked at each other then back at Dr. Connor. Both nodded.

"Okay then. I guess I'll see you tomorrow."

Cat and Billie were talking about the children's visit that evening when Jen poked her head into the room.

"Hi," she said.

Cat felt Billie tense. "I'll be right back." She rose from the bed, took Jen's hand, and led her out of the room.

When they reached the solarium at the end of the hall, Cat released Jen's hand and began pacing. Jen grabbed her on one of her many passes. "Want to tell me what's wrong?"

"Jen, Billie is jealous of you. Well, actually, she's jealous of the closeness you and I share."

"But... but, I have the same closeness with her. She has no reason to be jealous."

Cat placed her hand on Jen's arm. "You and I both know that, but we need to remember Billie's memories of our relationship—the one between the three of us—are no longer available for her to draw upon. All she sees is you hugging me, and me not pushing you away. She assumed I encourage your affections, and we have some sort of romantic relationship going on. Hell, after she spoke with you on the phone earlier today, she was convinced we slept together."

Jen gasped when Cat explained to her what happened after their phone call. "Cat, I'm so sorry."

"For what? You didn't do anything. Billie misinterpreted what you said."

Jen sat down on the edge of the couch. "I wish it was that simple."

"What does that mean?"

"Damn. How could I be so stupid?" Jen said. "I told her I was just leaving and you were in the shower because we were both pretty sweaty, but I neglected to tell her the sweat was from a power walk, not from a hot and wild lovemaking session."

"Jen, it's not your fault if she misinterpreted what you said."

Jen stood up and paced across the room a couple of times before stopping in front of Cat. "I was purposely vague. I left out the details. I wanted to make Billie jealous."

Cat's voice raised three octaves. "Why the hell would you want to do that?"

"Well, I was kind of aware of the jealousy thing. I've been sensing for a while now that she's uncomfortable when I'm around. I was hoping to use it to spur some memories, to push her into admitting how she feels about you. I'm sorry. It sounds like I really screwed things up."

"No, Jen, you didn't screw things up. I think your plan worked. It's just her reaction was a little more volatile than is healthy for her."

"I'm sorry. I'll back off. Maybe I should go home and let you two be alone."

Cat took Jen's hand. "No. I want you to stay, and I don't want you to change the way you are around Billie and me. Please don't change. It is one of your most endearing qualities. I've told Billie how I feel about our friendship. She already knows I'm not willing to give that up."

Jen's voice was choked with emotion. "I don't want to cause problems between you two."

"Billie has to realize there's no threat here. The old Billie knew that. The new Billie has to learn it as well."

Jen whispered, "I'm sorry."

Cat wrapped her arms around Jen. "Well, I'm sorry too—sorry life sucks so much right now for all of us, but it's bound to get better. I know it will."

Cat stepped back and wiped a tear from her eye. "Let's go face the music."

Jen tensed as they entered the room. Sensing this, Cat squeezed her hand. "Just go with it," Cat whispered.

Jen released Cat's hand and walked right up to Billie, sat on the edge of the bed, and leaned in to kiss her on the mouth. "How are you feeling, tough guy?"

Billie couldn't help but smile at her boldness. Surely Cat told her about the misunderstanding. "I'm fine. Thanks."

"Cat tells me you're just about ready to run the hundred-yard dash down the hallway. Is that true?"

Billie willed herself to relax. For Cat, she thought and grinned. "Want to race?"

"Billie, you know the rules, No running in the hallways," Laura said from the doorway.

"Geesh, Laura, you're no fun," Billie said as Laura pulled her walker around in front of her.

Laura looked at Jen. "Hi, Jen. Have you come to see Miss Show Off strut her stuff?"

Jen raised her eyebrows. "Strut?"

"Hey, I've got to do something to draw attention away from my bald head."

Jen planted a kiss on top of Billie's head. "I kind of like your bald head, my friend."

"All right, missy, let's go." Laura grabbed Billie's hat and planted it on her head before holding the walker for her to pull herself up.

Soon, the entourage headed down the hall, stopping at the solarium for a breather. Billie made two round-trips, and they returned to her room.

"Well," Jen said as she perched on the arm of Billie's chair, "I've got to get home and get dinner for the family." She leaned in and placed a kiss on Billie's head. "I'm proud of you, girl, and I love you very much. You know that, don't you?"

Billie just nodded.

Jen rose to her feet and opened her arms to Cat. She held her close for several moments before releasing her. "Walk me to the elevator?"

Cat leaned in and kissed Billie on the cheek. "I'll be right back." She locked arms with Jen and walked out of the room.

Doc arrived with the kids after dinner. While Tara and Skylar climbed into Billie's lap in the chair, Seth hid behind Cat.

After several minutes of hugs and kisses, the girls climbed out of Billie's lap and onto her bed to play with the bed controls. Seth, still hiding behind Cat, pushed her in front of him as they walked over to Billie. Billie drew her brows together as she watched him maneuver his way over to her.

"All right, scout, what's up?"

Cat took a step sideways, exposing Seth to his mother. He reached up and removed the baseball cap he was wearing.

Billie's eyes flew open. "You shaved your head!"

"Yep. Just like you."

Billie brought her hand up to her mouth and laughed, then opened her arms to him. She held him close and whispered into his ear, "Thank you. That was so sweet."

"Grandpa took me to get it cut."

Billie looked over at Doc, who was studying her chart. "Oh, he did, did he?" She caught Doc's eye and winked at him. "Well, I like it."

Several times through the visit, Cat saw glimpses of the old Billie come through: small signs, gestures, expressions, terms of endearment she most often used with them. It was apparent her body was starting to remember, but her mind was still resisting. All in all, the signs were positive. Cat realized that only with the children did Billie really relax.

I've got to get her home. I just know things will improve once she's home.

Finally, it was time for the children to leave. After hugs and kisses, they said their good nights, leaving Cat and Billie alone in her room.

Billie yawned, signaling the end of a long and tiring day. "I'm beat." She rubbed her hand over her eyes.

"Are you all right?" Cat asked. "You don't have another headache, do you?"

"No. I'm just tired." Billie yawned once more. "How about helping me to bed?"

"Now that's an invitation I can't refuse. I'll take you to bed any day."

A sudden tension fell between them as their eyes met. It was on the tip of Cat's tongue to apologize for her comment, but instead, she adopted a wait-and-see attitude.

"Cat, I... Maybe you should go home and sleep in your own bed tonight. I know you're not sleeping well with us crammed together on this small bed."

Cat's first instinct was to refuse, but Billie was offering her a convenient escape from the tense situation she had created with her careless comment, and she did the very thing she so didn't want to do. She agreed to go home.

After feigning a yawn and a stretch, Cat assisted Billie from the chair to her bed and tucked her in for the night. Leaning in, she intended to kiss Billie on the lips, only to brush her cheek when Billie turned her head at the last moment.

Cat stepped back and tried to hide the awkwardness. "All right then. I guess I'll be going. I'm scheduled to anesthetize a surgery tomorrow morning, so I'll stop in before I scrub to say hi. I'll see you in the morning. Sleep well, my love."

Cat chided herself all the way home for the verbal slip that made Billie so uncomfortable. Up to that point, things had been progressing in the right direction. Billie had stopped pulling away every time she touched her. She even allowed Cat to kiss her without recoiling. Cat surmised the growing familiarity between them caused her to forget Billie still felt uncomfortable with her insistence they were lovers.

She pulled into the driveway, stopped the engine, and rested her forehead on the steering wheel. Intense sadness washed over her as despair filled her heart and mind. She sat in the dark for a long time, fearing that one careless comment had destroyed all the trust and comfort she had worked so hard to build between herself and Billie since the operation.

Feeling chilled, she climbed out of the car and went into the house, only to find herself pacing across the living room, too restless to sleep and too distracted to focus on a book or television show. The minutes ticked by as she paced. By eight o'clock, she was climbing out of her skin and anxiety had a firm hold on her stomach.

"Get a grip, Cat," she said to herself. "You'll be of no use to Billie if you work yourself into a stupor. So you opened your mouth and inserted your foot—so what? Get over it." She tried to convince herself she hadn't ruined her chances with Billie.

When she couldn't take it anymore, she picked up the phone. "Jen?" she asked when her friend answered the phone. "Jen…" Cat didn't know what to say or even why she had called her.

"Cat, where are you?"

"Home."

An audible click was heard as the phone fell silent. Cat stared at the receiver, trying to decide whether she should call Jen back.

The decision to make a second call became unnecessary as the kitchen door swung open. "Come here, you," Jen said as Cat rushed into her embrace. "Now tell me what happened."

"I blew it. I blew it."

"What do you mean, you blew it?"

Cat broke away from Jen's embrace and wiped her tears with the sleeve of her shirt. "Billie made a comment tonight about being tired and asked me to help her to bed, and stupid old me had to make light of it with an off-color remark of my own, one that left no doubt as to how willing I was to take her to bed."

A small grin appeared at the corners of Jen's mouth. "I see. So, how does that constitute 'blowing it'?"

"Well, considering she asked me to leave, I guess that pretty much speaks volumes, you think?"

"She asked you to leave?"

"Well, she didn't exactly tell me to go. She suggested I might want to go home and sleep in my own bed. She thought I would be more comfortable here at home than crammed into the small hospital bed with her. At least that's the excuse she used."

"And you don't believe her?"

Cat started pacing the kitchen floor. "You should have seen her face when I made the sexual comment. She was like a deer caught in the headlights. No, I don't believe her. I think it was a convenient excuse to send me home and avoid confronting the intimacy issue."

Jen crossed her arms and shifted her weight to one hip. "And here you are, at home right where she wants you to be. Since when did you lose your backbone?"

Cat stopped pacing and narrowed her eyes.

"Don't you give me that look. I'm not the bad guy here, at least not this time. Who are you more angry with right now, Billie or yourself?"

Cat reacted like someone had thrown cold water in her face as she understood what Jen was trying to tell her. She grabbed her car keys, hugged and thanked Jen for once again being there when she needed her, and headed out the door.

Chapter 35

Billie was awakened the next morning by an elbow in her ribs. "Umph. What the hell?" she muttered under her breath as she rolled over and realized Cat was in bed with her. Being careful not to wake her, she maneuvered herself onto her back, raised both arms above her head, and rested them on the pillow. Staring at the ceiling, she went over the sequence of events that ended with Cat leaving the hospital the night before.

It had still been early, not even seven p.m., but an exhausting afternoon PT combined with a visit from the children had wiped out Billie's reserves. She was falling asleep in her chair and asked Cat to help her to bed, which Cat apparently saw as an invitation, considering Cat's suggestive comments. Billie did the only thing she could think of at the time. She asked Cat to leave. It was a request she regretted almost as soon as it was made.

After Cat left, Billie lay awake. She stared at the ceiling and fought with the emotions and feelings that seemed both alien and familiar to her at the same time. A burning sensation formed in the center of her abdomen. Her legs weakened, and her respiration became choppy. An undeniable tension ran rampant through her body, and she couldn't relax as she watched the minutes tick by on the clock beside her bed. After an hour, the feelings subsided and she willed her body to sleep.

Now, several hours later, she found herself once again lying awake, tension gripping her midsection, only this time, the source of her discomfort was a mere hair's-breadth away.

Daring a glance, Billie realized Cat was awake. "I thought you went home last night."

Cat pushed herself upright and off the bed. "Good morning to you, too."

"I'm sorry. Where are my manners? Good morning," Billy said, hoping to repair any damage she might have caused by her abruptness.

Cat went into the bathroom without responding.

"Shit," Billie said as the door closed behind Cat. "Damn it. Why does this have to be so hard?"

A few minutes later, Cat emerged and climbed onto the foot of Billie's bed. She sat cross-legged in front of Billie and rested her elbows on bent knees. "It almost worked."

Billie was confused. "What almost worked?"

"You sending me home last night. It almost worked. I paced across the living room beating myself up for what I thought was an inappropriate comment, until someone talked some sense into me."

"Jen?" Billie asked sarcastically.

"Yes, Jen. Nice try, but you ain't getting rid of this chick so easily next time." Cat leaned forward. "Like it or not, you're my wife, and yes, I would like nothing more than to take you to bed and make love to you all night. You may not remember it right now, but our physical relationship is almost as important to us as our emotional one, and I, for one, miss it."

Billie avoided Cat's eyes.

"Billie, look at me," Cat said. "I'm sorry if I made you feel uncomfortable yesterday, and I'll try not to do that again, but let me make one thing very clear. I will never again allow you to chase me away. You got that?"

Billie nodded while trying hard to ignore the feelings of arousal brewing deep within her soul.

"Okay, Billie, on your feet," Joseph said.

Billie planted her feet on the floor and, using the walker, pulled herself off the bed into a standing position.

"All right, hold on to my shoulders."

"I don't think I'm ready for this."

Joseph bent over the walker. "Don't be a coward. You've been cruising the hallways for three days now on this thing. It's time you give it up and move on."

Billie was uncertain and held fast to the walker.

"I'm going to count to three, then I'm going to pull the walker away, so you'd better be holding my shoulders by then."

Billie maintained eye contact with him and wondered whether she should call his bluff.

"One, two, thr..."

Billie let go of the walker and grabbed Joseph's shoulders. She made no attempt to mask the anxiety on her face.

"Good girl. We're going to try out some crutches today. Laura…" he said.

Laura handed a pair of forearm crutches to Joseph and took the walker away.

"All right, these cuffs fit around your forearms like this." He fit a cuff of one crutch onto her right arm as she continued to hold his shoulders.

Once he had the cuff attached, he motioned for Laura to join him. Laura held onto Billie's belt while Joseph lowered the first crutch to the floor.

"Okay, hold on to the grip and let the crutch help you balance while we attach the other one. Laura's gripping the belt. You won't fall."

Billie teetered toward the crutch side. She could feel the belt tighten around her midsection. Laura applied pressure to keep her upright as she struggled to maintain her balance. Joseph attached the second cuff and lowered the crutch to the floor. Billie, her forehead drawn and tense, concentrated on balancing on two support points, rather than the four afforded her by the walker.

"Okay, try to regain your balance, using the crutches as anchoring points. Try not to lean on them. That's it, stand up straight. Good," he said as she brought herself up to her full height. "Over the past several days you've gained a great deal of control over your leg muscles, so you shouldn't have much trouble moving them forward on command. What we need to work on is balance and your sense of rhythm while you walk," Joseph said. "Do you understand?"

"Yes, I think so."

"All right. Let's get started. When you move forward, you'll need to move the opposite crutch. In other words, you move the left leg and right crutch together, and vice versa. Okay so far?"

Billie nodded.

"Good. Laura's holding onto the belt, and I'll be here in front of you, so don't be afraid of falling over. Now, let's go, left foot, right crutch."

Billie teetered side to side but managed to keep her balance. She looked at Joseph in awe. She redistributed her weight to her left leg and moved the right foot and left crutch together. Again, she teetered, but didn't fall. She grinned. Five minutes later, she managed to move ten feet across the room.

When she reached the other side, Joseph wrapped his arm around her waist to give her extra support as she pivoted around. Within minutes, she walked back to the edge of the bed where she started.

"Can we go again?" Billie asked.

"Sure." Joseph led her to the other side of the room and back once again. "Okay, let's walk over here to the chair and learn how to get on and off your feet using the crutches."

For the next half hour, with Joseph on one side and Laura on the other, Billie practiced raising and lowering herself in and out of the chair. She did fine while they held her arms, but the moment she tried getting up on her own, she lost her balance and fell forward into Joseph's arms.

"Keep your weight over your legs. Don't lean forward," Joseph said.

After several more failed attempts, she managed to lift herself out of the chair and stand erect. By the time she accomplished this much, a sheen of sweat covered her body. Exhausted, she lowered herself into the chair and called it quits for the morning.

Joseph squeezed her shoulder. "You're doing a great job. Keep it up, and you'll be out of here in no time."

"Thanks," she said and watched him leave.

Before Laura left, she moved the walker within Billie's reach. "No trying the crutches on your own for a while, okay? You've gotten pretty good with the walker, so as long as you have someone to walk with you, go ahead and use it, but stay off the crutches unless Joseph or I am with you. All right?"

"Got it."

"Okay then. I'll see you later this afternoon. Maybe we can take it down the hall if you're up to it."

Cat had not returned from work by the time Billie's lunch arrived. She ate alone in silence and thought about everything that had happened to her in the nine or ten days since she'd been in the hospital.

She found it incredible she was involved with someone like Cat. When she first woke up, she didn't remember being attracted to women. As she began remembering who she was, her sense of self returned but without memories of Cat. Over the past few days, she realized what she was feeling for Cat was not sisterly affection. She felt different around her. Cat made her feel special, wanted, loved.

She was also beginning to feel stirrings at the very center of her being that she tried to suppress, but as of late—especially after Cat read her the riot act that morning—the stirrings had become too strong to deny.

She looked forward to waking up each morning next to Cat. Sending Cat home the night before was something she regretted as soon as the suggestion passed her lips. She was glad Cat came back during the night.

She loved sharing a bed with Cat. Sometimes she woke up before her and just enjoyed the feel of Cat's head on her shoulder. The aroma of Cat's jasmine shampoo sent tentacles of warmth straight to her heart. Sometimes she could sense Cat looking at her. She reveled in the attention but didn't let on she was aware of the voyeurism. She loved the way her skin tingled when Cat touched her, the way her heart skipped a beat when she hugged her, the way fingers of warmth spread through her when Cat kissed her.

She loved to watch Cat with the children. It made her heart soar to realize Cat treated Seth like he was her own flesh and blood. Billie hated the way she felt when others were affectionate with Cat—especially Jen. She hated the feeling of loneliness when she was away from her for long periods of time—like now.

Billie leaned back in the chair. "My God," she said out loud. "I'm in love with her. I love her. I do. I love her!" Her heart pounded with excitement as she let herself acknowledge the fact. "I love her," she said again, liking the sound of it.

Billie had no way of knowing how long she sat there, a stupid grin on her face, before Dr. Connor arrived.

"A penny for your thoughts," Dr. Connor said from somewhere in front of her.

Billie's eyes focused on her. "I didn't even notice you come in. Please sit down."

"Will Cat be joining us?"

"I don't know. She had surgery this morning. She hasn't come back yet."

"I see. You had a very happy expression on your face when I came in. Want to tell me about it?"

"I love her."

Dr. Connor folded her arms across her chest. "I know."

Billie was still smiling when Laura arrived for her afternoon PT.

Laura placed the crutches in front of Billie and held her elbow as she rose to her feet. When Billie was standing, and they were face-to-face, Laura touched her cheek and said, "So, you've finally realized it, huh?"

"Realized what?"

"Cat?" Laura said.

Billie blushed.

"Thought so." Laura tightened the belt around Billie's waist. "Okay, let's get to work. We've got a redhead to impress."

For the first fifteen minutes, Billie practiced moving around in her room on the crutches. When she was more sure of herself, they ventured into the hall. It didn't take long for Billie to set up a cadence, making jerky but continuous progress down the hall. A full half hour later, she reached the solarium where she sat down to rest before making the long trek back to her room.

Cat rushed back to Billie's room from the OR. The surgery she anesthetized that morning was long and difficult, and at one point, the surgeons almost lost the patient. The expected four-hour surgery lasted eight, but now Cat was free for the rest of the day.

When Cat reached Billie's room, she found it empty. She checked her watch. It was time for Billie's afternoon PT. As she stepped into the hallway, she saw Billie and Laura making their way back toward Billie's room. Cat was surprised to see Billie on crutches instead of her walker.

She was drawn like a magnet toward Billie, walking in her direction until she was standing in front of her. They stopped and looked at each other, both of them oblivious to Laura, who stood off to the side, providing Billie with gentle support with her handhold on the belt. Cat caressed the side of Billie's face, and Billie leaned into the touch.

Cat's eyes misted over with happiness. "I'm so proud of you."

Billie's forearm cuff pivoted as she released the hand grip and cupped Cat's cheek. "We have to talk."

Without breaking eye contact, Cat nodded. "Yes, we do."

The sound of Laura clearing her throat reminded them they had company. "Okay, ladies. What do you say we finish our walk and you'll have the rest of the day to spend together?"

Billie made her way back to her room, with Cat and Laura in tow. Laura helped her into bed and ran her through a series of stretching exercises. She gave her a thorough massage and rubbed the soreness out of her much-abused muscles before leaving for the evening.

Laura left Billie on the bed with the head of it raised so she was sitting up. When they were alone, Cat shut the door and pulled the chair up to the side of the bed, but Billie patted the bed. Cat sat where Billie indicated.

Billie took one of Cat's hands, placed Cat's palm into hers, and closed her fingers around it. "Nice fit, huh?"

Cat studied their entwined fingers. "Yes, it is."

"Cat?"

Cat's gaze rose to meet Billie's. "Yes?"

"Cat, I love you."

Cat caught her breath. "Are you sure?"

Billie nodded. "Very sure."

Cat cupped the side of Billie's face. "Do you love the Cat you see before you now, or the one you met five years ago?"

Billie's eyes clouded over. "I don't know the Cat I met five years ago. I'm sorry, but I still don't remember you—or us."

Cat closed her eyes to hide her disappointment. She inhaled deeply to regain control of her emotions then opened them once more.

"I'm sorry," Billie said.

Cat kissed her. "At least it's a start," she said before once more claiming Billie's mouth in a searing kiss that left them both breathless.

Chapter 36

Billie screeched the car to a halt in the parking lot and ran into the building. She scaled the stairs, three steps at a time. The apartment door was ajar. Her first thoughts were for the children. She ran to each of their rooms but found them asleep in their beds.

She raced toward their bedroom. "Cat! Cat, where are you?" She pushed the door open. The scene before her overwhelmed her senses as an uncontrollable rage filled her heart and mind. She pounced on Brian, who was in the process of zipping his trousers.

Billie landed a roundhouse kick to Brian's chin. He slammed into the wall but stayed on his feet. "You bastard! You son of a bitch! I'll kill you!" She jammed her elbow into his solar plexus. He gasped for air and retched the contents of his stomach all over the floor. He made a break for the door. She swung her leg again and hit him square on his nose. He was airborne briefly, then slammed into the bathroom door and sank to the floor, unconscious.

"Billie! No!"

Billie bolted upright. Sweat poured down her face, and her body trembled. Her eyes were wild with terror. She looked around frantically and found Cat lying on her side next to her, sleeping. Billie took a few minutes to bring her breathing under control before she reached over and touched Cat's shoulder, assuring herself she was really there, and safe.

She lay back down on the bed, covered her eyes with her arm, and tried to remember the dream. Cat... Brian... rape... feelings of murderous rage, but no more than that. All she could see were glimpses in time. She rolled over to spoon herself behind Cat and pulled her close. *I'm scared, Cat. I need to remember. We can't be whole until I do.*

Cat lay with her back to Billie, her eyes wide open. She felt Billie bolt awake but fought the urge to react. She hoped with all her heart Billie had been startled from a sound sleep by a memory, and she waited for Billie to wake her, to no avail. All she felt was Billie's light touch on her shoulder before being enveloped in her arms.

Lying there, wrapped within Billie's arms, she felt safe and warm in the present but far from certain about their future. Billie loved her. She said as much, but without the years of memories they had built together, Cat wasn't sure they could rebuild the same beautiful relationship they enjoyed before. Their present was built on their past. Without the past to shape their future, she fretted it would never be the same.

She closed her eyes and mourned the loss of her life with Billie. They spent years building their lives together and forming the incredible bond they shared. Gone were the precious memories: the moment Skylar was born, screaming and kicking in protest while announcing her presence to the world; attending Seth's Little League games and seeing the pride in Billie's eyes as she watched him; Tara asking her if Santa would still know who she was after her name was changed to Charland; the vows they had shared when they pledged their lives together in front of family and friends; the intense feeling of pride and accomplishment she felt when Billie reversed the state's ban on same-sex marriage. All of this was lost—all of this and more.

An intense feeling of hopelessness washed over her. *Please come back to me, Billie. I need you—all of you.* She willed herself to relax and enjoy the feel of Billie's arms around her. Slowly, she fell into a tortured sleep.

Cat was scheduled for surgery every morning for the rest of the week. While she worked, Billie put all her energy into her therapy. Over the next two and a half days, she gained enough mobility and balance on the crutches that Laura no longer maintained a constant hold on the belt. At the end of each day, Laura stretched and massaged Billie's limbs before leaving her in Cat's care. Evenings were spent cuddling and talking, or lying in each other's arms, enjoying the closeness.

Billie's OT and speech therapy sessions were discontinued, and sessions with Dr. Connor were reduced to every other day. With Cat in surgery, Billie attended these alone. In one particularly grueling session, she told Dr. Connor about the dream she had.

"It was horrible. I found myself rushing home from work. Fear gripped my chest, and I couldn't breathe. Somehow I knew Cat was in trouble. I burst into our bedroom and found my ex-husband, Brian, had raped her." Billie tried hard to hold the tears back as she wrapped her arms around her midsection.

"How did you react to that?" Dr. Connor asked.

"I nearly killed him. My martial arts training kicked in, and I beat the shit out of him. Cat stopped me, or I might have crossed the line. At that point, I woke up, terrified."

"So, tell me, do you think this was only a dream, or was it a memory?"

"I don't know for sure. Cat told me Brian had raped her. That was how Skylar was conceived, but Cat spared me the details of the rape, so I don't know if what I dreamed was recall or my mind's fabrication of what the rape might have been like for Cat."

"Have you told her about the dream?"

"No."

"Why not?"

Billie wiped tears from her cheeks with the back of her hand and sniffled before replying. "Cat wants our lives to be the way they were before. She wants me to regain all memory of us—of our lives together. It tears my heart out each time I have to tell her I don't remember. I can't bear to see the pain in her eyes. I refuse to hurt her any more. That's why I didn't tell her."

Dr. Connor covered one of Billie's hands with her own. "Keeping things like this from Cat won't lessen her pain. It will only serve to heighten it if she believes you don't trust her to handle it. Cat's a strong woman. She loves you with every fiber of her being. A blind man could see that."

Billie shifted under Dr. Connor's scrutiny.

"You know, Cat may be able to help you if you let her."

"What do you mean?"

"If this incident was indeed recall, and not just a dream, Cat would have been there. Talk to her about it. She'll be able to validate for you whether this is real or fabrication."

Billie narrowed her eyes. "Doc, how long ago did Cat and I begin seeing you?"

"Let's see, it's been almost five years. Why do you ask?"

"If the dream is true, it would've happened just about then. Wouldn't we have talked to you about it?"

Dr. Connor folded her hands in her lap. "It's not for me to say whether this incident was real or not. What I can say is this… if Cat confirms this is recall and not just a dream, it's a memory you share. She's the best person to help you deal with the details of it."

"And if it's not a memory?"

"You and Cat must understand permanent memory loss is a very real possibility. If that happens, you'll have to accept the past is gone and begin building the future on new memories. That may be something you'll both have to decide whether you can live with."

Billie frowned as Dr. Connor's meaning sunk in. "Are you saying Cat may not be able to live with it if the memory loss is permanent?"

"As painful as it sounds, yes, that's a real possibility."

Billie brought both hands to her face as she allowed the dam holding back her tears to burst. Dr. Connor waited while Billie let down her guard and released the feelings she'd been holding inside for days.

"I can't lose her. She's my lifeline."

Dr. Connor rubbed Billie's back. "Talk to her about the dream, Billie. If it is real, then there's hope the rest of your memories will return, but if it isn't, both you and Cat will have to focus on what's ahead rather than dwelling on what's lost. If you love her and she loves you, there's a very good chance you'll be able to work this out together."

* * *

Bright and early Thursday morning, on Billie's fifteenth day in the hospital, Joseph showed up at Billie's room, just after Cat left for work.

"Good morning," Joseph said.

Billie sat on the edge of the bed eating the last of her breakfast. "Joseph. To what do I owe this honor? Where's Laura?"

"Laura's preparing the PT room for your therapy. I'm here to escort you there, but first, we have a little exercise to do."

"Exercise?"

Joseph walked over to Billie and moved her breakfast tray out of the way. He held out his hands to her. She placed her hands in his and pulled herself into a standing position.

"All right, balance yourself," he said.

While Billie concentrated on keeping her balance, Joseph released one of her hands. Fear overwhelmed her when she realized what he was planning to do. He released her other hand and she looked down at her feet. Joseph grabbed her by the shoulders, when she started to teeter, and steadied her. "No. Look here," he said, pointing to his eyes.

Once again, while maintaining steady eye contact, he released her. For long moments, she stood on her own with no support from a walker or crutches or Joseph. When her balance started to weaken, he grasped her shoulders.

"Well, Billie. If today's therapy sessions go as well as this, you might be going home tomorrow."

Billie's eyes widened. "Home?" she asked as she accepted the crutches from Joseph.

"Billie, that's wonderful news!"

Billie looked beyond Joseph to see Jen standing in the doorway. "Hi," she said as Jen crossed the room and hugged her. "Cat's working this morning."

"I know. I'm here to see you, not Cat. Want some company during your PT?"

"Sure."

Billie's PT that morning consisted of stair-climbing techniques. Cat had provided a description of their home to Joseph very early on. She pointed out potential problems with the stairs to the family room in the basement and to the bedrooms on the second floor.

Billie scanned the layout of the PT room and noted Laura set up two configurations of stairs, one with railings and one without. "I'm not sure I can do this, Joseph."

"Of course you can," Joseph said. "Stair climbing requires a combination of three components: muscle strength, muscle control, and balance. You stayed in shape through regular aerobic exercise and running prior to your illness, so you should have more than enough muscle strength to do this. We've also been working on your balance for the past two weeks. All we have to do is combine those components to negotiate the stairs. You can do it, Billie. I know you can. Do you have any questions?"

Billie shook her head.

"Okay then. Let's get started."

In no time, Billie mastered the stairs with railings, as she was able to use her arms to help pull herself up and to restrain her descent down the stairs. The stairs without railings were more difficult. Billie worked very hard, while Jen watched. For two hours, Billie concentrated on climbing up and down the stairs with crutches as Laura stood close by to catch her should she stumble. Finally, Joseph called a halt and sent her back to her room. Jen followed close behind.

Laura left Billie sitting in the chair by the window while Jen sat on the edge of the bed facing her. Billie was very quiet.

"Are you all right, Billie?"

Billie frowned at Jen. "I'm sorry, what did you say?"

"You're nervous about going home, aren't you?"

"Yes, I am."

Jen knelt in front of Billie, took her hands in her own, and sat back on her heels. "It'll be all right, you know. Cat loves you very much. I know she'll make it as comfortable for you as possible. Don't be afraid."

"I still don't remember her. I don't remember you or the girls. I'm afraid I never will." Her eyes misted over.

Jen reached up and smoothed the worry lines from Billie's brow. "I think being home will help. You'll be in familiar surroundings. Maybe it'll prompt memory recall. But if it doesn't, if for some reason, your memory fails to come back, know you'll be among people who love you."

Billie just nodded.

Just then, Billie's lunch arrived.

Jen rose to her feet and placed a gentle kiss on Billie's head. "I've got to go. There's something I need to do before tomorrow. Tell Cat I stopped by and to give me a call tonight, okay?"

Billie nodded as Jen kissed her again. "Love you, big guy. I'll see you tomorrow."

Cat arrived at Billie's room just as she finished her lunch. She kissed Billie on the lips. "Hi. How was PT this morning?"

"Stair climbing."

"I'm sorry I missed it."

"That's okay, Jen was there. Oh, and by the way, she wants you to call her later."

"Okay. Thanks for letting me know."

Billie seemed withdrawn and quiet. The expression on her face worried Cat.

"Billie, What are you afraid of? I can see the fear in your eyes."

"Joseph said I'll probably be able to go home tomorrow."

"That's wonderful! I can't wait to have you home. The kids will be thrilled." Cat hugged her.

Cat pulled back when she realized Billie was unresponsive. "Billie?" She searched Billie's face for some clue about how she was feeling. "What's wrong?"

"I… I don't know if I belong there. I still don't remember you. It isn't fair to burden you with this."

Cat was angry. She walked a couple paces away. "Damn it, Billie. Of course you belong with us. There's no way you'll be a burden on us. How dare you even suggest such a thing?" Cat approached Billie and knelt down in front of her. She took Billie's hands in her own. "Sweetheart, I'm thrilled you're coming home tomorrow. I just know you'll recover faster there. Please give us a chance. What have you got to lose?"

"It's what you've got to lose that I'm afraid of. What if I never remember? What then?"

"You said you loved me. Do you, or were you just telling me something you think I wanted to hear?"

Billie's brows knit together. "I do love you. I don't know why, but I feel as though I always have. I just don't know you. That terrifies me," she said. "I'm afraid, Cat. I'm afraid."

Cat placed her fingertips under Billie's chin and lifted her face until their eyes met. "Well, that makes two of us." A play of emotions ran across Billie's face.

"I have something to tell you," Billie said.

"What is it?"

"I had a dream the other night. At least I think it was a dream."

"Tell me about it. Please."

Billie held Cat's gaze with her own. "Was I there when Brian raped you?"

Cat gasped as the question left Billie's lips. She regained her composure before answering. "You weren't there during the rape. You came in just after it was over."

"What did I do?"

"You kicked his ass clear across the room. You nearly killed him. I think you might have if I hadn't stopped you."

Billie squeezed Cat's hands as a tear fell from her eyes onto their entwined fingers.

"What is it, Billie?"

Billie smiled through a cloud of tears. "My dream was real. It wasn't a dream at all. It was a memory."

Laura came to collect Billie for her afternoon PT while Cat discussed her discharge with Doc and arranged to schedule her own vacation time for the next two weeks. After the paperwork was finished, she called Art to let him know Billie would be going home the next day, and he was free to visit whenever he wanted. The last call she made was to Jen.

"Hello?"

"Hi, Jen. It's Cat."

"Oh, I'm glad you called. I see you got my message. So you must know by now Billie's being released tomorrow."

"Yes, and by the way, thanks for spending time with her today. I hated that I had to work this week. I missed a lot of her PT sessions. In fact, she's in one now that I need to run to as soon as I'm finished with you."

"No problem. Hey, I was thinking I could pick your kids up tomorrow from your mom's, and Fred and I could arrange a coming-home party for Billie. What do you think? We could have a small cookout in the backyard. Just our two families. Anything else might overwhelm her."

"I think that's a great idea. You might want to warn Fred, Stevie, and Karissa, that Billie might not recognize them."

"They already know. I've been keeping them up-to-date on Billie's progress while she's been in the hospital. I'll get the ball rolling on this end."

"Jen, what would I do without you? You're such a wonderful friend."

"Oh pshaw. Enough of the mushy stuff. You know how I feel about you guys. In fact, the big guy better get her act together and get her memory back, 'cause if she doesn't, you're mine. You got that?"

Cat laughed. "You're such a nut," she said before remembering her conversation with Billie earlier in the day. "Speaking of Billie getting her memory back, she had a dream— well, it was actually a recall. She remembers kicking the shit out of Brian after she walked in on the rape."

"Just like Billie to start with one of the most difficult memories. That's great news. Let's hope it's a sign of more to come."

"Keep your fingers crossed that it is."

"Fingers, toes, even my ringlets will be crossed," Jen said. "Okay, sweetie, I know you want to get back to the PT session. Oh, oh, oh, wait a minute, I almost forgot. Billie is worried and nervous about coming home tomorrow. You might want to talk to her about it tonight."

"I've already talked to her. She's more than nervous, she's downright scared. This isn't going to be easy. It's going to take a lot of time and patience. I just hope she comes back to us. The dream is a good start. I miss her." Cat's voice choked up at the end.

"Don't lose faith, all right? I have a good feeling about this. You'll see. Keep your chin up."

"I will. Thanks for listening. I'll call you tomorrow when I know what time we'll be coming home. I'll talk to you later. Goodbye."

Billie's PT went well. In addition to stair climbing, she practiced walking through the parallel bars. Using a minimum amount of support from the railings, she concentrated on keeping her balance as she placed one foot in front of the other through the length of the bars. Cat stood off to the side with Joseph, and Laura walked behind Billie, ready to reach out and support her if necessary. The going was very slow, but she managed to get through with only the lightest touch of her fingertips on the rails. It would be some time yet before she would be able to walk unassisted, but it was an encouraging start.

After the session was over, Billie climbed onto her bed and lay back to wait for the stretching exercises and massage to begin. Laura approached her and stood beside the bed, her arms crossed as though in thought.

"Cat, come here, will you?" Laura said.

Cat approached the bed.

"Since you're the one who'll be doing this for her at home, you might want to participate in this session."

"Are you sure?"

"It's okay. You've been watching me for two weeks. You should know what to do by now. Here, let me help you get started." Laura came around behind Cat and took her hands to direct her in how to exercise and massage Billie's muscles. After a few moments, Cat took over while Laura released her and stepped off to the side to watch, providing verbal direction every now and then.

Billie enjoyed the rubdown. She closed her eyes and savored the feelings and emotions Cat generated with her hands.

For her part, Cat tried very hard to keep the massage as clinical as possible. Her goal was to provide therapeutic relief, not sexual stimulation. However, glancing at Billie's face, she wasn't sure which one she was accomplishing. By the end of the massage, she was very warm, her face was flushed, and her heart beat rapidly in her chest. *This is one job that's going to be very difficult to get through each night.* She took a step away from the bed and noticed the disappointed expression on Billie's face.

"Good job, Cat," Laura said when she finished. "Don't you think so, Billie?"

"Oh, yeah," Billie said in such a way it was obvious what she thought about the rubdown.

Cat blushed and looked everywhere but at Laura.

Later that evening, Cat and Billie lay in each other's arms, too nervous about Billie going home the next day for either of them to sleep.

"Jen's going to pick the kids up and bring them home for us tomorrow," Cat said.

Billie nodded.

"Sweetheart, I know you're nervous. I'm nervous too."

"What's the house like?" Billie asked.

Cat climbed off the bed and grabbed the pad of paper and pencil Dr. Connor had left for Billie to write down her feelings. She sat cross-legged beside Billie and drew out the floor plan of all three levels of their house.

"The main floor of the house holds the living room, a big eat-in kitchen, bathroom, and a guest room. We'll have to avoid the family room for a while, since it's in the basement. I don't think you're quite ready for that flight of stairs. All of the bedrooms are on the second floor, as well as a second bathroom. Since our bedroom is one flight up, you'll have to stay in the first floor guest room for a few days."

Cat noticed Billie tense when she mentioned their bedroom. She let it pass without comment. *No pressure, Cat. No pressure.*

"An open porch with a bench swing graces the front of the house, while the back has a closed-in porch. We've shared many wonderful evenings on the back porch watching violent thunder and lightning storms."

"We watch storms?"

Cat wiggled her eyebrows. "Oh, yeah. An intense thunderstorm is quite stimulating, if you know what I mean."

Cat was making Billie uncomfortable with her remarks, so she changed the subject.

"We have a fenced-in backyard, complete with a tree house. You put a lot of time and effort into fixing it up for the kids. You even installed a manual rope elevator for them."

"I did?"

"Absolutely. Oh, before I forget, Jen and Fred are organizing a small cookout in the yard for when we get home tomorrow. Kind of a welcome-home party."

"Who's Fred?" Billie asked.

Cat was startled. "Oh my God, that's right, we haven't spoken to you about Fred, have we? Fred is Jen's husband."

"Jen's married to a man? When I asked if she had a partner, I assumed it was a woman."

"Yes. And as you already know, they have two children, Stevie, who's Seth's age, and Karissa, who's a year younger than Tara."

"She's not gay?" Billie asked, surprise evident on her face and in her voice. "But she's so affectionate with you... and me. How can she not be gay?"

The question startled Cat as she finally realized why Billie felt so threatened about her relationship with Jen.

"No she isn't. Not that you haven't tried to convert her on several occasions."

Billie's eyes flew open. "I have?"

"Yes, you have. I've lost track of the number of times you tried to convince her she needs a woman."

"Why would I do that?"

Cat took Billie's hands in her own. "Sweetheart, you and I have a unique relationship with Jen. When we first moved into the neighborhood three years ago, we were pretty much shunned for our lifestyle, but one evening Jen's house caught on fire and you risked your life to save Fred and the kids from certain death. You went into that burning house three times and pulled them out while Jen and I waited outside. They actually lived with us for a few weeks while repairs were done on their home. Jen proclaimed herself an honorary sister and has become a very important part of our lives. We've become the same to her and her family. Jen is the closest thing you'll ever have to a real sister. She loves us and will do anything for us."

Billie fell silent.

Cat rubbed her arm. "You've grown quiet all of a sudden. What are you thinking?"

"I'm sorry. I've been a fool. I assumed some things that weren't true. I was jealous. I know that's not an excuse, but it is an explanation."

Cat knew what Billie was talking about. "I should have told you from the start Jen was married to a man. Come to think of it, that piece of information might have made a few things easier on both of us. It's just that part of me still doesn't get that you have no memory of our lives together. I've made some bad assumptions myself. I'm sorry. Forgive me?"

Billie nodded. "Did I really save them from a fire?"

"Yes. As catastrophic as it was to them, it was a godsend for us."

"What do you mean?"

"You were a real hero, Billie. After that, the entire neighborhood came around and Jen became an instant soul mate to both of us."

"That's an amazing story."

"Every bit of it is true."

Billie yawned, interrupting their conversation.

"Well, either I'm boring you to death, or you're tuckered out from your PT today."

"I guess I'm more tired than I thought," Billie said.

Cat placed the paper and pencil on the nightstand and crawled back into bed beside her. "Come here."

Billie rolled over into Cat's embrace, placed her head on her shoulder, and draped her arm over Cat's abdomen. Cat placed a kiss on Billie's forehead and said, "Pleasant dreams, my love. Sleep well."

Minutes later, both women drifted off to sleep.

Chapter 37

Cat was awakened the next morning by a rhythmic clicking sound. She opened her eyes and noticed Billie wasn't in bed. Alarmed, she sat up and saw Billie pacing across her room, her crutches clicking with each step she took.

She noted the distress on Billie's face as she paced. "Billie, is something wrong?"

"Did I wake you?" Billie said. "I'm sorry."

Cat climbed out of bed and walked over to her. She wrapped her arms around her and rested her head under Billie's chin. Billie lowered her cheek to the top of Cat's head.

They were still standing in this embrace when Doc walked in several minutes later. "Good morning, daughters."

Cat stepped away and hugged her father. "'Morning, Daddy."

"Good morning, Doc," Billie said.

"Well, are we ready to go home?" he asked

"You bet," Cat said, a sentiment not echoed by Billie.

"All right then. After breakfast, Billie, we'll put you through one more series of tests to baseline your condition and draw up a training and therapy schedule you can do at home. We'll also need to take a blood sample this morning to check the level of anticonvulsant to make sure it's at the right therapeutic level to keep the epilepsy under control. If all goes well, you'll be out of here by midafternoon."

"Great," Cat said. "I better run home and pick up some clothes for you to wear. I'll just jump in the shower and go while you have breakfast."

Billie nodded as Cat collected her shampoo, towel, and clean clothes and headed for the bathroom.

"Doc," Billie said, "this epilepsy thing, are there any restrictions that come with it? You know, like operating machinery or driving a car?"

"Unfortunately, yes. All fifty states restrict driver's licenses for persons with active seizures that aren't controlled by medication. That can be waived if the person has been seizure-free for a specified period of time, usually three to six months. It also requires a statement issued by their physician confirming the individual's seizures are controlled, and if the person is licensed to drive, he or she will not present an unreasonable risk to public safety."

"I was afraid of that. Getting to work once I'm back on my feet might be a problem."

Doc squeezed Billie's shoulder. "Let's not worry about that right now. Our first goal is to get you well. I'm confident we can control the seizures, and in no time, life will be back to normal with little to no restrictions."

"I'm not sure I know what normal is, Doc. I may never remember what I once knew. I'm afraid I may have to start over."

Doc shoved his hands into his pockets. "Billie, I know this must be terrifying for you. You'll feel like a stranger in your own home. But know this. Cat and the children love you very much. The decision to stay or go is yours to make, but be sure you've given it a fair try before you do anything. All right?"

"I will. I promise."

"I once told you I couldn't replace your own father, but I'd be honored if you'd let me try. I still mean that, regardless of what happens here. I hope even if things don't work out with Cat, you'll still allow an old man to spend some time with his only grandson."

Billie could hear the emotional quiver in his voice. She lowered her eyes to the floor and nodded her head. "Of course." Her voice broke as her shoulders shook.

Doc wrapped his arms around her and comforted her.

As planned, Cat ran home to pick up a change of clothes while Billie was having breakfast and her morning baseline session. While she was home, she planned to meet with Jen on the afternoon's festivities. As she stepped into the kitchen, she heard the sound of power tools coming from the living room.

"There. That ought to do it," she heard a man's voice say.

Cat walked through the kitchen into the living room and gasped in surprise when she saw Jen and Fred putting the finishing touches on a new set of handrails going up both sides of the stairs to the second story. "What would I ever do without you two?" she said as she ran into Jen's arms and kissed her before moving on to repeat the process with Fred.

"I reinforced the basement stairs too," Fred said. He puckered up to get another kiss.

Jen punched him in the arm. "You're such a pervert."

Before long, Cat was on her way back to the hospital while Jen hurried home to make salads.

Joseph and Laura had Billie about halfway through her baseline testing when Cat arrived. An hour later, they finished the tests and were formulating a therapy plan that they reviewed in detail with Billie and Cat. The exercises were simple and repetitious, to be done twice a day, followed by stretching and a massage at the end of the day. In between, Billie was encouraged to walk as much as possible with the crutches and to practice without them as long as she had handholds close by to grab for balance. Laura gave Billie's belt to Cat to take home, instructing her on how to use it to help Billie with walking.

Another hour later, the blood tests came back with Billie's anticonvulsant blood levels. They were at the low end of the therapeutic range, so instructions were given to increase the dose and to repeat blood work in a week.

Soon it was time to leave. Saying goodbye to Laura was difficult for Billie. She had grown very close to her over the past two weeks and considered her to be a friend and ally.

Billie hugged her. Emotion made her voice quiver. "I'm going to miss you."

"Ditto on this end," Laura said. She handed Billie a piece of paper. "Here's my number at the hospital. Call me anytime. And keep me posted on your progress. Promise me you'll give it your best shot with Cat. Give it some time. I know it'll get better."

Billie hugged her again. "I will. I promise."

She turned to Joseph, who stood there as arrogant as ever, arms crossed in front of his chest. Billie smiled. "Well, Ivan the not-so-terrible, you're a real pussycat under all that toughness, you know."

"Don't let that get out, Charland. You'll ruin my reputation. By the way, I still don't get what you see in her," he said, motioning with his head toward Cat.

She winked at him and turned to Cat. "Ready to go home?"

"I'm more than ready."

Billie refused the wheelchair and insisted on using her crutches to leave the hospital. "I've seen enough of that chair to last me a lifetime. I'll walk, thank you very much."

* * *

On the drive home, Cat prepared Billie for the cookout that awaited them. "Jen will be there, along with Fred and the kids," Cat said.

"What are the kids' names again?"

"The boy's name is Stevie, the girl is Karissa. They're best friends with Seth and Tara."

Billie looked around at her home with nervous anticipation as Cat pulled into the driveway. Cat got out of the car, walked around to Billie's side, and opened the door for her. Billie scowled. "I can do this myself, Cat."

Cat backed up two steps and crossed her arms. "You're right. I'm sorry." She waited while Billie struggled out of the car and set herself up on her crutches. When Billie cleared the door, Cat pushed it closed and earned herself another scowl.

"What?"

"I'm not an invalid."

"Fine!" Cat stomped into the backyard and left Billie to struggle across the uneven grass on her own.

The kids spotted them the moment they rounded the corner of the garage. Tara was the first one to reach Cat as she jumped into her arms and nearly knocked her over. Seth ran to Billie and hugged her around the middle. Skylar attached herself to one of Billie's long legs while Tara scrambled out of Cat's arms and joined her brother and sister in welcoming Billie home.

Billie's whole demeanor changed when she was around the children. "Whoa, there, hold on a minute. Let me sit down at the picnic table so I can greet you without falling down, okay?" She hobbled over to the table and lowered herself into a seated position then opened her arms to the three squirming bodies, showering them with hugs and kisses. "I've missed you guys so much."

As expected, Skylar climbed into Billie's lap, curled herself into a ball, and tucked her head into Billie neck. She stayed there as the other two became bored and ran off to play with their friends. Billie kissed Skylar on the head.

Skylar sat up. "Mommy, are you going away again?"

Cat held her breath as she waited for Billie's answer.

"Sky, sweetie, why would you ask a question like that?"

"I don't want you to go again, Mommy. I missed you," she said and buried her head in Billie's neck once more.

Billie rocked her back and forth. "I don't want to go again either, lovebug."

If Cat expected a commitment from Billie, she was mistaken. Billie had avoided Skylar's question, leaving it hanging unanswered in the air around them.

Jen walked up behind Cat and wrapped an arm around her waist. Cat recognized the comforting embrace and leaned her head into Jen's shoulder.

"How is she?" Jen asked.

"Nervous, edgy, scared. She's already snapped at me twice since we got here."

Jen kissed her on the side of the head. "This is going to take time and patience. There's bound to be good days and bad. We'll just need to ride it out and hope we all come to a safe stop at the end."

Cat patted the hand Jen had wrapped around her waist. "You're a good friend. I'm so glad you're here."

Jen came around to face Cat. "I'll do anything to help—anytime, day or night. Promise me you'll call when you need me, even if all you need is a shoulder to cry on."

"Don't I do that already?" Cat hugged Jen before releasing her. "I love you, Jen. You're the best friend anyone could ask for."

The cookout was a marginal success. Billie spent a great deal of time laughing and playing games with the children. She was introduced to Fred, whom she seemed to like instantly, and she even helped cook the burgers and hot dogs on the grill. To an outsider, all was well, but it became obvious to Cat that Billie was avoiding her.

Partway through the cookout, Art and Marge showed up. Cat was in the house mixing a new batch of fruit punch for the children when they arrived. She watched the reunion from the kitchen window. Billie recognized Art immediately and rose to her feet. She struggled across the yard with her crutches to meet him halfway. He opened his arms and Billie went into them.

Art was a big man and absorbed Billie into the circle of his embrace, while Marge stood off to the side, waiting. She slapped Art on the shoulder with the back of her hand. "Hey, I want some of that too," she said, taking Billie into her own arms.

It was early evening before everyone left. Jen offered to take the kids for the night, but Cat insisted Billie would feel more comfortable with them home on her first night.

The kids led Billie on a tour of the first floor while Cat put away leftover food, straightened the kitchen, and did anything else she could think of to avoid dealing with Billie. When her excuses ran out, she joined them in the living room, where the four of them were cuddled on the couch, watching a movie on TV.

Cat curled up in a chair off to the side and watched her family enjoy the show. Every once in a while, she would catch Billie's eyes and smile. Each time, Billie looked away. After a few minutes, Cat asked, "Who wants popcorn?" Four pairs of eyes lit up at the suggestion, including Billie's. Popcorn was one of her weaknesses.

Cat went into the kitchen. A short time later, she heard the clicking of Billie's crutches as she approached. Cat held her ground at the stove and kept her back to Billie.

Billie moved closer and soon stood behind Cat. "Cat, I'm sorry for the way I've been treating you since we got home."

Cat remained with her back to Billie, trying hard to fight the emotions threatening to run away with her. "It's all right. It's been a hectic day. I understand."

Billie leaned in and placed her chin on Cat's right shoulder. "No it isn't all right. I've hurt you and I'm sorry. Forgive me?"

Cat faced her as Billie righted herself to her full height. She saw such utter sorrow and despair in Billie's eyes, her heart melted. This time, there was no holding the emotions in check. A tear escaped her eye as she touched the side of Billie face. "Of course, I forgive you."

Billie lowered her head and kissed Cat on the mouth. A beep drew their attention to the microwave oven.

"Popcorn's ready," Billie said.

Cat followed Billie back into the living room with the large bowl of popcorn and waited until Billie settled herself on the couch before placing the bowl in her lap. Cat started toward her chair when Billie interrupted her.

"Cat. Right here." Billie patted the couch beside her.

Cat climbed into the jumble of bodies that were snuggling up close to Billie. The children flowed in to fill any gaps between themselves and their mothers, all managing to get closer to the bowl of popcorn.

"This is good," Billie said.

"Thanks. You never could resist a good bowl of popcorn, could you?"

Billie shook her head. She shoved another handful of fluffy kernels into her mouth as she became absorbed once more in the movie.

When the movie ended, Cat and Billie were surrounded by sleeping children. Seth lay on Cat's right, his head in her lap. Skylar leaned against Cat with her legs spread out across Billie's lap, and Tara was curled up in Billie's left arm.

Cat and Billie exchanged an amused look as they nudged each child awake. "Come on, lovebugs. Off to bed with you."

Seth and Skylar grumbled as they came awake. Tara refused to budge.

Billie gently shook Tara. "Tara, honey, do you remember what happens when you don't behave?"

Tara opened her eyes and grinned at Billie. "To the moon, Alice?"

"Yep."

Cat sat there, wide-eyed at the old joke that passed between them.

"Okay, okay, I'm going," Tara said as she sat up. Before she climbed down, Tara wrapped her arms around Billie's neck and kissed her. "I'm glad you're home, Mom. I missed you."

Billie lowered her forehead to Tara's. "I'm glad to be home too, sweet pea."

"All right, off to bed," Cat said as the three children climbed to their feet and gave both mothers hugs and kisses. After a round of good nights, they headed for the stairs as Billie watched them go.

"I'll tuck them in and be right back," Cat said.

Twenty minutes later, she descended the stairs to the living room and Billie was gone. A brief search found her in the kitchen pouring hot water into two teacups. Cat stood there and watched, as Billie opened the cupboard and pulled out the honey. She spooned the sweet liquid into both cups and stirred them before reaching for a cinnamon stick from the canister on the counter, breaking it in half and dropping one into each cup. *It's as if she knows where everything is.* Hope rose a little higher in Cat's breast. *Part of her remembers.*

Billie moved the cups to the table one at a time, while maintaining her balance with the other crutch. "Tea?"

"You bet." Cat sat down at the table with her.

After they finished their tea, Cat rinsed both cups, placed them in the dishwasher, and turned to Billie, who was still seated at the table. "Are you ready for bed?"

Billie appeared nervous. "Cat—"

"Billie, like I said at the hospital, I think you should sleep in the downstairs guest room for a while. That way you won't have to worry about negotiating the stairs right away. I'll sleep on the couch. I want to be nearby in case you need anything in the middle of the night."

"Cat, you don't have to sleep on the couch. Why don't you sleep in your own bed upstairs? I'll be fine."

Score one for Cat, she thought as she saw the tension leave Billie's face. Sleeping together in the hospital with very little threat of anything sexual happening was one thing. Sleeping together in the privacy of their home was another thing altogether. Cat wanted to take the pressure off Billie by making it clear to her things would move at her pace. "No, for the first night or so, I'll take the couch. We'll take this one day at a time, okay?"

Billie reached for Cat's hand. "All right, thanks."

Cat rose to her feet. "Come on, let's get you settled."

Cat granted Billie the privacy she needed to change into her nightclothes while she fetched a couple of blankets and a pillow from the hall closet to use on the couch. After making her bed, she returned to the guest room and found Billie already under the covers, the room lit only by moonlight. Billie was still awake.

Cat sat down on the edge of the bed and traced a pattern across Billie's brow and down her cheek with her fingertips. "Pleasant dreams, sweetheart." She bent over and placed light butterfly kisses on her lips.

"Good night," Billie said as Cat rose to her feet and walked toward the door. "Cat," Billie said, stopping her short, "I love you."

Cat smiled from across the room. "I love you too. Good night." She stopped in the hallway just outside Billie's room and leaned against the wall to regain her composure. "Good night, my love," she whispered before heading to bed on the living room couch.

Chapter 38

Billie awoke the next morning to find a warm body snuggled against her back. She rolled over, expecting to see Cat there. Instead, smiling blue eyes looked up at her.

"Sky, honey. You surprised me. I thought you were Cat, I mean, Mama."

Skylar snuggled in closer and leaned her face into Billie's neck. "Mama's sleeping on the couch."

Billie wrapped her arms around the child. "Mama's still sleeping? Are Tara and Seth up yet?"

"They're watching cartoons in the living room."

"With Mama sleeping right there?"

"Yes."

Boy, that woman can sleep through anything. I wonder how she ever made it to work on time before we met? She frowned. *Now where did that thought come from?*

"Mommy, how come you didn't sleep in your bed last night?"

"Because my legs need more practice before I can climb that many stairs, sweetheart."

"How come Mama didn't sleep with you? She always sleeps with you."

Billie swallowed hard. *How do I explain this one?* "Ah... Mama wanted to make sure I slept well. Mama's a bed hog, you know, kind of like a little four-year-old rugrat I know," Billie said, hoping the child would accept the answer.

"Me?"

"Yes, you. Do you know what I do to bed hogs?"

Skylar's eyes grew wide as she shook her head no.

"The claw! Arrrrgggghhhh," Billie formed her hand into the claw and tickled her.

Skylar screamed in delight as Billie tickled her into submission.

Suddenly, Cat ran into the room, her hair a mess and her nightshirt askew. "Who screamed?"

Skylar poked her head up from behind Billie. "I did. Mommy was tickling me."

Cat walked over and sat on the edge of the bed. "Sky, did you wake Mommy up this morning?" she asked, with a hint of reprimand in her voice.

Billie came to her rescue. "No, she didn't. She was sleeping, and I almost rolled over on top of her."

"Mommy said you were a bed hog," Skylar said, laughing.

Billie grabbed Skylar and put her hand over her mouth while shooting Cat an apologetic look.

Cat raised her eyebrows to Billie. "Oh she did, did she?"

Skylar nodded her head yes while Billie still held her hand over her mouth.

"Well, I think Mommy is exaggerating a bit. You know what we do to people who exaggerate?" Cat asked first Skylar, then Billie.

An expression of comical worry crossed Billie's face. "The claw?" she said in a little girl voice.

"The claw!" Cat pounced on Billie and started to tickle her. Skylar shrieked with glee before joining in. Soon Tara and Seth came into the room. Within seconds, they had joined the melee as an all-out tickle war ensued. After a time, Billie and Cat both fell victim to the kids, who quickly ganged up against them. Soon, the war was over and the kids claimed the victory. Their promised reward was a blueberry pancake breakfast with link sausage.

The kids ran back to watch cartoons while they waited for breakfast. Cat swung her legs off the bed and got up. "Well, I guess I'd better go start breakfast."

"Wait, I'll come with you. I think I might be able to cook the sausage links without too many of them committing suicide on me."

Cat grinned and waited for her to climb off the bed and grab her crutches. Billie rose to her feet and looked down on Cat from her height advantage. "I sure could use a good-morning hug."

Billie didn't need to ask twice. Cat slid her arms around Billie and rested her head on the space between Billie's chin and breasts. Billie leaned into Cat for support. She raised one arm to circle Cat's back and held her close. She stood like this for long moments, savoring the feeling of closeness.

Cat broke the embrace. "As much as I'd like to stay like this all day, I need to get breakfast started."

Billie lowered her head and kissed Cat full on the lips. One long kiss followed by several light butterfly kisses. "Okay, let's go."

"Keep kissing me like that, and the kids will be making their own breakfast." Cat took a deep breath and led Billie into the kitchen for breakfast duty.

Billie sat at her usual place at the kitchen table while the kids dug into the stack of pancakes and sausage. She had a full cup of coffee in front of her, and Cat stood at the stove flipping the last batch of cakes.

"Who wants more pancakes?" Cat asked, holding the spatula over a tall plate of cakes.

Seth and Tara held out their plates.

Billie shook her head, smiling at how much the children could eat. Suddenly, a loud ringing started in her ears and a wave a heat rose from her chest into her neck and head. Billie gripped the edges of the table to keep her balance. A sound from the kitchen doorway drew her attention. In the doorway, she saw a battered vision of herself standing there, holding Skylar in her arms.

Billie winced as she walked toward the table where she placed Skylar in her seat and sat down in the empty chair beside her. She opened her arms to the older children. Both of them rose from the table and approached her warily.

"It's all right. Come here." She tried hard to stifle a painful grunt as they ran into her arms. She wrapped her arms around them and held them close. With a kiss for each child, she sent them back to their seats to finish their breakfast.

Gingerly, she rose to her feet once more and approached the counter where she poured herself a cup of coffee and refilled the cup Cat was drinking from. She carried them both to the table.

Cat followed her with a clean plate and utensils. "Sit. Help yourself." She placed a stack of fresh pancakes and sausage in the center of the table.

Billie shook her head to clear the confusion. She saw Cat dish pancakes out to the children and drop a few on two other plates for the both of them. Cat slid one of the plates over to Billie. "Eat up. You'll need your strength for therapy today, love."

Billie reached for her fork and the plate of sausages. She was in a daze, still trying to understand the vision she had seen.

After the children were settled, Cat sat down, and joined the family for breakfast. "Billie, are you all right?" she asked.

"Huh? I'm sorry. What was it you said?"

"You've been sitting there staring at your plate for several minutes. Are you sure you're okay?"

"Yeah, I'm fine. I'm just a little overwhelmed. Sorry for drifting off like that."

Cat reached over and stroked Billie's face. "Is there something you need to tell me?"

"Later," she said, nodding her head in the direction of the kids. "What was it you were asking about, Cat?"

"I was just talking about your therapy schedule for the week."

While the adults talked, one by one the children excused themselves from the table. They rinsed their dishes, placed them in the sink, and went into the living room to watch cartoons.

When they had both eaten their fill, Cat rose, took Billie's plate from her, and loaded it and the rest of the breakfast dishes into the dishwasher. She refilled their coffee cups and announced she was going to run out to the mailbox for the morning paper.

Billie sat at the kitchen table nursing her coffee while she waited for Cat. Without warning, a pain tore through her skull as the loud ringing began anew. Billie looked up as Cat came back into the house.

Billie sat back and pushed a chair out with her foot. "Sit down, Cat."

"No, I think I'm fine right here." Cat continued to lean against the door with her arms crossed in front of her.

"I asked you to sit down. I won't be so nice the next time. Now do it."

Cat's defiance matched Billie's anger. "I don't think so. You're my wife, not my boss."

Billie placed her elbows on the table and held her head between her hands. A moment later, she slammed her fist down onto the table. "Damn you, Cat. Get your ass over here before you make me do something I'll regret."

"Judging by those photographs, I'd say you've already done something you'll regret."

"I promised my son I wouldn't hurt you. Otherwise I'd give you the beating you so deserve."

"Billie, Billie," Cat said as she shook her.

Billie's eyes darted around in confusion. She examined herself and saw no evidence of injury. There were no photographs and no fear in Cat's eyes.

"Cat, I hurt you."

"What are you talking about? Honey, you've never hurt me."

Billie's eyes filled with tears. "Here, in this kitchen. I pinned you against the door. I... I wanted to hurt you."

Cat's eyes flew open wide. "You're remembering!"

"I hurt you," Billie said again.

Cat took both of Billie's hands in hers. She kissed the knuckles and pulled them in to rest over her heart. "No, you didn't hurt me. You couldn't. You stopped yourself."

"Why did I do it, Cat? Why did I treat you like that?"

Cat released Billie's hands and walked a few paces away. "Billie, we received some photographs in the mail, very disturbing photographs depicting you in compromising positions with a blonde woman. I freaked out when I saw them. I never gave you a chance to explain. I flew off the handle and assumed the worst. I'll never forgive myself for treating you like that."

"Where did they come from? Who took them?"

Cat sat next to Billie and covered her hand with her own. "What do you remember about your life with Brian?"

Billie frowned as she turned her hand over and grasped Cat's, interlacing their fingers. "Glimpses, only glimpses. It's odd. I know who I am. I remember working at the firm. I remember Seth, and if Brian walked in here right now, I'd know who he was, but I don't remember much about being married to him."

"Not remembering your life with Brian is in some ways a blessing."

"What does my marriage to Brian have to do with the pictures?"

Cat looked away.

"Don't avoid the question. Please—I need to know."

"Brian staged the pictures years ago when Seth was still a baby. Brian is a sick son of a bitch. He used the pictures as blackmail to keep you from divorcing him."

Billie's eyes grew large as a wave of fear filled her. The loud ringing was back, and she fought the nausea growing in the pit of her stomach. Somewhere on the periphery of her consciousness, she felt someone squeezing her hand and asking if she was all right.

Brian backed her up against the wall and slammed her head into it over and over. "You belong here with me, taking care of that little bastard in the other room, not out screwing everything in sight."

"I wasn't."

"Don't lie to me, you filthy whore."

"Brian, stop… please."

"I'll teach you to run out on me, bitch."

While he reached for his belt buckle, Billie kicked him in the shin. He let out a howl and fell to the floor, releasing the hold he had on her neck only when she fell on top of him. She scrambled away, but he caught her foot and yanked on it as hard as he could, twisting it at the same time and causing an audible snap. He climbed up and sat across her stomach, throwing blow after close-fisted blow toward her face. About half of the blows landed on target, the other half blocked by Billie's flailing hands. When he stopped, he removed his belt and whaled it across her back until stripes of blood could be seen through her blouse.

Billie yanked her hand from Cat's grasp and covered her face. "Oh my God. Oh my God," she cried in anguish as she rocked back and forth.

Cat jumped to her feet and circled behind Billie, wrapping both arms around her. "It's okay, love. I've got you. I've got you. You're safe now. He'll never hurt you again. I promise."

After a few moments, the tremors subsided. Billie removed her hands from her face and clung to Cat's arms, still wrapped around her from behind. She leaned her face against Cat's.

"I'm so sorry, my love," Cat whispered in Billie's ear.

"You have nothing to be sorry for. You're right. Brian was a monster. I remember the beating… and the pictures. He's pure evil. I hope to God he didn't pass any of those traits to Seth."

Cat released Billie and sat down at the table. She took Billie's hands in her own. "There's no way Seth inherited any of Brian's traits. He's pure sweetness. Seth's compassion and inner beauty comes from you. Please believe that."

Billie nodded.

Cat cupped Billie's cheek in her palm. "Do you remember anything else?"

"I had another memory just as breakfast was starting. I saw myself in the kitchen doorway holding Skylar. I was... I was..."

"You were injured, weren't you?"

"Yes, like I'd been beaten."

"You were. You attempted to drown your sorrows in one the seediest bars in town, and you were assaulted. Art brought you home to me the night before the event in your vision." Cat lowered her head as a wave of shame filled her heart at the way she had overreacted to the pictures.

"What is it, Cat?"

"I've already told you I overreacted when I saw the pictures we received in the mail. I'm afraid I caused you tremendous pain and heartbreak by accusing you of being unfaithful to me. Things wouldn't have escalated the way they did if only I'd listened to you."

"Cat, I'm the one who hurt you. My God, the vision. I can't believe I treated you so rough. I'm so sorry."

"Your anger was justified. I was wrong to accuse you of infidelity. If I hadn't done that, you wouldn't have left, or gone to that bar, and you wouldn't have been injured. Don't you see? It's my fault, not yours."

"Nothing justifies the manhandling I saw in that vision. I'll never forgive myself for doing that to you."

Cat turned her head and kissed the inside of Billie's palm still resting against her cheek. "It's in the past. Please let it go."

Billie closed her eyes and whispered, "I'll try."

"Good. I'm so happy you're starting to remember. Sweetheart, do you remember anything else?"

Billie shook her head. "Not right now."

For most of the morning, Cat worked with Billie on various therapeutic exercises while the children played in the yard. Around midmorning, Cat was walking backwards in front of Billie, helping her cross the living room without her crutches, while Billie walked forward, her hands lying on top of Cat's palms.

Suddenly, Jen barged into the living room. "Hi there, ladies," she said, scaring both of them out of their skins and distracting them to the point Cat stepped over her own feet and fell on her butt. Billie landed right on top of her and pinned her to the floor.

Billie was worried she'd hurt Cat. Coming awkwardly to her knees, she reached out to Cat who was holding her stomach. "Are you all right?"

Cat held her hand up to Billie and gasped a couple of times. "I'm okay. I got the wind knocked out of me, that's all. Are you okay?"

"I'm fine."

Cat and Billie glared at Jen, who was trying hard to control her laughter.

Billie grew indignant and sat back on her heels. She crossed her arms and scowled. "Okay, Miss Neighbor Extraordinaire, you think this is so funny, get your ass over here and help us up." Her anger abated under Jen's constant chuckling.

Jen approached them and offered her hand. Billie glanced at Cat, grabbed Jen's hands, and yanked her down into a pile with them on the floor.

"Whoa!" Jen said.

"Hold her down, Cat. She needs to pay for her insolence."

Cat held her down while Billie administered the claw to her midsection.

"No! Stop. I'm sorry," Jen said between bouts of laughter. "I promise. I'll knock next time."

Billie and Cat ceased torturing Jen and let her sit up. All three women sat there, leaning on each other, their sides aching from the laughter, before they regained enough composure to climb to their feet.

Cat and Jen prepared lunch, while Fred took all five children to McDonald's and then to a minor league baseball game. It would be late in the day before they would return.

After lunch, Billie took a nap while Cat and Jen dragged the stationary bike and free weights up from the makeshift gym in a corner of the family room downstairs. They placed the bike in a strategic corner of the living room where it could be ridden while watching TV. It would become an important part of Billie's afternoon workout routine. That accomplished, Cat made a pot of coffee and sat down to tell Jen about the flashbacks Billie had that morning during breakfast.

"It sounds like she's starting to remember," Jen said, "and man, she sure picked some tough memories to start with. Maybe being home has something to do with it."

"Maybe. Daddy said being in familiar surroundings sometimes has a dramatic effect on memory recall. He also said once the memories start to surface, it wouldn't be uncommon for them to come back rapidly. We've only been home for a day, but already, I've seen her fall into familiar habits. She made us tea last night and knew where everything was and how I drank mine. We got into a tickle war this morning with the kids, and she was so like the old Billie, it was as if this entire nightmare never happened—and now the flashbacks. I just wish the memories that are returning were the good ones."

"Well, like it or not, she won't be truly whole until all her memories are back, including the bad ones."

"I know you're right, but it's painful to watch her recall something unpleasant."

"It's only been a day, Cat. Give it time."

"I hope you're right, Jen. I really hope you're right."

The afternoon therapy session was very tiring for Billie. After several passes of walking across the living room, with Jen standing close by for balance and Cat holding onto the belt around Billie's waist, she moved to the exercise bike and then to the free weights. By the time her workout was over, her clothing was damp and her muscles quivered with exhaustion.

She sat at the kitchen table and enjoyed a tall glass of iced tea while Cat filled the Jacuzzi with hot water. Jen came up behind her and wrapped her arms around Billie's neck and shoulders. She pressed her cheek against the side of Billie's head.

"I'm afraid I don't smell very good right now," Billie said. "You're going to need a bath yourself if you keep doing that."

"What's a little sweat between friends, huh? Someone's got to hold you up in the shower. I thought I'd volunteer for the job."

"I don't think Cat will appreciate that."

"Cat won't appreciate what?" Cat said from the doorway.

"Busted," Jen said.

"Cat won't appreciate what?" Cat asked again, hands on her hips.

Billie smirked at Jen. "You're in trouble now, girlfriend. Let's see you worm your way out of this one."

"Um, um, Cat wouldn't appreciate… Is that Fred I hear calling? Got to go. See you later." Jen escaped out the kitchen door.

"Coward," Billie said as she watched her flee.

A few moments later, Billie reclined in a tub of hot swirling water, a rolled up towel behind her neck and candles providing muted lighting. Classical music played from the cassette player on the vanity. Billie soon fell asleep.

Billie stood to her full height and scooped Cat into her arms then slowly lowered her into the warm water before settling in behind her. She poured two glasses of wine and handed one to Cat.

Cat's head rested against Billie's shoulder as Billie's fingertips drew lazy circles around her left nipple.

"Hmm, that feels good. Damned appendix. I finally get you alone and naked, and I can't do anything about it."

Billie kissed the side of Cat's head. "I know. I've been waiting for this moment almost since I laid eyes on you. You're so beautiful. You've no idea what you're doing to me right now."

"Sorry."

"How long did your doctor say you had to wait?"

"Four to six weeks before engaging in strenuous activity."

"Four to six weeks? You're killing me here."

Cat chuckled. "You're not the only one dying."

"You're right, of course. As hard as it'll be to wait, I want our first time to be without restriction. We'll just have to wait until you're fully recovered to make our dream come true."

"Thank you for being so understanding, Billie. You were willing to risk your heart, and despite everything you had going on in your life, you made time for me and Tara."

"You're worth any risk I may have to take. I love you."

"I love you too."

Cat settled in once more with her back to Billie and her head resting on Billie's shoulder. For several moments, neither of them said a word.

"Billie, I never thanked you for watching Tara when I was sick. Hell, I never even asked you to stay with her, but I'm so glad you did. She's rather taken with you."

"It's funny how she wriggled her way into my heart." Billie chuckled. "I have to admit I was shocked when Gail opened your door that day. When I knocked on your door, the last thing I expected was a strange woman in a negligee."

"Gail. Ugh. That's a mistake I'll never make again."

"Tara said you had a fight with her, over me no less, and you asked her to leave."

"That daughter of mine sure has a big mouth. I'll have to talk to her about that." Cat paused. "Yes, we did have a fight, and yes, it was about you. She threatened to leave me in the lurch without day care if I continued to see you. You can imagine how that pissed me off. No one tells me how to live my life. Not even my parents. She was stupid enough to pull this on me after I'd spent a day and a half throwing up and doubled over in pain with appendicitis. It didn't take me long to tell her to pack her bags and get the hell out."

Billie laughed. "Speaking of your parents, I can't believe how incredibly accepting they've been of Seth and me. They don't even know us, yet they're treating us like family."

"They know you better than you think. Heaven knows they've heard enough about you over the last few months. While they were in Florida, I talked to them two or three times a week. Hell, they knew I loved you before you did."

"It's obvious they don't have a problem with our relationship. Your dad was pretty blunt about it."

"Billie, my dad means well, but don't let him push you into something you're not ready for. I heard his comment about the marriage thing and—"

"I didn't say his talk of marriage bothered me."

"Billie Charland, are you proposing to little ole me?" Cat asked in a fake Southern accent.

Billie stiffened, worried that Cat's flippant attitude meant rejection.

"I love you with all my heart, Billie. Nothing would make me happier than to be your wife."

"I think we'd better wait to see what happens with Seth before you commit yourself. I know you said you wanted us to be a family, but if your father can't help him, the future may not be so rosy."

Cat swiveled around. Her sudden movement splashed water out of the tub and onto the floor and spilled her wine into the tub. "What did you say?"

"I said that you need to go into this with your eyes open."

Cat pinned Billie to the back of the tub by her arms. Their faces were a mere breath's width apart. "Is that what you really think of me? Do you think I'd turn tail and run as soon as things got rough? Damn you."

Billie suddenly awoke. She sat up, momentarily confused. Once she realized where she was, she relaxed and reclined against the back of the tub. She stared at the ceiling and thought about the dream. "You're worth any risk I may have to take. I love you," she said under her breath.

After the kids were bathed and tucked into bed that evening, Cat asked Billie to sit on the couch while she went to the bookcase in the family room and found the video of Skylar's first birthday party. Cat slipped the disk into the DVD player and sat next to Billie. She reached for Billie's hand and held it in her lap while the video began.

Billie's gaze never left the TV screen as the home movie played. She squeezed Cat's hand several times, especially when the children were on screen.

"There's Seth," Billie said. "That's how I remembered him in the hospital. He must have been what, seven in this video?"

"He was actually eight. He was seven when Sky was born, and this was her first birthday party."

"So Tara was about five then?"

"Yes, that's right."

"I see Doc and Ida. Oh, there's Jen and Fred. I see everyone but myself. Was I the photographer?"

"Right again, but there's a scene coming up soon with you in it."

Billie watched intently as everyone sang Happy Birthday to Skylar and a small chocolate cake was put in front of her. When the camera zoomed in on a chocolate-faced Skylar diving into her birthday cake, Cat could have sworn she heard Billie say under her breath, "Smile for Mommy, baby."

"Here comes the scene with you in it." The picture on the screen showed Jen approaching the photographer and taking control of the camera. Billie was seen joining her family at the table.

She frowned when she saw the bandage on her head. "Why was my head bandaged?"

"You rescued the kids and me from Brian. He was holding us hostage, right here in the house, demanding custody of Seth and Sky. You broke into the house and ambushed him, but not before he managed to shoot you. We almost lost you on the way to the hospital. It was only by the grace of God you survived. It's because of that gunshot to the head that scar tissue formed and we're here today trying to recover your memories."

When the video finished, Cat squeezed Billie's hand. "Did anything look or feel familiar?"

"I'm sorry. I don't remember. I'm so sorry."

Cat rubbed her temples. "I don't understand. You've recalled memories that include me, the rape, the photographs. How can you recall me, yet still not know me?"

"I don't know how to explain it. I know through the recalls that you were a part of my life, but I don't have memories of loving you. That feeling of knowing your heart and your soul isn't there. I'm so sorry."

Cat struggled to force a smile onto her face.

"That's okay. It will come back. I know it will," she said.

Billie yawned loudly. "God, I'm tired."

Cat shut off the TV, helped Billie up, and walked arm in arm with her to the guest room.

"Let me rub you down. You'll sleep better." Cat removed Billie's clothing without waiting for a reply. Soon, Billie was naked, except for her panties, and lying facedown on the bed, her hands crossed under her chin. Cat began a deep massage and worked the stiffness out of Billie's tired muscles. She started at Billie's neck and massaged her entire body, down to her feet. Then, rolling her over, she repeated the process on Billie's front side, avoiding her breasts.

Cat forced herself to stay focused throughout the massage. *Remember what Laura said—your job is to massage, not stimulate. Keep it under control, Cat. You can do it.*

When the massage was over, Cat studied Billie's face and thought she saw desire burning in her eyes. *Don't go there, Cat.* She pulled a T-shirt over Billie's head, tucked her under the covers, and kissed her. "I love you. Pleasant dreams."

Billie grabbed her hand before she could walk away. "Thank you, for everything. And I love you too."

Cat kissed her once more, said good night, and retreated to the couch, where she knew sleep would be a long time coming. *God, Billie, I'm on fire from touching you. So much for sleeping.*

Billie stared at the ceiling. *God, Cat. Do you know what your touch does to me? So much for sleeping.*

Chapter 39

The next morning, Billie was up bright and early before the rest of the household. She made her way to the kitchen, set up the coffeepot, and returned to her room to throw on a pair of shorts. Using her crutches to maintain her balance, she slipped her feet into her tennis shoes and made her way down the porch steps. She hobbled over to the mailbox to collect the morning paper.

An hour later when Cat woke, Billie was on the exercise bike, reading the paper as she pedaled. Cat sat up on the couch. "Good morning," she said. "Getting a head start?"

Billie lowered the paper. "Good morning. Sleep well?"

"Yeah, okay I guess."

"Good. Coffee's made."

"You're a lifesaver." Cat climbed off the couch and headed to the kitchen.

Billie watched her go, all disheveled, hair a mess. *God, Cat, you are so sexy all mussed up like that.*

Cat came back into the living room carrying a full cup of coffee. She stopped next to Billie. "Did you go out to the mailbox for that paper?"

Billie grinned. "Yep."

"Cool." Cat sipped her coffee. "Oh, this is so good."

"Thanks. I want to thank you for the massage last night. It was wonderful."

"You're welcome. We need to do that every day to keep your muscles from becoming too sore after therapy. Feel up to walking outdoors today?"

"How far?"

"Just to Jen's house and back. She lives two doors down the street. She's invited us all to lunch today, and I thought the walk could replace part of your therapy session. What do you think?"

"All right. I also want to practice stair climbing today, okay?"

"Sure. Why don't you finish up on the bike, and I'll fix us a quick breakfast? The kids should be up soon, and we'll get started."

"Great."

As Cat predicted, over the next several minutes, the kids started making their appearances. Each one stopped to kiss and hug Billie before going into the kitchen for something to eat.

Seth was the last one up. As he approached Billie, she stopped.

"Good morning, scout."

"'Morning, Mom."

"Do you know where I can find a handsome young man to escort me to the kitchen?"

In a very grown-up fashion, Seth offered her his arm and they made their way to the kitchen table. He pulled out her chair and held it for her as she lowered herself into it.

"Oh, no you don't." Billie caught his arm. "You're not getting away without a hug and a kiss." Billie held him close. "Thank you, sweet love."

"You're welcome, Mom."

When breakfast was over, the kids ran off to get dressed.

Cat collected the breakfast dishes and rinsed them all in the sink.

"Let me help you with that." Billie started to get up.

"No worry. I've got it covered. You just sit there and rest. You've got a busy morning ahead of you."

Billie sat back down and watched Cat load the dishwasher. Each time Cat bent over to put a dish on the bottom rack she presented Billie with a fine shot of her backside. Billie found herself wishing they had dirtied more dishes, as the show was over way too soon.

Cat started the dishwasher and turned around. The expression on Billie's face was that of a kid caught with their hand in the cookie jar.

"Ready to go to work?"

"Yep." Billie got to her feet and, with her hand on Cat's shoulder, walked through the living room toward the stairs that led to the second story. Cat carried her crutches for her to use at the top of the stairs.

The kids suddenly came charging down the stairs, nearly running into them. Cat grasped Billie's waist to prevent her from falling.

"Whoa, slow down there. You almost knocked Mom over," Cat said. "How many times have I told you not to run in the house?"

All three children stood there with guilty expressions. Billie nudged Cat to get her attention. When Cat looked at her, she saw the most pitiful pair of puppy dog eyes she had ever seen.

Cat shook her head. "What am I going to do with the four of you?"

"We're sorry, Mama," each child chimed in.

Cat looked at Billie and saw a pout on her face. "All right. Just slow down, okay? Someone will get hurt one of these days."

"Ma, can we go over to Stevie and Karissa's this morning?" Seth asked. "Stevie has this new Nintendo game that I want to play."

"I guess so. We're having lunch with them today anyway. Seth, could you tell Jen we'll be there around noon? Oh, and Tara, include your sister, okay? You and Karissa have a tendency to shut her out."

"All right, Mama." Tara took Skylar's hand and dragged her along as the kids ran out the door.

Cat punched Billie in the arm.

"Ow! What was that for?"

"For giving me that cute little pouty face. How can I be the disciplinarian when you look at me like that?"

Billie grinned. "You thought it was cute?" She wiggled her eyebrows.

"What am I going to do with you?" Cat said. Seeing the suggestive leer on Billie's face, she added. "Don't play with fire if you don't want to get burned, Billie. Come on, we've got work to do."

"I'm thinking a little heat might not be a bad thing."

"Be careful what you wish for. Don't make me do something you'll regret later."

"Who says I'll regret it?"

Cat faced Billie and placed both hands on her hips. She cocked her head to the side. "Billie, I'd like nothing more than to heat things up between us, but be sure you're ready for that before you tease like this. I don't know whether to take you seriously or not, so I'm going to chalk this one up to your good mood this morning."

Billie had no trouble negotiating the stairs, thanks to the rails Fred and Jen installed. She climbed and descended them twice, before climbing them a third time with the intention of exploring the second floor. She stopped at the top of the stairs and faced the hallway. Her eyes widened and she grasped Cat's arm. "Cat, this is familiar!" Pointing, she said, "That's Seth's room, that's Tara's, and on this side is the bathroom, and Sky's room, and our room at the end."

Cat smiled. "Yes. You're right."

Billie took the crutches from Cat and moved down the hallway, stopping in each room as she went. Her eyes became fuller and fuller with unshed tears as the memories of the house came flooding back. When they reached the master bedroom at the end of the hall, her hand shook as she reached for the doorknob.

She pushed the door open and stepped inside. Intense feelings of déjà vu overwhelmed her. "I can sense it, Cat. I belong here."

"God, I've waited so long for you to realize that. What else do you remember? Who else do you remember?"

"I'm sorry. I remember the house, but I still don't remember you, at least not all there is to remember about you."

Cat narrowed her eyes. "What do you mean by 'not all there is to remember'?"

"I had another recall. I saw a vision of you and me in a hot tub. We were talking about Seth being in a coma, and you were pissed at me."

"I remember. I was so angry with you for not trusting me, for not believing I could handle Seth's condition, no matter what."

Billie nodded. "Yes, that's it." She allowed a heavy pause to fall between them. "Cat?"

"What?"

"Are we still in this together? I mean, all I ever seem to do is disappoint you. I'm so afraid you'll decide one day you've had enough."

Cat put her hands on either side of Billie's face. "When we got married, I pledged my love and my life to you until the end of time. I meant that. I still mean it today."

Billie stared intently at Cat as the ringing in her ears intensified.

"Billie, are you all right?"

She took a few steps backward and leaned against the wall. "I'm okay. Just give me a minute."

"Billie and Caitlain have written their own vows that they'd like to share with you now. Caitlain, you may begin."

Cat cleared her throat and began to speak. "Billie, I have loved you for all eternity. I believe we were destined to be together through all time, through many lives, past and present. You are my reason for living, the keeper of my heart, and the other half of my soul. You are my lover and my protector. You are in my thoughts from the moment I rise, until I lay my head down to sleep at night. You fill my dreams with sweet music. You lift my soul to the very heights of heaven. I will love you until my dying day and beyond. I pledge my love and my life to you until the end of time. Billie, I love you with all my heart, and I'm honored to be your wife."

Billie composed herself and prepared to deliver her own vows. She took a deep breath and began. "Cat, you came into my life at a time when I was emotionally destitute. You healed my soul and lifted my heart to new heights. You have given so much of yourself to me while asking so little in return. You are everything I could ask for. You are bright, intelligent and beautiful. You are the mother of my children and my true soul mate. You complete me, Cat. Like you, I believe our destiny was linked many years ago. For that, I will forever be grateful. I offer to you everything that I am. I promise to love you and protect you until the end of time and beyond. You are my one true love. I am honored to be your wife. Thank you for loving me."

"Well," the minister said, "I believe there's no doubt as to how these two women feel about each other, so without further ado, Caitlain, please present your offering to Billie."

Cat held the ring in front of her. "Billie, this ring signifies our bond. It is a never-ending circle of commitment. Please accept this token as your consent to be my wife."

Billie offered her hand and Cat slipped the ring onto her finger.

Billie held Cat's ring tightly in her fist until her knuckles were white. "Cat, I hold our love close to my heart, as I now hold this ring. I will fiercely protect you and our family, and I ask you to accept this ring as a symbol of that love and protection and as your consent to be my wife."

As Billie slipped the ring onto Cat's finger, their hands interlocked and their eyes met in an unwavering gaze of love.

The minister held her arms out wide. "In the eyes of this church and our God, and in the presence of their friends and family, I declare Billie and Caitlain to be joined as one for all time." Then, she turned to them and said, "You may kiss the bride."

"Billie, are you all right?"

Billie opened her eyes. "I remember our wedding."

"You do? That's wonderful!"

"I'm sorry, Cat. I'm sorry for putting you through this. It's so close, just beyond my grasp. I'm sorry for not remembering more."

Cat grabbed Billie's arms. "Damn it. Stop that. You've done nothing to apologize for."

Billie nodded and looked around the bedroom again. "I think I'll take a shower as long as we're here. I'm kind of sweaty from all that work on the stairs. Okay?"

"Sure. I'll just be downstairs. Please don't come down the steps by yourself. I'll be close by. Call to me when you're ready. Agreed?"

"You've got it, Sarge."

The master bath was large and contained mirrors on opposite walls to provide the right angle for looking at the back of an outfit. Billie stepped in between the mirrors and took off her T-shirt and shorts. Out of curiosity she glanced in the mirror. Her world came crashing in on her. Pain tore through her head and drove her to her knees. She grabbed her head and fell to the floor, pulling her body into a fetal position.

Cat was in the living room, folding the blankets she used on the couch the night before, when she heard a painful keening sound. She took the stairs two at a time and made her way to the second floor master bedroom. She found Billie curled up on the bathroom floor. Her body visibly trembled and wretched sobs tore from her throat.

Cat fell to her knees and lifted Billie's head into her lap, cradling her like a baby. "Billie, what happened? Did you fall? Tell me, please."

Incapable of coherent speech, Billie just clung to Cat.

"I've got you, love. It's okay. I've got you."

A short time later, Billie calmed down enough to take a deep breath and continued to draw in short, hiccuping gulps of air. After a time, she spoke.

"I… I remember the welts on my back… Brian… the man at the bar…" Billie was unable to continue as she clung to Cat once more.

Cat held Billie for a long time before she was able to convince her to lie down for a nap. Cat helped her to her feet and walked her into the bedroom. She drew down the covers on their bed and tucked her in. She reached for the telephone.

"Hi, Jen, it's Cat. Billie and I won't be making it for lunch. No, she's all right. She had another recall, a painful one from her first marriage. She's in bed right now. I'm going to stay with her for a while. She's pretty wrecked emotionally. What's that? Sure, if you don't mind. Okay I'll pack their pajamas and clean clothes for tomorrow and run them over to you after Billie's asleep. All right, and Jen, thanks. I'll see you in a while. Bye."

She looked at Billie and found blue eyes staring back at her. Cat reached over and ran her palm down the side of Billie's face. "Jen's going to keep the kids tonight."

Billie nodded. "Can you hold me?"

Cat was under the covers with Billie in seconds, pulling her into the circle of her arms.

Billie slept well into the afternoon. Cat packed an overnight bag for the children and ran it over to Jen's. Jen wouldn't let her leave until she sat down and told her all the details of the recall.

"There isn't much to tell. She remembered the beatings at Brian's hands and the guy who beat her up in the alley behind the bar a few weeks ago. She was devastated. I've never seen her so terrified of anything in my life." Cat rubbed her forehead. "On the plus side, she's recalled memories of our wedding. Can you believe it? Unfortunately, she remembers everything about the ceremony except how she felt about me. Go figure."

"Billie is such a lucky woman to have you. How you're managing to stay strong through all of this is beyond me. Just know you don't need to go it alone. We're here to help, okay?"

"You're already helping. Keeping the kids for us is a godsend." Cat looked at her watch. "I want to be there when she wakes up, so I need to get going. Kiss the kids for me when they come back from the park. Tell them I love them, all right?"

"I will. Now go take care of your lady, and call me if you need help."

* * *

Dinner that evening was very quiet. Billie awoke late in the afternoon with no intention of doing further therapy that day. After dinner, she insisted they both return to their room for the night. For a long time, she lay in Cat's arms in silence. Finally, she spoke.

"Cat, I've spent a lot of time trying to figure out what I did to deserve the abuse. I just don't have an explanation for it."

"It doesn't warrant an explanation because there isn't one. You did nothing to deserve it. You were the unfortunate victim of a sick mind. Nobody asks for that kind of abuse."

"I can't help but think... if only I was a better wife, or better mother."

"Stop it. Stop it right now. This isn't about how good or bad you were. It's about how sick and twisted and controlling Brian is. This is about power and control, not about levels of goodness. And by the way, I happen to think you're a wonderful wife and mother."

"I don't know about that. I don't feel worthy of you right now. You're putting up with so much shit from me and because of me."

"Billie, when I look at you, I see the most wonderful, beautiful, worthy individual I've ever known. You're perfect. You're good. Please don't ever change. I love you just the way you are."

Billie held Cat while she cried. And cry she did, releasing all the emotions she'd kept in check since the beginning of Billie's illness. A full quarter hour later, the sobbing reduced to whimpering, and then to even breathing, and ultimately to sleep.

Chapter 40

Billie woke the next morning with a splitting headache. She maneuvered herself into a sitting position against the headboard and took a few moments to orient herself. Her eyes scanned the room until they fell on Cat sleeping beside her. Billie studied her for several moments. *Why do you love me, Cat? You're so smart and so beautiful. Why have you chosen me?*

Billie leaned her head back and closed her eyes. A wave of heat began to rise as the ringing in her ears increased, accompanied by the expected panicky feeling. She willed herself to relax as a memory surfaced.

"Billie, I have never been happier in my life. All through my teen years, I was ridiculed for my preferences. My so-called friends had me convinced I would never have a normal, happy life, never have children or a stable family. Then you came. You changed my life forever. I've never loved anyone the way I love you. I'd die for you, you know."

Billie opened her eyes and closed them again against the intense pain. She struggled out of bed and made her way to the bathroom in search of painkillers. While she searched the medicine cabinet, she heard Cat call out her name.

"I'm right here." Billie stepped into the bedroom. "I have a headache. I needed to find something to get rid of it."

Cat held her arms out to Billie. "Come here."

Billie made her way over to Cat and laid the crutches on the floor before crawling across the bed and laying her head in Cat's lap. Cat massaged her temples until the pain subsided and the painkillers started to take effect.

Billie lay there, on her back. "Cat, when did you know you loved me?"

"From the first moment I saw you. That fateful day when I walked into your aerobics class five years ago."

Billie closed her eyes as a pressure started to build behind them.

She had red-blonde hair and a well-toned build, china-doll features, full lips, and the most startling emerald green eyes Billie had ever seen. "My God, I wonder if the woman knows how striking she is."

"Now, on the count of four," Billie said, "we're going to take this two steps to the right, then two steps left, Okay?" Billie once again came up behind Cat. She wrapped her arm around Cat's waist and pulled her close, locking her in place against her chest. Watching the two of them in the mirror as they moved together looked so right. Billie's arm wrapped around her waist, Cat's head rested on Billie's shoulder. Soon her eyes were closed as they floated back and forth across the room.

Billie opened her eyes and saw the concern on Cat's face.

"You went away there for a few moments. Are you all right?"

"I'm fine." Billie rolled herself up into a sitting position.

"Is your headache gone?"

"Almost. We'd better get to work on my therapy."

"Are you sure you're all right?"

"Damn it. I said I was fine."

"Okay. You don't have to be such a grump about it," Cat said as she climbed off the bed.

Billie, feeling guilty from her treatment of Cat, declared a refreshment break right in the middle of her stair climbing therapy. While Cat went to get two tall glasses of ice water, Billie sat at the bottom of the stairs, thinking of a way to apologize for her thoughtlessness.

Cat handed her a glass of water and sat next to her on the stairs. "Thanks," Billie said, leaning sideways to bump shoulders with Cat. "I'm sorry for snapping at you. I don't know what came over me." She flashed a crooked smile at Cat. "Still love me?"

"Of course I do."

Billie gasped as memories flashed through her mind. She looked at Cat and quickly regained her composure. "Well, I was acting like a fool. I'm sorry. I do love you, you know."

A pain shot through Billie's head. She reached up with one hand to quell it. "Oh God."

Cat took Billie's glass from her. "Billie, what is it?"

"My head. Still hurts."

"Billie, maybe you're overdoing it. You're not Superman, you know. You need to rest."

Billie lay in the hospital bed, her head swathed in bandages. She opened her eyes to see Cat sitting beside her. Her face was a mask of worry and concern.

"Hey, love," Cat said. "Thank God you've come back to us."

Billie tried to focus through the haze of sedatives. "The kids?"

"Brian broke Seth's arm, but otherwise, the kids are okay, thanks to you."

"Brian?"

"The police have taken him into custody. He won't be able to hurt you or the children anymore."

"Good. How serious are my injuries?"

"The bullet lodged in the frontal lobe. Daddy is hopeful for a full recovery. Don't think I'm not grateful, Billie, but you could've been killed."

"You and the kids were in danger. I had to do something."

"Well, the next time you need to stop a speeding bullet, call Superman, got it?"

Billie closed her eyes and shook her head to clear the confusion. "Maybe you're right, Cat. I'm going to lie down for a while." She reached for her crutches.

"Do you want me to carry those for you while you climb the stairs?"

"No, I think I'll just lie down in the guest bedroom. It's closer," she said as she headed to the guest room for a short nap.

Cat remained sitting on the stairs for some time, contemplating Billie's strange behavior. She was still there when the kids came home around lunchtime, followed by Jen.

After lunch, the kids retreated to the backyard to play with Stevie and Karissa. Cat and Jen sat at the kitchen table, enjoying glasses of iced tea.

"So how's it going?" Jen asked.

"Something's happening. I can feel it. Billie's been acting strange all morning."

"What do you mean, strange?"

"Well, she keeps blanking out and staring into space. She has a headache that seems to come and go. I'm betting it's more memory recall, but she isn't saying one way or another. I'm worried about her."

"Worried about who?" Billie said from the kitchen doorway.

"Billie," Cat said. "You scared me. How are you feeling?"

"Headache's gone." She hobbled over to sit at the table.

"You've been giving your lady here reason to worry. Are you all right?" Jen asked.

Billie looked at Jen, a blank expression her face.

"Look. The Swensons' house is on fire. I already called 911," Cat said.

Billie saw flames dance along the roofline of the house down the street. "Holy, shit. We've got to do something. Where are my boots?" She located them quickly and shoved her feet into them.

"Where are you going?"

"I'm going to help them. I have to. I wouldn't be able to live with myself if I didn't."

"I don't know how to thank you," Jen said. "We've treated you and your family so bad, how can you ever forgive us?"

Billie wiped the tears from Jen's cheeks as she realized this woman was no older than Cat. "Shhh, let's not talk about that right now. How are Stevie and Fred?" She prepared herself for the worst.

"They're both alive, thanks to you. Fred is resting comfortably and should go home tomorrow. Stevie's in intensive care. He inhaled a lot of smoke, but the doctors think he'll be well enough to go home in about a week." Jen paused. "That is, if we had a home to go to."

"You have a home to go to. Ours."

Billie saw only confusion on Jen's face.

"I'm under strict orders from the boss lady to bring you home with me. Our home is open to you and your family for as long as you need it."

"I don't know what to say... except thank you."

Billie gave her shoulders a squeeze. "That'll do."

"Earth to Billie." Jen waved her hand in front of Billie's face.

Billie shook her head to clear the fuzziness, her brows knit in confusion.

Jen placed a hand on her arm. "You're remembering, aren't you?"

Billie looked from Jen to Cat and back to Jen. "Yes," she said.

"You're remembering?" Cat asked. "Are they memories from our life together, not your marriage to Brian?"

"Yes," Billie answered, not meeting Cat's eyes.

"Billie, why didn't you tell me?"

"I wasn't sure until now. They're isolated. Nothing connected. Glimpses in time."

"What have you remembered?'

"I remember the day I first met you, our aerobic lessons. I remember bits of conversations. Do you remember calling me Scrooge because I didn't want to go Christmas shopping?" She watched Cat nod. "I remembered that."

"I remember saving Fred, Stevie, and Karissa from the fire, bringing Jen home with me from the hospital after their house burned, and thinking she wasn't much older than you," Billie said as Jen grinned. "I remember events, glimpses, but it's not enough. They're disjointed. There is no continuity. I still don't know who we are. I need that."

Cat got up and circled behind Billie. She wrapped her arms around her neck and rested her head on Billie's shoulder. "It will happen. I can feel it." Billie closed her eyes.

"Well, lovebirds," Jen said, "I've got to go get dinner started." She walked around to where Cat stood behind Billie and wrapped her arms around both of them for a group hug. "Hold it together. This will happen. I just know it will." She wiped a tear from the corner of her eye. "Cat, you can send the kids home when you get sick of them, okay?" She beat a hasty retreat.

Billie looked up at Cat. "You know, that friend of ours is quite a mushball."

That afternoon, Billie ventured with Cat into the family room in the basement for the first time since being home. As with the second story of the house, strong feelings of familiarity invaded her mind as she walked around the room. She stopped in front of the fireplace and ran her hand across the mantel. "Seth's Lego castle was here, wasn't it? I remember Tara and Seth rebuilding it after it was destroyed by a collision in the hallway. I was studying for the bar exam at the time."

Looking over the audience, Billie finally located Cat. Such an intense wave of love passed between them that it was almost palpable. Billie transferred the tassel from one side of her hat to the other as she descended from the stage and headed back to her seat.

"Billie?" Cat placed a hand on her arm as she stood there, staring at the mantel. "Another memory?"

"Graduation."

Cat took Billie's hand and led her to the couch. "Come sit with me. I want to show you something."

Cat removed a couple of photo albums from the bookcase and sat next to Billie. She opened the first book across both of their laps and started to page through it. The previous five years of their lives were about to be laid out before them.

Tara at age four, sat side by side with Seth, age six, in his wheelchair the day Seth came home from the hospital.

After teaching her aerobics class, Billie went to collect the children and found Tara sitting in a chair, holding a cloth with ice in it to her lip. Seth was sitting on the floor playing with some race cars. "It was his fault, Mom," Tara said, pointing to another boy who sat in the opposite corner, his hands crossed in front of his chest, a sour expression on his face and a bruise darkening around his left eye. "He was mean to Seth. He called him a cripple, so I punched him, and he punched me back."

Billie ran her fingertips over the pictures of the children. A smile crossed her face at the memory.

She saw a photograph of a very pregnant Cat, sitting in the park, writing in her journal, unaware her picture was being taken. "I remember the day this was taken."

"Cat, When we first found out you were pregnant, I have to admit I was upset, angry, and jealous, but—"

"Jealous?"

"Yeah, jealous that I couldn't be the one to give you this child." She paused. "Anyway, I had mixed feelings at first, but now I'm so looking forward to this baby. Our baby. This child binds us together. It's the one true link between Seth and Tara. Don't you see? We've always been a family in spirit, but with this child, we're a family in blood. I don't care if the child isn't technically mine. It's mine in my heart, and I'll do everything in my power to be a good parent. Thank you for giving me this chance."

A picture of Skylar, no more than a few days old.

"Okay, now, push," Billie said in her best coaching voice.
"Aaahhhhh!"
"Come on now, Cat." She pulled Cat against her chest a little tighter. "That's it... push."
"Damn it, Billie. If you want this so bad, you push!"
... Billie took Cat's hand in her own and lifted it to her mouth, kissing the back of each knuckle. "We have a beautiful daughter, Cat. She looks like you, red hair and all."

Billie's eyes were heavy with unshed tears. "I remember them, Cat. I remember the children. You were so angry at me when Sky was born. You said, 'Damn it, Billie, if you want this so bad, you push.'"
"That was the most wonderful day of my life, Billie. Our baby girl was the most precious gift I could ever give to you. She made us a family. She became the bond that drew us all together. Thank you for being there for her and for being there for all of us."
"Cat, I loved you so much at that moment," Billie said as tears coursed down her face.
Cat pulled Billie's face down for a kiss and wiped the tears away. "Are you all right? Do you want to go on?"
Billie nodded. "I need to be whole again. Help me to remember. Please."
Cat opened the second album to their wedding photo.
Billie stared at the picture for a long time before closing her eyes.

Billie dropped to one knee in front of Cat, holding a diamond engagement ring in front of her. She looked into Cat's tear-stained face. "Cat, I love you with all my heart. You're the mother of my children and the other half of my soul. You complete me and I can't live without you. Will you marry me?"

Several moments later, Billie reached out to Cat. She kissed the back of Cat's hand and then the palm. Cat closed her eyes and felt the arousal building inside her.

Cat opened her eyes, making no attempt to hide the desire burning in them. "I love you, Billie."

Billie held Cat's hand as she continued to thumb through the photo album.

Adoption day. A photograph of all five of them, with the words "The Charlands" written across the bottom of the photo. Jen had taken the picture. Billie smiled as the memories returned.

Tara rubbed her eyes. "Are you my dad?"

"Cat, she asked me to be her dad," Billie said.

"And how do you feel about that?"

"How do I feel? How can you even ask that?" Billie said. Then seeing she had hurt Cat's feelings, she added. "The real question is, when do we start adoption proceedings?"

Finally, pictures of this past Christmas: the children opening their presents and playing with their new toys. Billie remembered Tara being so worried about Santa finding her because her name had changed from O'Grady to Charland after the adoption.

"Santa knows you, regardless of what your last name is, just like Mama and I know you. Changing your name doesn't change who you are here, inside. You're still Tara, and nothing will change that. Santa knows that. He'll find you, sweetie. I promise."

… "Cat, this is the best Christmas I've ever had. All I ever wanted I have right here in my arms and in my heart. My love, my wife, my children. We're a family in name as well as in blood."

Billie closed the photo album and moved it to the coffee table. She laid her head in Cat's lap and allowed her mind to process all that she had remembered. Cat stroked her head as they sat there in silence.

Finally, Billie spoke. "I'm so close, Cat, so close. But I still don't have you. I see you in my life, but I don't feel you. Come back to me, please."

Cat and Billie's silent contemplation was interrupted by the children charging down the cellar stairs. "Mom, Stevie and Karissa are tenting in their backyard tonight, and they want us to sleep over. Can we? Can we? Please?" Seth said, his pleas echoed by his sisters.

Billie sat up and looked at Cat then at the children. "What does Jen have to say about this?"

"Jen is fine with it," a voice said from the stairs. "They're more than welcome," Jen said.

"Can we, Mom? Can we?" Tara said.

"Sure, but we don't have any sleeping bags, do we, Cat?"

"The only thing they need to bring are their pillows," Jen said.

"All right then," Billie said.

"Yeah," the kids cheered. They hugged and kissed both of their mothers and ran off to collect their pillows.

Cat looked at Jen. "Are you sure about this?"

"Hey, it's Fred's idea. He's the sucker, not me." She walked over to her friends. "Photo albums, huh? A trip down memory lane?"

Cat smiled. "Indeed. It's helped a great deal."

Jen looked at Billie. "How are you doing?"

"Better than expected. A lot has come back. Thanks for taking the kids. It'll give me a chance to process what I've remembered without interruption. That means a lot."

"No problem," Jen said. "Anytime. You two have a good evening, okay?" She dropped a kiss on their heads before going up the stairs.

After a quiet dinner, Billie spent some time on the stationary bike while Cat updated her journal. There was a slight tension in the air, an anticipatory feeling, like something was about to happen.

Cat filled the Jacuzzi in the master bathroom for Billie to relax in after her workout and avoided the bathroom while Billie was soaking. The rubdown she knew was coming was enough to arouse her almost beyond control. She didn't need to further torture herself beforehand by watching a naked Billie lying relaxed in a swirling hot tub.

Soon, Billie was finished with her soak and was lying facedown on the bed with a towel thrown over her bottom, waiting for Cat to start the massage.

Billie closed her eyes as Cat's hands started kneading her muscles. Suddenly heat began to rise in Billie's chest, spreading to her neck and face. She grabbed her head with both hands. "Oh God."

Cat stopped the massage and moved to Billie's head. She knelt on the floor beside her and rubbed her temples. "Honey, what's wrong?"

Billie opened her eyes and sat up in the middle of the bed, mindless of her nakedness. She stared at Cat, her eyes wide as the memories rushed in.

Cat moaned and tilted her head to one side to give Billie greater access. Billie responded with a more intense sense of urgency.

"Oh God, I want you so much."

"Patience, my love, patience." Cat pulled out of Billie's embrace. "Stay right here." She put her wineglass on the nightstand next to the bed and returned to Billie in the center of the room. Slowly, she circled Billie and lightly ran her hands over Billie's breasts and stomach. Billie struggled to maintain control.

"You've no idea what you're doing to me right now," Billie whispered.

"Oh, I think I do." Cat walked behind Billie and pressed herself against her back. She reached around to the front and unbuckled Billie's belt. Cat slapped Billie's hands away when Billie became impatient and attempted to help.

Cat unzipped Billie's jeans and slid her hands into the front of Billie's panties.

Billie gasped when Cat's fingers delved into the warm, moist crevice.

"Oh God, you're so wet." Cat pushed the jeans off Billie's hips.

An arousal began at the very center of Billie's being, so intense she couldn't hold it back. She looked at Cat, tears freely falling down her face.

"Billie?"

"I need you, Cat."

"Have I come back to you?"

Billie sobbed. "I remember. I remember everything. My God, I love you."

Cat flew into Billie's arms. "Please. I've missed you so much."

"I need to feel you," Billie whispered between kisses. "I want you so much. I want to fill you with my soul. I want to take you to heaven and back. Let me love you." Billie lowered her mouth to smother the whimpers of passion coming from Cat's throat as her tongue was welcomed into Cat's mouth. The kiss was deep and probing, threatening to consume them in flames of passion. Groans of pleasure escaped as desire coursed through their veins.

Billie pulled Cat onto the bed and lay down beside her. Her hands caressed Cat's body, squeezing, grabbing, and kneading. The frustration and anger of the past few weeks melted away. She grabbed the front of Cat's shirt and tore it open.

"Oh God, Billie!" Cat leaned her head back. "Please take me, please. I need to feel you inside me." Cat ran her hands over an already naked Billie.

Billie began to explore the exposed territory, kissing and biting, leaving marks on Cat's throat and neck that would show evidence of their passion for days to come.

Cat grasped Billie's head and closed her eyes in the heat of passion, as Billie left a trail of kisses along her neck and shoulders.

Billie pushed the remains of Cat's shirt from her shoulders, slid it down her arms, and threw it across the room. She reached around Cat and released the catch on her bra, allowing her full breasts to escape their prison. Lifting Cat's breasts in her hands, she met them halfway, suckled one swollen bud, and circled it with her tongue.

Cat's moans only served to entice Billie as she bit down on the sensitive nub, causing Cat to wriggle against her. "Billie, oh God. I need you. Please."

Billie kissed her way up Cat's neck and chin and once again ravished Cat's mouth with abandon, while her hands found and unzipped Cat's jeans. She slid her hands under silk panties. Deeper, she pushed until she grasped firm buttocks, kneading them until they were warm, all the while pulling Cat's lower body closer to her own.

Cat tried to push the denim material off her hips. Billie too was anxious to remove the barrier between them. She sat back, pulled the jeans off Cat, and threw them across the room. The panties soon followed.

"God, Cat, I need you so much. I want to ravish you, to touch your body and your soul to help me feel whole again. To help us feel whole again. I feel like I'm bursting inside. I want you. I want to make love to you over and over. I want to hear you call out my name at the height of desire. I want to plunge into your depths. I want to taste you on my breath. I want to drive you to the edge of madness and catch you when you fall back to earth. Let me love you, Cat."

Cat looked into her eyes and said in a raspy voice, "Billie, I want all of you. Do you understand? All of you. All that you are and all that you have to give. No holding back. I've been aching with need for a very long time. I need you to love me with everything you are."

Billie responded by capturing Cat's mouth in a brutal kiss. She trapped her smaller body beneath hers and ravaged every inch of Cat's skin.

"Oh God, Billie, yes. More, please."

Billie left trails of bite marks along Cat's neck, shoulders, and breasts. Cat dug her nails into Billie's back, each one driving spikes of desire through her. A low guttural growl formed in the base of Billie's throat as she pressed her core into Cat's abdomen.

Billie pinned Cat's hands against the bed above her head. "Tell me what you want," she said, her mouth hovering over Cat's, her tongue flicking out to taste Cat's lips. "Tell me."

"I want you, Billie. I want you inside me. Please. I need to feel you."

Billie kissed Cat before moving lower. Kissing every inch of skin along the way, she stopped to worship at Cat's breasts and teased the darkened nubs to attention. She trailed her tongue down Cat's abdomen, dipped her tongue into her navel, and grinned when she prompted a squeal of surprise.

Cat squirmed with desire as Billie caressed her skin. Cat's hands pressed on Billie's head, urging her lower. Billie stopped momentarily and looked up at Cat.

"Please?"

Billie lowered herself between Cat's legs and dove into the depths of her core.

Cat's hips arched high off the bed. "Oh God, Billie. God, baby, oh God." Without warning, Billie plunged her fingers deep inside of her.

Cat grabbed the bed sheets as she pressed her head back into the pillows. "Billie. Oh my God," she screamed into the night. "Harder, please," she demanded, and Billie increased the speed and intensity of her thrusts. "Billie!"

Billie continued to thrust as she felt Cat reach the heights of ecstasy. For several moments afterwards, Billie held her, wrapping her long frame around her and enveloping her in strong arms while aftershocks racked her body.

"I've got you, my love. I've got you," Billie chanted over and over as Cat recovered from the assault on her senses.

"I love you, Billie, with all of my heart."

Billie leaned down and placed a light kiss on Cat's mouth, allowing Cat to share in her own essence.

Cat's eyes opened wide with realization brought on by the kiss, reigniting the fire in her veins.

Surprising Billie, she locked legs with her and rolled Billie onto her back.

Pulling Billie's arms upward and pressing them into the pillow beside her head, she leaned in and kissed her passionately. "Stay here. I'll be right back." Cat walked over to the dresser and placed a CD into the stereo. Soon the sounds of romantic music filled the room.

Cat approached the foot of the bed and crawled her way up Billie's body, until they were lying face-to-face. She tasted and kissed every bit of skin on Billie's body, working her way down her face, over her mouth, jaw, and throat, biting earlobes, and flicking her tongue inside Billie's ears along the way. Kisses found their way across Billie's shoulders and down her breastbone between her breasts. Billie moaned, and Cat continued downward, trailing her tongue across Billie's abdomen, across her right hip, down her leg. Billie jerked in reflex as Cat bit the tender skin on the inside of her right knee.

Cat moved to the other leg, kissing the inside of Billie's thigh before heading upward once again. She stopped at Billie's breasts and took each one into her mouth in turn, biting and nipping. She kissed every part of Billie's body except the place that Billie wanted her most.

"Cat, I need you, please."

"Soon, my love."

Cat ended her journey straddling Billie's waist. She felt her own desire escalating as Billie attempted to take control.

Billie reached up to circle Cat's slim waist, pulled her down closer, and raised her hips to grind her abdomen against Cat's moist center. Cat buried her face in Billie's neck as bolts of desire shot through her. "My God, Billie," she moaned.

Cat sat up and once more pinned Billie's hands to the pillow above her head. "Slow down." She smiled at the pained and impatient expression on Billie's face. "All in good time, sweet love."

Cat released Billie's hands and reached for the generous mounds that greeted her eyes. She took one in each hand and caressed them. Marveling at how soft Billie's skin was, she let her thumbs roam around the soft buds, causing them to harden with excitement.

Billie gasped, leaned her head back, and closed her eyes as Cat ran her tongue and teeth across the erect nipples.

"Cat. I need you, please." She heaved upward against Cat. "I can't believe how turned on I am. I can't take this torture anymore. Your seduction is driving me insane with need."

Cat leaned forward to whisper in Billie's ear. "Who am I?"

Billie closed her eyes. "You are my heart."

"And who are you?"

"I am your lover, your wife, and the mother of your children."

"I love you, Billie. I want you, and I need you."

"Now, Cat, please."

Cat explored further as she worked her way down Billie's body, caressing the secret places that made her scream out in ecstasy.

"That feels so good. Please, I need more."

"Close your eyes."

Cat could sense she had pushed Billie as far as she could. She worked her way down Billie's body and hovered close enough for Billie to feel Cat's heated breath on her most sensitive parts, yet not close enough for contact.

"Cat, please," Billie urged.

"Shhh," Cat said. Still, she waited.

Billie gyrated her hips upward.

When she was sure Billie was on the edge of anticipatory madness, Cat plunged three fingers inside of her while sucking her soft bud into her mouth.

The room filled with loud cries of release as Billie screamed Cat's name.

When Billie came back to herself, she was wrapped in Cat's arms, her head resting on Cat's shoulder.

"By all that's sacred, I love you," Billie said, barely able to lift her head to look into Cat's eyes.

"I love you too, with all I am." Cat kissed her on top of the head.

"Cat?"

"Yes, my love?"

"I missed you."

"I missed you too. Welcome home, Billie."

Chapter 41

"Billie, how are the burgers coming?" Cat called from across the yard as she spread the cloth over the picnic table.

"None of them are committing suicide yet, so I guess they're okay. I'm surprised you're trusting me to do the cooking. You must not like our guests very much."

Cat approached Billie and rubbed her back. "You don't have the fire on high again, do you?" She spared a glance at the burgers.

Billie pointed at the dial on the front of the grill. "See for yourself. It's on halfway."

Cat stood on tiptoe and kissed Billie. "Just keep an eye on them and spray them periodically with that water bottle. Once both sides are cooked, move them to the top rack. And you're right, we're all familiar with your culinary skills, or lack thereof I should say. I'll stop by every few minutes, and between us, we'll get them cooked just about right. The goal is to not poison our guests. They should be arriving soon."

"Is that sarcasm I hear in your voice?"

Cat batted her eyelashes. "Would I do that?"

Billie flipped several of the burgers over. "You're the one who said I have many skills."

"Yeah, but cooking isn't one of them. How are you doing, by the way?"

"So far, so good." Billie lifted the one crutch she was using for support. "This crutch is enough to keep me balanced, and I've got a chair close by in case I need to sit."

"This cookout was a good idea, Billie. It's a chance to thank everyone who helped us through the past few weeks."

"I agree. I know we've already had a coming-home event for me, but I have to admit I wasn't on my best behavior. Now that I'm back to my old self, I plan to enjoy this one much more."

Billie put the spatula on the side wing of the grill and wrapped her arm around Cat's waist. "You're smiling. Want to share?"

"You're very cute with spiked hair."

Billie ran a hand over her head. "Do you really like it this short?"

"To be truthful, I'm kind of partial to it long, but like I said when you were in the hospital, you're a beautiful woman, no matter how long your hair is."

"I like it long, Mom," Seth said as he approached his mothers. "Where do you want this salad?"

"On the table, sweetie."

"Mama, Grandpa and Grammy are here," Tara called from the back porch.

"Thank you, sweetie. Tara, could you send the paper plates and cups out with your sister?"

"Where are they?"

"In a bag on the kitchen table."

"Okay."

Moments later, Doc, Ida, and Skylar made their way across the backyard with Doc carrying the bag of paper goods.

'Hi, Daddy, Mom." Cat hugged her parents and looked at Skylar. "I see you talked Grandpa into doing your dirty work."

Skylar beamed. "He wanted to carry it."

"Guilty as charged," Doc said.

Cat took the bag from Doc and handed it back to Skylar. "Okay, you're off the hook this time. Run these over to the table for me, okay?"

"All right," Skylar said as she took the bag.

Doc draped his arm around Billie's shoulder. "So how are you, Billie? Does it feel good to be home?"

"Yes, it does. Cat put me in charge of cooking. She said no one else can cook a burger like me. I guess I'm pretty good at it, huh?"

"You've got that right. No one else indeed." Doc turned to Cat and raised his eyebrows. "I think I'll help scout bring the salads out," he said.

Cat wrapped her arm around Billie. "You are so bad, Billie Charland."

"Who, me?"

"Yes, you. Oh, good, Fred and Jen are here." Cat waved her hand. "Jen, over here."

Jen approached Cat and hugged her tight. She went to hug Billie and stopped in her tracks.

"Hi, Jen," Billie said as she flipped another burger.

Jen took Cat's arm to walk a few steps away. "You're letting her cook?"

"She insisted," Cat said.

"And you expect us to actually eat the burgers?"

"Come on, Jen. Give her a chance."

"If you say so. It's a good thing we brought extra salads."

"Hey, Jen," Billie called from the grill.

Jen turned back to Cat. "She's calling me. Give me a minute and I'll help set the table." Jen approached Billie and wrapped her arms around her waist. "Hi, big guy. How are you feeling?"

"Not bad, actually. I think I could get used to this new life. Maybe it won't be so bad. I mean, I've got a great house, great kids, and Cat is wonderful. Best of all, I feel needed."

"What do you mean?"

"Well, take this cookout for example. Apparently, Cat has always depended on me to do the grilling. I don't remember much about it, but it seems I'm pretty much a master chef on the grill."

"Master chef, huh? Ah... you wouldn't happen to have any beer or wine, would you?" Jen asked.

"Sure, in the cooler beside the picnic table. Are you thirsty?"

"Yeah, that's it."

"Help yourself."

"Thanks. I think I'll give Cat a hand setting the table while I'm over there." Jen walked directly to Cat. "Oh my God!"

"What is it?" Cat said.

"She thinks she's a master chef on the grill. Holy Shit. I hope her memory comes back before the end of this cookout."

Cat laughed. "Come on. I think you're exaggerating a bit."

"Can you say, hockey pucks? That's like letting Fred cook."

"Did I hear my name?" Fred approached Jen and Cat.

"As a matter of fact, you did," Jen said. "Look at Billie. She's cooking."

Fred's eyes opened wide. "Wow, Cat. You're brave. That's like letting me cook."

"My point, exactly," Jen said.

"Maybe I should go help her."

"No!" Jen and Cat shouted together.

"Geesh. Make a guy feel appreciated, why don't you," Fred said.

Cat handed Fred two bottles of beer. "Here, take one of these to Billie."

Cat and Jen watched Fred walk away. "Phew, that was close," Cat said.

"You got that right."

"Okay, let's get this table set. There are also a few more dishes in the refrigerator, not to mention the condiments and hamburger buns."

After a few minutes, Cat and Jen had the table organized. On their way back toward the house, they met Art and Marge coming through the gate.

"Art, Marge," Cat said. "Thanks for coming. You remember Jen?"

"Of course we do," Marge said.

"We're on our way to bring the rest of the food out. There's beer and soft drinks in the cooler by the picnic table. Help yourself."

"I'll give you a hand," Marge said.

"Where's Billie?" Art asked.

"She's grilling."

Art looked at Cat like she had antennae growing out of her forehead. "Don't tell me you're letting her cook."

Jen snickered.

Cat elbowed Jen in the side. "Come on. Give her a chance. It makes her feel needed."

Art grimaced. "I suppose." He glanced toward the grill and watched her spray the burgers with an exaggerated flourish. "Maybe I can give her a hand."

"Good luck with that. She seems to think she's some sort of gourmet chef or something," Jen said. "If she had her memory back, she wouldn't even think of cooking."

"You have lots of other food, right?" Art said.

"My point, exactly," Jen added.

Cat looked at Marge. "Is he always like this?"

"When it comes to food—yes. You have to admit, Billie's a pretty awful cook."

"Well, we'll just have to make the best of it. Let's get the rest of the food on the table," Cat said.

Billie watched Art cross the yard to join her and Fred at the grill. "Hey, Art. I'm so glad you could come."

Art hugged her. "How are you doing, Billie?"

"I'm doing okay. Getting better every day."

"I see you're feeling well enough to cook. How's that going?" Art asked.

Fred snickered, earning him a dirty look from Billie.

"It's going well. I hope you're hungry. We've got a lot of food."

"Do you need any help with the grilling?"

"Nope—got it covered. It appears I'm pretty good at it. You could get me another beer though. It's in the cooler near the picnic table."

Cat, Jen, and Marge walked past the grill at that moment, carrying salads, chips, and rolls. Cat winked at Billie on the way by. "How are the burgers coming along?" she asked.

"They're just about done. Would you mind getting me a container to put them in?"

"Sure. Let me get rid of these salads, and I'll get it for you."

"Fred, Uncle Art," Seth yelled from across the yard, "Grandpa is going to play touch football with us. Do you want to play?"

Art and Fred looked at Billie. "Go ahead, guys. I wish I could join you, but between these crutches and the fact that my cooking skills are needed at the grill, I'm pretty much stuck here. No reason for you two not to join in on the fun. I'm going to turn the grill on high for a few minutes to finish them off. I'll let you know when we're ready to eat."

Billie chuckled as they stared at one another with a dismayed look before they hurried away.

Cat stopped by the grill on her way back to her guests to drop the hamburger tray and a roll of aluminum foil off to Billie.

"Are you having as much fun playing with their heads as I am?" Cat asked.

"Oh yeah." Billie lifted the cover on the grill. "How do they look?"

"Did you cook them on medium heat and spray them like I said?"

"Yep. I moved them to the top rack after both sides were browned. I'm just about ready to put cheese on them, then they'll be ready to go."

Cat poked one of the burgers with a fork. Light pink fluid ran out. "They appear to be nice and juicy. Good job."

"No hockey pucks this time," Billie said. "Thanks for helping me out."

Cat kissed her. "You're welcome. Go ahead and shut the grill off and put the cheese on them. Take them off in about five minutes, and I'll have everything else ready by then."

Ten minutes later, Billie, Cat, their children, and all of their friends and family sat around the picnic table. Before they filled their plates, Billie rose to her feet and lifted her glass. "I'd like to make a toast."

Everyone fell silent as they waited for Billie to speak.

Cat sat beside her and held her other hand.

Billie looked at each and every person. "I want to begin by thanking all of you for coming today. Your presence here means more to Cat and me than you can imagine. We've worked hard to put on an appetizing spread for you today. Little did I know, I'm apparently the go-to person for backyard grilling. Go figure." Billie paused and watched the expressions of disbelief on her guests' faces.

She struggled to maintain a straight face as she continued. "Anyway, these past several weeks have been very difficult, not only for Cat and me, but for every one of you." Billie directed her attention to Doc and Ida. "Mom, Dad, what can we say, except we love you and we appreciate you. Doc, if not for your skills I'd either be dead or a vegetable right now. You've given my life back to me. Ida, your unwavering support for both Cat and the children has put us eternally in your debt. My mom and dad are no longer with us, but you both have stepped into their shoes and loved me as though I was your own. I love you dearly. Dad, you once said you would be honored to be my father. Well, I'm honored to be your daughter."

Ida wiped a tear away and reached for Doc's hand. Doc raised one eyebrow at Billie as he nodded his head.

Billie next turned toward Jen and Fred. "Jen, what can I say? While I was in the hospital, Cat told me you are about as close to a sister as I'll ever have. She was right. I couldn't love you more if you were related by blood. If ever I had a straight-girl crush, it would be you. You've been our rock through this whole ordeal— especially for Cat. I have to admit that the first time you kissed me right on the lips in the hospital, I thought we beeped in the same orbit, if you know what I mean. But in reality, you have the most wonderful and loving heart I've ever known, save for Cat. As awful as it may sound, your house fire several years ago was the best thing that ever could have happened to Cat and me. It found us you. It found us this wonderful community we live in. You've been our friends and our family. You've been surrogate parents to our children. I can't imagine our lives without you."

Jen grabbed a napkin from the table and wiped away the tears that fell freely. "We love both of your very much, Billie. Thank you for coming into our lives."

Fred wrapped his arm around Jen. "That goes for both of us."

Billie held her glass up to Art. "One of the principle rules of business is not to mix business with pleasure. Art, I'm so glad you chose to ignore that. You're so much more than my boss. You're my friend. Out of love and concern for me and my family, you nearly kicked me off the McBride case. Why? Because you knew how it might affect me personally. You put my needs before the needs of the firm. Not many bosses would do that. You're truly a good friend. You and Marge opened your home to me several weeks ago when I needed shelter. You treated me like family. I'll never forget your generosity."

Billie paused for a moment and allowed her gaze to fall on Cat. "Cat, you are my heart. You own me, body and soul. Without you, life isn't worth living. For the longest time, I didn't completely understand how devastating it was for you to not have all of me. So much of our present, and so much of our future, is based on our past. You were unwilling to settle for anything less than full recovery. Even in the darkest hours, you stood by me and never gave up hope. You fought for me—and for us. I love you, Cat. I love you with every fiber of my being. You are the mother of my children, whom I love dearly. You are my lifeline. Thank you for standing by me and never giving up on us."

Cat made no attempt to hold back the tears as she folded her hands as though in prayer and held them in front of her mouth. "I love you too, Billie."

Billie scanned the faces of everyone at the table. "If I had to use just one word to describe everyone at this table, it would be 'family.' Family is always there for each other. Family never gives up. Family loves unconditionally. I'm so proud and blessed to be part of all of you. Thank you for being there for me."

A round of applause erupted from the table. Billie remained standing until it died down.

"There are two more things I need to say. First, it should be obvious to you now that I've recovered my memory. I'll never again take for granted the memories I've made with all of you. When you lose them, you lose part of yourself. I'm so happy I found you all again, and Cat, I am so very happy that I have found us. Life would not be worth living without us.

"Second, on a lighter note, Cat and I have enjoyed watching each of your reactions to me cooking. I couldn't resist taking advantage of the memory loss angle to play it up. Let me make something very clear... I know how bad I am at cooking. Like Cat said, I have many skills, but cooking isn't one of them. So, without further ado, I invite you to feast on this wonderful meal, including the juicy burgers—not hockey pucks—cooked by me, but under the watchful guidance of Cat. Oh, and by the way, you guys were way easy to fool. Now, dig in."

The picnic went well into the afternoon. Jen and Fred were the last to go, refusing to leave until the trash was collected and dishes done.

"Thanks for your help, guys," Billie said. "We appreciate it."

"No thanks necessary," Jen said. "We had a good time." Jen hugged Billie. "I'm so happy you're back. It was really rough watching the two of you struggle to find each other again."

"Me too. We couldn't have done it without your help. And Fred's too. I can't imagine it was easy on him for you to be gone so much and to have our kids practically living at your house."

Jen watched Fred toss the football around with Stevie and Seth. "Fred's a good man. He's a good husband and father too. He loves your kids as much as I do. You needed us. There was no way we weren't going to help. You'd do the same for us."

"You're right. We would. Anyway, just know that we love you and appreciate you very much."

"Ditto, my friend. Ditto."

"Dishes are done," Cat said as she came out of the house.

"Walk us home?" Jen said.

"You bet."

"Fred, we're heading home. Are you coming?" Jen called.

"I'm right behind you." Fred threw the ball to Seth and joined the women.

Moments later, they stood in front of the Swenson's house. Jen hugged Billie then Cat. "This has been one hell of a run," Jen said. "It's time for things to settle down. Time to relax."

"It's been crazy for all of us," Cat said.

"You know, we should do something together, just our two families. Something fun," Jen said.

"Like what?" Billie asked.

Jen shrugged. "I don't know. We should go somewhere on vacation together. Somewhere far away from the hassles of our day-to-day lives."

"That sounds great. Let's make plans," Cat said.

"Cool. Okay. Tell Stevie and Karissa they need to be home by eight."

"You got it. Good night."

Cat slipped her hand into Billie's back pocket as they walked home side by side, in cadence to the clicking of Billie's crutches.

Photo Credit: Song of Myself Photography, Provincetown, MA

About the Author

Karen D. Badger was born in Vermont. She is the second of five children raised by a fiercely independent mother who, in addition to being the strongest influence in Karen's life, is also one of her best friends. Karen holds a BA in Theater Arts and Elementary Education and a BS in Mathematics. She is a Semiconductor Engineer with 34 years of experience behind her and plans to continue that work as long as it remains challenging.

Family is the most important and rewarding priority in Karen's life. Her sons, Heath and Dane and their beautiful ladies, Kacie and Daisy, are at the center of Karen's universe. Heath and Kacie have expanded that universe with three gorgeous grandchildren who are the apples of their Nona's eye. Kyren is sixyears old, and is very protective of his two sisters Ariana, who is nearly five, and Ellie, who is three.

Her life wasn't quite complete until she met the love of her life, Bliss, at the 2007 Golden Crown Literary Society's annual Writers' Conference in Atlanta, Georgia. They currently live in Vermont and enjoy kayaking, camping, and motorcycling in the Green Mountain State. They also spend time working on their homes, which seem to be in a constant state of renovation, in New Mexico and Vermont.

Karen D. Badger, better known to her online fans as "kd bard," is the author of *On a Wing and a Prayer* and *Yesterday Once More*, winner of the 2009 Speculative Fiction Golden Crown Literary Society Award. Her third book, *In a Family Way,* is the first installment in *The Commitment* series. *Unchained Memories* is the second title in this series. All of Karen's books are published by Blue Feather Books Ltd.

Karen is currently editing the third book in *The Commitment* series, *Happy Campers, NOT!,* as well as penning a new standalone book, tentatively titled *The Blue Feather.*

Recommended Reading from Blue Feather Books:

Cresswell Falls, by Kerry Belchambers

Alicia Sanders has suffered constant humiliation at the hands of her unfaithful husband and, as a consequence, has been the victim of malicious gossip in the small town of Cresswell Falls.

Christina Brewster suffered through a painful upbringing, which left her believing she's incapable of falling in love. After she retires from her high fashion runway modeling career, she returns home to Cresswell Falls.

These two women meet and even though they are very different from one another, they are instantly drawn to each other. Alicia is confused by the strange attraction she feels towards Christina because she's never been with anyone except for her ex-husband. Christina believes she'll only hurt Alicia and her beautiful little boy, so she pushes Alicia into the arms of Tony Simmons.

When professional circumstances force them to tread the same path, their mutual attraction grows wildly out of control and they discover a deeply rooted history that ties them closer, making it impossible for them to stay apart. A secret buried in their pasts leads to a shocking suicide that tears both their worlds apart.

Despite the tumultuous events that transpire, the small town of Cresswell Falls helps these women find forgiveness, redemption, love, and happiness.

My Soldier Too, by Bev Prescott

"I wish I'd known love in this life." Captain Madison Brown strained to hear the dying soldier's last words in the makeshift hospital on the fields of war-torn Iraq. The lieutenant's final comment haunted Madison for the remainder of her tour in Iraq and then followed her home to Massachusetts. Ironically, Madison wanted no part of love for herself—or so she thought until she crossed paths with Isabella Parisi, an idealistic young social worker who challenged her to love again.

Isabella, a dedicated professional from a tightly knit Catholic family in Boston's North End, has a seemingly perfect life: a satisfying job, a family she adores, and a devoted boyfriend. A chance encounter with Captain Madison Brown causes Isabella to question everything she thought she believed in. And the emotionally guarded Captain Brown gives Isabella even more reason to doubt the feelings swirling within her.

Isabella's family, Madison's commitment to the Army, and their fears about what it means to love each other conspire to keep them apart. Just when it seems they've finally dodged all of the landmines between them, Madison is deployed to Afghanistan.

As an officer in the Army, Madison swore herself to be a guardian of freedom and the American way of life. Can Isabella accept Madison for the person—the soldier—she is? What price duty? What cost honor? How much must one sacrifice in exchange for the promise of love?

Not all of the ravages of war happen on the battlefield. What happens to Isabella and the relationship between the two women when Isabella must confront the fact that Madison is not just her lover, but her soldier too?

Available now, only from

Make sure to check out these other exciting Blue Feather Books titles:

Confined Spaces	Renee MacKenzie	978-1-935627-98-2
If the Wind Were a Woman	Kelly Sinclair	978-1-935627-97-5
Two for the Show	Chris Paynter	978-1-935627-80-7
Possessing Morgan	Erica Lawson	978-0-9822858-2-4
Merker's Outpost	I. Christie	978-0-9794120-1-1
My Soldier Too	Bev Prescott	978-1-935627-81-4
The Chronicles of Ratha	Erica Lawson	978-1-935627-93-7
Encounters, Volume I	Anne Azel	978-1-935627-96-8
30 Days Hath September	Jamie Scarratt	978-1-935627-94-4
From Hell to Breakfast	Joan Opyr	978-0-9794120-7-3
In a Family Way	Karen Badger	978-0-9822858-6-2
Yesterday Once more	Karen Badger	978-0-9794120-3-5

www.bluefeatherbooks.com

CPSIA information can be obtained at www.ICGtesting.com
Printed in the USA
LVOW130326010313

322219LV00002B/117/P